Peter Watt has spent time as a soldier, trawler deckhand, builder's labourer, salesman, private investigator, police sergeant and adviser to the Royal Papua New Guinea Constabulary. He has lived and worked with Aborigines, Islanders, Vietnamese and Papua New Guineans and he speaks, reads and writes Vietnamese and Pidgin.

Good friends, fine food, fishing and the vast open spaces of outback Queensland are his main interests in life. Peter lives at Finch Hatton in Queensland and is currently working on the sequel to his novel *Papua*.

Peter Watt can be contacted at www.peterwatt.com

Excerpts from emails sent to Peter Watt since his first novel was published:

'Hi there, I have just finished reading the Duffy/Macintosh trilogy and thought it was brilliant! I hope that Wallarie's narrative at the end of *Flight of the Eagle* continues in a future novel of yours.' Nick, England

'At last Australia has its own Wilbur Smith! Keep on writing (PLEASE!).' Mike, Australia

'Thanks for coming to the rescue. I have just finished all of Ken Follett's books, have read all of Clive Cussler's books, and then was stumped for someone new.' Noel, South Africa

'I just wanted to let you know both my husband and I have just finished reading the *Cry of the Curlew* trilogy – please, please, please don't tell me that's the last we have heard of the Duffys and Macintoshes! We were staying up until one or two in the morning reading, now we are lost.' Nigel and Donna, Australia

'I have read the novels and series of many authors including Wilbur Smith, Bryce Courtenay, Jeffrey Archer and Jean Auel and right down to Len Deighton's spy series and thoroughly enjoyed them all. But the enjoyment I derived from your trilogy surpassed all of the aforementioned . . . Please keep up your imaginative writing and don't make us wait too long for another novel.' Martin, Australia

Also by Peter Watt

Cry of the Curlew
Shadow of the Osprey
Flight of the Eagle
Papua

TO CHASE THE STORM

PETER WATT

MACMILLAN
Pan Macmillan Australia

First published 2003 in Macmillan by Pan Macmillan Australia Pty Limited
St Martins Tower, 31 Market Street, Sydney

National Library of Australia
Cataloguing-in-Publication data:

Watt, Peter, 1949– .
To chase the storm.

ISBN 0 7329 1187 7.

I. Title.

A823.3

Set in 13/16 pt Bembo by Post Pre-press Group
Printed in Australia by McPherson's Printing Group

For my much loved aunt Joan Letitia Payne, nee Duffy, of Tweed Heads, one of Duckie's Daughters

Acknowledgements

As always, my special thanks for the hard work of turning a manuscript into a novel go to my publisher at Pan Macmillan Cate Paterson, ably assisted by Chris Mattey, my editor Simone Ford and patient copy editor Jan Hutchinson. For the artwork my thanks again to Deborah Parry and, for the ongoing support with regards to publicity, to Jane Novak. Special thanks go to an old friend – also my agent – Geoffrey Radford of Anthony Williams Management. I would like to extend my thanks to Rea Francis of RF Media for her continuing support as well as Brian Cook from the Manuscript Appraisal Agency. For ongoing technical advice from my old mate Phil Murphy in Cairns, my many thanks. Also to my sister and brother-in-law, Kerry and Ty Mckee, for helping in the transfer from Tweed Heads to Finch Hatton. To my wonderful mother, Elinor Watt, and all my family for their unstinting encouragement to keep writing – I cannot thank you enough.

To my old *wantok* Robert Bozek and Nadine, whose flow of information in cyberspace keeps me up to date on so many matters, my thanks.

Since the publication of my last novel, *Papua*, I have lost three very important people from my life. I would like to acknowledge their importance to me personally and professionally. My wonderful agent, Tony Williams, who passed away October of 2002: I will miss his company and conversation as much as his sound advice. To his sister Leonie and family in Perth I send my heartfelt thoughts. Beverley Harper, a truly great writer in this genre, also passed away last year. I will miss the times we spent around the barbecue laughing at ourselves and discussing the ins and outs of being authors. Fortunately Bev lives forever in our memories and in the words she has written. Finally, my aunt Marjery Leigh passed away last year and I will miss the support she gave me when I was struggling. Like some of my Aboriginal friends, I believe that their spirits now shine as brightly as stars in the constellation of the Southern Cross. We see them forever.

Not least of all my love and gratitude goes to Naomi Howard–Smith. She is there when times get hard.

And he sees through the rents of the scattering fogs,
The corroboree warlike and grim,
And the lubra who sat by the fire on the logs,
To watch, like a mourner, for him.

'The Last of His Tribe', Henry Kendall

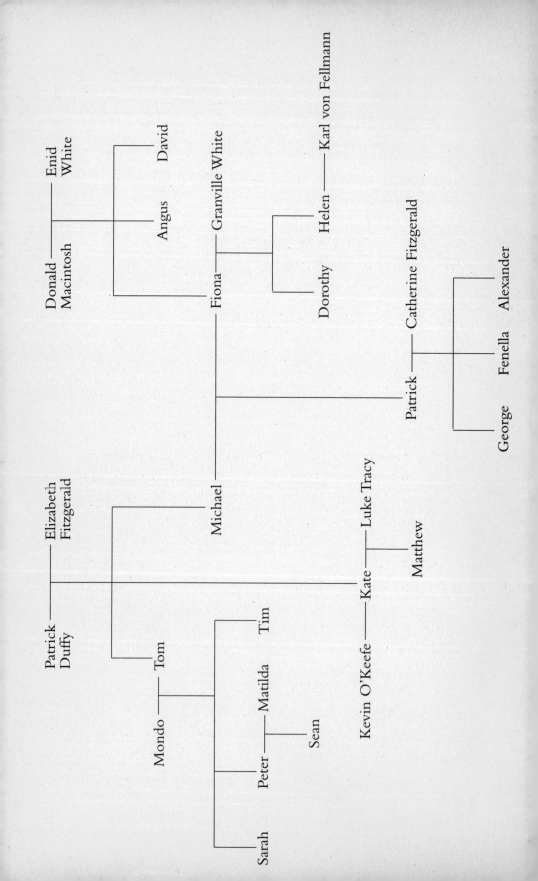

With deft fingers the Aboriginal bushranger – as he had once been labelled by the white man's law-makers – curled off a piece and tamped it into the old clay pipe he produced from his lap. With a burning twig from the fire he lit the leaf and puffed until it smouldered with a bright glow. Dragging on the pipe, he again sighed with pleasure.

Sean watched the ritual and wondered at this very European habit of the old Nerambura man. As if reading his thoughts Wallarie confided, 'Your grandfather taught me to smoke when we were young men together. That was when he taught me the killing ways of the white man.'

Sean nodded dutifully. He was less afraid now but understood that he should not speak unless asked to by the old man squatting on the other side of the fire. A long silence followed as Wallarie continued to puff on his pipe and stare with dreamy eyes into the flickering flames. When he finally spoke it was almost as if Sean was not present. Many of the Nerambura words he used were unknown to Sean with his limited knowledge of the dialect of his ancestors. Wallarie spoke of many things of great importance, telling the stories that the old men once told in the shade of the bumbil tree by the side of the creek that flowed gently as the blood of the land. He spoke of things that were sacred and should be remembered forever. He spoke through the night and the possums in their trees came to listen as the dingo, wild dog of the plains, howled mournfully. The moon rose and set over an endless sea of grey scrub and the curlews cried to each other the song of lost souls.

Outside Matilda shivered as she crouched amongst the rocks in this place of Dreaming, wondering at what might be happening in the sacred place of the men. Finally she fell asleep. When the sun came to touch her face, waking too the rock wallaby from its rest and warming the goanna, she was aware of her son squatting beside her, staring across the dry and sunburnt scrub.

'It is done?' she asked as she sat up.

Sean nodded and placed his head on his folded arms. He remained still for some moments before rising and Matilda could see in her son's face a terrible burden. She knew then that the old man, to whom she had for so many years brought the occasional supply of white man's food, had initiated her son into the blood of his father. Perhaps not in the traditional ways of the Darambal people but in another way, born of the necessity of the times. She also knew that she could never ask her son what he now knew. This was not the way of his Darambal customs.

When he rose to his feet Sean cast a long look back at the entrance to the cave. Had the old Nerambura warrior flown from the sacred place on the wings of the giant wedge-tailed eagle, he wondered, as the Kalkadoon had once believed after the terrible battle that decimated their people. Sean had been reborn of his people and he must never forget all that he had been told. He tried to understand as best as he could. From now on he had a new name granted to him by the old man of the cave. He was to be known by all as Nerambura Duffy. A man of two worlds.

END OF
A CENTURY

1899

PROLOGUE
1899

The woman wore an old cotton shift that recorded the circumstances of her life. It had been torn and patched many times and the red dust of the brigalow scrub plains had turned the once white dress to a deep pink.

Beside her walked a tall young man dressed in the garb of the Australian stockman: flannel shirt and long moleskin trousers tucked into knee-length, calf skin boots. Each was deep in thought as they walked. The young man was barely fifteen years of age but on the frontier, in the hard and sometimes dangerous world of mustering the white man's cattle, he was already considered a man.

Sean Duffy's face reflected the mixed blood of his ancestry: part Aboriginal, part Irish, part Chinese. It was a handsome face in any land and his mother, who walked with him, had also been pretty in her youth. But more than a decade of toil, working long, arduous hours as a station domestic, had drained her beauty. She carried a hessian sack containing a few of the staples of frontier life for both blacks and whites: sugar, tea, tobacco and flour.

The sun over the vast, seemingly endless dry plain was losing its punishing sting when they finally reached their destination. They had set out from the Glen View homestead early that morning. The woman, known by the white man's name of Matilda, now stopped to re-acquaint herself with the landmarks that had become familiar to her over periodic visits. Yes, there was the lonely old gum tree in the clearing. And the piled rocks amongst the grasses!

Her son also knew the place. He had first visited the clearing as a chubby baby, holding his mother's hand and toddling beside her. But now he stopped, using the back of his sleeve to wipe the sweat from his face and brushing idly at the persistent cloud of bush flies that clung to the salty sweat of his body. Without a word, he strode towards the small clusters of stones that marked the final resting place of three men – two of his blood – and gazed down upon them. His mother remained at the edge of the clearing with the sack of precious supplies intended for the living, watching her son pay his respects to his paternal great-grandfather, the big Irishman Tom Duffy, slain by the Native Mounted Police forty years earlier. He then turned his attention to the grave of his father, Peter Duffy, also killed fifteen years earlier by an officer of the Native Mounted Police not far from where he now lay. Sean scarcely gave the third grave a glance, for it contained the bones of an old Aborigine from a place far to the south. His spirit was the concern of his own people of the Murray River area.

'We will go now,' his mother said quietly when Sean turned to walk back to her. 'He is waiting for you at the sacred place.'

She spoke the words in an almost forgotten dialect. It was the language of a people brutally dispersed forty years earlier when the Mounted Police came to kill them, considering them as no more than vermin competing with precious flocks of sheep. Matilda had learned the language over the years from an old man who knew the sacred ways of the Nerambura clan of the Darambal people. The old man was the last full-blooded survivor of those terrible times and his name was still spoken with awe – and sometimes fear – amongst the station employees, Aboriginal, Chinese or European. Old Aboriginal nannies would frighten children out of the dark with threats that the spirit of Wallarie would come and snatch them away if they did not come inside to bed. White governesses would warn the same children that if they strayed too far from the homestead the old warrior would spear them.

But Sean Duffy did not fear the terrible bogy man of his childhood companions, for his mother had told him other stories about the legendary Darambal warrior who had once ridden with Sean's own father as well as with his grandfather, the bushranger of Burkesland, Tom Duffy.

No more words were needed as they continued their trek to the low range of hills that dominated the vast red plains of central Queensland. Sean Duffy was about to meet the man whose name had for so long dominated the tales his mother told him. As the sun began its descent towards the western horizon they reached the craggy, most conspicuous hill in the ancient range, which itself resembled the protruding backbone of the earth.

Following a well-worn trail first used by the hunters and warriors of the Dreaming, they struggled up the hill until they came to a rock overhang which concealed a large cavern, the very heart of the Nerambura people.

Matilda passed the sack to her son and gestured for him to go inside. He could see his mother's fear and knew that it was justified – no woman should ever step inside the sacred place of the men. Taking the sack, Sean hoped his mother could not see his own fear, for was it not said by all at Glen View that this was a cursed place?

Taking a deep breath, Sean brushed aside a tangle of exposed roots growing down the rock face. Inside he could see a fire burning and suddenly felt a wave of strange and overpowering fear such as he had never experienced before. There was a presence here that transcended all that he had ever known in the living world. The young man stood petrified, as still as the stones of the hill itself. He would go no further.

'Your white blood causes you the fear,' said a voice that seemed to come from the flickering fire itself at the centre of the dark place. 'But you are also Nerambura and you belong here.' As his eyes adjusted to the dim light Sean could see that the voice did not come from the fire but from a dark figure, sitting with his legs crossed. 'Come sit with me.'

The young man obeyed. Drawing near, he could see the shadows of firelight flickering on the face of an old man with a long, grey beard. This was not the man he imagined from the stories told by the other station children. Wallarie did not have razor sharp teeth or horns growing from his head. Nor were his eyes blood red and burning. The face was that of a man who had seen much tragedy but it was also a gentle face, reconciled with the cruelty of mankind.

'You have brought tobacco?' the old man asked in the Nerambura dialect.

Sean nodded and rummaged in the flour sack for the twist of tarry leaves. He passed it to Wallarie who sighed as he fingered the precious leaf.

ONE

The silent people on the street seemed to be running rather than walking. Horse-drawn carriages and drays were weaving in and out of the milling crowds at a break-neck speed. The grainy black and white images flickered to the accompaniment of a rhythmic clattering interspersed with gasps of wonder from those watching. The film spread its magic throughout the room.

'Oh look, Father! I can see the David Jones building,' Fenella exclaimed in awe. 'It's so real!'

Patrick Duffy smiled at his fourteen-year-old daughter's child-like wonder. She was not as grown up as she would like all to think. The demonstration of this new device they called a moving film projector by his old military colleague of the Sudan campaign, Arthur Thorncroft, could entrance his daughter and take her back to a time when dolls were more important than her debut into Sydney's colonial society.

9

'Yes, the images do look real,' Patrick agreed. 'But then they were real when Mr Thorncroft filmed them.'

The short film clattered to an end and Patrick's two boys, George aged fifteen and Alexander aged twelve, both moaned in unison that the magic lantern had nothing else to offer – they had wanted it to go on forever!

Arthur Thorncroft turned to the young man who had assisted him and nodded his approval. In his late thirties but with the receding hairline of an older man, he looked small next to Patrick Duffy. Though they were of a similar age, Patrick's hair was still thick and curling despite a distinctive dash of grey peppered through it. With his clean shaven face dominated by startling emerald green eyes, Patrick stood tall and broad-shouldered, still bearing the ramrod posture of the military officer he had once been when fighting Her Majesty's colonial wars in Africa. His was not the finely chiselled, handsome face of an English aristocrat but that of the Irish rebels of his father's ancestry. Although perhaps not fashionably handsome, his rugged presence nonetheless turned the head of any lady in a room, although it was not a power he seemed conscious of.

Patrick glanced across at his three children, still glued to the deep leather chairs of the Macintosh library. Arthur pulled aside the long, heavy curtains, allowing the sunlight to flood the room. The delicate beauty of the two eldest children, George and Fenella, was revealed. They reflected their mother's aristocratic looks, but when the Australian sun shone on Alexander, it revealed his remarkable likeness to his father. Physical similarities to their parents aside, it was the very different personalities of the three children that often enough would puzzle Patrick. Fenella may be the mirror of her mother in appearance and mannerisms, but there was also a snobbishness that was not hers alone.

10

Alexander was reserved to the point of being timid; not unlike his cousin Daniel, he was an easy target for George to bully – which the latter did with an unhealthy enthusiasm. Patrick secretly hoped that his youngest son would, in time, learn to stand up for himself.

Then there was George himself, a strangely sullen boy with a tendency to cruelty and deceit. Patrick shuddered at the thought that passed through his mind with the haunting presence of a rotting corpse. He did not want to compare his eldest son with a man who had been so instrumental in bringing misery to two families for so many years, a man who was dead but whose evil legacy still echoed down the corridors of time. Was it possible that people could inherit characteristics from those who had gone before? Was it possible that George displayed some likeness to a young Granville White? Patrick reflected on this with his inborn Celtic superstition for the unexplainable. Even Lady Enid Macintosh, Patrick's maternal grandmother, had remarked to him once that the boy had an uncanny similarity to Granville.

'It's the future, Patrick.' Arthur's words cut across Patrick's brooding thoughts. 'A means of unlimited possibilities. Imagine: we could record events as they happen and then take those moving pictures to any place in Australia to show people the closest thing to being there. Or record on film someone as famous as Miss Deborah Cohen performing her arias before royalty. All Australians – even those in the most remote areas – could then share the splendour of her fame.'

'Miss Cohen is renowned for her voice,' Patrick countered quietly. 'How would your moving pictures have any meaning with just an image and not her voice?'

The dapper little man thrust his hands in his pocket and

glanced across at his assistant. Patrick followed his look and wondered if the young man was another of Arthur's many lovers. It was something that he would never dare ask; some things were better ignored between friends.

'Ralph has thought about that for some time and come up with the answer,' Arthur replied. 'You explain to Mr Duffy, Ralph,' he said with a triumphant smile.

The young man coughed nervously and shifted his feet. 'We use a gramophone in conjunction with Miss Cohen's image on the screen, Mr Duffy,' he replied softly. 'All we have to do is synchronise voice and film. A bit tricky, we concede, but it can be done by trained projectionists.'

Ralph looked visibly relieved as Patrick nodded his head approvingly at the young man's answer. 'On that matter you have answered my question, Arthur. But I can assure you that I will probably have many more questions after I discuss the question of incorporating your moving pictures into the Macintosh companies with Lady Macintosh.'

Arthur smiled again, sensing that he had won his friend's financial support and could now visit Europe and America to further his knowledge of this new technology and its limitless possibilities. Arthur Thorncroft had a vision. All he needed was money – a lot of money – to see that vision realised.

'Would people pretend to do things on the moving pictures one day, Mr Thorncroft? Make up stories like those in stage plays?'

This was an echo of Arthur's own thoughts and he turned towards the one who asked the question. 'They would one day, Miss Macintosh. Just like the great actors and actresses of the stage today. They would be seen by more people in the world than ever before.'

Fenella's enigmatic smile went unseen by all in the room

except the man who had answered her. She has the vision, Arthur mused. 'It might be that one day you will be one of those people that the world will see. You are certainly beautiful enough, like your mother.'

The young woman blushed at the compliment but was bold enough to stare into his eyes when she replied softly, 'I will be, Mr Thorncroft.'

Patrick glanced up from the cumbersome projector he had been examining with scientific interest. 'First you finish your education, young lady,' he growled gently. 'Then I think you will meet a young gentleman fitting your station in life and get married.'

'Oh, I will do that some day, Father,' she replied lightly. 'But I have so many things to do first. Just like Mama wants to do now.'

His daughter's reply had a barb that stung Patrick. Catherine's restlessness had been all too apparent over the last year and it was obvious that the tension between them had not been missed by their daughter. She was too perceptive for her age, he thought. What is between a man and a wife is their concern only, not that of mere children. He was tempted to reply to the barely concealed challenge but checked himself. 'I think it is time you children thought about music practice,' Patrick said gruffly.

There was no moan of protest. All three Macintosh children knew better than to argue with the gentle but strong man who ruled their lives with love and discipline in equal amounts. They dutifully bid him and Arthur a good afternoon and slouched off for the detested hour on the piano under the sharp nose and beady eyes of their music tutor, Miss Graham.

Patrick turned his attention to his guests and finalised plans for their next meeting on the matter of finance before escorting them to the grand entrance of the Macintosh family home, where a carriage waited to carry them the few miles back to the growing city of Sydney. Patrick waved to Arthur then turned back towards the house and walked to his grandmother in the drawing room. There was much to discuss. He only wished Catherine had been with him this afternoon to witness the miracle of the moving pictures.

Lady Enid Macintosh was an impressive woman even in the first years of her eighties. Her frailty was only visible in the transparent, smooth skin of her face which seemed delicate as rice paper but otherwise was barely marked by the signs of time. From her face burned the emerald green eyes that marked the women of her family, eyes that Patrick also had inherited through his mother, Fiona, Enid's daughter. Her once raven hair was now snow white but carefully groomed into a bun on her head.

Enid sat with her hands in her lap, where a pair of spectacles lay. Her vanity did not allow anyone to see her wearing them when she perused company reports or read the newspapers. Although she had been dozing when Patrick entered the room his presence was immediately sensed and the green eyes, now only slightly opaque with age, were open as he took a seat opposite. The room seemed strangely devoid of ostentation, given its location in a house that could afford any luxury available in the colony of New South Wales.

Enid smiled warmly. 'Mr Thorncroft has departed?' she asked. 'I hope your meeting was fruitful.'

'You would have enjoyed yourself, Grandmother,' Patrick said. 'The moving pictures are not the work of the devil as you might believe.'

'Oh, I know that. But I fear that people will use the invention for the devil's work some day. Perhaps that does not make sense to you, but I have a feeling nothing good can come of such an invention.'

'It can make money.'

'Well, that is a good thing for the company, I suppose,' she replied with a sigh. 'And that is what it is to be a Macintosh.'

'I'm not all Macintosh,' Patrick reminded his grandmother.

'I know it was hard for you to allow your children to take my name,' she said with a hint of compassion. 'But it was arranged with your Uncle Daniel a long time ago, Patrick. A necessity, so that against all odds the Macintosh name should survive. Did you know that your Uncle David was fascinated by photography?' Enid continued as she reflected on the complexity of family relationships. 'I think he would have been very fascinated by Mr Thorncroft's project.'

'Does that mean that you will give your approval to any proposal I put to our bankers to finance Arthur?' Patrick asked.

'I think so. I know that is what David would have wanted. Perhaps it is also possible that moving films will capture all that is good in people's lives.'

'Thank you, Grandmother,' Patrick said, rising to kiss her.

Enid waved him down, indicating that she had not yet finished with business. 'I have received a letter from Germany this day. A letter from Helen.'

Patrick sank to his chair. His grandmother could never bear to refer to Helen or Dorothy as his sisters – or at least half sisters. The old animosities that once existed between Enid and his mother prevented her from doing so, he thought.

'I hope she is well and enjoying life in the von Fellmann family,' he said politely. 'Are we to see her one day?'

'It seems so. She and her husband will be travelling to

Sydney and then on to Queensland. Her husband has a post with his Church up there.'

Patrick had never met his half sister's husband. Karl von Fellmann was one of his Aunt Penelope's twin sons. A few years younger than Helen, he had married her after his ordination as a Lutheran pastor. Penelope's other son had followed in his father's footsteps and taken a commission in the imperial German army.

'Then her visit is more than just social.'

'Yes,' Enid replied with a slight frown. 'Her husband is seeking missionary work in Queensland amongst the Aboriginal people. Helen has requested that we grant her and her husband land at Glen View to set up a mission station.'

Patrick raised his eyebrows in surprise. 'A bit late for missionary work around Glen View,' he commented pragmatically. 'The dispersal of '62 took care of that. The only blackfellows at Glen View are the ones we brought in from surrounding districts to work the cattle.'

'Apparently Helen knows that but she feels her husband can provide a central place to minister to all the dark brethren that might be displaced in the districts around Glen View. They feel they could provide a place for them on Glen View.'

'What is your view of her request?'

'I have my thoughts,' his grandmother replied thoughtfully. 'But I would rather hear yours first, as the owner of Glen View. It is only right.'

Patrick knew from experience that whenever his grandmother made such a statement she had already decided that her thoughts would be opposed to his. He shifted uncomfortably in his chair before replying. 'My two grandfathers are buried on Glen View,' he replied. 'So also my cousin Peter Duffy, not to mention my Uncle Angus. The property

16

is more than just a money-making enterprise. It might be one of many properties we own but even you must appreciate its family significance to both you and me, and to your great-grandchildren.' He examined her expression for a reaction and was pleased to see just a hint of self-doubt.

'You are right,' she finally said. 'We cannot give up one inch of Glen View for any reason whatsoever. God has given us the land and Helen will just have to understand.'

'I am sure that if she and her husband approach the Queensland government they will be more than sympathetic to a request for land to be used as a mission station,' Patrick said rather lamely. 'I know the government up there is seeking a solution to the Aboriginal problem by spreading Christianity amongst them.'

'They have been steeped in their heathenism for so long with their primitive beliefs,' Enid said with the conviction of her Christian devoutness, 'that I sometimes despair that our faith will ever truly take root amongst them.'

Patrick found himself silently agreeing with his grandmother. What he had learned of the Aboriginal people mystified him. Aided by the Native Mounted Police, his maternal grandfather had launched a deadly and thorough expedition to slaughter every man, woman and child of the Nerambura clan of the Darambal people on Glen View. By 1868 only one full-blooded man survived and even now he remained a legend amongst the frontier communities in the colony of Queensland. While Wallarie lived so too did the Nerambura people. Although Patrick would never approve of the methods his grandfather used to disperse the Nerambura he did at least understand them. His grandfather had been at war with the land, carving out a place fit for good Christian men and women. The Nerambura had resisted his holy crusade and so had to be eliminated.

But could such terrible violence go unavenged? So many violent deaths had come to both the Duffys and the Macintoshes over the years for no apparent reason. It was as if both families had unleashed a primitive curse upon themselves.

'Patrick? You are miles away,' his grandmother interrupted. 'What is bothering you? Is it Arthur's proposal?'

He realised that his withdrawal was disturbing her. His grandmother was sensitive to his moods and might construe his reflective silence for worry. 'No. I was thinking about something else. I'm sorry if I seem to be distracted.'

He rose again and kissed her gently on the forehead. Reaching up to touch his face with her delicate, frail hand, Enid said perceptively, 'Life has a way of going on despite all our worries. One day our family will find the peace we seek.'

'I know,' he replied. 'I just hope it comes in our lifetime.'

Patrick left his grandmother alone in the drawing room, taking his troubled thoughts with him. But Enid harboured her own troubled feelings. Had she made the right decision to side with her grandson and leave Glen View firmly in Macintosh hands? Or should she have conceded to her grand-daughter's request to provide a place for the Aboriginal people? For many years she had harboured the fear that all the problems that had beset the family had a source far away on the brigalow plains of central Queensland, a force released by the bloody slaughter of an ancient people whose soul was the land itself. The more Lady Macintosh tried to justify their decision, the more she was reminded of a name that always seemed to be present in the shadows of her life, the strange heathen name of a warrior: Wallarie.

TWO

The teak inlay and expensive brass fittings of the room reeked of opulence and an assurance that the food served here would be the finest in the colony. Catherine Duffy's appearance in the hotel restaurant caused the heads of a couple of colonial matrons to turn. Whispered comments concerning her public appearance without her husband were made as their eyes followed the beautiful woman to a table where a man sat, obviously awaiting her company.

'I am so pleased to see that you could join me for dinner, Catherine,' Brett Norris said as he rose from his chair. 'I feared you might have trouble getting away.'

Brett Norris had journeyed to Sydney to explore future prospects for his family's enterprises. But his first order of priorities had been the renewal of an old acquaintanceship with the beautiful Catherine Duffy, nee Fitzgerald. From his first meeting with her he had confirmed his belief that she had learned the error of her ways in marrying the Australian. Catherine had a discontentment that he knew he could exploit and their rendezvous in the hotel restaurant was the fourth time they had met to dine and talk. But Norris wanted more than talk. He wanted the wife of Patrick Duffy more than he wanted any financial opportunities that the Australian colonies could offer.

Catherine flashed a smile as she allowed the waiter to assist her into her chair. Brett Norris could not help admiring this woman with the beautiful green eyes, milk white skin and long, fiery titian tresses piled elegantly on her head. 'Patrick is more interested in managing Lady Enid's companies and playing soldiers with his regiment than my whereabouts,' she replied with an edge of bitterness.

'His regiment might be called on to campaign in South Africa against the Boer, the ways things are going,' Norris cautioned. 'How would you feel about him leaving you?'

Catherine accepted the crystal flute of champagne poured for her by the waiter. 'He has seen enough war,' she replied, sipping from the flute. 'Knowing my husband as I do, I doubt that he will leave his grandmother to go away, even if his regiment is called to service in Africa.'

Brett Norris pursed his lips in disagreement. He was a handsome man, approaching forty, and now controlled his father's companies. Iron, coal, railways, arms of war and textile factories in England were the mainstay of Norris & Son and the company now sought further afield for the raw materials of their industry. 'I think, knowing the little that I do of your husband,' he said, 'that he could not bear to relinquish his command of the regiment in time of war. Men like your husband have misguided ideas that they must be prepared to lay down their lives for men who need their courage and leadership.'

Catherine gave him a quizzical look. 'You sound like you actually admire my husband.'

'Don't misinterpret me, my dearest Catherine,' he replied smoothly as he sipped the excellent French champagne. 'I am only saying his kind of values are not my kind. No, I prefer wealth and power as any normal man would to the possibility of a painful death on an obscure battlefield in some godforsaken place. And I think you know that I was right about what I said that night at the dinner your grandfather invited Captain Duffy to. Do you remember?' Catherine frowned as Norris continued, 'I told you that we were meant for each other.'

'That is either arrogance or presumption on your behalf,' she replied. 'Either way, you do not know me as you think you do.'

'Oh, I know how restless you are to find something in your life for yourself. Until now you have borne the duty of a good wife and mother, but that is not you, Catherine. You have always sought to be your own woman, and I think I know just what you want.'

Brett Norris's eyes seemed to bore into the secret places of Catherine's being; he spoke with such conviction. Could he really know what she wanted when she was sometimes not sure herself?

'What do I want then?' she challenged.

'You want your grandfather's estate, which of course I currently own. And furthermore, I suspect that you really want the Hill of Cuchulainn, even more than the house.' He noted her reaction and smiled triumphantly before continuing. 'When I purchased your grandfather's place after the death duties could not be paid, I suppose I always hoped you would take your rightful place as mistress of the house. You would then be able to undertake your dig on the hill and write papers on your findings. I think I am right in saying that the Hill calls you with its ancient Celtic songs of seduction, Catherine Fitzgerald. This miserable country is not your land. You belong back in Ireland with your faerie people.'

Catherine listened to his persuasive words as if in a dream. He really did know what she wanted. 'What would I need to do to be with my faerie people?' she asked softly, faintly aware that the man opposite had taken her hand in his own. A soft hand with long tapering fingers, the sensual hand of a man who desired her.

'You would sell your soul to the devil,' he answered with a smouldering intensity that made her think he just might be the devil himself. 'You would return with me to Ireland. If you stay with me for one year I will sign your grand-father's estate over to you and you alone.'

'And what of my children?'

'You would leave them here for one year before they joined you in Ireland. I want just one year to allow you to see how much more of a woman you could be away from all that has taken up your life.'

'I do not think that I could leave my children under the circumstances you propose.'

'You could arrange to have them sent to England to finish their education. That is a reasonable suggestion, con-sidering that, as their mother, you would have a say in their future. But for now, why not return to Ireland with me?'

Listening to his words, Catherine was suddenly fright-ened. *But what about Patrick?* She found herself thinking of him as dispassionately as if he were a complete stranger. It was then that she admitted to herself – without misgivings – that she no longer loved him. But nor did she love Brett Norris.

'I will consider what you propose,' she said quietly, and

felt Norris give her hand a gentle squeeze. 'But if I accept do not presume that I am making any declaration of love for you.'

'I would make no such presumption. I told you that you were making a pact with the devil.'

Even as he said the words, Catherine made up her mind.

THREE

The old bull's emaciated frame belied its cantankerous nature. He was full of fight and swung his head, attempting to gore the rider's horse close on its flank. Ben Rosenblum expected the worst but still swore angrily as he pulled down on the reins to swerve away.

Red dust exploded and his mount hit a knee-high termite nest. The concrete-hard tower held strong and Ben found himself flung into the thick dust as his terrified horse fought to stay upright while avoiding the old scrawny bull. The pain in Ben's chest spread to the very tips of his fingers as the sky swirled above him in a red haze, and his breath came in ragged gasps. He was not aware of the sound of a horse galloping towards him.

'He almost got you,' a voice yelled down. Saul swung himself expertly from the saddle. 'Are you all right?'

Ben grunted, trying to ease himself into a sitting position.

'I'm going to shoot that bastard,' he muttered painfully through the pain. 'Should have shot him last year, the mongrel.'

Despite Ben's regular threats, his son fully knew that his father would not shoot the old bull. The animal had come as a calf with him from Townsville all those years ago when he first took his lease of land. He had named the property Jerusalem in honour of his Jewish roots – and because it was to be his new promised land. But the disastrous economic depression of the '90s, coupled with one of the severest droughts in the colony's history, had meant his dreams of success eluded him still. He knew that he should have cut his losses years earlier and walked away, but the property had been settled at the cost of the life of his beloved wife Jennifer. A man does not walk away from that which he loves most.

Saul helped his father to his feet. The young man was himself as hard as the termite nests that dotted the dusty red plain north of the Queensland town of Cloncurry. Sporting a long black beard below the sun-blackened face of an Australian bushman, Saul had known no other life than the gruelling work of a stockman alongside his father. Once he had been sent to live with his wealthy relatives in Townsville, Solomon and Judith Cohen, but he had yearned for the wide open spaces of Jerusalem and made his way back to the property leaving his young sister, Rebecca, and his brother, Jonathan, behind. Saul had no regrets.

While he was helping his father to his feet, two other horsemen galloped over. Terituba, an Aboriginal man of Ben's age, was a survivor of the terrible war fifteen years earlier when the fiercest of all the Aboriginal tribes, the Kalkadoon, were slaughtered in a pitched battle in the Godkin Ranges north of Cloncurry. Wounded, he had made his way with the remnants of his family to Jerusalem to be employed by the Jewish cattleman. The young man who rode beside him was his only surviving son Jacob, whose name had been bestowed on him by Ben.

'You bin wrestle with old King,' Terituba said with a twinkle in his eye as he surveyed the scene. The old bull was now trotting towards the distant and sparsely scattered scrub. 'You bin lose 'im pight with old King.'

'Yeah, you old black bastard,' Ben scowled, looking up at his friend sitting easily astride the mount. 'Like to have seen you do better.'

'I bin leave 'im alone, boss. Mebbe I'm smarter than you. Mebbe you too old to go chasin' old King,' Terituba said with a chuckle.

Such misfortunes as being unseated in a muster were not uncommon and often the cause of some light-hearted merriment amongst the tough stockmen, both black and white.

Saul could not help joining in the laughter as his cursing father limped after his horse. But he suddenly ceased as he followed his father's limping chase with worried eyes. Turning to the Kalkadoon man, Saul saw an expression on his normally passive face that mirrored his own.

'He looks a bit crook,' Saul said. 'You think he will be all right?'

'Me tink 'e should go 'ome,' the old warrior said softly. 'Mebbe lie down by an' by.'

'I think so too,' Saul replied softly in the Kalkadoon language, so as not to be overheard. His father had never bothered to learn the language but it had been natural for his son to as he grew alongside his boyhood friend. 'He has had bad nights with chest pains. I don't think the fall would have done him any good.'

'I agree, Bumbil. He a sick man – should be sittin' in the shade with his woman.'

Terituba used the name given to Saul many years earlier. It was an honour to be named after the hardy tree that provided so much. For the settlers the wood of the bumbil was used for building material and fence posts. For the Aborigines it was a tree from which were made the wooden weapons of war and hunting. Saul was a man who understood both worlds, and together the old Kalkadoon warrior and young stockman conspired to guide Ben back to the tiny ram-shackle homestead that nestled in the encroaching scrub of the dusty plains north of Cloncurry.

When the four men rode in just on sunset they were met by a solitary figure. Standing near the tank stand, a short distance from the bark slab hut that was home for Saul and his father, the well-dressed young man was covered in dust but beamed with delight at the horsemen, who now broke into a gallop to reach him.

'Hey, Jonathan! What are you doing out here?' Saul whooped as he brought his mount to a sideways halt beside his brother. 'You get sick of city life?' Swinging himself from the saddle, Saul embraced him in a crushing bear hug.

'Time came when I thought I should see you both. After all, it's been three years,' Jonathan replied with some effort. 'I need to talk to you and Dad. Uncle Solomon sent me.'

Saul stepped back from his brother. The mention of Solomon's name caused an ominous shiver of concern. It had to be about the property.

'What's Uncle Solomon want with us?' Saul asked suspiciously, but his brother ignored the question as he greeted his father and nodded to Terituba and Jacob.

Ben led the way to the hut to recover a precious bottle of gin he had stored for special occasions, while Terituba and his son led the horses away to be brushed down and yarded. The visit of his son guaranteed the bottle would be emptied that night.

Inside the hut the air was hot and oppressive so once the bottle was found the three men went out to the makeshift verandah, a bark shingle lean-to held up by two rickety posts. They sat down on logs that passed as chairs while the patriarch of Jerusalem poured three tumblers of gin.

'Mazltov,' Ben said, raising his glass.

Jonathan cast his father a curious look. 'I have never heard you say that before, Father,' he commented. 'Have you come back to our ways?'

'Maybe not as much as I should have,' Ben replied as he took a long swig on the fiery liquid, causing his eyes to water. 'A man has a lot of time to think out here under God's heavens.'

Jonathan nodded. He was a devout man who donated to the Synagogue whenever possible. Working in the vast enterprises accumulated by his uncle over the years had made him prosperous. He could easily afford a nice home in one of Brisbane's more affluent suburbs. Jonathan turned to his brother. 'Have you also come back to our ways?'

Saul gave his brother a cheeky grin. 'Me? My religion is Kalkadoon, so I guess you would consider me no better than one of your philistines.'

'You should not joke about such things, Saul. Our religion is very important to our identity.'

'Out here most people know me as one of the best stockmen in the district. That's my identity. Maybe you need religion to know who you are, but I don't. I know who I am and where I belong.'

Jonathan's audible sigh of disapproval annoyed Saul. He could be a toffy bastard when he wanted to, he thought. Always wanted to be a city man.

Ben moved to check the animosity between his two sons, who from birth had been like chalk and cheese. 'How is little Becky?' he interjected. 'Has she plans to marry her young man?'

'Becky is fine. She plans to marry David in six months. He is doing very well in his position in the bank in Brisbane,' Jonathan replied. 'The ceremony will be in the Synagogue.'

'Ahh . . . A Jewish banker then, is her young man,' Ben said, teasing his serious son. 'She will be his princess and live a good life.'

Saul was also pleased at the news. Rebecca's frequent letters to him and his father were treasured documents. He had missed his little sister and often wondered what sort of young woman she had grown into. Did she take after his mother with her long blonde hair and gentle ways?

'I hope you two will be at the wedding,' Jonathan said quietly. 'It would mean a lot to her if you were.'

Saul was about to protest that the property kept them tied down when his father put his tumbler of gin down beside him in the red earth and said in a flat voice, 'You have come from Solomon to tell us that we are finished. That is why we would be able to go to Becky's wedding, isn't it?'

Jonathan's expression was grim on hearing his father's unexpected observation. 'I'm sorry, Father,' Jonathan mumbled. 'But everyone suffered from the crash. Uncle Solomon stretched himself as far as he could to finance Jerusalem and keep you here. He knows what this place means to you and Saul.'

'He has been more than generous over the years in extending the loan,' Ben said with a sigh. 'I understand that and will always be grateful. I have known for a long time that this day would come. Maybe it is God's will.'

'Be buggered!' Saul exploded. 'With the war coming in South Africa we could make a lot of money from beef. All we need is a bit more time to pay back everything we owe.'

'No, Saul!' his father roared angrily. 'We do not live on charity. We have our strength and I know you could get work anywhere from here to the Gulf. No, it's time we learned to cut our losses and pay back what we have lived on for so many years.'

The tough young stockman turned to his father and saw in his eyes a lost soul, beaten down by the harsh land that surrounded them. 'What about Terituba and Jacob?' Saul pleaded. 'Their women are long dead and they are alone like us.'

'Old Terituba will never be alone in this land,' his father said in a tired voice. 'He belongs out here, whether we exist or not. I learned that from my old friend a long time ago. No, he will continue to live on when we are gone from here. Jacob is probably as good as you as a bushman and with my recommendation will get work on Franklin's lease. He will be all right.'

'And me? Where do I go?'

'You are strong and capable.' Ben flared at his son's self-pitying question. 'My old friend Kate Tracy would get you work if you asked her. She once employed a worthless boy from Sydney and gave him responsibilities far beyond his years. She would do no less for that man's son whose snivelling makes him just about as bad as I was those years ago.'

Saul bowed his head and fumbled with his broad brimmed hat. His father was right! The inevitable had happened and he could work somewhere else. He did not need to apologise for his weakness to his father, who knew him better than any person on earth.

'Saul will make preparations tomorrow to go to Towns-ville,' Ben said. 'I will follow soon enough.'

'Don't you think you should come with me, Father?' Jonathan asked gently.

'No. I have things to do before I leave and it is good that Saul goes ahead to find us a place until we get work. I will be all right. Terituba will be with me. Now we will break bread together and be happy for Becky's coming happiness. I know your mother would have wanted us to. And then we finish the bottle.'

The three men ate that night and talked of all things except the coming foreclosure on Jerusalem. They drank outside under the magnificent, slowly swirling canopy of southern stars until their heads swam and the stars blurred, arcing streaks across the black velvet sky. Then they slept where they fell in the red dust of the land. Only Ben awoke in the early hours of the morning when he heard the distant mournful sounds and felt the pain grip his chest with its familiar vice-like fingers.

On unsteady legs he tottered towards the silhouette of the big pepper tree and smelt its pungent scent on the cool, early morning air. He crumpled to his knees beside the carefully tended mound that marked his beloved wife's grave, here at the foot of the tree she had once so lovingly nurtured as a struggling sapling, far from its South American home. A dark shape suddenly appeared at his side out of the night's shadow.

'Terituba? I hope that's you.'

'Yes, boss.'

'I'm dying, aren't I?'

'Yes, boss. Not long to go.'

'Good. I swore to Jennifer a long time ago that I would never leave her alone out here.'

'No, old friend of mine. Not good to leave your woman. Her spirit wanders alone waiting for you,' the old Kalka-doon man answered softly in his language.

It did not matter that the white man did not understand his words. What was important was that his friend would not be alone when he died. He had sensed death very close and knew whose dying it would be. Terituba squatted in the powdery dust a short distance from Ben. He was aware that the old man had a need to be alone with the spirit of his dead wife. Many times over the years, the white man would sit beside the mound and talk to her spirit. Her soul was now the spirit of the spreading tree, with its cooling shade in a land of sparse comfort.

'My darling Jennifer, I promised that I would never leave you,' Ben said with tears brimming in his eyes. The gentle tears were not for himself but for the memory of a young girl standing forlorn amongst the tents of the Palmer River gold miners after the terrible floods of '74. He had been a young man then with the veneer of an independent tough bushman, working alongside Kate Tracy hauling in the desperately needed supplies for the starving miners and their families. The stolid bullocks had crossed rivers swollen by flood, climbed bone-breaking mountains and faced the spears of the fierce Merkin warriors along the way. But his tough veneer had been shattered forever when this frightened and half-starved young woman had come into his life, never to leave his side until the fateful day when a snake had struck, protecting its own young.

He wiped ineffectively at his eyes with the sleeve of his shirt and sniffed. 'I have missed you for so long, your laughter and the way you smiled. I have missed you more than you could have ever known.'

He paused and stared up at the silent sky above. The constellation of the Southern Cross was low on the horizon and across the dusty yard he could see the outline of their hut where Jennifer had once baked bread and waited anxiously for his return from the dangerous places where the Kalkadoon stalked the unwary. Turning to look down at the mound, he could make out the now desiccated posy of wildflowers he had left a week earlier. As he reached down to touch them, the pain came to his body in a way that he knew it would never again.

Terituba saw Ben slump forward with a low groan. The old Kalkadoon warrior rose from the earth. He padded to the body and squatted beside his old friend, crooning a song softly so that he did not disturb the spirits of the night. He sang until the Southern Cross was gone from the dark sky then rose to his feet and walked away. No-one would ever again see the last true warrior of the Kalkadoon.

In the morning Ben's two sons found their father slumped over their mother's grave, clutching a dry posy of flowers as if taking them into the next world to greet her. Jonathan's was the greater grief, the guilty sorrow of a man who had long been away.

'He died alone and without the prayers,' Jonathan cried quietly. 'Someone should have been with him to say the prayer for the dead.'

'He did not die alone,' his brother said. His keen eyes had read the footprints in the red dust beside his father's body. 'He had a friend with him.'

Jonathan glanced at his brother with a questioning look but Saul only shrugged and walked back to the hut to fetch a shovel. Jonathan would never understand the spirituality of the Kalkadoon, Saul thought as he walked towards the bark hut that had been his home.

Together the brothers buried their father beside their beloved mother. Despite Ben's apparent return to the religion of his ancestors he was also at one with the spirits of the red earth, lagoons, rocks and trees.

The old bull stood under the shade of the scrub trees, eyeing the young man who was afoot. He watched with suspicion as the man raised a stick-like thing to his shoulder and pointed it at him. Annoying flies buzzed around his thick and powerful head and he snorted irritably.

Saul trained the foresight of the Snider rifle squarely below the thick neck and over the scrawny bull's heart. It was better to kill the stock than leave them to the mercy of the savage land of drought and flood. It was an easy shot, and the old bull would finally be freed from its harsh life in the scrub, Saul thought.

But the shot was never fired. The rifle was lowered and the young bushman smiled. 'You have sired a family that has learned to live in this land, you old bastard,' he said softly. 'Maybe your progeny will be around when we are all gone from these lands. You have earned the right to live.'

He hefted the rifle over his shoulder and strode back to where his horse grazed contentedly on the wild grasses of the vast inland plain. With easy grace he swung himself into the saddle and pointed his rifle at the sky. The shot rolled its echo through the scrub, causing the old bull to turn and trot away. The sound was like that of the stockwhip and the old bull knew its stinging bite.

FOUR

For as long as men have gone to war, barking voices have harried civilian recruits into untidy squads, platoons, companies and eventually battalions. The voices that abused their motley assemblies as poor excuses for fighting men belonged to the senior non-commissioned officers of the army: corporals, sergeants and, above all, sergeant majors. And mere hours after the news that Britain had declared war on the Boer Republics in South Africa, the barking voices were mustering their unruly flocks at military depots across the length and breadth of the colonies of Australia.

Major Patrick Duffy stood by the brigadier's window and gazed out onto the parade ground of Sydney's Victoria Barracks. Although a major with a colonial regiment, Patrick was not in his military uniform but wore a suit, the more familiar uniform of his daily working life. He watched with a certain amount of nostalgia as straight-backed sergeants with quivering moustaches waxed to pencil points bawled incomprehensible orders at the civilians. Soon they would be soldiers in the mounted infantry, facing new terrors in the coming battles against the Dutch farmers across the sea. These recruits could ride and shoot with all the skills of their soon-to-be adversaries, tough men from the colony's Outback where they had worked under the southern skies like the Boer. The sights and sounds were all so familiar to Patrick and he was momentarily transported back to the British army campaigning in Egypt and the Sudan.

'Patrick, old chap, so good to see you again after all these years.' The man who had entered the office offering his hand and a genuinely warm smile stood almost as tall as Patrick. He wore the uniform of a Scottish Highlands regiment and the rank of colonel.

'Good to see you, John,' Patrick replied as he grasped the hand of Colonel Hughes. 'Must be at least fifteen years since we last met in Suakin.'

'Must be, old chap,' the colonel replied. 'I remember then I was trying to talk you out of resigning your commission with us.'

'You still have me, in a manner of speaking. If you can call command of a colonial militia regiment being part of the British army.'

'My opinion is that your Tommy Cornstalks will well and truly be a part of Her Majesty's imperial army in South Africa. This is not going to be like it was back in the Sudan in '85 when all we faced were spear-wielding fuzzy wuzzies. I have spent time in the Boer Republics and our experience at Majuba a few years back has shown us the Boer is a tough customer. My views – not necessarily shared by my colleagues in London – is that our colonial troops are just the right material we need to fight fire with fire. But that is an opinion I fear puts me off side with the War Office, old chap.'

'So that's how you ended up here,' Patrick grinned. 'They shuffled you off to the colonies as your punishment.'

'Sort of,' Colonel Hughes said with a frown. 'That and a posting to damned intelligence.'

'At your rank it must be a command posting of staff? Sounds rather mysterious.'

The colonel gestured for Patrick to take a seat on the other side of the dark timber desk clearly meant to be functional rather than decorative. He felt comfortable around Patrick, with whom he had soldiered in two North African campaigns. Despite the difference in rank and the resulting formalities between soldiers, in private they related as old friends who had shared much together in a way that only seasoned soldiers could understand: desert, dust, flies and violent death.

'It is a command well enough,' Hughes replied bitterly, 'but not one that I sought. I wanted to command a brigade – not a bloody desk.'

Patrick nodded his head in sympathy. Soldiering was really about the comradeship of soldiers facing the enemy, not endless files and staff meetings. Hughes' views on the tenacity of the Boers must have bordered on heresy to bring about such a posting.

'But so much for my woes,' the colonel sighed. 'What I cannot understand is why one of Britain's finest colonial officers would ever decline the command of a colonial regiment. It's almost inconceivable, Patrick. Absolutely inconceivable.'

'I can assure you that my decision now is no less painful than the one I made when I resigned from the regiment back in '85,' Patrick replied.

Colonel Hughes could tell from Patrick's voice that the decision not to take his regiment to Africa was probably one of the most difficult he had ever made in his life.

'Family matters?' he asked gently.

Patrick nodded. 'I have a duty to my family as much as I have a duty to my regiment. And under the rather difficult circumstances of managing the family concerns I have a particular duty to my grandmother.'

'Lady Enid Macintosh,' the colonel said. 'A fine woman, I have heard.'

'God almighty – I would give my life to be with the men when they sail,' Patrick continued in an agonised tone. 'I feel like a damned deserter.'

Although Patrick did not elaborate further, Hughes guessed that all was not well at home, but it was not his affair to make further inquiries in the matter. Upon reaching Sydney the colonel had been stunned to hear of his friend's decision. And while Patrick's men in the mounted infantry had been bitterly disappointed by their commanding officer's decision, there was also some understanding of the heavy responsibility 'the boss' had in managing the Macintosh companies. Hughes had hoped at this informal meeting to perhaps persuade him to retain his command, but he also had another agenda. A more distasteful matter in relation to his new appointment as the head of military intelligence for the War Office. A matter that directly involved his friend.

'Despite the fact that you have decided not to go with the regiment to Africa, I would presume your loyalty to Her Majesty is in no doubt?' Hughes asked, noticing the expression of disbelief on Patrick's face.

'That's a rather insulting question,' Patrick growled. 'I will continue in Her Majesty's uniform and seek a training command.'

'I'm sorry, Patrick, but I had to be sure. And from your reaction I have not the slightest doubt of your loyalty. You see, I have to confess that I arranged this meeting for reasons other than just renewing our acquaintance. It happened that, before I sailed for Sydney from London, I received a file on someone close to you as part of my briefing.'

'My father?' Patrick asked hopefully. 'He is alive?'

The colonel shook his head. 'I'm sorry. Not your father. It's your cousin, Father Duffy.'

'Martin?'

'Father Martin Duffy S.J. A rather colourful – and some would say dangerous – man.'

'Martin dangerous!' Patrick exclaimed. 'Martin's just a priest. How could that be dangerous?'

The intelligence officer rose and walked across to a wooden filing cabinet, opened it and rustled through folders until he found what he was looking for. Returning to the desk he sat down, flipping open the manila folder and peering at the reports relating to a Jesuit priest trained in Rome, but originally from the Colony of New South Wales.

'How much do you know about your cousin?' he asked quietly.

Patrick frowned as he recalled the boy he grew up with. Martin was reserved to the point of timid. How could such a boy grow to be a man considered dangerous by the might of the British Empire?

'I have not seen Martin in over twenty-five years. Unfortunately my choice to renounce my Catholic religion put me on the wrong side of the Duffys. Only my Aunt Kate in Townsville still corresponds with me. So there is little I know of Martin – I heard through Aunt Kate that he had gone to Rome to be ordained as a Jesuit priest. Then I heard that he was on missionary work in Africa . . . Africa!

That's the connection, isn't it?' Patrick exclaimed suddenly.

'Yes,' the colonel replied. 'That, and his anti-British activities in Ireland. I think under the circumstances, old chap, I can tell you a certain amount, without compromising secrecy. Most of what I will tell you is common knowledge in Ireland and Africa. Father Duffy is currently in Ireland covertly recruiting young men to join an Irish Brigade to fight on the Boer side,' Hughes said grimly. 'He had a rather lot of success recruiting around the mines and goldfields in the Boer Republics when he was in Africa. We fear he may also have secret contact with the Kaiser's people in Germany in his crusade against us. We have been assured by the Vatican that his secular work is not condoned by the Catholic Church.'

Patrick sat in stunned silence as the colonel outlined the picture of a fearless, if misguided, fighter for Irish freedom from Britain – a picture of a man so much the opposite of the one he remembered when his cousin and he were growing up together at the Erin Hotel in Redfern.

'Why doesn't the Church discipline him then?'

'They would if they had proof. Your cousin is a Jesuit and it seems that they have trouble controlling the Soldiers of Christ,' Hughes answered with a note of sarcasm. 'The founder of the Jesuits, Ignatius Loyola, was once himself a mercenary soldier of some enviable repute and I suppose some traditions die hard. From what I have heard even the occasional excommunication of the Jesuits does not seem to deter them.'

'I was taught by Jesuits when I was young,' Patrick said quietly. 'They are the brightest and toughest the Church has.'

The colonel nodded. He had a grudging respect for priests whose rigorous training and dedication were not unlike those of a good soldier. They had a reputation as fearless and learned warriors of God, and their crusades had taken them to some parts of the world long before the great imperial powers of Europe reached them officially. From India to Japan they had gone, at great risk to themselves, and now one of them had taken on a crusade against his own government in the name of justice for the Irish. A very dangerous undertaking!

'I know there is little you can do,' the colonel said gently, seeing the pain in his friend's face, 'but if Father Duffy ever returns to Sydney you might attempt to reason with him. Point out that his activities also put Australian lives at stake in a war with the Boers, that he has a greater loyalty to the land of his birth than to the land of his fathers.'

'What makes you think he would listen to me, a man who has renounced the religion that Martin was ordained into? I am probably just as much an enemy to him now as the British government.'

'You are right in all you say, Patrick, but at least it's worth a try. There are others around me who would prefer to just quietly do away with him. Any violent act that might be exposed against him by those same people naturally cannot be entertained. Should it become public knowledge that a priest was summarily executed it would bring down international sympathy on his side. There are too many damned Irishmen in the United States with growing political power to allow that to occur. Not to mention the record of Irish rebellion in the Australian colonies over the years – Vinegar Hill, the Eureka Stockade . . . No, better that your cousin somehow be persuaded to give up his secular cause and concentrate on ministering to his congregations.'

Patrick felt stiff with tension. He stood and again walked to the window overlooking the parade ground outside the solidly built sandstone barracks. He gazed across the sacred ground of sergeant majors, deep in thought.

41

Finally Patrick turned to speak. 'I know the Duffys. Their blood runs within me. They have been fighting the British as far back as my grandfather and his war did not end in Ireland. He was one of the miners who stood at the Ballarat goldfields back in '54. You may not have any other option than to do as you say − quietly remove him.'

Patrick's cold-blooded statement surprised the colonel. He was a man used to making difficult decisions in battle but the colonial major's quietly delivered words chilled his soul. Something must have died in Patrick, perhaps after his terrible experiences wandering in the Sudanese desert after the advance on Tamai village. How else could a man condone the possible killing of his own blood? There was only one question that remained and he was reluctant to ask it.

'If the circumstances ever arose, Major Duffy, could you bring yourself to remove your cousin?'

There was a cold dead look in the eyes that stared into his. Patrick slowly nodded his head before replying. 'If my cousin's actions in any way put the life of even one of my men in peril, then he is a sworn enemy of mine.'

On the carriage journey back to his offices through the streets of Sydney, Patrick felt the air of gaiety in the crowds thronging in and around the shops. The news that the colonies would be sending troops to assist the British lion was welcomed as a chance to show the English that their colonial cousins were more than equal to the task as fighting men.

Those who had misgivings about the war against a small nation of farmers wisely elected to remain silent amongst the fiercely loyalist Sydneysiders. For now, the important conferences planning the uniting of the colonies as one nation under one Australian flag were forgotten. All that mattered was a patriotic outburst from the crowds to prove the worth of those transplanted sons to the Southern Hemisphere.

Patrick had not found the festive mood contagious. He brooded about all that had occurred in his meeting with Colonel Hughes and struggled with his deep-seated sense of guilt at deserting his regiment on the eve of war. But something else had influenced his decision, something he could never tell Colonel Hughes or anyone else: the sense that had he gone he might return to a life without Catherine. Her many mysterious absences ate at him – he could not bear the thought that she might be having an affair, but if she was he hoped that it would simply burn itself out and she would return to him. To date he had not questioned her activities away from the house. A matter of trust, he told himself. But the trust was growing thin.

Patrick returned to the harbourside mansion late that evening. The two-horse carriage trundled up the gravel driveway, through the impressive established garden, to deliver him at the front door. He was met by Betsy, the domestic who had been with his grandmother for many years. She greeted him politely and informed him that the children were already in bed and that Lady Enid had taken supper with them. It seemed that his grandmother had stepped in once more to fill the children's need for a mother. He thanked Betsy for the news and requested that the cook bring his supper to the verandah, a place where he could be alone and take in the salty smells and lulling sounds of the broad expanse of water below.

It was a pleasant, balmy evening and under other circumstances he might have shared it with Catherine. In the

43

past they had often sat here, enjoying the peace and the wonderful climate of Sydney. But tonight Patrick would pick at his supper alone and probably get very drunk on a couple of bottles of excellent colonial wine.

As he seated himself in one of the cane chairs, the cook brought his supper. Cold mutton, pickles and bread on a silver salver were placed beside him on a small table. He requested two bottles of sauterne and his cigars from the library and when the cook returned with them he settled back to reflect on his life. The cigar glowed in the dark, its thick grey smoke curling lazily away on a gentle evening breeze. The wine was superb but Patrick ignored the supper and stared across the dark harbour at the tiny lights that marked fishing boats and houses on its lower reaches. The night air carried the rough voices of fishermen to him as soft whispers.

'I thought you might be out here,' Lady Enid Macintosh said, jolting him out of his thoughts as she took a chair beside him. 'Betsy told me you were home. Has it been a bad day?'

'A different day, Grandmother,' he replied distantly, trying to keep his feelings to himself.

But Enid knew her grandson well and understood from his reply that he was troubled. 'Is it Catherine?' she asked bluntly. 'It has been apparent to me that you have been rather melancholy lately.'

'Catherine, my decision not to remain with the regiment – a lot of questions I have no answers to.'

He did not see the expression of relief on his grand-mother's face at his mention of leaving the regiment. She had almost lost Patrick to another war and he had since become the most precious being in her life – possibly even more precious than her desire to retain the Macintosh name.

'The children also wonder about their mother,' Enid said. 'She is never at home lately. She leaves the house without saying where she is going. Or who she is meeting.'

'She has always been very independent,' Patrick said defensively. 'I suspect that her absences from the house will cease soon.'

He took a long swig of the wine as if to drown his own doubts. He had taken little notice of Catherine's restlessness until it had been too late; he knew that now. And although he would not admit his fears, Lady Enid suspected. Had not she lost a daughter to a young Irishman almost forty years earlier? Was her grandson now a victim of that terrible unspoken curse that seemed to haunt the family?

'I pray that you are right, Patrick, but I fear that you need her in your life more than she needs you.'

Enid's blunt statement caused Patrick to glance sharply at her. His grandmother had a perceptiveness that had proven itself in her business dealings over the years, but he was surprised to see that same perceptiveness displayed in matters of the heart.

'I can see you would prefer to be alone,' she continued gently, 'so I will bid you a goodnight.'

Patrick rose to offer his arm as she got to her feet, even though she did not require it. She was still a strong woman. He kissed her on the forehead as she waved off his offer to help her to her room, and when she was gone Patrick sank again into his chair and his troubled thoughts. He knew that he was lost and he knew why. And there was nothing he could do about it.

FIVE

More than a thousand miles north of where Patrick Duffy sat on the verandah overlooking the beautiful harbour of Sydney, three people also sat on a verandah overlooking another harbour. The boy – though more a young man now – sat beside his mother, an attractive woman in her early fifties. Matthew Tracy was a strapping lad of fourteen years and could have passed for eighteen. He had inherited the broad-shouldered build of the Duffy men rather than the lankiness of his American father, gold prospector Luke Tracy, known only to Matthew through legend, having disappeared between Townsville and Burketown on the arid plains outside Julia Creek at the time of Matthew's birth.

The tall young man with the long, dark beard opposite them wore the clothes of a bushman and his floppy hat lay on the wooden plank floor of the verandah beside his chair.

In his lap he balanced a delicate china saucer as he sipped at a cup of India tea. The house was large and cool, designed to capture the occasional breezes of the tropics. But for the moment Townsville harbour was perfectly still and all three sweated even in the cooling darkness of the evening.

Kate Tracy, nee Duffy, who had also once been known by her married name of Kate O'Keefe, fanned herself with an ornately splayed Chinese fan. It had been a gift from her old friend John Wong who she regularly did business with importing and exporting to the Far East. Little was said amongst the three as Kate was still taking in the tragic news that the young bushman had brought of the death of his father, Ben Rosenblum.

Saul had ridden into Townsville that afternoon to deliver the news to the woman who had once been not only his father's boss but also a lifelong friend and to comply with a wish his father had expressed during his living years. He returned a small, battered case that had once been polished mahogany. Inside it snuggled a huge Colt cap and ball revolver. 'He always said you were to have this back on his passing, Mrs Tracy,' Saul had mumbled, awkward in the presence of the legendary woman of the frontier. 'Said something about not needing insurance when he was gone.'

The tears welled in Kate's grey eyes as she stared down at the battered case. A distant memory of a boy hardly older than her own son came to her. A boy who stood as awkwardly beside the giant bullock wagon as the young man now before her. She had given the new pistol to Ben when he had first set off with old Joe Hanrahan to take supplies to the far-flung, isolated properties west of Rockhampton. But then she had not been very old herself in those days. So much had happened in her fifty-five years; a deserted seventeen-year-old girl perilously ill with fever and losing

47

her first baby had become the ruler of a financial empire that spread its influence across the oceans as far as America. With some persuasion she convinced the tough young bushman to stay on at her Townsville house for as long as he needed to. He accepted self-consciously but with some gratitude, as he had no lodgings arranged before his journey south to Brisbane.

Over dinner Kate had marvelled at the similarities of the young bullocky that Ben once was and this young man sitting at her table.

'Will you visit your sister in Brisbane, Saul?' Kate asked after a long silence. 'I have heard she will be married.'

'I suppose I will,' he answered. 'If I have time.' Kate's questioning look caused him to continue, 'Goin' south to join up with the Queensland Mounted Infantry, Mrs Tracy. Hope to get down there before I hear they might be sailin'.'

Glancing across at Matthew, Saul noticed a sudden attention to their discussion that had gone unnoticed by the boy's mother.

'You wouldn't consider a job on my Balaclava property?' Kate asked, hoping to detour the young man from the path to war.

He shook his head. 'Have a need to get away for a while. Joining up now seems the best way to do that.'

'I was very sorry to hear about the foreclosure on Jerusalem. Just damned bad luck with all that has happened in the last few years,' she said angrily.

Saul was surprised to hear this woman, who he considered to be a true lady, swear. He would have been even more surprised to learn that her time walking beside the big bullock wagons in far north Queensland had given her an even more colourful vocabulary of words rarely used in public.

'We did our best,' he replied and shrugged his shoulders. 'Just wasn't good enough it seems.'

Kate gave Saul a closer look. There was a tough fatalism in the young man's statement that she feared might get him killed in a war. The trait was shared by her brother Michael who had lived life not caring whether he saw the sun rise. Perhaps it was the way of men who did not have families. 'The offer of work will stand when you return from South Africa,' she reiterated gently. 'I have a feeling you are very much like your father, and that alone is enough to recommend you.'

'Thank you, Mrs Tracy,' Saul mumbled awkwardly. 'My dad was a good 'un.'

As they sat for another hour chatting, Saul noticed that Matthew said little but took in a lot. When Kate excused herself to retire for the night leaving Saul and Matthew alone on the verandah, the young man finally found his voice.

'I'm going to enlist with you,' he said quietly.

Saul was about to laugh off the boy's impulsive statement but when he looked into the boy's eyes he could see a burning ambition that was not about to go out.

'Why would you want to leave all this behind and run away to a war?' Saul asked. 'Anyway, you're too young to join up. You won't get past the front door of the recruiting depot.'

'Your own father was only a couple of years older than me when Mother gave him the Colt. I know because she told me the story. That's not much different to what I'm going to do.'

Seeing the fire in Matthew's grey eyes, Saul felt uncomfortable. He could see that Matthew meant every word. 'Your mother would have me horse whipped if she even suspected I would help you,' he replied. 'She's a good woman and there's no way I would want to do anything that might cause her pain.'

Matthew leant forward and stared the bushman directly in the eyes. 'My mother would never know you helped me enlist,' he said in a pleading yet firm voice.

Saul could see that the boy was used to commanding others. It was in his bearing and, he guessed, probably as a result of his upbringing as heir to his mother's fortune. 'I just need you to support me when the time comes to produce my birth certificate,' Matthew continued. 'Sort of back me up.'

'You won't get far on your birth certificate,' Saul said with a chuckle. 'I heard most of the recruiting people can read and write.'

'I have a forged birth certificate in the name of Matthew Duffy. That was my mother's maiden name.'

Saul stared suspiciously at the boy. 'How did you get your hands on a forged birth certificate?' he growled.

Matthew smiled mysteriously and leant back in his chair. He could see that he was slowly winning. But he was not about to mention his contact.

'I have and that's all that matters,' Matthew replied.

'If I was to help you, what's in it for me?'

A triumphant look crossed Matthew's face. 'You and I both know that you need to get to Brisbane in a hurry if you are going to join up in time to steam to Africa with the regiment. And we both know that you were going to try and ride south. How long will that take you?'

Saul frowned. 'A bloody long time.'

'Then you might just miss the boat. Unless you were to take a boat from Townsville to Brisbane. It's the quickest way to get there.'

'You can do that?' Saul asked with a sudden respect for the boy. 'You got the money to get us a ticket on a coastal going south?'

'Enough for both of us. And we can leave first thing after lunch tomorrow. I just need a few hours to get things in order.'

'What about your mother?' Saul asked with a touch of guilt for his seeming betrayal of her faith in him.

Matthew fell silent for a short time and stared across the bay. The muddy water was flat and stagnant looking. 'I will miss her but I'm going to leave a note to say I've decided to go off and see Queensland for myself for a year.'

The bushman shook his head. 'You really think she will believe that?'

'She married my father,' he replied with the ghost of a smile. 'And from what I've heard of him he was always going walkabout. I think she will blame him for my sudden need to head out west. Sort of something in the blood I can't help.'

'Jesus, boy, you could get me killed before we even get into a war,' Saul laughed softly. 'You better make sure, no matter what happens, that my name never comes up as the person who helped you get in the army. If it does, I promise you I will kill you myself.'

Looking at the tough, bearded bushman Matthew had no doubts that he would carry out his oath.

It was a full day before Kate realised her son was missing. When she found his letter and read his lie, tears flooded her eyes as she remembered how a tall, lean American prospector had kept coming and going in her life. She loved that man still and even now she felt his ghost at her elbow, as if

51

Luke Tracy were trying to tell her something was not right, that she could easily lose her son forever to some great tragedy. She did not suspect in a million years that the tragedy had a name – and that name was war.

SIX

The end of October saw the rain come to Sydney, but it did not deter what seemed to be the whole population of the city thronging the route between the military barracks in Paddington and the embarkation point at Circular Quay. For the second time in its short history the city was farewelling brave young men off to fight in the Queen's name. Patrick Duffy was one of those who took his place in the crush to watch his regiment march past with rifles at the shoulder and bayonets fixed.

He stood against the drenching rain under an umbrella and listened morosely to the unbroken roar of cheering and singing. He felt the loneliness of the deserter as the crowds became part of the spirit of the soldiers, soon to be Queen's crusaders in far-off Africa. In places, the crowds hemmed in the New South Welsh contingent to the point where the bands and the infantrymen could hardly move. Small

Union Jacks festooned the tips of bayonets as well-wishers pressed forward. Pretty young ladies kissed any soldier they could reach. Shops and buildings displayed the colours of the Union Jack from walls and windows and red, white and blue predominated in the grey streets lashed by rain. Snatches of 'God Save the Queen' and 'Rule Britannia' blurred together in the jubilant singing.

Patrick stood in front of a bill board displaying a patriotic slogan: 'The Lion and the Kangaroo will put old Kruger through.' He could not see the marching men but neither did he have a great wish to. It was bad enough that his decision to remain at home and attempt to save that which was most precious to him, his marriage, meant that he could not sail with his men. Even if he had second thoughts it was too late now as officer appointments had been made and signed by the War Office in London.

He was not sure whether the wetness on his face was from rain or tears but he knew he had enough of the desolation he felt. Even his faithful secretary could not resist proudly boasting of his own son's enlistment in the regiment now sailing for the war. With his chest stuck out, and tears behind his spectacles, George Hobbs had related how his son would show the English the prowess of Australians on the battle-field. Patrick had listened and wondered whether George truly understood that the war was not some grand cricket match. How could he deflate the proud father with his own recollections of war: dying men screaming for their mothers, others cursing the very existence of God as they clawed at bowels hanging from ripped stomachs, and always the ever-present stench of decaying flesh, thirst and numbing fear. Instead he had mumbled his own admiration for such courageous patriotism and then taken his umbrella to join the rest of Sydney farewelling her troops.

With some difficulty, Patrick now pushed his way through the crowd until he came to a hotel. Most of the patrons were out on the street and very few stood at the bar. Patrick was aware of someone tugging at his sleeve as he forced his way through the door past a pack of young men with beer glasses in hand boisterously toasting the Queen. He turned to see Arthur Thorncroft at his elbow.

'Thought I might join you,' Arthur said with a weak smile. 'A bit too much for me out there.'

Having shared a campaign and similar scenes of departure, Patrick welcomed his friend's company. It was humid inside the hotel's main bar as the spring rains heralded the coming of a hot summer.

'Like this when you left for Suakin?' Patrick asked as he fronted up to the bar with the smaller man beside him.

'Not much different,' Arthur replied as he shook off the rain and unfurled his umbrella. 'Except we didn't have the crowds the boys have now.'

Patrick ordered two pints of ale which had improved considerably since the early years of the colony. It no longer poisoned a man – just got him drunk.

'They deserve the gratitude of Sydney,' Patrick mumbled as he sipped at his beer and stared at the painting behind the bar of a woman reclining naked on a couch. She smiled at him and he felt an ache for Catherine along with the sense that she was gone from his life, although he could not yet admit this to himself. 'The memory of this day is going to have to get them through a lot of hard days and nights ahead,' he continued sadly.

Arthur nodded grimly. They had soldiered together as officers under the blazing sun of Sudan's arid lands and faced death together. That would always be a special bond between men, just as the birth of children was between women. 'Anyway, it will all be over by Christmas,' Arthur offered lightly, hoping to reassure his friend. 'The lads will be back before Easter. Might not even get to see any action for that matter. The British regiments will probably roll up the Boers before they get to Capetown. After all, they are only up against a rabble of peasant farmers.'

'I'm not so sure,' Patrick replied quietly. 'I've seen how they operate – any man who could kill my father has to be more than a peasant rabble. No, it will not be over by Christmas.'

Arthur sipped his ale and said nothing. He knew of Patrick's search many years earlier for his father, the legendary Michael Duffy. And he knew of the determined defence that father and son had put up from under the cover of an ox wagon on the African *veldt* against a force of mounted Boers – a defence that had cost the life of the big Irish soldier of fortune so that his son might live.

'Your daughter, Fenella, certainly has an interest in my work,' Arthur said, attempting to distract Patrick. 'She badgers me to allow her to see my other work.'

Patrick's mood shifted slightly at the mention of his daughter. 'It would do her no harm. I will arrange for her governess to take her to your studio to see how moving pictures are produced.'

'I think that you should come and have a look yourself. It would do you no harm either.'

Patrick smiled. 'You don't have to sell me, Arthur,' he said. 'My grandmother has already approved finance for you to travel to Europe. You know that. And you don't have to change the subject because of my apparent melancholy. I will adjust in my own good time.'

Arthur sighed with relief and took a long swallow of his cool ale. 'I know you will, Patrick,' he said, wiping the creamy froth from his moustache. 'All will work out for the best.'

But his last statement was delivered without conviction, for he knew what the rest of Sydney knew: Patrick Duffy's beautiful wife was most often seen in the company of the English capitalist Brett Norris at the city's cafes, theatres and hotels. Rumour had it that she was known to stay all night with the suave and elegant millionaire at his rooms in the city's best hotel. But not even Arthur dared bring the matter to his old friend's attention. If he didn't know already, better that he find out in his own way.

The two men passed the afternoon drinking together. They talked mostly of Arthur's coming voyage to Europe and what he hoped to achieve, and they reminisced briefly on their experiences in the Sudan campaign. Finally they departed the hotel and rolled out onto a street covered in the backwash of a farewell party: lank red, white and blue bunting strewn in gutters where a downpour had attempted to wash the colours away. The rain had finally driven most of the party-goers from the street and both men were able to hail a Hansom cab. Arthur bid his friend a good evening, thoughts on his young man and a warm place by the hearth of the studio they shared. But for Patrick there was only the return to a sprawling mansion. It was a lonely place to be.

When Patrick arrived at his residence he slumped into his chair in the library. The room was his retreat from the world and his children had come to respect that this was not a place to enter unless summoned. So the timid knock on the door and the sight of his youngest son Alexander surprised him.

The boy stood awkwardly, framed by the open door

awaiting permission to approach. Patrick nodded his assent and it was only when Alex came close that Patrick could see the bruising and swelling on his son's face. Alex stood anxiously before him, his expression alternating between fear and resolve.

'What is it, son?' Patrick gently asked.

The boy's battered face was twisted in anguish. 'Do you want to tell me something about why your face appears as if it was kicked by a camel?'

'I . . . I don't think . . . ,' Alex stammered as his courage dissolved and he realised his question was beyond his daring to ask.

Patrick reached out to grip his son's shoulders gently. Displays of affection were not normally encouraged in the house of Lady Enid and so his father's compassionate gesture gave the boy courage. He took a deep breath and let the question tumble over itself.

'Are you a coward, Father?'

Patrick was stunned by the question. 'Who says I am a coward?' he redirected quietly. Alex stood mute. 'Someone I know?'

His son shook his head vigorously. But his answer was a lie. How could he tell his father that his own brother George had accused his father of cowardice?

Patrick sighed and slumped back into his chair, leaving his son gazing at him forlornly. 'Do you think I am a coward,' he asked the boy in a tired voice, 'because I didn't go with my men to war?'

'No, Father. I think you stayed because of Mother and us. But . . . ' he trailed away as he realised that he had almost mentioned his brother's name.

'But what?' Patrick asked.

'Nothing important.'

'Is that how you got your beating?'

'Yes,' Alex answered uncertainly, and then lied a second time. 'Some boys from school.'

He could not say that he had received the beating from his brother after flinging himself at him, the accusation levelled at the man whose strength he idolised more than he could bear. George had taunted him after the beating and Alex had cried in shame at his inability to put right a wrong.

'Has your mother seen the state you are in?' Patrick asked, his love for his youngest son hurting as much as the aching distance that had grown between he and Catherine.

'No, Father. She has not come home yet,' he replied with tears in his eyes. 'She telephoned Grandmama this afternoon to say she would be home tonight though.'

'And I don't suppose she told your grandmother where she has been for the last few days,' Patrick muttered angrily to himself before realising that he was unduly bringing his youngest son into a matter over which he had no control. 'No matter,' he added quickly to deflect any answer the boy might feel he should give. 'I will no doubt see your mother tonight.'

Gazing at his father, Alex now knew his answer. He could see that his troubled question had been unnecessary. His father had fought in other wars, he knew from the stories, and had been very brave. He was only staying at home because he truly loved them. At least he had the satisfaction of knowing his brother was wrong.

As he guided his son to the door of his bedroom Patrick did something he had not done in a long time. He kissed Alex on top of the head and gave him a hug. Embarrassed, Alex quickly disengaged himself, and went into his room after bidding his father goodnight. Patrick closed the door and walked slowly back to the library. So there were those who questioned his physical courage . . .

Although he had been determined to remain awake in the library and await his wife's arrival, the gentle ticking of the tall grandfather clock in the corner along with the steady beat of the rain on the roof and the effects of the ale consumed during the afternoon lulled him to sleep. It was a sleep the likes of which he had not known for many nights when he tossed alone in the bed that Catherine had all but abandoned.

Old habits die hard and when the rain ceased Patrick woke. He came awake with a start, shaken by the memories that had crept into his world of dreams. Memories of nights spent wandering alone in the Sudanese desert behind enemy lines, surviving with nothing more than animal cunning. The sticky wet feel of warm blood on his hands as he slit the throat of some unsuspecting desert nomad slumbering by his campfire had merged into erotic dreams of Catherine's creamy, pale breasts which under his kisses turned into two hills. Hills thousands of miles apart and yet sacred places to the ancient peoples who had lived around them.

He sat up in the big leather chair, sweat covering his body. Peering at the face of the clock in the corner, the hands told him it was three in the morning. Except for the clock, the world was as silent as that distant desert of his past. With some effort he heaved himself to his feet. Catherine should be home by now, he thought. He would go to her.

When he opened the door to their bedroom he could vaguely make out her outline under the sheets. Her long red hair spilled across a pillow. She was deep in sleep. He padded across to the big bed and sat gently on the edge so that he might not disturb her. Watching her breathing softly, with her mouth slightly agape, Patrick felt a massive surge

60

of love for the woman who had travelled across the sea from her home in Ireland to marry him a decade and a half earlier. Catherine, my beloved, what is happening? He gazed down upon her sleeping body. How could a love as strong as ours just fade away?

As Catherine turned on her side in her sleep Patrick could see the sensuous shape of her hip taut against the sheet as she nestled into her pillow. Memories of the wild and abandoned passion they had once known came back to him. Their passion seemed to have died over the last twelve months. His wife appeared to be at war with herself although he had not noticed until the last battle was fought in the past few weeks. Had it been that she had called out for his help and he had been so preoccupied with work that he had missed her call?

Catherine stirred in her sleep and rolled over onto her back. The sheet fell away revealing the swell of her breasts under her silk nightdress. Patrick felt a yearning as he gazed upon his wife. He would wake her with gentle caresses and they would make love in the early hours of the morning as they once had.

Sliding his hand under the sheet, he found the hem of the long nightdress. Carefully moving his hand along the contour between her legs, he leant forward and gently kissed her exposed throat. As his hand made its way softly along the inside of her thighs his tongue traced a silky path to her lips. As Catherine began to react to his caress, Patrick experienced a powerful feeling of overwhelming passion for the first time in many months. He would ask no questions. He would only accept that the love he knew she must have for him was somehow temporarily lost in her war.

Catherine's eyes were now open and she stared at him in confusion as his lips covered hers. His hand was between her legs and his fingers gently probed.

'Don't,' she pleaded desperately as she became fully awake.

Patrick suddenly realised why his wife had attempted to twist away from him. The wetness his fingers had discovered was unmistakable and he recoiled in shock.

'Who was it?' he snarled as he stood back from the bed, his overwhelming feelings of passion shattered as surely as if he had been hit with a bullet in the spine. A savageness that had long been dormant in him fought with what remnants of love he felt for his wife.

'It does not matter,' she replied as she snatched the sheet up, as if to shield her body from the fury in his eyes. She had never before seen the normally gentle man in such a deadly mood and she was afraid. The room seemed to be electric with a mixture of betrayal and pain. 'What matters is that I cannot live with you any longer, Patrick.'

He stood in the shadows of the room, his shoulders slumped as if he had fought a fight and been beaten. 'Do I know him?' he finally hissed in a low and deadly tone.

Catherine could now see that the man she had married was in control of his passion, but the knowledge caused her a new wave of terror as memories returned to her. She had once heard stories of such control from Arthur Thorncroft. A drunk Arthur told of her husband surviving in the Sudanese desert by raiding dervish camps at night and cutting the throats of the nomadic bedouin he encountered. Arthur's tales were recounted with something like pride for the man she knew he idolised, and it had been almost impossible for her to understand until now what kind of man could so cold bloodedly kill another in such an intimate manner.

Now facing her husband's steely self-control, Catherine knew that Patrick's emotion was directed not at her but at the man who had taken her from him. She feared for her lover's life. But for Patrick to turn and walk out of the bedroom without another word and without even a desire to know why she had betrayed him was even worse.

Alone in the bed, she sat shaking uncontrollably. It was never meant to happen this way, she thought. She never meant to hurt him. But deep down a tiny voice laughed at her denial. What else could she expect? Her husband was, after all, the son of Michael Duffy, and the blood ran hot in his veins.

Catherine sobbed. Something had gone terribly wrong. Had she not only that afternoon gone to tell Brett that she could not go to Ireland with him? And in doing so, had she not made the decision to return to her husband and attempt to rediscover that which had once been so wonderful between them?

But the suave English capitalist had wooed her to his bed one time too many. The little harm she thought it could do had instead brought possibly the greatest disaster of her life. What chance she had to forget the past few weeks had walked out the door and she was left with just one option.

SEVEN

Matthew Tracy and Saul Rosenblum stepped ashore in Brisbane from a coastal steamer and hoisted their swags on their shoulders. They needed to find accommodation for the night, and as Matthew had a considerable amount of cash in his pocket, they decided on a hotel. The next day they would enlist in the contingent that the Colony of Queensland was sending to South Africa.

As they trudged along a dusty, wagon-rutted road, Saul was deep in his unhappy thoughts. What if the boy managed to enlist and got himself killed? How could he ever face the woman who had been so important to his father? And in a battle situation the boy's demise seemed almost inevitable to Saul. Although physically mature, he was still in many ways a boy. Sure he was big enough to pass for eighteen or so. But sometimes on their trip south he sounded just like a fourteen-year-old straight off the rugby playing fields. It was as if the boy saw what lay ahead as just a glorified game of football.

The closer they came to Brisbane town the more determined Saul became to thwart the boy's attempt to enlist. It would not be easy. Matthew Tracy had learned to ride and shoot on his mother's property at Balaclava during school holidays, and it sounded as though the boy had learned quickly. If he was as good as he said then he might just fool the recruiters. And yet he felt guilty that the boy's money had got him to Brisbane in time to join up. Matthew had a winning way about him that made betrayal hard. He had to think of something before they went to the military barracks in Brisbane to sign up.

They arrived at a hotel that looked good enough for a cold beer, good meal and night's accommodation. As Saul signed them in, the publican eyed the roll of pound notes fingered by the tall, broad-shouldered young man beside the sun-blackened bushman. Must be twenty quid, he thought avariciously, already counting in his head the amount of grog that could buy, including a bit of short changing as the evening wore on and the alcohol took hold. The war in far-off South Africa had been good to the unscrupulous publican as young men from the bush flocked to Brisbane to enlist in the great adventure.

Saul and Matthew threw their swags onto the metal cots on the hotel verandah and were greeted by other men who had streamed out of the bush to the recruiting depots. The hotel was packed and only the sight of so much cash had induced the publican to find space for them in his already crowded establishment. Saul soon found a couple of men he knew from the Cloncurry district who had ridden in days earlier to join up and the party adjourned to the noisy bar.

As Matthew tried to act as if a hotel bar was familiar territory to him, Saul noted with some disappointment that the boy was settling in too well with the rough and tough men from the bush. He introduced himself as Matthew Duffy, eighteen-year-old stockman from the Balaclava run, out west of Rockhampton. Fortunate that the Cloncurry men knew few of the Balaclava stockmen, he was able to parry any questions on horses and cattle from that area.

But the flow of beer that came with the numerous shouts of the bushmen was another matter. At home Matthew occasionally sipped on a sherry or port after dinner in the company of his mother, and at his Catholic boarding school he joined other boys in drinking small quantities of purloined altar wine, provided by altar boys for a fee. But he was out of his depth with the hard-drinking men from the bush and the afternoon seemed to fade into a happy blur of laughter, boasting and more beer. Saul watched Matthew quickly becoming inebriated as the afternoon wore on and smiled to himself. He no longer felt any guilt for what he planned. Young Matthew had a long way to go if he were to join the company of men.

Matthew did not know how he came to be on his cot on the verandah of the hotel fully clothed. All he knew was that when he awoke in the morning it was to the rough shaking of the publican, who said that his time was up and he had to leave or pay another day's accommodation.

Matthew groaned as he sat up, then made a scramble for a bucket at the end of the verandah. He prayed for merciful death as he painfully retched but it did not come to free him of his self-inflicted pain. His first hangover was one that he would not forget. When he finally rinsed his mouth, he reeled unsteadily back to his swag and gazed around bleakly at the world. With rising concern he noticed that Saul was gone. Why had he not woken him?

Matthew's question was soon answered when he arrived at the recruiting depot. A steely-eyed army sergeant sat behind a desk perusing the crumpled birth certificate before him. 'Mr Matthew Duffy, is it?' he asked. His mocking tone told Matthew that something was wrong. 'Mr Matthew Duffy, from the Balaclava run out of Rockhampton?' Matthew nodded, and his head felt as if it would either split or fall off.

'Yes, Sergeant.'

The sergeant's waxed moustache quivered comically, and Matthew would have laughed were it not for the look in the man's eyes. 'Don't bullshit me, boy,' he growled, pushing the paper back across the table as the young man stood to attention as best he could. 'The only reason I don't call the coppers is because you get marks for trying. I give you credit fer guts.'

Matthew felt his world dissolve as he realised his ploy had failed. The sergeant continued in a more friendly tone. 'I got a tip you might try to pull a fast one on us. I was told that you might be able to ride and shoot. And if you got past me that would mean we might end up sending you over to fight the Dutchmen. Wouldn't do having a kid in the ranks whose mother might one day have my hide for letting her precious little boy get killed, would it? If I hadn't been given the tip-off, you just might have fooled me with this bit of paper, all things being considered.' He leant back in his chair and eyed Matthew. 'But you might just fool those Whalers down south,' he said with just the ghost of a smile. 'So, I would be advising you to go straight home to your mother and not be thinkin' of going south to try and join up.'

Matthew folded the crumpled certificate and placed it in his pocket. Smiling bleakly at the burly sergeant, he thanked him politely for his consideration, and pushed his way through the crowd of young men waiting outside.

As the recruiting sergeant watched Matthew leave, he could not help but think of his own enlistment many years earlier when he too had joined up under the required legal age. This one had the stamp of a young man who would one day make a bloody good soldier, he mused to himself. The few vacancies in the regiment were eagerly sought and only the cream of manhood were allowed to die for the Queen. The rest were allowed to stay home and have families. With a wry smile the recruiting sergeant shook his head and chuckled. He knew the boy was smart enough to pick up his meaning. He had seen the flicker of cunning behind the boy's bloodshot eyes at the mention of fooling the recruiting officers of New South Wales. Ah, but what went on in the recruiting offices outside the Colony of Queensland was not his concern.

'Next,' he bellowed and another hopeful stumbled apprehensively into his office.

Matthew pushed his way past the mass of bodies in the drill hall, fuming. Saul had dobbed him in! He picked up his swag from where he had left it and hoisted it onto his shoulder. Someone muttered, 'Bad luck,' as Matthew strode towards the door but he ignored the sentiment. Bad luck for Saul Rosenblum if he ever caught up with him again, he thought bitterly. There would be a settling to be made.

Outside the drill hall he found the shade of a gum tree just off the dusty street and sat down in the dry grass. He wanted to curl up and sleep off his hangover but realised that he needed to move fast if he was to have any chance of joining up. He took stock of the little money he had left and figured he still had enough for a boat fare to Sydney – with just a little left over for a couple of days food and accommodation. It was a gamble, but he was the son of two tough pioneers who had fought overwhelming odds most of their lives, and he was not going to take a step backwards.

Matthew rose to his feet, shook off the dust of Queensland, and headed in the direction of the Brisbane River wharfs where the coastal steamers could be found. He was going south to Sydney.

EIGHT

Arthur first noticed the young man as he lingered long after Arthur had completed filming the Sunday crowds strolling in the Domain. The amateur orators were surrounded by clusters of hecklers and supporters as they stood on their soap boxes to deliver their tirades against the devil, papists, the idea of federation and any other subject that was bound to arouse passions on a balmy spring afternoon.

The magnificent view from the Domain gardens took in the harbour below so some of the people attending just simply sat on the grass and enjoyed the afternoon. The orator attracting the most hecklers was a tall, gaunt man speaking out against the colony's involvement in a war across the sea, a war, he declared, that had nothing to do with Australian interests. His Irish accent was distinct, and the hecklers were kept in check by a group of tough-looking men who supported the speaker's views.

But the gaze of the tall, broad-shouldered young man with the tousled hair had remained on Arthur alone as he ground away at the cranking handle of his camera. Dressed in the clothes of a working man and his face tanned by the sun, he seemed to have no interest in the colourful characters delivering their sermons and tirades. Assisted by Ralph, Arthur began to pack the cumbersome camera. He has an intelligent look about him, Arthur mused as he returned his camera to its polished wooden case.

It was then that the young man approached and spoke. 'I've read about cameras that take moving pictures. How do they work?'

Arthur was mildly taken aback by his educated accent despite his shabby working clothes of a labourer.

'You are interested in cameras then?'

The young man smiled sheepishly, confirming his youth. Somewhere between fifteen and twenty, Arthur guessed.

'I've never seen one before. Only read about them.'

'You want to be a camera operator then?'

'Not really. I've come to Sydney to sign up for the war in South Africa,' Matthew said politely. 'But the camera and how it works interests me.'

'Better to learn how to use a camera than a Lee Metford rifle, young man,' Arthur replied. 'The people we shoot with a camera stay alive. I know what I am talking about.'

'You don't believe we should be fighting for the Queen?' Matthew asked without rancour.

Arthur ceased his packing and turned to stare at him. 'How old are you?'

'Eighteen,' Matthew lied, his eyes fixed on those of the older man. 'My name is Matthew Duffy, sir,' he said, offering his hand.

Arthur took it and felt the firm grip.

'I am Arthur Thorncroft, formerly of the New South Wales Contingent that once sailed for the Sudan to fight the Queen's enemies. I am pleased to make your acquaintance, Mr Duffy. It seems you share your family name with a very dear friend of mine.'

At this Matthew involuntarily started a little, but he knew the man's words were mere coincidence. There were many in the colonies with the surname of Duffy. 'I thought that with your experience serving the Queen you would have been all for us fighting the Boer, Mr Thorncroft,' he said.

'Time – and a bit of wisdom that comes with age – makes one more questioning of crusades. But please don't misunderstand me. I applaud the courage of the boys who sailed from here not two weeks ago. Their intentions are honourable and their courage unquestioned. It is just the wisdom of committing so many fine young men to fight a people with so much in common with ourselves that I question.'

'I still intend to sign on. I have heard New South Wales is going to raise a publicly subscribed regiment to join the first contingent in South Africa.'

'The Bushmen's Rifles, I hear they will be called from my dear friend, Major Duffy.'

At the mention of his friend's name and military rank Matthew suddenly paid attention. His mother had spoken to him of her brother's son's military involvement in the colony. There could be few other Major Duffys than his own cousin. He glanced away lest the older man should see the recognition in his face.

'You will have some rather stiff competition to join the ranks of the new unit should you muster for enlistment,' Arthur continued. 'Many will be called but few chosen.'

'I'll get in, Mr Thorncroft,' Matthew stated with the confidence of youth. 'No matter what happens.'

'I'm sure you will. But until then, allow me to extend an invitation to join my assistant and myself for supper, Mr Duffy. There I will be able to show you the soon to be great industry of moving pictures.'

He could see that the boy – as he thought of him, despite the age he had proffered – now wore an expression of gratitude. He was a handsome lad of intelligence and good breeding, Arthur thought. And there was something about young Matthew Duffy, with both his forthrightness and naivety, that made him appealing.

Matthew sat in the living room of the smart, dark brick house that was both home and studio to Arthur and his assistant. Ralph said very little but in his occasional veiled glances there was a hostility that Matthew did not understand. But Arthur made him feel welcome. The roast mutton with potatoes, pumpkin and minted peas was a change from the monotonous fare of this last week at the boarding house where he had resided. Hefting bricks all day working as a labourer on a building site had toned his boyish fat into muscle. He had already been accepted by his older workmates for the age he claimed to be and in some ways he was beginning to wonder where the years between fourteen and eighteen went. And the port he carefully sipped on was a change from the beer he had swilled like a veteran at the Ultimo Hotel with his workmates.

When Arthur offered him a cigar Matthew accepted, but watched Arthur carefully as he prepared his own. Matthew was careful to appear as if he knew what he was doing. When they were settled in with the port and cigars Ralph left them with a surly goodnight, saying he had work to do developing the day's film.

'Where do you call home, Mr Duffy?' Arthur asked as he watched a ring of smoke rest on the still air of the small but comfortable room.

'I come from Queensland. From a property up there.'

'Your parents' property?'

'No. My father died a long time ago. My mother works in Brisbane as a seamstress,' Matthew lied smoothly. 'Lost track of her when I went out west to work.'

Arthur's smile at this went unnoticed by Matthew. 'No relatives in this colony?'

'None,' Matthew answered, taking a sip from his port then a puff on his cigar.

'Then I can presume you are pretty well alone in Sydney.'

'Pretty well, except for my mates where I work. But none of them are staying in the same boarding house as me.'

'You are welcome to take up lodgings here and work with Ralph and myself if you wish.'

Arthur's sudden offer took Matthew by surprise. He liked the cottage with its well kept gardens and unconventional residents. In fact, all of Sydney had a wonderful unconventional atmosphere compared to the country town feel of Brisbane or Townsville. From the moment he had stepped off the coastal steamer from Brisbane and onto the shores of Sydney, Matthew had fallen in love with the city on the harbour. It seemed a place that held a promise of not knowing what the morrow would bring, and already a new opportunity had presented itself. He could move away from the squalid boarding house that stunk of boiled cabbage and sweating bodies. Besides, Sydney was the original home of his mother and of many relatives he had never met but had heard much about.

'You would not be paid much, I'm afraid, Matthew,' Arthur said apologetically as he watched the boy think over

74

his offer. 'But I'm sure you would be learning a craft that could one day take you far. At the very least, the food is probably much better than you are getting at your boarding house. I would deduct your board and lodgings from your wages each month.'

'Your offer is most kind, Mr Thorncroft. I think I would like to learn to be what you call a camera operator. I've never heard of anyone else being called such a thing before.'

'A unique title for a unique young man,' Arthur said with a smile of satisfaction, extending his hand to seal the deal between them.

Given the new and exciting world of moving pictures, the boy might forget his foolish notion of running off to war, Arthur thought as he shook Matthew's hand. Even now, he still remembered that terrible day when he had stood beside a young Captain Patrick Duffy in the Sudanese desert and gazed upon the rotting bodies of young Scots soldiers killed by the dervishes. The obscenity of war had become a reality that day. And now another Duffy had come into Arthur's life. And for some reason he did not want this young man to lose either his life or soul to war. Whether it was in the name or his appearance, Matthew Duffy was very much like Patrick.

'He is a Mr Brett Norris,' Lady Enid Macintosh said as gently as she could. 'Catherine has gone away with him. I believe they sailed for London two days ago.'

Patrick bowed his head and stared into the murky white tea in his cup as a butterfly fluttered to a rest on the edge of the garden table. The morning was magnificent, a zephyr of a breeze playing amongst the masses of blooming flowers amidst the lawns of the house. The spring air tempered a soft kiss to the bright sunlight and close by tiny birds twittered as they sought out the nectar of the flowers with their curved beaks.

Enid gazed at her grandson with sadness. She too felt the weight of his crushing pain. He looked so strong and hand-some in his uniform, she thought. And how could any woman not love him for his gentleness? A week earlier, Patrick had visited his old friend Colonel Hughes and asked for a commission as a special services officer with a regiment in South Africa. His request was granted and now it was only a matter of time before he sailed for the African continent.

'It's probably a good thing that I did not know it was Norris,' Patrick sighed, his shoulders slumping as he sat with the cup and saucer in his lap. 'If I had known, I think I would have killed him.'

'He is not all to blame, Patrick,' his grandmother cautioned. 'It takes two people to be involved in such matters.'

Patrick rose from his chair. Placing the cup and saucer on the table, he stared across to the harbour and the numerous boats plying the placid blue waters. Busy steamers heading for all the ports of the world passed frolicking little sailing skips.

Enid noticed her grandson's distant expression. Her efficient intelligence network had proved as reliable as always with the name of Catherine's lover and the places and dates they had been seen together reported to her over a period of weeks. But Enid had not told Patrick of her information for fear of what he might do – a fear he had now confirmed. 'Do you know this man Catherine is with?' she asked.

'I met him once in Ireland when I was on leave from the regiment,' he replied without turning. 'That was the same time I first met Catherine.'

Enid frowned. She had liked the young girl who had first come to her in Sydney from Ireland to seek out Patrick. The girl had good breeding, despite the fact that she was Irish by birth. For a time she had been a good wife to her grandson but now Enid was bitterly disappointed by Catherine's betrayal.

Patrick resumed his chair at the table with its immaculate white linen tablecloth and stretched his long legs in front of him, affecting a relaxed manner which did not fool his grandmother. 'Well, I will have enough to worry about looking after my men,' he said casually, as if able to dismiss his past so easily. 'They are going to need me.'

'Make sure that you look after yourself first,' his grandmother chided gently. 'Your children need you too . . . and so do I.'

'Me? You know nothing can happen to me. I have the luck of the Irish – along with my Anglo-Scots blood,' he answered as he leant forward to grasp her fragile hands in his own broad fists.

She gave a wan smile in return but she did not feel so sure about his reassurances. Something terrible haunted the family, she knew. 'You have seen war, Patrick, and you know it does not respect your optimism. Just be careful.'

As Patrick flashed her one of his now rare smiles, Enid was reminded of the young boy who stood in her library for the first time thirty years earlier. If only he could know how precious he was to her. But he had a new focus now: the tough soldiers he loved so much.

They discussed the children. In his year-long absence they would stay at the house in the care of a governess. And Enid had convinced him that she was more than capable of managing the family estates and companies in his absence. Over the years she had formed an efficient and reliable staff of advisers around her who would continue to ensure the expansion of the Macintosh financial empires.

'I should complete my preparations,' Patrick said finally, leaning back in his chair. 'I sail for Queensland in three days hence to join a unit steaming for Capetown. I promised the children I would spend as much time as I could with them before I left.'

'That is very wise, Patrick. I know they are confused by all that has happened in the last few days.'

'Fenella has told me that her mother said they would join her in Europe in a year,' Patrick said. 'It seems she failed to mention that they would be joining her and her lover,' he added bitterly. 'That will not happen so long as I am alive.'

'And if, God forbid, something should happen to you, I promise that they will never do so, so long as I am alive,' his grandmother flashed.

Patrick smiled at Enid's fierce loyalty. Her formidable nature may have been locked inside a body in its ninth decade, but the power she could still muster was ageless. She was certainly a long way from dead and buried.

NINE

'Have you finished in there yet?' Arthur called to Matthew.

'Yes, Mr Thorncroft.'

'Good. I have some dear friends I would like to introduce you to.'

Matthew clipped the last of the lengths of developed film onto a line and removed his heavy gloves. After washing his hands he pushed back his tousled hair and opened the door of the darkroom. The first thing he saw were two very curious and emerald green eyes staring into his.

'Mr Matthew Duffy, this is Miss Fenella Macintosh,' Arthur said. Matthew tried not to stare at the beautiful young girl.

'And this is Major Duffy, father of Miss Fenella and masters George and Alexander.'

Each boy stepped forward and shook Matthew's hand

without saying a word. Arthur continued directing Matthew's attention to a tall, well-built man wearing the khaki uniform of a New South Wales colonial officer. On his left breast the young man could see the impressive strip of brightly coloured ribands that marked his campaigns in previous wars. His Sam Browne belt and riding boots were highly polished and reflected the spring sunshine that poured through the stained glass windows of the living room. Surely this must be my famous cousin, Matthew thought as he took the major's extended hand. He looked so much like the photographs he had seen of his Uncle Michael Duffy.

'Major Duffy has come at Miss Macintosh's insistence to see our studio, Matthew,' Arthur explained.

Matthew felt his face flush for no apparent reason other than the presence of the young woman only feet away. He felt foolish at his uncontrolled reaction and hoped Fenella had not noticed. 'Are you interested in moving pictures, Miss Macintosh?' Matthew asked, attempting to hide his awkwardness. Her answering smile made him feel just a little light-headed.

'Although my daughter is only fourteen years of age,' Patrick complained affectionately, 'she thinks she is already starring in one of Mr Thorncroft's moving pictures. I believe her interest is the stage rather than the technicalities of your craft, Mr Duffy.'

'Mr Thorncroft believes that moving pictures will one day make ordinary people into famous ones,' Matthew replied with some pride.

'I also believe that moving pictures will make people famous,' Fenella added. 'And one day I will be one of those famous people.'

Matthew did not doubt that what this beautiful and self-assured young woman said would come true. Suddenly it dawned on him that in all likelihood Fenella was his cousin.

'Mr Thorncroft has informed me that you have a great interest in enlisting in the Bushmen's Rifles and going to South Africa,' Patrick interjected.

'Yes, sir. I came down from Queensland to sign up.'

'Why didn't you enlist in Queensland?' Patrick asked and Matthew was quick to note the dangerous question.

'The contingent had all the volunteers they needed,' he replied quickly. 'They suggested that I should try down in New South Wales.'

Fenella cast him an approving look at his declaration of patriotism and he felt pleased that he had gained her esteem.

'Do you have any relatives in Sydney?' Patrick continued. 'As we share a name I thought that we may be related.'

'My family went to Queensland directly from Ireland,' Matthew lied, feeling uneasy under the scrutiny of the famed colonial soldier and praying that his fear of revelation was not showing in his face.

Patrick nodded, apparently satisfied by his answer. Then Arthur spoke, breaking the tension Matthew was experiencing.

'Maybe you would like to show Miss Macintosh and masters Macintosh around, Matthew, while I have a talk to the major. You know enough after two weeks here to explain all that we do.'

Matthew nodded. He was grateful to be out of Major Duffy's presence.

While Patrick followed Arthur outside to the privacy of the garden Matthew took the three Macintosh children into the darkroom where he cautioned against touching anything as the chemicals were dangerous. Showing them outside to a shed where the cameras and other equipment were kept, Matthew spoke using the technical language he had picked up from his mentor. He was a quick learner and Arthur had been pleased with the work of his new assistant, especially as Ralph had recently left to visit his family in South Australia for a time. While continuing his demonstrations and explanations, Matthew took every opportunity to steal glances at Fenella. She, in turn, acted as aloofly as a young lady should whenever she caught him doing so.

Her brothers were quick to notice their sister's strange behaviour, however; she would be in for some teasing when they got home. Matthew had taken a dislike to George. He had caught the boy sneering behind his back at the idea that moving pictures might one day be an industry. But there was also something else about the boy that Matthew did not like. Possibly it was in the way he dominated his younger brother. But Matthew liked Alexander. He seemed a curious and genuinely interested boy.

After the three Macintosh siblings had departed with their father, Arthur informed Matthew that they had been invited to afternoon tea with Lady Enid Macintosh the very next afternoon. Matthew tried to look indifferent. Asking as casually as he could if Miss Macintosh would also be in attendance, Arthur grinned widely and replied, 'No doubt she will be, Matthew.'

The afternoon tea was intended as a farewell function for Lady Enid's grandson who would depart on a coastal steamer for Brisbane the following day. Major Patrick Duffy's friends and family would not see him again for at least a year – if ever.

Enid had invited only a handful of Patrick's closest friends to share the magnificent spring afternoon in the beautifully manicured garden. The afternoon was intended to be gay with laughter. However, it was subdued in a way that made Enid wish she had not sent the invitations.

The men talked of the shock reverses the British army was suffering at the hands of the Boers, an army better equipped in artillery and small arms than the British had expected. Modern artillery pieces from Germany were blasting holes in the stolid ranks of British infantry while the latest in small arms technology, the Mauser rifle, was being employed to fire a smokeless cartridge. It gave unseen marksmen the deadly ability to fight and flee – and the cold steel of the British bayonet was proving no match. In all, the news being telegraphed to the world painted a picture as bleak as any known to the Empire in many a year, and it was to the Boer-dominated *kopjes* and *veldt* that Major Patrick Duffy was going.

Matthew did not feel out of place amongst the important guests at Lady Macintosh's afternoon tea. As one of the wealthiest people in the Colony of Queensland, with holdings in mines, pastoral properties, transport and numerous other enterprises, his own mother had often hosted such functions and entertained equally as important people at their home in Townsville.

The suit purchased for him only that morning by Arthur fitted Matthew well. He had accepted Arthur's kind gesture on the understanding that he would pay it off out of his wages over a period of time. It was ironic when he remembered the suits that he had left hanging in wardrobes at his home in Townsville. But, as he reminded himself, he was no longer Matthew Tracy. He was now Matthew Duffy and his real identity must remain a secret if he was to be successful in enlisting.

Upon introduction to her, Matthew's impeccable manners

impressed Lady Enid. Alone in the company of Arthur, she complimented him on his choice of an assistant. 'I hope he is nothing more than your assistant in your work, Captain Thorncroft,' she said sternly, fixing him with a steely stare.

'Nothing more, Lady Macintosh,' Arthur replied with feigned shock.

After his introduction, Matthew looked around for Fenella. He finally found her under a marquee on the lawn in the company of a tall young man, about sixteen years of age and dressed in the clothes of one born to wealth. From a short distance away Matthew thought that Fenella's companion paid an undue interest in her. He waited impatiently until the boy was called away before making his approach.

'Can I fetch you a glass of lemonade or a buttermilk, Miss Macintosh?' he asked. Fenella shook her head, looking up at him from under a delicate sunbonnet. 'Mr Bryant is looking after me, Mr Duffy,' she replied sweetly.

'Is Mr Bryant that bloke you were talking to?' he glowered, unthinkingly using a term he had picked up from his workmates on the building site. 'Bloke' was not good English.

'That *bloke*,' Fenella said teasingly, 'is the son of one of the wealthiest families in Sydney, Mr Duffy. Some day he and I shall marry.'

'I thought you were going to be in moving pictures,' he muttered, before her smile confirmed that he had stumbled into her trap.

'Yes, I shall be famous first, then I shall marry,' she said. 'Or possibly I shall not marry at all.'

'Well, it doesn't matter to me either way what you do. I'm off to South Africa as soon as I can join up.'

Matthew's retort, delivered with a shrug of his shoulders, brought a response he did not expect. He felt Fenella's hand on his and a sudden shift in her mood. She did not say anything but turned and walked quickly away from the guests in the garden towards a winding path that led down to the edge of the harbour through a blaze of brightly flowering shrubs.

Confused, Matthew stood for some moments before following. He found her sitting on a wooden pier that jutted into the harbour, feet dangled over the edge and long skirt drawn towards her knees, exposing milky white legs. She stared across the blue waters at the ships moving slowly towards the twin sandstone heads that acted as the gateposts to the harbour.

As Matthew sat down beside her he could see that she was crying and felt a strong urge to put his arm around her shoulders.

'I'm sorry if I said something to upset you,' he said softly, watching the tiny silver fish flash beneath their feet in the water.

Fenella wiped at her eyes with the back of her hand. 'It's just that Father sails away from us tomorrow and Mother has already gone. I don't know if I will ever see either again and I'm frightened.'

'Your father is a good soldier. He will come back.'

'And Mother?' Fenella asked sadly. 'Will she come back to us?'

'I don't know, Miss Macintosh. I did not know that she had gone away.'

'No-one speaks of her anymore,' Fenella continued bitterly. 'It is as if she never existed. All I know is that she told us she would only be gone for a year to do something important in Ireland. But if it was that important why didn't Father go with her?'

'I don't know,' Matthew replied helplessly.

All he knew of Fenella's mother was what he had been told by his own: that she was an Irish beauty distantly related to the family on her own side. He wished now that he had asked more but such matters of faraway family relationships bore little interest to a young man.

'Would your father not be with your mother if something was that important?' she asked with a little sob.

'My father is dead. He died when I was born,' Matthew said flatly. 'I never knew him . . . just about him.'

'I'm sorry, Mr Duffy. It must have been hard for your mother.'

'It was. I think she still loves him even though he has been dead for over fourteen years.'

'But that would only make you a year older than me,' Fenella replied in a puzzled tone. 'Mr Thorncroft said you were eighteen.'

Matthew blushed furiously. He had tripped himself up!

'You have been telling lies about your age,' Fenella continued in an accusing tone that caused him to squirm.

Matthew did not know how to reply.

'Is Matthew Duffy really your name? Or are you telling lies about that also?'

'My name is Matthew but I cannot tell you my real family name. All I can do is beg you not to tell anyone what you know of my age,' he pleaded. 'It is important that I get in the army. The most important thing in my life. It is something I must do for my father who I never knew. Please keep my secret.'

As Fenella stared at him he could see doubt in her eyes. Was it all over? Would she tell her father and all would then be revealed? His life hung on the tiny thread that was a young girl's whim. 'I will not tell anyone, Matthew. I think that you are one of the most remarkable young men that I have ever met.'

'Even more remarkable than your Mr Bryant?' Matthew asked with a sheepish grin.

'Even more remarkable than that silly young man. He is not half as brave as you.'

Then she leant over and gave him a quick kiss on the cheek.

Matthew sat stunned until Fenella swung herself away from the edge of the pier, stood up and brushed down her dress. He pushed himself up to stand beside her. Without a word she placed her hand in his and together they walked up the winding path. When they reached the top and were almost in sight of the guests she let his hand go as if nothing had occurred between them. But Matthew was in love for the first time in his life.

A NEW
CENTURY

1900

TEN

The hot, still summer air over the African *veldt* shimmered ahead of the outriders from the column as they fanned out along the high ground that rose up into a cluster of rocks that the Boers called *kopjes*. Private Saul Rosenblum no longer felt the sweat that continuously covered his body under his heavy khaki tunic. Nor was the exhaustion of the forced march to Bloemfontein a consideration. It was something that he had long learned to live with over the four months he had campaigned in South Africa.

His tough little mount endured the same conditions of searing heat by day and bitter cold by night. If they were not sweating they were shivering. Not even the summer storms that came to lash the seemingly endless miles of rolling plains gave comfort to the soldiers advancing relentlessly towards the Boer capital in the Orange Free State under the command of General Lord Roberts.

The regular swish of the horses' legs through the tall grasses was suddenly drowned by the shattering crack of Mauser rifles firing from the *kopje* ahead of the flanking outriders of the Queensland Mounted Infantry. Private Rosenblum was wrenched from dreams of a decent beef stew, a hot bath and clean sheets as his mount reared, the deadly rounds plucking at her body. She crashed to the ground, flinging her rider free.

'Into 'em, boys!' Saul heard Major Duffy roar amidst the terrifying crash of the high velocity rifle fire. He crawled painfully away from his horse as she thrashed helplessly on her side in the tall grass, her terrible dying whinnies of confusion and pain adding to the trooper's fear. Although he still clutched his rifle in his hands despite the heavy fall, he realised that the bandolier of Lee Metford rounds slung diagonally across his chest had been flung away from him when he hit the ground.

Desperately feeling around for the precious ammunition, Saul soon found it a few feet away. Around him, horses' hooves pounded the earth as the rest of the flanking party charged the knoll of rocks. A lethal hail of Boer bullets plucked the tips of the grass around him and Saul hugged the ground as if trying to be absorbed by the very earth itself. He knew from past experience that the Dutch farmers could be deadly accurate with their modern German rifles, so he dared not raise his head above the concealment provided by the tall grasses. But as quickly as the incoming rifle fire had rent the hot air, it tapered off into a spasmodic sound of distant shots. He guessed the Boers had employed their ruse of harassing fire and then escaped down a reverse slope to their waiting mounts. There was no hope of catching the expert horsemen as they galloped away to do the same further up the track. Their own horses had been pushed far too long and were in no state to gallop after the Boer skirmishers.

Major Duffy appeared above him astride his mount and glanced down with an expression of concern on his face. 'You've been hit, Private Rosenblum?' he asked with a note of concern.

Saul eased himself into a sitting position and reached for his broad-brimmed hat. 'No, boss. But it looks like old Nelly copped it.'

As Patrick reached down to help Saul to his feet the trooper gazed across to the rocky knoll at the rise of the undulating grassy *veldt*. With bayonets fixed, his comrades were on foot, searching amongst the rocks. Although Saul could not hear them, he guessed they were cursing the elusive Boer guerillas, who refused to stand and fight a pitched battle.

'Anyone else injured?' Saul asked the special services officer who had been attached to his unit of Queensland Mounted Infantry.

The QMI rode to a battle like cavalry men but fought on foot like infantry whilst their horses were held in the rear by a handler. On the seemingly endless plains of the South African campaign this strategy proved highly effective against an enemy that used the mobility of the horse to strike at the less mobile British army which was hampered by a cumbersome logistics system.

'We were lucky – this time,' Patrick replied. 'Lost a couple of horses and Private Grady hit in the leg. Not serious. Wasn't one of those damned explosive bullets of theirs. You can take Grady's horse.'

'Thanks, boss,' Saul replied as he chambered a round to put his own horse out of her misery.

She no longer whinnied but lay on her side snorting in

laboured breaths, blood oozing from five holes in her broad chest. Her big brown eyes rolled in pain as Saul levelled the rifle at her head and fired. She jerked at the impact and then relaxed. The pain was gone. Major Duffy turned sharply and cantered towards the knoll to rally the flanking party and take stock of what they may have found for intelligence purposes.

Saul limped across to Grady's horse grazing quietly on the grass. The rider was sitting beside his mount holding his leg and pulling a face as he gritted his teeth but making no audible complaint. Saul knew Grady from Brisbane where he was renowned as a rugby player. He was also an easy-going soldier liked by his comrades.

'I'll get you down to the medical wagons, Harry,' Saul said, bending over to give his comrade a sip from his water canteen. 'The boss has given me your horse.'

Grady grinned up at him when he had swallowed the warm water. 'Better a bullet than to die of the shits,' he said, knowing that enteric fever and dysentery had taken a terrible toll on the expeditionary force since it had arrived.

'Yer not going to die of that wound, Harry. Probably get sent home to boast about how yer got it in the charge against the Dutchmen.'

'Trouble is I didn't. I went down before I even heard the shots. Never got a chance to follow Major Duffy up the hill. I suppose if he hadn't given the order so quick we might all be lyin' out here dead,' Grady reflected grimly. 'Didn't give them Dutchmen a chance to pick us all off. Just straight into 'em before they knew what was comin'.'

Saul nodded. Although he did not have direct command over them, Major Duffy was extremely popular amongst the men of the unit. Major Duffy's posting was more like a liaison role between the British staff of the column and the colonial soldiers. But he had a habit of spending his time wherever he thought the bullets might fly and his cool courage and competence had earned him the enviable title of 'boss' rather than the formal 'sir' that the British officers insisted on.

'You able to get on yer horse?' Saul asked as he helped his colleague get to his feet.

Grady nodded, wincing when he placed weight on his leg where the bullet had lodged in his thigh. The rest of the troop were filing down from the *kopje* as Saul helped haul Grady astride his mount. Four months was more like four years, Saul thought as he doubled with O'Grady and reflected on his time in South Africa. All he had to do was survive another eight months and he would be free to go home. War was not as romantic as it had been portrayed by the cheering crowds in Brisbane when they had departed. It was just downright dirty, dull and dangerous.

General Roberts' strategy was to thrust north along the axis of the vital railway track to Bloemfontein and hence the capital of the Boers, Pretoria. He planned to capture the seats of Boer government and in turn force the Boer armies to abandon their sieges of Ladysmith, Kimberley and Mafeking, names that had become rallying points of patriotism for the people of the British Empire. But in doing so he was forced to march his column at a relentless pace. To advance the required ten miles a day meant rations of only three hard biscuits, a quart of tea and half a pound of tinned beef per man, with little fodder for the horses and mules. The column's route was marked by the carcasses of hundreds of horses and mules which had simply died of exhaustion and starvation. To the men of the colonial contingent the pitiful sight of brave animals dead and dying was heartbreaking. These were men who valued the horse as a companion, men who had traversed the great Outback of Australia's colonies prospecting for gold, mustering sheep and cattle, or riding the boundaries where the horse is often the best means of staying alive in a hostile land.

But Roberts, bestowed with the Victoria Cross at Kandahar many years earlier, knew that his strategy might bring the war to a close and so the men of the column marched and rode with a desire to fulfil his aim and go home.

It had not all ended by Christmas 1899 as many had predicted, however, with the Boer armies inflicting some of the worst defeats in recent history on the British army in the closing days of the century. And now in the dawn of a new century, Private Saul Rosenblum faced the terrifyingly quick-firing guns known as pompoms, which threw explosive shells almost as fast as a machine gun. When the explosive projectiles burst open they would shower an area of ground with red hot fragments of iron shrapnel. He had also faced the barrages of the larger artillery guns of the Boer army which shook the earth under him as he hugged it, hearing it tear through men's bodies and inflict terrible, ragged wounds of smashed muscle and bone. He had seen men and animals disembowelled, limbs torn from bodies, and heads smashed to pulp by the effects of the heavier shrapnel fired on them from the big field artillery pieces. These were sights that would haunt him for as long as he lived. Often he despaired of ever seeing the wide, sun-baked plains of the Queensland Outback again but, like all soldiers, he did not admit his fears to those who rode with him. What counted was that he did not let his mates down when they needed his courage and skill in battle.

Saul squatted by the small wood fire he shared with two other troopers of his squadron. They collected sticks of dry timber as they advanced across the *veldt* and the precious supply was pooled every evening. Around them other Queenslanders were doing the same. On the fire, an old pot recovered from a deserted Boer farmhouse boiled water for tea. Stirring in the tiny black leaves with the end of a twig taken from the fire, Saul sat back to reflect on how close he had come to dying earlier that afternoon, an introspection on life and death that had become all too frequent for him. But the trooper who sat opposite broke his silent mood as he noticed the big major moving amongst the resting soldiers.

'Hey, boss! You want a cuppa?' he called to Patrick.

'Wouldn't mind one, thanks, Private Berry,' he replied and sat down beside the fire.

Berry called for a spare cup and poured from the steaming billy. He handed the mug to Patrick.

'You think the Boers will put up a fight for Bloemfontein?' he asked, as Patrick sipped his hot tea.

'I think so,' Patrick frowned. 'There's a range of hills just four miles outside of the town they could easily fortify with trenches.'

'Means the buggers will give us a hot time,' Saul said quietly.

'Maybe more for the poor bloody English infantry who will no doubt be used to engage their front while we outflank the Dutchmen's positions,' Patrick replied, turning to Saul. 'We might just frighten them off the high ground. Their tactic of not allowing themselves to be trapped on any position will mean they will fall back without much of a fight. They can't afford to lose men. But, in our present condition, I doubt that we would have the ability to cut off their escape.'

Berry nodded in agreement. The major knew so much because he worked with General Roberts' staff headquarters.

What's more, he kept the men of the colonial contingent up to date, and to know what was really going on was important to even the lowliest private.

Berry excused himself suddenly as the dysentery he suffered hit him with stomach cramps. He hurried away into the night. Then the other trooper rose to retire for some badly needed sleep. Saul and Patrick were left alone by the gently burning fire in the shallow hollow.

Patrick was pleased for the opportunity to speak with Saul privately. He had learned of the soldier's relationship with his Aunt Kate in a rare letter that he had just received.

'I believe you know my aunt, Kate Tracy, Private Rosenblum,' he said.

Saul glanced at Patrick with an expression of surprise. 'How did you know that, sir?' he questioned.

'She wrote to me just after you went south to enlist in Brisbane,' Patrick replied, poking the fire with a twig. 'About the same time young Matthew took off. Do you know anything of his mysterious disappearance?'

Saul flinched under the question. The major had a way about him that did not invite untruths. At least his conscience was clear as he had sabotaged the boy's attempt to join up.

'I first met Mrs Tracy when I was a kid and the old man sent us to Townsville during the trouble with the Kalkadoon around the 'curry way. Only other time I saw Mrs Tracy was when I was on my way through town to tell her of the old man's death.'

'And you met Matthew then?'

Saul squirmed and avoided the officer's piercing green eyes. 'He came with me to Brisbane of his own accord. When he tried to join up I made sure he didn't get in. I knew he was only about fourteen or fifteen.'

'Fifteen now,' Patrick sighed. 'But his mother hasn't seen him since.'

Saul glanced up sharply. 'I know for sure he didn't get in. I missed the first contingent as they were only taking men with military experience. I had to wait for the second lot and didn't leave Queensland until January. He wasn't on the *Maori King* when we sailed.'

Patrick's expression in the flickering firelight reflected uncertainty. He stared into the gentle flames that were dancing their fiery ballet and sipped at the black tea. 'How did he expect to get in at his age?' Patrick mused more than questioned.

'He's a big lad for his age,' Saul said between sips of tea. 'A bit like you, boss – in looks and build. And he had a forged birth certificate in the name of Matthew Duffy. He . . . '

Saul was taken aback by the expression that suddenly clouded the major's face. It was almost the stricken look of a man who knew he was dying.

'He came to Sydney and we met!' Patrick exclaimed as the truth dawned on him. 'I suppose I was thrown because he was not under his birth name of Tracy and at the time I met him I had a lot on my mind. He certainly fooled me. What an idiot I am. He's probably going to try and enlist in Sydney under the Duffy name.'

'Be buggered!' Saul exclaimed. So the little bastard had not been deterred! 'You think he might get in?'

Patrick pulled a face. 'If he is anything like the stories I have heard of his father . . . and he has Duffy blood through his mother . . . he's likely to succeed. Excuse me, I have some letters to write and dispatch as quickly as possible.'

Patrick rose and quickly downed the precious tea before thanking Saul and striding towards the column's headquarter wagons.

Saul sat alone, cursing himself. He could have told the major about Matthew a long time ago if only he had known of the family connection. The last thing he wanted on his conscience was the possible death of Matthew Tracy. But four months had now passed. Other contingents had been raised in the Australian colonies for service in the campaign. Maybe it was too late.

That night Saul slept fitfully under the stars of the African *veldt*. Every noise woke him. His nerves were stretched taut by how close he had come to death the previous day. Occasionally he would sit bolt upright and snatch for the carbine by his side, staring out into the dark. Exhaustion fed fear and fear fed his body with adrenalin.

Overhead, the shells from the British artillery sighed before whistling down onto the low range of hills where they exploded in silent plumes of dirty smoke. Seconds later the 'crump crump' of their explosions drifted to the weary men. Slouched in their saddles, they watched the bombardment just outside Bloemfontein.

Saul scratched at his jaw and adjusted the chinstrap that held the battered brimmed hat on his head. His mount shifted and twitched with each shock wave as the ground beneath her hooves came alive. Although at this distance he could not see the Boer defenders, he knew they were still there. He did not feel any pity for the men under the terrible crash of exploding artillery rounds. He felt nothing.

At least they had not been ordered up to cut the fences that impeded their advance on a wide front, he thought with some relief. The New South Wales Lancers had scored that unenviable task and risked exposing themselves to the inevitable Boer snipers. A messenger from the front galloped past on his mount. Dark blood covered the horse's shoulder from a gaping wound. The flesh was peeled open like an obscene leer. Shrapnel, Saul thought idly as he watched the horse pass. The Boers are probably hitting the Lancers with a pompom.

As usual Major Duffy was astride his mount and far from the relative safety of headquarters. He rode slowly along the column of colonial mounted infantry, murmuring cheerful words of support. The tough colonial volunteers privately took heart from his encouraging words. His quiet courage was infectious.

'All well, Private Rosenblum?' Patrick asked when he rode up to Saul.

'No problems, boss,' Saul replied. 'Just hope you're right about the Dutchmen getting the hell out of them hills.'

'They will,' Patrick replied casually as he stared up at the distant range bare of vegetation. 'You'll see.'

He moved on and continued talking softly to the rest of the men in the column, exchanging jokes and good-natured banter as he went.

After an hour the order was given to dismount and the troopers sprawled around on the *veldt*, legs stretched and smoking pipes or propping paper on water bottles to write letters home.

Saul used the time to stretch out on his back and slip his hat over his face. He soon fell into deep sleep. When he woke it was just on dusk and the shelling had stopped.

'What's happening?' he asked a trooper sitting nearby and chewing on a blade of grass.

'Boers have scooted,' he answered with the blade still in his mouth. 'Looks like we have to fight 'em in the town.'

Saul moaned his disappointment. He had almost hoped that the war would be over when he awoke, but it was just one of those stupid, futile dreams soldiers knew too well.

But the next day the word went down the column from man to man that the mayor and his officials had met Lord Roberts with the keys to the town. The Boer army had melted away, leaving Bloemfontein to the British. A month's hard march had been rewarded. Soon around fifty thousand troops would descend on the five thousand or so inhabitants of the Boer capital. This was where the seeds of war had in fact been planted at the 1899 conference, when unreasonable British demands on the independent Boer Republics under Paul Kruger had given him little choice other than fight for the freedom of his people and their way of life.

The beginning of autumn in southern Africa also signalled the beginning of a more far reaching change in the resistance that the free-ranging Boer commandos would offer the British expeditionary forces. But for Private Saul Rosenblum a more personal turning point awaited him on a dusty street in the little town. Her name was Karen Isaacs.

ELEVEN

In the Northern Hemisphere spring had arrived in the green fields of Ireland. From where Catherine stood atop a huge, round mound she could see the tiny village across fields blooming yellow with marigold.

Beyond the stone houses and narrow cobbled streets she could see the tiny harbour with its small fleet of fishing boats and the grey Atlantic Ocean beckoning them. Turning to gaze south, the stained glass windows of the house of her birth caught the sun in a dazzling display of rainbow-coloured reflections. A gentle breeze pushed upwards from the hedged fields below. It played in the wisps of Catherine's hair that had escaped the securing pins and plucked cheekily at the hem of her white linen skirt, causing it to whip around her legs.

The surrounding circle of fir trees gave off a wonderfully fresh scent and a mass of shed needles covered an inlay of ancient patterned stones beneath Catherine's feet. She shaded her eyes and peered down through the gaps in the trees at the tiny figure of a man trudging the winding road behind that led past the mound to the Fitzgerald manor. As the figure drew near, Catherine could distinguish the black cassock, and she smiled with pleasure at the sight of an old friend.

She had been expecting him for some time, but duties had kept Father Eamon O'Brien in Rome and away from his parish for several weeks. As the priest paused to gaze up at the hill, Catherine waved and he returned the welcoming gesture. Cutting across the field of marigolds, he steadfastly puffed his way to the top to join her. Although only in his late thirties, the sedentary life of a priest at the Vatican had dulled his physical fitness.

'Ah, Catherine Fitzgerald,' he said, beaming with slightly myopic but intelligent eyes behind spectacles. 'You have grown even more beautiful in those far-off heathen lands.'

Catherine returned his smile and gave him an affectionate peck on the cheek.

'How many years, my dear lady?' Eamon asked as he stood back to appraise her. 'Fourteen . . . fifteen?'

'Too long, Father O'Brien,' she replied softly, a note of both happiness and sadness in her reply. 'Too long away from home.'

Eamon looked about for somewhere to sit, finally lowering himself onto a rounded, lichen covered stone.

'No need to call me Father O'Brien, Catherine,' he sighed as his body recovered from the short but sharp climb. 'You are not of the Faith and we have known each other for some years. And, from what I have heard, Patrick has now dropped the rosary beads in the Macintosh name.'

Catherine nodded. She preferred to address the man

rather than the priest and she was a long way from the young barefooted girl who once haunted this strange and magical place.

'Thank you, Eamon,' she said. 'I would feel more comfortable addressing you as a colleague rather than a priest if we are to work together on this dig. You know I could never accept your Christianity any more than I did my grandfather's Protestant faith.'

'I have always suspected that you were one of those pagan Celtic ladies of the old times,' the priest replied with feigned indignation for the rejection. 'The Morrigan I always imagined you really were. But God forgive, one day you might find the teachings of Saint Patrick and save your immortal soul. If not, then you will be doomed to go to that pagan heaven of yours surrounded by warriors and their blood-drinking gods.'

'You sound almost envious, Eamon,' she teased in return. 'That your heaven is so boring.'

'Ah, let us not go into talk of the next world when we have enough talk of this world – and the venture ahead of us.'

'You are right. We have much to organise if our findings are to be accepted by the academic world of learned scholars. We will need a team of reliable men to dig. Not men used to digging up potatoes, but men who will be patient enough to scrape away at the earth with trowels. And we will need a photographic record of our excavations for the journals. Not to mention –'

The priest put up his hand to halt her enthusiastic flow of plans. 'First, I think I would be liking to go down the hill and see if your grandfather left his supply of whisky. There we can sit down and discuss what is needed. Besides, I'm curious to see if the new owner has changed the old place from how I remembered it when your grandfather was alive. I hear Mr Norris has kindly consented to fund our work?'

'He has,' Catherine replied just a little evasively, avoiding his gaze. 'Mr Norris has a great interest in Irish history.'

'Or is it you that his interest might be in, Catherine?' the priest asked quietly.

'Do you ask me as a priest or as a man, Eamon?' she retorted gently. 'Because, whichever you choose, I will tell you a lie.'

'Ah, that would be a sin, and it is not my role to cause you to sin. Only you can do that.'

'Then we understand each other. I know that we have a common cause in this place and we can leave the subject of Mr Norris out of our discussions. Does that offend your sensibilities as a priest?'

'More my sensibilities as a friend,' Eamon replied. 'I do not think highly of Mr Norris and wonder what you could ever see in him when I remember the other men in your life.'

At this Catherine glanced at Eamon, puzzled, until suddenly remembering that he well knew of her young love for Michael Duffy, the Irish soldier of fortune who came to the village of Duffy to visit the place of his birth. A legendary mercenary, his hands held the ability to both create beauty through his paintings or to kill a man. Their wild, passionate interlude as she followed him across Europe would stay with her always but it was the son of that same man she had truly loved and eventually married.

'Brett Norris is not like either of those *other men* you refer to, Eamon. He is a man of culture and charm.'

'You do not have to defend him to me, Catherine,' Eamon replied. 'It is obvious you know what you want out of life.'

'You are both a man and a priest,' she returned. 'I do not expect you to understand what a woman wants.'

'On that point I concede you are right,' he answered with a wistful smile. 'I sometimes suspect that He did not know what He was in for when He allowed Adam to create Eve. Things just got out of control and have not been the same since.'

Catherine could not help but laugh at the priest's light-hearted approach to life and religion. She knew she would like working with him on the dig. A sense of humour would be a definite asset in the back-breaking hours ahead of sifting soil.

They descended the hill together, talking amiably as they crossed the yellow fields to the brooding, two-storey stone house.

The Fitzgerald manor was more like a small castle than a large residence. To Eamon's mind there was only a subtle change in the house. Maybe it was just the absence of old Fitzgerald, the tall and erudite man with whom he had shared many an evening, poring over his notes on Celtic artefacts. With a whisky in one hand and his spectacles in the other, Fitzgerald would deliver his theories on the region before Saint Patrick's time. The staff were long gone and an elderly woman from the village had moved in to assist with the running of the large house.

Eamon sat in the musty library, gazing around the cluttered room. At least the library was still the same with its floor to ceiling library shelves, stuffed birds and untidy collections of old papers.

Catherine shifted a pile of notes in one corner and located a dusty bottle of her grandfather's whisky. 'I hope whisky gets better with age,' she said, brandishing the bottle. She poured the amber liquid into a tumbler for Eamon.

'Like a good woman,' he responded cheerfully without thinking.

Catherine laughed. 'You don't sound like an Irish priest

at all,' she said, pouring herself a small tot and sitting down in her grandfather's old leather chair by the fireplace.

'I remember a young colonial officer saying that to me when we first met at my presbytery,' Eamon replied as he let the whisky catch the back of his throat. 'Ah, but that seems a lifetime ago.'

'Patrick,' Catherine said soberly.

She stared into a corner of the library, remembering how Patrick had stood, tall and arrogant, when she had first been introduced to him by Eamon in this very room.

Eamon noted the sad expression on Catherine's face and regretted his reflection on times past. 'I suppose it is my English education and Roman ordination that has tempered some of my Irish nature,' he said tactfully, to change the course of the conversation. 'I am not always sure of my Irish Catholicism and that is a terrible thing for an Irish parish priest to be saying when he has to minister to the souls of a devout congregation such as mine.'

'If you saw the people of this land from my viewpoint, Eamon, you would be seeing the most pagan people in this Christian world of yours. You know the people in your village have a thousand customs that link directly with their pagan past. For example, the idea that piercing a young girl's ears would guarantee good eyesight. A superstition no doubt buried in pagan custom and yet accepted as harmless by your Church.'

'True,' he mused. 'And banshees and little people all have links with the past. I know they are just folklore but they persist in the minds of the people despite us scoffing at them as silly superstition. You might be right in thinking that the Irish Catholic Church stands steadfastly on a pagan religion. I suppose my interest in archaeology has a spiritual motivation. I suppose I feel the deeper we dig into that hill out there the closer I will come to finding the answers to my quest for Irish Catholicism. That the Lord did indeed overcome the old pagan gods of the Celts in an unrecorded battle.'

'My husband . . . ' Catherine frowned and checked herself. 'Patrick has told me of a story that persists in his family on his father's side. It is a superstition about another and older people. A story of an Aboriginal curse on the Duffys and the Macintoshes that seems to have been unleashed when grandfather Macintosh helped the Native Mounted Police to kill off a tribe on Glen View. Patrick believes that a supernatural force was unleashed to wreak misery on both families. A black force, whose home is a hill on the property that the Aborigines held sacred to their religion. Though I could never understand why the Duffys should have the curse on them when his father's father was apparently murdered trying to save one of the survivors of the massacre.'

'I have heard the stories that both families have suffered an undue amount of tragedy,' Eamon replied. 'If such a curse existed then it would only be logical that the curse be upon the Macintosh family – not the Duffys. If you ask me, I would say that Patrick still has a lot of Irish blood in him which causes his superstitious introspection.'

'Oh, it is not only Patrick,' Catherine said, gazing at a stuffed owl watching them with glass eyes from the top of a desk. 'Even his grandmother, Lady Enid, has quietly expressed that they are all under some kind of curse. Is not the God of the Old Testament a vengeful figure who would destroy the people He created on a vast scale if they displeased Him? Did He not lay waste whole populations to protect His chosen people? Patrick said he knew why the curse was visited on both families and at the time his answer terrified me.'

'How?' the priest asked as he leant forward with obvious interest. 'How could he have the answer?'

As Catherine looked away the priest could see an unexpected fear and anguish in her face. 'Patrick says that he is the reason why the Duffys too are cursed. That when his father, a Duffy, and his mother, a Macintosh, conceived him, they crossed their blood in him, and in so doing unwittingly extended the vengeance of the spirits of the Nerambura people to all those with his blood as well.'

'Your children,' Eamon concluded softly, now understanding her fear.

'If he is right, yes, then my children are cursed. And so will their children be cursed.'

'Catherine, you are a highly intelligent woman who knows that such things are the realm of ignorant people. They are the stories we invent to scare ourselves.'

'A part of me believes that, Eamon. But . . . '

'But nothing,' he scoffed, swallowing the last of the whisky. 'In the meantime you should be thinking of how we are going to go about the business of the dig. You have a lot to do.'

Catherine nodded but the priest's attempt to dispel her seemingly irrational superstition was not completely successful. After Eamon excused himself saying he must return to the parish to hear confessions, Catherine escorted him to the door and bid him a good afternoon. But an uneasy feeling remained with her as he trudged away. A storm was rolling in from the sea and Catherine hoped that he would make it back to his church before the rains came to lash the marigolds.

When Eamon passed by the strange hill he paused to gaze at it. What secrets would they find in the ancient place of the pagan Celts? Lightning flashed a blue-white jagged fork to the ocean beyond the hill and thunder rumbled ominously in the distance. The priest shuddered. For in the voice of the thunder he remembered the echoed warning of his old housekeeper, Mary Casey: Tis not a good thing to go disturbin' the final restin' place of the old ones, Father O'Brien.

Instinctively Father Eamon O'Brien crossed himself and hurried home.

TWELVE

Major Duffy lounged in a canvas field chair with his long legs stretched in front of him. The sun was on his face and all around him the army prepared to move into the captured town of Bloemfontein. Beside him was a huge covered wagon that contained the mobile headquarters paraphernalia of Lord Roberts: map and dispatch boards, telephones and tiny, fold-down desks for his staff to scribble off situation reports and orders to his field commanders.

Senior NCOs bawled orders at tired men and mules brayed as their African handlers put them in the traces to haul the last mile. A bugle's familiar note pierced the morning air as it called men to parade. All these sounds were as familiar to the soldiers as the noises of the city are to a civilian. But the seemingly disorganised noises were evidence of a single purpose and from the cacophony would emerge the trundling rumble of wagons and the steady plod of hooves.

Patrick had snatched a rare chance to sit in the autumn sunshine and relax. He closed his eyes to block out the dull colours of camouflage all around him, but his privacy was interrupted by a shadow that fell across him.

'Major Duffy?'

Patrick opened his eyes and stared up at a civilian wearing the khaki dress of a war correspondent. The man spoke with an Australian accent.

'At your service, sir,' Patrick replied without attempting to change his position.

'I am Andrew Paterson, sir, correspondent for the *Bulletin*.'

'You hardly need any introduction, Mr Paterson,' Patrick said as he stood up to shake the other man's hand. 'My grandmother, Lady Enid Macintosh, is an avid reader of your poetry. As a matter of fact my youngest son is currently attempting to memorise your poem, "The Man from Snowy River", so I have been told.'

'You did not mention yourself, Major Duffy, as a reader of my poetry.'

'I must confess, sir, that I am more a reader of Mr Kendall's poetry. I particularly liked his poem, "The Last of His Tribe". It has somewhat an aptness to my family's history.' Patrick paused. His thoughts had been, ironically, on his family just before the well-known poet and journalist had interrupted his privacy. 'As you know my name, I presume that you have come in search of me for a purpose?'

'An officer on Lord Roberts' staff suggested that I talk to you about the Queenslanders of the Mounted Infantry. He said you had the most first-hand experience to speak of their performance in this campaign.'

'I would hardly think that a man with your considerable experience at the front lines would need to ask me, Mr Paterson,' Patrick said politely. 'You have followed the campaign with us and have as much knowledge as I of how finely they have performed under fire.'

'I have been told that you have served in Africa at Tel-el-Kebir and the Sudan campaign. Did you know my former colleague Mr Lambie from that campaign, Major Duffy?'

Patrick suspected that the journalist was indirectly testing him on his attitude to the press by his question. 'I'm afraid I never had the honour. All I knew of him was that he was shot in the leg when he rode into a village full of fuzzy wuzzies. A brave man. I have since heard that he was killed with the Tasmanians while on patrol with them near Rensburg a few weeks back.'

'Yes. The Melbourne *Age* has lost a good correspondent and Australia a brave and colourful son.'

Patrick produced a packet of cigarettes and offered one to the war correspondent who declined politely. Patrick lit his own and sent a long trail of white smoke into the air.

'All I can tell you about the men of the Queensland contingent is that they are not unlike your Clancy of the Overflow I suppose,' he said. 'Bushmen who are proving daily to Lord Roberts and his staff that they are well and truly the equal to the Boers who ride in the commandos against us. These men have lived all their working lives on the back of a horse and with a rifle in their hands, the same sort of stock the hardy Dutchman is.'

'Do you think that we will win this campaign when we capture Pretoria?'

'No,' Patrick answered bluntly and the journalist's quizzical look prompted him to go on. 'We are already seeing a new pattern of warfare developing here. The Boers have deserted their trenches and now strike at our supply lines at will. I have no doubt that the Boers under men like De Wet and De la Rey will be prepared to wage a war not unlike the Spanish guerillas did to Napoleon's armies in Spain. Or even to an extent the kind of war we fought in the Sudan against the dervishes. They will try to wear us down with constant casualties, a cost that even the mine owners here will not tolerate. And finally a political victory in London with the public annoyed that their morning papers cannot herald as decisive a victory as they have known before. The British public will eventually demand that we pull out. The Boers are like the colonials: tough, self-reliant and inured to hardship. This is their land and they know it better than anyone outside the darkies themselves.'

'How would you suggest we bring this war to an end then, Major Duffy?'

Patrick's expression reflected his gloominess. 'I don't think we can win. Even if we lift the sieges we will have won nothing more than the towns. The Boer will own the countryside and each and every one of his farmhouses will become a base of operations. His women will work the fields, tend the cattle and feed the men. No, we cannot win unless we are able to starve the Boer into surrender and I dare not think how we would go about that. I fear such tactics would bring outrage from the rest of the world.'

'It may be necessary,' Paterson replied. 'I have heard many stories from men I have interviewed telling that they have come under fire from Boer farmhouses flying the white sheet of neutrality. And I have no doubt that many of those fellows who have sworn not to take up arms against us again simply do so to return to their farms for a bit of rest and resupply.'

'That is why I think this war is unwinnable. But I would not like you to quote me, sir. My observations are merely reflections on the situation as I see it and have no relationship to the war aims of Lord Roberts.'

'You are an honest man, Major Duffy,' the journalist grinned. 'First you admit that you are not a reader of my poetry when others lie to flatter me. But, at least I can promise you, sir, that your private opinions will remain out of the newspapers.'

'Thank you, Mr Paterson,' Patrick replied and held out his hand. 'Please do not doubt my enthusiasm to continue this war. It's just that I feel the world has not only entered a new century but is also seeing the future of a new kind of warfare. I only hope we can adapt in a military fashion to fight the new wars of this century or soldiers' lives will be wasted for nothing.'

'Rather well put, Major Duffy,' Paterson said as he took the offered hand. 'I wish you good luck and good health.'

'You too, sir,' Patrick replied.

Patrick watched the famed Australian walk away to gather his kit for the advance into Bloemfontein. That's about all he could hope for, Patrick thought. Good luck, good health, a hot bath, a square meal and clean sheets. A fleeting picture of his wife came to him lying naked against crisp bed linen, her beautiful tresses of red hair spread like a fan on the pillow as she smiled up at him. But such memories held nothing but emptiness for him now.

Patrick folded the canvas chair and threw it on the back of a wagon attached to the headquarters group. With long strides he crossed a field busy with men making last minute adjustments to their kit. At the horse lines his mount waited for him.

The troops of the column entered the town as a sorry looking spectacle of worn and weary men. Astride his mount Saul Rosenblum eyed the sombre crowd of men and women as they watched the conquerors of their town parade past. The rough-looking, big-bearded men scowled from under broad-brimmed hats from the verandahs of shops and Saul knew he could well have faced many of them along the barrel of his Lee Metford carbine only weeks or even days earlier. He had no doubt, from the surly looks that he was given, that he might see them again framed in the sights of his rifle in the weeks ahead.

His squadron was allocated an area at the edge of town to bivouac. Hardly had they set up camp before the mounted troopers began slipping away to explore the Boer capital, with or without leave from their officers. Saul was among those quietly making their way into town to enjoy for a moment the luxuries afforded by civilisation.

As he wandered through streets crowded with soldiers and civilians he could not help being reminded of the provincial towns of his own home Colony of Queensland. The neat and tidy homes with wide verandahs and struggling gardens were so much like those of Cloncurry or Mount Isa. Even from stands of blue gums imported from Australia wafted familiar eucalyptic scents. There were fine and substantial buildings like the Boer parliament house which was now being converted into a hospital for the sick and wounded of the column.

Wandering along the dusty streets, Saul could see the shops were empty of goods. The cutting of the railway from the south had ensured that the town was starved of supplies. In time it would be opened and thousands of troops and tons of supplies would flow in to bring a certain amount of prosperity again. But for now, to a soldier nostalgic for home it gave the town a desolate mood.

Saul's attention was drawn to raised voices in the crowd just in front of the Orange Free State military barracks. One of those speaking in the guttural tones of Afrikaans was that of an obviously distressed woman. Saul pushed aside a circle of burly Boer farmers surrounding the young woman in tears. A large, pot bellied man with a long beard was berating her. He raised a *sjambok* whip to strike as she cowered before him. But the whip did not descend. The pot bellied man suddenly felt the hard tip of a rifle barrel pressed firmly behind his ear. Angry voices were raised at the action of the Australian soldier but were dulled to loud mutterings as other soldiers of Roberts' column stepped in to help Saul disperse the onlookers.

'Don't do it, Dutchman,' Saul growled.

The Boer did not have to understand English to know what the soldier was saying to him. He slowly lowered the whip and snarled something in Afrikaans at the girl before reluctantly walking away, but not before he spat on the ground at the feet of a soldier who watched him cautiously. The soldier, a member of Saul's squadron, grinned defiantly into the man's face and drawled, 'See you on the *veldt* some time, Dutchie, and when I do it will be the last time I will ever have to look at you.'

The girl was shaking. She was not beautiful. Her hips were too slim and her dark hair was cut short and worn loose around her shoulders. But Saul was immediately taken by her deep, brown, intelligent eyes as she gave Saul a look of gratitude for his intervention.

'Are you all right, missus?' Saul asked, not really expecting her to understand his question.

'Yes, thank you,' she answered. 'They were not able to hurt me because you came to my assistance. I will be going now,' she added as she brushed herself down.

Saul was surprised when she replied in English and reluctant to allow the young woman to leave. He had not been in the company of a woman for a long time and, although it was a strange way to meet one, he felt he had a right to get to know her. 'What was all that over?' he asked. 'Why was that big Dutchman going to give you a hiding?'

'It was nothing,' she replied evasively. 'Nothing that you would understand.'

'You live here?' he asked.

'Ja. I mean no,' she contradicted herself. 'I am staying here. My home is in Pretoria with my father.'

'Where are you staying then? I can walk you home just in case that big bastard . . . sorry, missus . . . that big bloke is hanging around down the street.'

She seemed to consider the question. 'That would be courteous of you,' she replied with a weak smile. 'I will accept your kind offer.'

Saul was pleased and stepped beside the young woman to escort her. She pointed down the street and said she was staying with a friend, an English woman, two streets away. As they made their way through the crowd of soldiers and civilians the Queenslander took in her appearance through sidelong glances. He guessed she was about twenty years of age and had a prettiness that he had missed at first impression. Her dress was a simple, blue patterned skirt with a white blouse that came to a frilly collar around the neck. The fair skin of her face was smattered with freckles. Even to the less than worldly young bushman, the young woman who walked beside him was a contradiction. The manner of her dress and her very looks themselves just did not seem to fit. She appeared neither European nor one of the mixed blood people he had come to recognise on the *veldt*. Her English was accented, but without the guttural tones of the Boers who spoke English.

'My name is Saul Rosenblum,' he finally said to break the

silence as they walked. 'I'm with the Queensland Mounted Infantry.'

'You are an Australian,' she replied. 'I should hate you for being in this war which is not yours. Why are you here?'

'I'm here because . . .' he fumbled with his words. Why was he here? While he knew he was not really in South Africa for the same patriotic reasons his comrades espoused, he had never really questioned his motives for enlisting until this strange young woman had pinned him down with her blunt question. He took a deep breath and continued. 'I'm here because you needed my help a while ago. That's why.'

Her laughter took him by surprise. It was light and spontaneous. She stopped in the street and turned to the tall soldier from across the Indian Ocean.

'That is not why you are really here. But I like your answer.'

There was a merriment in her eyes he had not seen up until now. And it was as if something had passed between them.

'My name is Karen Isaacs, Mr Rosenblum. And, as you can see, we may share a common heritage.' She hesitated and frowned. 'You are an Australian Jew?'

'Sort of,' Saul responded uncertainly. 'My father was a Jew but my mother a gentile. Me, well, I don't exactly believe in all the stuff. But my father started to believe again, right before he died last year.'

'I am sorry, Mr Rosenblum,' she said as the merriment faded from her eyes and she touched his arm lightly.

'He had a good innings,' Saul replied.

'What does a good innings mean?' she asked, looking puzzled at the expression.

'Like in cricket. Scored a few runs before he was bowled out.'

'Oh, I understand now. But I was not saying I was sorry for your father dying. I was saying I was sorry that you did not follow the faith of our fathers.'

'Yeah, well, you don't get much time to think about religion when yer wrestling with some old scrub cow where I come from.'

'You are a man who works with cattle,' she said with interest as they began to walk again. 'Do you have many cattle?'

'Not anymore. We lost the property about the time the old man died. Guess the real reason I joined up was for a job that paid four and sixpence a day and all the biscuits you can eat . . . when we can get them.'

They came to a little house with a wide verandah and dirty white-washed walls. A low wire fence overgrown by desiccated, long grass surrounded the house and red dust filled the spaces between what had once been a nicely laid out garden trimmed with stones. Karen stopped in the space where a gate should have been and turned to Saul. He was desperately attempting to stave off the imminent separation. He wanted to get to know this young woman but did not give himself much of a chance in a town where fifty thousand other soldiers would probably be wanting to do the same.

'You didn't tell me why that Boer was going to give you a hiding,' he finally said, hoping the explanation might delay her just a little longer.

'I will tell you when you come to have supper with Mrs Ramsay and myself tonight,' she said, eyes twinkling. 'Five o'clock we dine. Is that convenient to you?'

'My oath! Sorry, Miss Isaacs, I meant that will be fine.'

'Good,' Karen said as she turned her back and walked away from him, her slim hips swinging under the cotton dress.

Saul watched her disappear into the house and turned to walk back into the town. As he did he found his thoughts remained focused on the eyes and enigmatic smile of the woman he had just met. There was something about her that haunted him in a pleasant way. But he was soon lost in the crowd of khaki soldiers roaming the African town.

THIRTEEN

April had come and was almost gone by the time the rains came to the tent city that had sprung up around Bloemfontein. The dusty soil turned to a quagmire of mud, making life miserable for man and beast.

Private Saul Rosenblum was more fortunate than his comrades who sat around in their clammy tents cursing the weather and praying for a chance to be back in the saddle hunting down the Boer commandos. He had a warm and cosy house to slip away to whenever he was granted leave – and sometimes when he was not. The gentle love that had blossomed between him and the mysterious girl grew stronger with each day in their lives.

Saul had learned that she was born in Holland and that her father was a gemstone buyer for De Beers diamond company. Her mother had died of malaria while they were in Portuguese territory en route to Rhodesia three years earlier and one of her brothers was killed riding with the Boer commandos earlier that year. Her other brother was presumably still living, his whereabouts unknown with a commando operating in the Transvaal. Her father, as he knew, resided in Pretoria, awaiting his daughter's return.

Karen told Saul how the Boers had accused her of collaboration with the English on the day he had rescued her from a public thrashing with the stinging *sjambok*. She said it was really because she was a Jew and also because she resided with an English widow, Annabelle Ramsay, whose husband had been killed in a mine accident at Kimberley two years before the war broke out in South Africa.

The Boers had focused their brand of anti-Semitism on the gold barons of South Africa, accusing them of being the real architects of the war. But the anti-Semitic feelings of the Boers were not restricted to them alone. Many protesting the war in England cited the universal Jewish conspiracy as the cause of war.

Mrs Ramsay was an old friend of the Isaac family from when Karen had lived in London for a time as a young girl to perfect her English. Saul's visits to the house and the walks he and Karen took together on the *veldt* soon led them both to the young Dutch girl's bed. She was sometimes unsure why the tall Queenslander had appealed to her above all other men she had known. Was it his gentle innocence despite his tough exterior? Or was it his slow smile and self-deprecatory sense of humour? In the old double bed with its brass metal bedhead, under the tin roof of Mrs Ramsay's cottage they would lie entwined and listen to the lullaby of the steady April rain. Together they found a universe that, however transient, transcended the inevitable moment when Lord Roberts had swelled his army sufficiently to march on the Boer capital of Pretoria.

Some nights Saul trembled in his sleep and screamed himself awake when the nightmares came, the ground thumping under him as the Boer artillery shredded men and horses with hot, flailing shrapnel. Arms, legs and entrails piled in steaming heaps as he struggled against the drowning tide of blood. On such nights Karen would press him against her tiny breasts and rock him with soothing words. At those times she would think of her dead brother whose body lay in an unmarked grave and wonder if the man she soothed in her arms might have killed him. But her guilt helped no-one. This was their universe and nothing else mattered when they were together.

Sister Greeves of the New South Wales Army Medical Corps held up a methylated lamp for the two rain-drenched colonial scouts who carried their comrade between them in the blanket they had used as a stretcher. With rifles slung across their backs, they struggled to get him into the makeshift hospital and onto the floor. In the converted former Boer military barracks enteric fever cases had taken most of the available beds.

'Doctor,' she called to the surgeon on duty. 'We have a man who has been shot in the upper body.'

The doctor hurried to join the nursing sister as she knelt by the big man and expertly stripped away the wounded man's blood-stained shirt to reveal a tiny hole to the right upper pectoral muscle. She knew from experience that the wound was caused by a high velocity Mauser round. She held the lantern close so that the army surgeon could make a diagnosis of the man's condition. He was conscious but refused to allow his obvious pain to show. His teeth were gritted to stop himself screaming out when the surgeon probed as gently as possible the entry wound with sterilised forceps.

'He looks too old to be riding around the *veldt*,' the doctor muttered angrily.

''E's only half the age of some of the Boers we've come across,' one of the tough-looking colonial scouts snarled. 'And I've seen some of them Boers no older than twelve shootin' at us from the rocks.'

The doctor glanced up into the face of the man who had made the statement. He was an Australian, as were many of the colonial soldiers in the local units raised to fight the Boer. Most had once worked the mines before the war, crossing the Indian Ocean from their own land to seek employment in South Africa when the recession of the '90s hit Australia. The doctor nodded. The independent scouts were not men who necessarily were awed by rank, nor was it wise to argue a point with them.

He scanned the rest of the wounded man's body and marvelled at the scars, obviously inflicted over many years and most probably by war. He was not young, perhaps close to sixty, and yet his body was as hard and muscular as that of a man half his age. Even in his wounded condition his face remained ruggedly handsome, despite the black leather patch over his left eye.

'This man should not be riding with you,' the sister exclaimed indignantly. She was unafraid of any living being except the matron of the hospital and the tough scouts did not frighten her in the slightest. 'How could the army let him enlist at his age – and with only one eye?'

'This old man, Sister, is none other than Captain Michael Duffy,' one of the scouts growled defensively, 'the best lion hunter in Africa, next to Selous that is, and a man who has seen more wars in his time than you've had

126

breakfasts. Them scars he got stretch back as far as the Maori Wars before you were even born. Not to mention the American Civil War, fighting the red Injuns, fighting Mexicans. And the rest just scars he got being mauled by lions. Kind of fitting he got another scar fightin' in this war.'

'We have a Major Duffy here in Bloemfontein, attached to Lord Roberts' staff,' the doctor said as he traced the route that the cupronickel projectile had taken along his patient's ribs under the skin. High velocity bullets rarely took a straight path when they hit a target. They had a habit of being easily deflected and following the least line of resistance, which in this case was under Michael's arm and down his ribs to lodge just under the skin at the lower end of his ribcage. 'Wouldn't be a relation, would he?'

'My son,' Michael winced as the doctor pressed on the outline of the bullet beneath the skin. 'But he'll be an orphan if you don't get the bloody bullet out soon.'

'You're lucky, Captain Duffy. The wound is clean and the bullet should come out with very little trouble. You seem to have a tough hide for someone your age. I'll have one of the orderlies fetch Major Duffy and tell him you are here.'

'Thanks, Doc,' Michael replied with a broad smile. 'Think he will be somewhat surprised to find he still has a father . . . or maybe not.'

'How did this happen?' the surgeon asked as he stood to prepare himself for the operation. 'I thought there wasn't much action out there for the moment.'

'We were reconnoitring well up the railway track when we stumbled into an ambush. Seems they didn't know I was too old to fight anymore.'

The doctor grinned at the Australian's quiet jibe. He was a tough bastard, he thought and wondered if the son was anything like his father.

Patrick stared at the rain-drenched hospital orderly in stunned silence, wondering if he had been sent as some elaborate joke by the Queenslanders in an attempt to break the monotony of their camp existence.

'Captain Michael Duffy?' Patrick repeated.

'Yes, sir,' the orderly confirmed. 'A big man with a black leather eye patch. He also says he is your father.'

Patrick quickly threw a groundsheet over his shoulders and followed the orderly through the tent city on the outskirts of the town. He was drenched when he arrived at the hospital in the early hours of the morning. As Sister Greeves eyed the tall major, Patrick knew she was making some comparison with the man who said he was Michael Duffy. From the expression on her stern but pretty face he knew he had passed her assessment. She held a lamp to lead the way between the rows of sleeping patients, some moaning in their restless fight with fever, others moaning in pain from their wounds.

By the time Major Patrick Duffy arrived at the hospital the surgeon had removed the bullet from his patient. The big Irishman had scorned the use of an anaesthetic for such a trivial operation, and did not scream out when the scalpel peeled open the flesh over his ribs to release the projectile. 'Send it to Count Manfred von Fellmann in Prussia,' Michael had grinned weakly as the doctor held up the bullet. 'Let the bastard know I'm still alive and his German bullets can't kill me.'

Sister Greeves led Patrick to a bed at the end of the ward

where the shadows of the lamp fell on a profile he had last seen fifteen years ago, crouching beside an ox wagon, with a Winchester rifle, waiting for the Boer commando to launch its night assault on them. Patrick stood beside his father's bed staring down at him.

Although Michael was in great pain he grimaced at his son. 'Hello, Patrick,' he said through gritted teeth. 'Or should I call you sir, as you seem to out-rank me.'

Patrick pulled a face and shook his head. He had only one question after fifteen years of presuming his father was dead.

'How?'

Michael attempted to drag himself into a sitting position. His son helped him prop himself against the wall behind the bed. 'Got a cigarette?' Michael asked when he was moderately comfortable.

Patrick produced a crushed packet and found a relatively dry cigarette which he lit and passed to his father. Michael inhaled deeply before answering. 'I was lucky. They hit me all at once and in the darkness and confusion I got hold of one of their horses. When they woke up to what had happened I was halfway down to the river. I got off the horse and took to swimming. The horse was still galloping away in the dark and the stupid bastards followed the sound of it away from me. It was as simple as that.' He took another long drag on the cigarette. As simple as that . . .

Patrick knew it had probably not been that simple but he also knew his father was not a man for elaborate explanations. 'Why in God's name didn't you contact me to say you were still alive?' he questioned in a cold voice, as if his father were an enemy to be interrogated.

'You know my life, Patrick,' the Irishman replied. 'I've been a dead man ever since you were born and there was no reason why I should disturb your life. And besides, it did not seem a good idea because you were rightfully with Catherine. I've never felt good about what happened.'

Patrick shook his head. In his mind the affair between Catherine and his father had long been buried. He did not blame his father for Catherine's infatuation with him – she had been very young then. Time had brought Patrick some wisdom in the matter long past. 'Do you know that you have a grand-daughter and two grandsons? Don't you think that they have a right to know you, even if I didn't seem to have that right?'

Michael smiled at his son's revelation. 'Ah, but that's a grand thing to know. Tell me about my grandchildren.'

Patrick sighed and sat at the edge of the bed, describing the three children to his father who listened engrossed as the cigarette burned down to his fingers. As Michael questioned his son on their lives, Patrick felt an unexpected closeness to this man who was almost a stranger to him. This was only the third time he had met his father in his life. The dangerous intrigue that was Michael's life had kept father and son apart.

When Patrick had answered his questions about his grandchildren, Michael moved on to the rest of the family. The answers came: Daniel Duffy was now a politician of some standing, fighting the Federationists with words, in favour of the colonies forming a republic on American lines. Lady Enid was alive and well and running the Macintosh companies in his absence. Aunt Kate, Michael's sister, was well and the wealthiest woman in the Colony of Queensland. Young Matthew had turned up in Sydney and enlisted under-age without his mother's knowledge. In response to his urgent inquiries, Patrick had just received a telegram from Arthur Thorncroft confirming the worst. Matthew was with the New South Wales Citizen Bushmen's Rifles en route to South Africa.

At this news of his nephew Michael growled his disapproval. Both men vowed that he would be intercepted and put on the first ship back to Australia, in irons if necessary. But they also agreed that Kate should not know of Matthew's foolhardy adventure until her son was located.

'Did you know of my mother's death?' Patrick finally asked.

His father looked away. 'I did not know,' he answered softly. 'When did she die?'

His son told his father all that he knew of his mother's peaceful death in Prussia. Michael nodded but no tears came. Instead he sighed and related a story from his own experiences.

'About ten years back I was doing some hunting in Bechuanaland, mostly lions. I had an opportunity to observe the big cats and the way they lived and I learned something that makes a lot of sense to me now. Maybe it always did. I learned that the female lion was happiest with her sisters. The females would hunt and live together and the old male would just prowl around as a solitary creature. The female only needed him when she came into season. For that privilege he was prepared to put his life at risk fighting off other competitors for the females. But when that time was over, she went back to her sisters, to live out her life. I don't think lions and people are much different.'

Patrick could understand what his father was trying to tell him. He knew of his mother's passionate love for her cousin Penelope and his story of the lions was his way of attempting to reassure his son that his mother had not been an evil woman.

'I do know of the matter of Catherine and yourself,

Patrick,' his father continued. 'Soldiers talk, especially about the private lives of officers, and I am truly sorry that matters turned out the way they did.'

'It's all just part of the curse that will never end for us,' Patrick said bitterly.

'If you mean that blackfella curse your Aunt Kate is so fond of espousing, then I could almost agree,' his father said. 'But if that is so, then I suspect that the curse was upon me, and not you, son.'

'It is a plague that infects the blood of both the Macintoshes, and the Duffys,' his son replied with a note of despair. 'It's not something we can fight like a Boer commando. It's an insidious force in our lives. Everything I have learned, from Lady Enid and others, points to that event at Glen View forty years ago. And I do not know of any way of putting an end to it.'

Patrick was surprised to hear his father chuckling softly at his lament. 'I think you have a bit of your Aunt Kate in you, son,' he said as he gripped Patrick's hand. 'And if you have then you will know how to take away the curse.'

'Then you too believe we are cursed,' Patrick said earnestly.

His father shrugged and lay back against the wall. 'Last month we were skirmishing along the Modder with a Boer commando of around a hundred *Uitlanders,* Americans, Frenchies, Germans and a bunch of Irishmen amongst them. My troop stumbled on their *laager* by the river just on sunset. We took them by surprise but they stood their ground and fought hard. It came down to the bayonet. When it was all over we had lost five good men but they had lost a lot more, including a few from our ancestral village in the old country. I learned that they had been recruited by Daniel's boy, Father Martin Duffy of the

Jesuits. So maybe the curse does exist if a priest of the True Faith would be rallying men to war to fight you and I. Especially a priest who is of our own blood.'

When Sister Greeves came to change the bandages of the grizzled captain's wounds, Patrick realised that he had sat talking with his father into the grey dawn. The ward was stirring with the appearance of more staff as he left his father in the tender care of the Australian nurses. Some local women had also volunteered to assist in the care of the sick and wounded, a generous gesture when their own men still rode the *veldt*, fighting the comrades of the soldiers the Boer women tended.

The rain had eased and the sun attempted to break through the low grey clouds that scudded across the sky as Patrick mused over the unexpected appearance of his father. At a time when he dreamed too often of death, perhaps his appearance was more than coincidence. Maybe it was meant to be, especially since his father had expressed his desire to return home to Australia as soon as he was released from hospital. He was weary of a life steeped in violence and dreaming of a pilgrimage to the graves of his own father and brother Tom. He wanted to sit with his beloved sister on the verandah of her big house in Townsville and talk softly of people past in their lives, Aunt Bridget and Uncle Frank, old Max Braun, Henry James and so many others now dead and buried and too soon forgotten. Michael Duffy was seeking retirement from the world of war he had known all his adult life but Patrick had other plans for his father. Just one last mission before he sought the peace he had never really known in his troubled life, something that only the legendary Michael Duffy could resolve. Next time he visited he would put the proposal to his father.

Patrick was weary as he walked away from the hospital. He had had little sleep in the previous twenty-four hours so the general order to attend an early briefing at headquarters brought him no joy. The young lieutenant dispatched to fetch him, one of the fresh new arrivals sent as reinforcement from England, saluted smartly as he delivered the command from above. Lord Roberts was obviously close to announcing the day the now-reinforced column would march north on Pretoria, Patrick thought grimly. He suspected that the Boers would fight fiercely to defend their capital.

Bringing his horse to an abrupt halt outside Annabelle Ramsay's house, Saul flung himself from the saddle and sprinted up the path to the front door.

'Karen,' he blurted as she hurried to greet him. 'We're on the advance. Just got through being briefed by Corporal Hastings a couple of minutes ago. Came straight here to see you.'

Karen's expression reflected her dismay. 'Pretoria?' she asked as she pulled Saul through the open door and held him.

'I suppose that is the general's plan,' he answered. 'I have to be back in five minutes. I promised that I was only duck-ing away for ten. We have to get ready this afternoon to move at first light tomorrow.'

They held each other in a crushing embrace motivated as much by their love as the shared fear that the war was sweeping them in different directions. A soldier was not a man who could choose where he went. He could not opt out of the army as a civilian might choose to seek other employment. Soldiering was a strange form of slavery, founded on loyalty and regulated by strict martial laws.

'You will think about all we have spoken of together

while you are away,' Karen said with an intensity that caused her slim body to tremble. 'That when you have finished with this war you will come with my father and I to Palestine to live.'

'I promise I will think about what you have said,' he replied as his arms crushed her to him and he bent to kiss the top of her head. The scent of her clean hair was a perfume he wanted to carry with him in his long days ahead riding the *veldt*. 'You promise me you will look after yourself. If anything was to happen to you . . . '

His words trailed away in a choking voice. He fought the tears that threatened to overwhelm him. He did not think of what lay ahead for him. At that moment he knew without hesitation that he would willingly lay down his life to protect this woman if needed. He reluctantly broke their embrace and gently kissed her on the lips. As he turned to stride back to his horse, his rifle slung over his back, he did not want to look back and see the pain he knew was in her face as much as it was in his. Although Saul had listened to Karen outline the plans she and her father had of travelling to Jerusalem and setting up a jewellery shop, he had hoped she would lose her enthusiasm. He had quietly spoken of Queensland, in hopes that she might travel back with him to the land of his birth. But it did not seem to be so. Yes, he would consider her plan to go to Palestine as soon as his enlistment was up at the end of the year.

As he swung himself into the saddle to ride away he was acutely aware that should he not choose to go with her to Palestine then he would surely lose her. He also knew he could be useful to her cause, as both an experienced fighting man and as a man who knew farming. He would have much more than just staying alive out on the *veldt* to consider. He would also have their future to decide on.

The next morning twenty-four thousand men and two hundred guns rolled out of Bloemfontein following the axis of the railway line that pointed north to Pretoria. At the same time, to the east of Lord Roberts' advance, General Hamilton led a column on a parallel course. In both columns the Australian horsemen rode ahead or on the flanks. They would be the first to engage the screening horsemen of any Boers between them and the capital. Major Patrick Duffy would ensure that he was in the reconnaissance parties as many times as possible on the advance.

FOURTEEN

The dig had begun with a disagreement. Catherine argued that they should dig down from the top of the hill, while Eamon suggested an excavation from the base, digging an exploratory trench from the side as if cutting a slice from a cake rather than a well into the centre. He reasoned that this method would also allow them to excavate to the heart of the mound, as Catherine desired. In the end they compromised and the dig commenced to one side of the mysterious ring of stones with a course descending towards the core of the small hill.

Eamon intoned a prayer for their success and the first symbolic spadeful of soil was turned by Catherine to mark the commencement of the enterprise. Two workmen from the village had been hired to carry out the manual work of excavation, both with experience channel digging in England. For two weeks the men toiled to clear a wedge-shaped trench pointing into the heart of the hill. But in that fortnight nothing had appeared in the carefully sifted spadefuls of soil.

Each day when Eamon arrived at the dig expectantly, Catherine would shake her head. Her journal recorded very little other than the fact that all that was being turned over was soil. But at least the soil itself indicated that the hill was not a natural feature. The priest had pointed out the probability that the earth had come from the plain below, surmising that a boggy marsh close to the Fitzgerald house had probably been created by the removal of soil to build the closely packed mound. The excavators shored up the sides of the trench to avoid the ever-present nightmare of a sudden cave-in caused by water seepage.

At the end of the second week Catherine called down to the two men sweating in their trench. They were to leave their work and start at a new point. Under Catherine's direction they carefully levered aside the ring of stones which a photographer had already recorded for her. The circle was a mystery as much as the hill itself. Their only theory so far was that the hill was in fact a giant burial mound constructed to honour a Celtic leader of high importance. Other than that, they had no idea as to what they might find.

Only a few hours into their new task, stripping away the topsoil in preparation for a large, square excavation from above, one of the workers cursed as his iron shovel struck stone with an arm-jarring clang. Catherine, under the shade of a canvas sheet heard the sound – and the blasphemous cursing of the digger that followed. She had been noting her reasons for changing the direction of the excavations and dropped the journal on a small camp table, hurrying over to the man rubbing his elbow.

Staring down at the area he had removed to a depth of six inches she caught her breath. The stone the shovel had struck was not of any kind she had seen in the surrounding countryside. Although its highly polished surface was now dulled, she did not have to be a geologist to recognise it as marble.

'Mr O'Connell,' she said breathlessly, attempting to keep her excitement under control, 'please be very careful with your spade. I would suggest that you use a trowel to scrape around the rest of the stone.'

Under her vigilant scrutiny the two men now knelt to begin the tedious task of scraping the soil away from the stone. It appeared that O'Connell, a big, raw-boned man in his late thirties, had struck the edge of what slowly revealed itself as a slab of polished, dark – almost black – marble. So engrossed were the three huddled around the excavation that they did not hear the Irish priest's approach.

'God in His heaven!' Eamon exclaimed as he leant over their shoulders to peer at the rectangular slab revealed beneath the earth. It was as long as a tall man and about the same width. 'I think it's of Roman origin.'

Catherine glanced up at him from where she knelt, startled. 'But it cannot be,' she said, a note of confusion in her voice. 'The Romans did not come to this part of Ireland.'

Eamon knelt beside her. Taking his spectacles from his nose, he wiped them with the hem of his cassock before replacing them to peer more closely at the stone. O'Connell had wiped the surface lightly with water and cloth and now the stone sparkled in the early summer sunlight.

'I have seen a similar artefact in the excavations at Pompei whilst I was assisting on a dig there,' he said with awe as his fingers stroked the wet surface. 'But even then we traced that marble to an earlier era of Etruscan civilisation.'

'If you were right, Eamon, how would you explain this?'

The priest frowned. He stood and gazed from the top of the hill to the grey sea beyond the village.

'The Vikings came in their longships to this coast a thousand years ago,' he reflected quietly. 'They had contact with the Byzantine Empire and there is a possibility that the stone came here via that contact.'

'Could the stone be of Norse origin?' Catherine asked but the priest shook his head.

'It is marble and that is not a medium they used,' he replied. 'I suspect that, as we excavate deeper, we will find that the slab is supported on a base. If my observations prove correct then I suspect that we have unearthed an unholy work of the devil.'

As Catherine glanced up at Eamon she could see the concern on his face. 'An altar,' she murmured. 'An altar of human sacrifice.'

The priest met her eyes. 'Yes. An altar of great rarity,' he reflected. 'I have seen only one other. It was in the excavations at that terrible place of human depravity, Pompei. I had access to a section that had been sealed off from the curious who came to tour the petrified city. There were orders from the Vatican that the public should not see what we had unearthed. It was thought that the revelations of man's most debased practices should be best left unrecorded and I saw why. The images on the walls of the room where the altar was found have haunted me still. It was a place of the devil himself. A bestial place of despair.'

The two workmen shifted uneasily as they listened to the priest relate his experiences in the ancient Roman city and they crossed themselves superstitiously.

Catherine returned her gaze to the polished marble slab and touched its surface with her fingertips. What horrors had this mysterious stone witnessed? And how did it come to be so far from another place and culture? 'We are only assuming,' she said softly as she stroked the smooth stone under her fingers, 'that this is an altar such as the one you saw at Pompei.'

'It is,' he answered in a flat voice. 'But I am sure further excavation will testify to my observation.'

By late afternoon he was proved right.

The workmen had gone home to the village leaving the young woman and older priest alone on the hill. The altar was now revealed for the first time in unknown centuries, the Roman writing engraved on the two square pillars supporting the black marble slab confirming Eamon's educated guess as to its origins. The engraved Latin writing was well preserved.

'Remarkable,' Eamon sighed, standing back to admire what had been unearthed. 'It has suffered no damage over the centuries. Not a chip out of it. It's as if it had been buried only yesterday.'

'It will certainly cause ripples in academic circles,' Catherine mused beside him. 'How will historians explain its presence in Ireland?'

'Perhaps they will be as mystified as we are, but I tend to think the stone may have been brought by the Vikings. For what earthly reason I cannot even dare a guess. It is something very much out of place. But if there is one thing I sense it is this stone is something unholy. Something that we should rebury.'

'That is silly superstition, Eamon,' Catherine chided. 'It is a valuable find, meriting a significant place in Irish history, no matter what your priestly feelings about good and evil.'

The expression on Eamon's face was immovable. 'During the third century before the birth of Our Lord the Romans imported many Egyptian and Middle Eastern religions. During the Second Punic War one of the imported religions was called upon against the famed Carthigian, Hannibal, to drive him from Italy. The Romans deferred to some works known as the Sibyline Books for inspiration. The books prophesied victory for the Romans only if they gave homage to the Great Mother cult of Asia Minor. And so a black meteorite symbolising the goddess was brought from Pessinus in Anatolia and paraded through the streets of Rome. The old goddess of Asia Minor was given a Roman name, Cybele, and her priests were known as the Galli. Such were the excesses – even by Roman standards – of the priests that Roman law soon forbade membership to the religion. The priests had a nasty habit of going into a frenzy and castrating themselves while playing exotic music and dancing. Despite such bizarre rituals, the religion grew popular, particularly in the second century A.D. Those Romans who were to be initiated into the religion would descend into a pit that had a wooden grate overhead. A bull would be brought over the top of the grate and slaughtered. Its blood would pour onto the initiates below.'

'Hardly evil considering the excesses of Romans at that time,' Catherine said quietly. 'I have read of worse things practised in the arena, Eamon.'

The priest removed his glasses to polish the lenses. It was his way of delaying an answer. 'Ah, but the religion did not end there,' he finally replied. 'More was revealed in the murals in that place of evil I visited. It seems the Galli also had a secret practice of subjecting young women to a perverse form of initiation. One that I am reluctant to even discuss.'

'It had something to do with the bulls,' Catherine said.

The priest nodded. 'Not only the bulls but also other

142

animals,' he continued quietly. 'They believed that the seed of the animal would give the woman's future child the virtues of that animal: the strength of the bull, the courage of the wolf and so on. Even leopards were used.'

Catherine was aghast. She was familiar with the mating of animals as she had grown up in the country. But the thought of a woman coupling with a bull was beyond her imagination.

'But how . . . ?' she whispered in her horror.

The priest knew exactly what she was thinking. 'It seems a frame would be erected over the altar and the bull's organ would only be allowed a short distance inside the woman. How they did this we are not sure. Nor do we wish to know. It is the perversity of the devil.'

'And you think this altar was used for such practices?'

'That would be a reasonable assumption, given its similarity to the one I saw and the accompanying Latin inscriptions I have deciphered,' he answered as he replaced his spectacles. 'So the stone has been corrupted in the eyes of Our Lord and this place is one of evil. Some places should not be interfered with by mere mortals,' the priest sighed as he continued. 'I think this is such a place. I think we should discontinue our excavations and bury what we have found.'

'No, Eamon,' Catherine said defiantly, turning on him. 'This is too valuable an archaeological find to simply bury for another thousand years or so. I intend to continue.'

'Then you do so without me, Catherine. I fear my soul would be in jeopardy should I assist you in discovering whatever other secrets this godforsaken place may reveal.'

'You are a learned man, Eamon,' she persisted. 'You know that such things as this altar and what it once meant are all part of man's heritage . . . his history. You know how important this find is.'

The priest shook his head and stared down at the altar. 'My search is over,' he said softly. 'I found that which I sought when the stone was unearthed. I found that I am as superstitious as my parishioners who, in my arrogance, I always felt superior to. Now I think that I am no better than they.' He shuddered although the afternoon was warm. 'I have a strong sense of an evil here that is almost tangible. If you persist then that evil may possess your very soul, Catherine.'

Catherine was unmoved. 'If you have decided to abandon the dig then that is your decision, but I cannot understand why you should.'

'I am sorry, Catherine, but you should consider reburying the altar,' he said, and made his way to the path that had been worn up the side of the mound. 'I will bid you good day and hope you see reason in what I have suggested.'

Catherine watched as Eamon disappeared beneath the crest of the hill and reappeared some minutes later, trudging with his head down across the field of marigolds. The sun was on the horizon and a cool breeze lifted the hem of her long dress, revealing her ankles. She gave the altar a final glance before she too turned to walk down the hill towards the house. Brett Norris was arriving that evening from London and she had not seen him in six weeks.

As she walked through the field of flowers her thoughts were in turmoil. Ahead of her was a meal with a man she did not think she loved. Behind her was a mysterious hill that had not given up all its secrets.

The trout served with fresh vegetables was excellent. So too was the wine that accompanied the main course. But Catherine picked at her meal listlessly, and Brett Norris

144

wondered at her lack of enthusiasm even when relating her discovery of the altar. He had expected that she would have been bubbling with excitement but this had not been so and he was baffled by her mood.

Catherine sat at the opposite end of the highly polished table deep in thought. The flickering candles highlighted her beautiful features as well as the pale, smooth skin above her dress, expensive and low cut, that clung to her shoulders. She had at least dressed to please him and Norris could feel his desire rising. Although she ate sparingly he did notice that she had filled her glass more than once with the claret he had brought with him from England.

'My trip to London was very successful,' Norris said lightly, by way of opening a conversation. 'The war in Africa has been a God sent opportunity for record profits this year in our iron foundries. Not to mention the need for arms.'

Catherine glanced up at him through the candlelight. 'I'm pleased to hear that someone is doing well out of the war,' she responded with an edge of sarcasm. 'Although I doubt that the soldiers would appreciate how good the war is for business.'

'Damn it, woman!' he exploded. 'I was trying to snap you out of your truculent mood. I haven't seen you in over six weeks and I had hoped that you would have been happy to see me.'

'When you make statements about how good the war is for your profits you cannot expect me to be sympathetic,' Catherine flared. 'Men from this village are fighting and dying on both sides over there. How can you expect me to react in any other way?'

'You are thinking about your damned husband, aren't you?' he said in a quiet but accusing tone. 'You are thinking about a man you don't even love anymore. Or am I wrong?'

'That is not the point,' she answered firmly. 'Naturally I am fond of Patrick in a way I don't expect you to understand. He is the father of my children.'

'Then you are welcome to return home to Sydney any time you wish. I will not force you to stay, no matter how much your leaving would break my heart.'

She stared into his eyes searching for insincerity but saw none. 'I'm sorry, Brett,' she said softly. 'It's just that . . . I don't know what is wrong with me at the moment. Possibly it is because Eamon has withdrawn his services from the dig. I relied on his knowledge so much. And I do worry about Patrick despite all that has occurred between us. It is only natural to worry when one reads the casualty lists in the paper every morning. I know what sort of man he is. He does not value his own life as much as that of others. He is the sort of person who is likely to take great risks in the war.'

'I know you, Catherine,' Brett snarled. 'I know you thrive in the company of powerful men like myself. I remember all those years ago when, in this very house, you clung to me rather than that pompous officer. Do you remember what I said then?'

'I remember,' she replied. 'You said I would eventually come to your bed when I realised what I wanted in life. Well, that seems to have happened, just as you predicted.'

'It was inevitable as you knew it would be,' he said as he rose from the table and went to her. 'As inevitable as you always being with me.'

She felt his mouth on her neck as he bent to kiss her, and his hands slid down to her breasts to cup them. 'Please don't, Brett,' she pleaded. 'I would fall pregnant if we went to your bed tonight.'

His hands ceased and he went very still. 'Damn it,

Catherine,' he swore. 'I want you tonight more than anything else in this world. Can't you see that?'

'I'm sorry, Brett. But tonight is not safe. Wait a couple of nights.'

'A couple of nights,' he fumed impotently. 'A couple of nights is forever. But if it must be so then I will wait.'

She reached up and took his hand. 'We will go to bed now and hold each other. I need that tonight more than you could know.'

Grudgingly he nodded. She pushed back her chair and he took her in his arms. His kiss on her lips was hungry with frustrated desire which frightened her a little.

Together they went to his room where he watched her undress by the light of the gas lamp. When her clothes fell to the floor revealing her shapely body he knew he truly wanted her more than the generous profits his companies were accumulating from the war in South Africa.

Catherine did not know what awoke her. Possibly it was the full moon, its light making a silver path from the huge window to the bed she shared with her lover. Beside her, Brett lay in a deep sleep. The night was hushed as if awed by the light the moon cast across the sleeping fields of marigolds and silent copses of fir trees. She eased herself from the bed and slipped on a long silk gown, a creamy colour like her pale skin. Her long red hair fell in a fiery cascade over her shoulders.

She padded to the window and stared across the fields to the hill, a brooding, dark landscape silhouetted against the night sky. A delicate mist covered the fields at its base under a sheet of white. No breeze stirred and it was as if the world Catherine gazed out upon had been frozen in time.

'Cuchulainn,' she whispered, thinking of the mythical ancient Celtic warrior who was both Patrick and Michael to her. 'Are you waiting for me on the hill?' Or something else, she thought with a faint sense of unease.

The mist swirled gently around Catherine's legs as she walked across the field. She did not feel the cold, wet grass beneath her bare feet. Nor did she feel the chill of the night air through the silk gown that clung to her body. She felt nothing except an overwhelming desire to climb to the top of the hill to find the mythical warrior of ancient Celtic stories. She was hardly aware of the climb to the top through the silent rows of heavily scented firs. It was as if the night was its own intoxication and she helpless to resist.

The marble altar shone in its pit with a glistening black light. Catherine stood at the edge of the excavation with mixed feelings of fear and elation: fear of the sinister object that Father O'Brien had shunned, and elation that she belonged in this place at this magical time of night. This was her hill and she had always belonged to the spirits that lived at the heart of the strange and ancient mound. Her elation overcame her fear and she found herself climbing down into the pit to go to the altar.

. . . some places should not be interfered with by mere mortals. Eamon's words uttered the previous day echoed in the back of her mind as she lay down on the cold, smooth slab. Her long tresses spread and splashed across the stone. The biting cold of the marble wet with dew bit into her through the silk gown but she was oblivious to any discomfort. She sighed and closed her eyes against the bright light of the moon and found herself in a world of darkness where vague shapes swirled like the mist and took on sinister but erotic forms.

. . . the stone has been corrupted and this is a place of evil . . .

There were men and women all around her. She was aware of their presence in her dark world away from the moonlight. Flames from the oil candles in their clay pots cast their shadows in the room filled with the pungent scent of their sex. Strange music filled the room, music that was sensual, hypnotic, and which lulled her senses and dragged her deeper into the pit. She was naked and knew that her body was desired by all in the room. But she also knew that they would bring the young bull to plant his seed deep in her body. She was exclusively for him to service.

Catherine moaned in pleasure as she spread her legs to allow his long organ to enter her. Her desire was all consuming and swept away any fear she might have known.

Suddenly her desire turned to fear as she felt strong hands grip her arms and legs and she was dragged along the altar to its edge. Frantically she tried to struggle. But the hands held her and other hands forced her legs apart. She could not scream. This was not a world where human sounds had meaning. Then she saw a shadow materialise at the foot of the altar and she was very afraid. It was a sleek young bull with fiery red eyes. His coat was as shiny as the black marble upon which she lay and from beneath his hind legs his bestial lust was blatantly apparent. He was led towards the altar and rose up to place his front legs either side of her. His huge head was between her breasts and she could feel his hot breath on her face. She cried out as his swollen shaft slid into her, its thrusts deep and strong as she lay helplessly pinned at the edge of the altar. Catherine struggled desperately to reach the light that was outside the world she had been dragged down into. When her eyes flew open, and she could see the moon above, she felt the bull's shaft suddenly pulse as his seed entered her.

'I woke and saw that you were gone from the house,' the

young bull seemed to say to her apologetically. 'I followed you here and could not stop myself from having you. You were so damned desirable laying stretched out on your altar.'

'Brett!' she hissed. 'What have you done!'

The priest's words echoed as a hollow taunt in her mind . . . *This was a place of evil!* And she had entered into a pact with the devil when she had gone to his bed.

FIFTEEN

In the Orange Free State Private Saul Rosenblum was fighting for his life. A hastily deployed rear guard action to hold a river crossing had turned into a desperate defence of their own lives as the Boer riflemen of General De Wet's field command swarmed forward towards the trapped squadron of Queenslanders.

Saul worked the bolt of his rifle and felt its sharp kick in his shoulder as he lay on his stomach on the cold earth. Around him, other troopers fired into the flitting shapes that appeared momentarily in their rifle sights. He did not know if his shots were finding targets and was hardly aware of his own rifle firing in the deafening crash of continuous sound. The ping and crack of incoming enemy rounds around his head blurred as a cacophony of death.

'Jesus, where's the covering fire?' he heard a trooper scream from nearby. 'The bastards have deserted us.'

Saul's protest was drowned out by the ear shattering high explosive that rained down on their position. A sizzling piece of shrapnel fell smoking in front of Saul's face. He did not have time to contemplate his near mutilation from the jagged metal fragment the size of his fist as a bullet plucked at his elbow, tearing a small hole through his shirt. Instinctively he jerked his arm closer to his body. Hell was the air around him filled with thousands of small, high velocity projectiles the size of wasps.

He refilled the magazine of his rifle and slammed it home. Beside him a small pile of empty cartridge cases shone under the African sun. The enemy were about four hundred yards out and firing from cover and Saul knew if they were allowed to creep closer their accuracy would improve and then they were all surely dead men. From only fifty yards out a Maxim machine gun chattered as it spat a steady hail of bullets into the prone ranks of dismounted infantry.

Saul turned his head to seek a safer position at the river itself. He felt sick in the stomach. The colonial horsemen to his rear were riding away, obviously unable to come to their aid.

He groaned in despair and snapped off a shot in the direction of the enemy, then checked himself. He was down half his ammunition and only had forty rounds left. Every shot would have to count if he was going to take as many of the Boer as possible with him to hell.

He did not hear the hoof beats of the horse galloping to their rear. Nor was he aware that Major Patrick Duffy had been informed by a distressed young lieutenant that his beloved Queenslanders were amongst the men pinned down and facing certain annihilation. But he did hear a voice bawling faintly above the crash of gunfire: 'Every man back to the river and mount up. Ride like hell and God be with you.'

The command had been given and the trapped men rose from the ground to sprint to the river behind them where their horses were waiting. The Maxim was swung on the major and its bullets sought him out.

Saul rose and ran zigzagging in a half crouch, trailing his rifle. He was aware that the gunfire had picked up as the Boer marksmen sought out the fleeing Queenslanders. He could see the major firing his pistol defiantly at the hidden enemy marksmen from astride his mount and his courage gave heart to the men who only moments before had given up hope.

Suddenly the major's horse reared with a shrieked whinny as the machine gun found its range. Patrick went down with the horse where he lay with his leg beneath the dead animal.

Saul flung himself over the edge of the river bank and down into a muddy flat below. The mud stank of horse droppings and stuck like glue. He gained his feet and looked about for the horse handler. Other troopers were snatching at the reins of their horses and flinging themselves into the saddle.

Saul found his mount standing alone with its eyes rolling in terror as some horses around it went down under the terrible fusillade of bullets pouring in from the now advancing enemy. Saul could hear the strangled cries of troopers hit by gunfire and the curses of men lying in the mud mortally wounded. The Boers were all around them. Private Berry was beside him mounted on his horse. 'Get yer bloody arse on yer horse and get outa here,' he yelled down at Saul.

'Major Duffy's down,' Saul called up to him as he slipped his foot in the stirrup. 'I've got to see if he's all right.'

'You haven't got a chance in hell of getting 'im out even

if 'e's alive,' Berry cried back as he leant along the neck of his horse and waded into the shallow river. Spurts of water erupted around him as he crossed the ford.

When Saul was in the saddle he wavered for just a second. Berry was right, he thought. To go back for the major was stupid, a suicide mission. But the major would probably have gone back for any of the men who were down.

'Shit! Up, up,' he swore as he forced his reluctant mount to breast the river bank. When he was over he had a fleeting regret that he had not followed Berry's advice. All around him the Boers were advancing and firing towards the river. Saul saw a Boer carrying a Mauser directly in front and only twenty feet away. The man seemed momentarily stunned to see the enemy apparently making a one-man counter attack and paused in his assault on the colonial officer who was firing his revolver from behind the carcass of his horse.

Saul charged the Boer and, when he was on him, swung his carbine down with one hand, braining him senseless. Others further out fired wildly at the lone horseman galloping across their front. Against the odds, Saul reached Patrick, who by now had disentangled himself from under his horse, and leant down. Patrick took his extended hand and hauled himself up behind Saul.

'You been wounded, boss?' Saul asked as he wheeled his horse around and put her head in the direction of the river.

'No. Nothing broken, Private Rosenblum,' Patrick answered.

Patrick snapped off his last shot at three Boers attempting to cut them off from the river. He missed but Saul's shot from the hip dropped one of the men. His mount leapt forward when he gave her a savage kick to the flanks and, with nostrils flaring and ears back, she galloped for the river, straight through a skirmish line of Boers. Both riders immediately saw the hopeless situation before them. The enemy had reached the river in force and was already turning to concentrate their fire on the galloping horse coming towards them. Saul could clearly see the big, bearded men dressed in farm clothes as they raised their rifles for the killing shots. They had only one option if they were to live. Saul's impulsive decision to save the officer he respected had brought captivity – if they were lucky. On the verge of slowing to a trot and throwing down his rifle, the regular chatter of a Maxim being fired on a sustained rate suddenly raked the line of Boers to their front, and those still standing scattered.

'Where in God's name is the firing coming from?' Patrick yelled over Saul's shoulder as he clung to him.

'Dunno. Hang on, we're goin' through,' Saul replied as he forced his exhausted horse into one last gallop.

The mare responded to his commands and raced through the ranks of the Boers seeking cover from the hail of machine gun bullets. They went over the edge of the river bank and splashed their way across the ford. The deadly hail of bullets passed close to their left then switched to their right. Whoever was directing the fire realised that they were attempting to escape the Boer cordon that had formed to trap them.

Saul reached the opposite bank and the horse scrambled up the gentle slope. On the other side of the river the Boers continued to follow their escape with a steady rain of bullets. After a few long minutes they reached a long shallow depression on the *veldt* where both men found the answer to their question as to who had provided the timely covering fire. Private Berry flashed Saul and Patrick a grin from where he stood beside the Maxim gun crew under the command of the young lieutenant who had first alerted Patrick to the danger the Queenslanders were in. The gun crew continued to pour a return fire back across the river as both weary riders flung themselves to the ground.

'Decided to go an' get some help for the boss,' Berry said.

That evening Patrick sat beside a small campfire and carefully wrote a brief account of Private Rosenblum's courageous ride to save him. It was not a report that he would tell Saul about until approval had been given on his recommendation. When that time came he would have great pleasure informing Saul Rosenblum of his promotion to corporal – and that he had also been recommended for the highest award the Queen could bestow on a soldier: the Victoria Cross.

SIXTEEN

The lone girl riding out from Bloemfontein did not attract much attention from the mounted patrols of English and colonial troopers. On the few occasions the slim young woman dressed as a Boer farmer was stopped and questioned, her explanation that she was attempting to reach her father's farm south of Pretoria seemed reasonable. Although they may have had suspicions she might be a Boer sympathiser, carrying information to the free-ranging commandos, they had no proof after searching her saddle bags. Nor was she armed with any weapon that could be considered a military firearm. Her only defence was a black powder, double-barrelled rifle of the type once popular with the elephant hunters of Africa. The large calibre weapon would provide a natural defence against any wild animals that might threaten her life alone on the *veldt*.

Fortunately for Karen Isaacs, the men of the English

157

patrols, as rough and tough as they were, respected the sanctity of womanhood. For had they carried out a body search they would have discovered the soft leather belt under her shirt which contained a small fortune in diamonds destined for the port of Lourenco Marques in Portuguese East Africa.

Her gamble had paid off so far and as Karen rode north she expected to encounter patrols from Pretoria where the Boer government still held on. They would provide her with an escort to the capital where her father would ensure that the diamonds were transferred east to the neutral port. From there, the precious cargo would be smuggled out to an imperial German navy ship in exchange for badly needed war supplies to bolster the beleaguered Boer forces in the field.

Despite Germany's fierce opposition to the English invasion of the Boer Republics, all that the Kaiser in Germany could do was give his Dutch brothers moral and materiel support in their war. He knew his own imperial navy was no match for the power of the British dread-noughts that still ruled the oceans of the world. But the Kaiser was attempting to rectify the imbalance of naval power and his industries were already producing the strategic chess piece in global politics to challenge Britain's powerful navy. German shipyards were busy producing their own dreadnoughts.

But as Karen rode across the rolling plains of long grass she felt uneasy. She could not understand her anxiety. She knew she was riding towards the people with whom she belonged. Was it that she had learned to live a life of lies in her own war against the English invaders, lying even to the man she had grown to love when between lovers there should be no lies? Yet from the moment she met the tall

158

young Queensland trooper she had spoken untruths. The Afrikaner who had threatened her in the street the day the English army had marched triumphantly into Bloemfontein had not accused her of treachery. His threats were based on his suspicion that she might have in her possession the diamonds rumoured for the Boer cause, a suspicion fuelled by the knowledge that she was the daughter of a well-known diamond merchant. Piet Bronkhurst feigned loyalty to the British, while it was assumed amongst the Boer commandos he was still loyal to their cause. But Piet knew only one loyalty and that was to his desire for personal wealth.

His hatred of Jews was well known in the district and he knew that Karen Isaacs was capable of extreme cunning. Piet Bronkhurst was proved right when the young woman had befriended the Australian trooper. His frequent visits to the house she shared with the Englishwoman had made it difficult to question her again as the occupying British swarmed all over the town and she was rarely alone.

Bronkhurst was no stranger to fighting the British. He had fought in the short war of 1881 when the Boers had routed the British forces on Majuba Hill and later had fought a small and personal battle with the Irishman, Michael Duffy, who had escaped after killing Bronkhurst's eldest son in a night skirmish thirteen years earlier. Bronkhurst had since learned that his personally sworn enemy had been brought wounded to Bloemfontein and then taken passage for Sydney in the British Colony of New South Wales. But now he sat astride his horse in the company of an English patrol that he had subtly recruited for the mission that he was about to undertake. The three English troopers and the Afrikaner watched the lone rider below them on the *veldt* from the rise of a small, grass-covered hill.

'That 'er?' the English sergeant growled as he handed the binoculars to the big Afrikaner beside him.

'Ja. Das is her,' he affirmed with a grunt. 'We will wait until she laagers tonight.'

The sergeant peered across the distance of swaying grasses between his patrol and the lone rider. 'You'd better be right, Bronkhurst,' he growled. 'About the diamonds. My neck could get stretched for 'elping you. If yer wrong, I promise you you won't be comin' back with us.'

The Afrikaner ignored the threat and spat on the ground. 'We both have a lot to lose, sergeant, if I am wrong. My people would shoot me if they knew what I do.'

The English sergeant licked his lips. He had been drunk in one of the town's hotels when the big Afrikaner befriended him. Bronkhurst was an astute judge of character and had measured the rowdy English soldier as a vicious and greedy man. His perceptiveness had paid off and Bronkhurst had been able to convince the man that, should he provide him with an excuse to ride out on a patrol, he would be rewarded beyond his wildest dreams. The sergeant had gained permission from his company commander to take the Afrikaner as a guide to reconnoitre a farmhouse that Bronkhurst had informed him was supplying sustenance to the commandos.

At first the company commander, an experienced soldier, had planned to send a larger patrol, but the sergeant had convinced him that the information was not much more than speculation and that he could reconnoitre with a minimum of men. If the information was valid, then the intelligence could be relayed back to Bloemfontein on the heliograph system with the other patrols in the area.

Hard riding had brought them on the trail of Karen within two days of her leaving Bloemfontein. Bronkhurst

160

did not see himself as a renegade to the Boer cause. He had given much for his Afrikaner brothers and sisters. Now it was time to retire on a well-earned pension. For the English sergeant the possibility of a small fortune spelt women and wine in unlimited abundance.

Karen did not stop riding until the dark was almost upon her. She prepared her camp carefully. She had collected a supply of precious kindling for a small fire and while she waited for some water to boil for coffee, she chewed some *biltong*, savouring the juices of the dry, leathery strips of meat in her mouth. A loaf of campfire-baked bread followed the *biltong* and the coffee washed it all down.

By the glow of the fire she spread her blankets out, the big hunting rifle always within reach, while her hobbled horse grazed on the wild grasses of the plain a short distance away. Weary from the long day in the saddle, Karen lay back and gazed up at the myriad stars of the African night, seeking out the cruciform constellation of the Southern Cross. Her thoughts turned to Saul and she sighed as she remembered their time together in the big double bed at Mrs Ramsay's house in Bloemfontein. Even if she had set out to use him as an unwitting protector, it had not ended that way. The mission to safeguard the diamonds stolen from the Rhodes mines was critical to the war effort. Her own remaining brother's life was at stake, should the badly needed supplies not get through. So too were the lives of other women's husbands, brothers and sons riding with the commandos.

At times she had fought her guilt that she was sleeping with one of the enemy by justifying her actions as a sacrifice for the mission. Then something inexplicable had occurred;

she had fallen deeply in love with Saul Rosenblum. Her passionate talk of travelling to Palestine to settle had indeed been the truth and Karen instinctively had included Saul in her plans. She smiled as she imagined herself, her father, brother and Saul walking the land that Moses had promised as the place of their destiny. Saul was strong and his skills, both as a farmer and a soldier, would be invaluable to the settlers of the Promised Land. Oh, but that he could only believe more in his heritage than he did, she thought wistfully. If only he could see with her eyes that their destiny was to return after two thousand years of persecution.

But Saul had the irreverent nature of his countrymen, who she had so often heard cursing God as they faced death in the fever-ridden hospital wards in Bloemfontein. Even the Christian pastors attempting to minister to the tough Australians had been shocked into mumbled requests to God to forgive the dying and unrepentant men as they stumbled away to the bedsides of their more pious British countrymen. The Australians had lived lives devoid of all help except that given by their mates in the lonely and desolate places of the harsh land they came from. Prayers had not been answered in times of drought and flood. Nor had the Almighty shown mercy on the dying stockman who lay with a broken leg with no hope of survival in some godforsaken part of the Outback. Death came slowly and painfully for him, his bloated or desiccated body to be found much later by a boundary rider or perhaps a mate who went in search of an overdue friend.

Saul was such a man. He did not see God's hand in the nature of life and death and believed only in the moment and the strength of his own abilities. Karen smiled as she remembered his lovemaking, at first clumsy but then more caring as he grew to understand her needs. She had known only one other lover in her life, a handsome Dutch boy she had grown up with in Holland and met again in Pretoria last year. He had been clumsy too but, unlike Saul, he had remained clumsy and uncaring for her feelings. She had left him and he was later killed, back in the early days of the war. Saul was not as handsome as her Dutch lover had been but he was, strangely, the most desirable man in the world to her now. His dark eyes were filled with laughter and his face always had a wry smile when she tried to be serious. He was a paradox; a combination of tough soldier and gentle man.

And when the terrible dreams of death came to him in the nights they were together, Karen would hold a little boy against her breasts as he gasped for air, fighting the scream and crash of imagined shells around him. She would hold him and rock him with soothing words and pray that the terrible war would end so they could find a life together away from Africa. Oh, how she missed having his arms around her now. To feel his strength protect her when she needed that security.

She was vaguely aware of the tears on her cheeks as her eyes finally focused on the Southern Cross. It belonged to Saul and perhaps somewhere he too was gazing up at the constellation that marked the Southern Hemisphere.

Suddenly, Karen's horse stopped grazing and snorted as he lifted his head to stare into the night. Her instincts well honed, Karen immediately reached for the gun beside her, all thoughts of Saul set aside. She knew from her experience on the *veldt* that her horse had sensed something unusual in the night. It may be nothing more than a harmless wild animal roaming the plains. But it could be something more dangerous.

Cautiously she sat up and brought the heavy rifle to her

lap. It was loaded and capable of bringing down the largest of African animals. As she heard the soft swish of horses' legs brushing the long grass as they approached, she stood, peering into the night.

'Hey, missus,' an English voice called reassuringly from the dark. 'Don't be worried. We're just a British patrol comin' in.'

Karen was not reassured. Her pretence of English sympathy was based on a lie and they were still the enemy. She forced herself to appear relaxed while keeping her finger on the triggers of the lowered hunting gun.

Three men appeared out of the shadows and into the light of her campfire, the sergeant and his two troopers smiling as they dismounted.

'Saw your fire and decided to have a look,' the sergeant said. 'Didn't expect to meet a woman out 'ere, though.'

Something was wrong, Karen sensed, and then it dawned on her. They were speaking in English as if they knew she could understand their language. Any woman out here would normally be assumed to speak Afrikaans.

Karen raised the hunting gun again, and when she saw Bronkhurst materialise behind the three English soldiers her suspicion turned to extreme fear. The expression on his face spoke as clearly as if he had said he was going to kill her. But the smile on the face of the English sergeant disappeared when the gun exploded with a blast. She had tried to swing on Bronkhurst but had fired prematurely. Both barrels discharged their heavy lead slugs almost simultaneously and the two soldiers standing beside their sergeant cried out as the bullets slammed into them, flinging them to the earth.

Instinctively the sergeant and Bronkhurst flung themselves to the ground. Realising that the slight young woman had to reload the cumbersome gun before she could do any more damage the sergeant reacted quickly. He sprang like a leopard and tackled her, knocking the big gun from her grip.

'You bloody bitch,' he screamed as he smashed his fist into her face. 'Try an' kill me, would ya?'

His rage was heightened by how close he had been to the heavy slugs that ripped into the troopers. One of the soldiers had died instantly but the other had taken the bullet in his stomach, and was groaning in agony. Bronkhurst snatched up the dead soldier's carbine and expertly flipped off the safety catch. The sergeant straddling the stunned woman immediately snatched up his own rifle and swung on the Afrikaner.

'Drop it,' he menaced. 'Drop it now or I'll kill ya as you stand.'

'I was going to kill the wounded man, Sergeant,' Bronkhurst replied calmly. 'Not goot he die like this.'

The sergeant's feverish expression took on a cunning look. 'Do it, Dutchman,' he said quietly. 'Then drop the rifle.'

Bronkhurst fired a shot into the badly wounded soldier's head, killing him instantly. He released the rifle knowing full well that he would not have a chance of reloading before the English sergeant shot him. 'We blame the Jewess for killing your man, Sergeant,' he said as the rifle lay on the ground beside him.

Karen could taste blood in her mouth and felt that the blow from the soldier's big fist had smashed some of her teeth. Her head throbbed with pain as the raw nerve ends of where her teeth had been felt the cool night air.

'You look through her saddlebags,' the sergeant commanded. 'An' I'll search this bitch meself.'

The Afrikaner obeyed as the sergeant reached down and ripped open the front of Karen's shirt revealing her small, firm breasts. The soldier felt his lust rising at the sight.

'Where you got the diamonds hidden, girlie?' he asked with a snarl. 'Got 'em in yer fanny?' he continued as he rose to his feet and stared down at her with glazed eyes. 'Maybe I should 'ave a look.'

Karen knew that she was a dead woman. She knew with the certainty of her love for the men she treasured in her life – her father, brothers and Saul – that neither Bronkhurst or the English sergeant would let her live. They would use her – probably torture her when they did not find the diamonds – then kill her. She remembered that the sharp knife she had sliced the *biltong* with was beside the fire. The sergeant had not seen it. Now, with all the strength she could muster, she rolled sideways to snatch up the knife.

Her hand wrapped around the handle and she hurled herself at the startled English soldier. He tried to step back but stumbled and fell heavily on his back. She was on him and the knife came down in a deadly arc, slicing along the side of his face and severing the lobe of his ear. He screamed as Karen raised the knife to deliver the killing thrust to his chest. But it did not come. She reeled back from the bone-snapping blow of a rifle butt to the side of her head. The knife fell from nerveless fingers as she sprawled on the grass, staring up with open eyes.

Bronkhurst stood holding the barrel of the rifle he had snatched from beside the soldier killed moments earlier. The sergeant rose shakily to his feet clutching the side of his face where the blade had carved him open from eye to ear. 'The bloody bitch is dead,' he moaned. 'You killed her, you stupid Dutchman.'

'Mebbe better she kill you, ya?' Bronkhurst replied as he

crouched beside Karen and expertly ran his hand inside her trousers. 'She is not carrying the diamonds on her. No diamonds anywhere.'

'So all this was a bloody waste of time,' the sergeant snarled as he used a handkerchief to stem the profuse bleeding along the side of his head. 'There never was any bloody diamonds. All I got is two dead men who I've got to explain back in Bloemfontein.'

'She had diamonds,' the Afrikaner said quietly as he crouched beside Karen's body. 'She was very smart. She has hidden them somewhere we will not find.'

'Leaves us with burying my men and getting back. And I'm goin' to need you come back with me. You can tell how it happened here with the exception of a couple of minor points and that should stop any embarrassing questions. You get what I mean, Bronkhurst?'

'Ya, I understand, Englisher. Ve vill bury your soldiers. But the Jewess, she can stay here for the animals.'

Bronkhurst dug two shallow graves and the soldiers were buried. When the work was complete the two men mounted their horses and led the other horses, including Karen's, back towards Bloemfontein. Neither man realised that Bronkhurst had almost found the leather satchel of diamonds as he dug. For Karen Isaacs had prepared her camp very well. She had scraped away some tussocks of grass and buried the bag containing the precious stones a few yards from her campsite. Then she had carefully replaced the tussocks to conceal her hiding place. Bronkhurst had only been mere inches from digging them up. In the morning the scavengers of the *veldt* would come to tear apart the body of the woman Saul Rosenblum loved.

SEVENTEEN

The housemaid, Betsy, was immediately impressed by the man with the black leather eye patch who stood tall with the arrogance of a man who feared nothing. She was further charmed when he remembered her name after a period of fifteen years and flattered when he said that she had not aged in all those intervening years. She blushed like a young girl, not a spinster in her early forties.

Michael Duffy was escorted to the library where Lady Enid met him. Tea was ordered and Enid gestured for him to sit in the big leather chair that Patrick so often occupied when he was home. She took a seat behind the great mahogany desk. Having received a letter from Patrick to say that he would be visiting, Enid was not surprised to see Michael.

'I must say that you are looking exceptionally well for a man reported dead so many times,' Enid said with a touch of mirth. 'Remarkably well, Mr Duffy. Or is it Mr O'Flynn?'

Michael's grey eye reflected the warmth of a smile for his old adversary. 'Mr O'Flynn, Lady Macintosh,' he replied. 'I'm afraid there is no statute of limitations on a charge of murder in New South Wales. Not even after almost forty years.'

'Patrick has told me the events surrounding your meeting in South Africa. And of your latest wound,' Enid said with a note of genuine sympathy. 'I do hope that you are well recovered.'

'Yes, thank you. I was once again fortunate with Lady Luck.'

'He also informed me that you would like to meet with your grandchildren,' Enid added. 'You are fortunate too that they are all here today.'

'I am glad, as I have come for that very reason,' Michael replied softly. 'But I would prefer that they meet me as Michael O'Flynn, and not as their grandfather.'

Enid looked at him in surprise.

'I have my reasons,' Michael answered her unasked question. 'Reasons that may not make a lot of sense – except to me.'

A light tap at the library door distracted them as Betsy entered the room with a silver salver upon which she balanced a sterling silver coffee pot, china cups and a small silver jug containing thick, yellow cream. Enid thanked her as Betsy placed the tray on the library desk and left the room.

'If I remember correctly, you do not take cream in your coffee, Mr O'Flynn,' Enid said as she poured.

'You have a good memory,' he commented with a warm laugh. 'You forget nothing.'

169

'I have forgotten much, I'm afraid,' she frowned. 'But I have not forgotten the mistakes that I have made in my life.'

'We can do little for what is in the past,' he said to reassure her. 'I have long learned to live with where I am and who I am with in the present.'

'Thank you, Mr Duffy,' Enid said. 'I have a need to hear your forgiveness. What I have foolishly done in the past has cost us both the same woman.'

'Your daughter and I were never meant to be together,' Michael said gently as he accepted the cup and saucer from her frail hand. 'I believe that she found her truest love with the countess.'

'I hope God will forgive her the transgressions of her strange love for my niece,' Enid sighed. 'I was finally able to reconcile her love for another woman. And I doubt that the Lord is half as judgmental as I. If I may ask,' she changed the subject that had brought pain to them both, 'what are your intentions when you leave Sydney, Mr O'Flynn?'

'I intend to go north to Townsville to see my sister. Her son has enlisted and gone to South Africa with the Bush-men's Rifles, as no doubt you are now aware from Patrick. She will be in need of my company.'

'Yes. I had the good fortune to meet your nephew here at this house but I'm afraid none of us suspected who he really was at the time. Otherwise, I would have used my influence to thwart his attempts to enlist. He is a fine boy and I pray the Lord will protect him. Captain Thorncroft was most dis-tressed losing his services as a photographic assistant. He had a promising future as something called a camera operator, Arthur said, just before he left for England.'

'I'm sure young Matthew will return safely,' Michael said. 'I knew his father and knowing him I feel the boy will survive.'

'Will you be staying with your sister for a while then?' Enid asked.

'Long enough,' Michael answered. 'Then I will travel the far reaches of the colony in an attempt to paint again. It is something that I yearn to do before I die.'

'You appear a long way from death, Mr O'Flynn,' Enid said with a warm smile. 'I suspect that you will fill a wagon with your paintings before then.'

'Well, I hope so. I've got this far and I have no intentions of ever seeing another war.'

Enid's expression suddenly changed and it was as if something had only now dawned on her. 'Mr O'Flynn,' she said, 'I have a rather unusual proposition to put to you.'

The last time Lady Enid Macintosh had put a proposal to Michael he had ended up in the Sudan seeking his son, only to find that she had reneged on the deal. She noticed his concern.

'Oh, do not appear so worried. No, my proposition is that you take your youngest grandson, Alexander, with you to stay for a short while at our property of Glen View. I know you may not have been considering such a detour in your itinerary, but I hope you might warm to the idea when you meet him.'

'I would have no objections to having Alexander accompany me,' Michael replied. 'In fact I would like to visit the grave of my father on Glen View while I'm out that way.'

'Good,' Enid concluded, as if closing a business deal. 'With both his parents away I know Alexander would benefit from your company on the trip north. I shall write to the manager of Glen View to inform him that you will be coming. You will also have the opportunity to meet Fiona's eldest daughter, Helen, and her husband while you are there.'

'Fiona's daughter,' Michael echoed, suddenly reminded that his own son had two half sisters. 'Isn't Helen married to one of Count von Fellmann's sons?'

'Yes, his son Karl,' Enid answered. 'He is a Lutheran minister seeking to establish a mission station for the blacks,' she continued. 'Helen has requested that the family turn Glen View over for a mission station, but Patrick and I have rejected her request. The property is where my husband and eldest son are also buried, not to mention your father and that nephew of yours.'

'Peter Duffy,' Michael offered. 'He was the son of my brother and a darkie girl called Mondo.'

'Oh yes, I am sorry, I had forgotten his name. But, as you probably appreciate, the land has great meaning to both our families and as none of the original blackfellows who once inhabited the land around Glen View are left it makes little sense to establish an Aboriginal mission station now. There are many other places Helen and her husband could choose.'

'I agree, Lady Macintosh,' Michael said. 'The old days have gone and the blackfellas have lost their land forever.'

'I see you understand,' Enid said. 'It would be different if any of the full-bloods still lived but it does not appear so. They are all gone.'

'If any of the full-bloods still lived would that have altered your decision on Glen View?' Michael asked quietly. 'Would you have turned the property over to a mission station?'

His question brought a cloud to Enid's face. He could see the struggle in her expression as she fought to find an answer. 'If even one full-blood still lived then I would con-sider my grand-daughter's request, Mr O'Flynn,' she finally answered. 'Then, possibly, we could make recompense in a small way for the injustice we brought down upon these people. I firmly believe that the consequences of that day, almost forty years ago, continue to haunt our present lives. There's a kind of heathen curse we will never understand. I know I sound like a silly old woman but the passing years have only strengthened my conviction in this. But let us not dwell on things beyond our control. If you have finished your coffee, perhaps it is time to meet your grandchildren.'

EIGHTEEN

Pretoria fell to the British army in early June.

A young lieutenant of the New South Wales Mounted Rifles under the command of Lieutenant Colonel De Lisle, the commander of the Mounted Infantry Brigade, rode alone into the town under a flag of truce to meet with the Boer commander, Commandant General Botha.

Lieutenant Watson from Sydney had tied a white handkerchief to a riding crop and passed through the Boer lines to meet with the famous commander at his private residence. Mrs Botha kindly served tea and sandwiches to the young Australian officer who had not eaten in two days. The British column, under the overall command of Lord Roberts, had pressed relentlessly forward despite a constant hail of bullets and shells.

Botha agreed to meet with Lord Roberts the next day at Lieutenant Colonel De Lisle's camp. The surrender was followed by Roberts marching twenty-six thousand of his troops into the last of the Boer capitals to fall to his army.

Saul Rosenblum was struck by the quaint beauty of the town that nestled in a hollow between picturesque hills. The houses reflected their Dutch origin: round turrets and wide verandahs set amongst shady gardens. But everywhere the dust of the *veldt* left a thin sheet of crimson as thousands of iron shod hooves churned up the earth. What also struck the young colonial soldier was the absolute silence of the Afrikaners who lined the streets to witness the bitter acceptance of their defeat against the hated *rooinek Uitlanders.*

Saul searched for the street where Karen had told him her father lived. An Englishwoman finally gave him directions and, after his squadron took up a campsite just outside of town, Saul slipped away.

The house was just as Karen had described to him, reflecting a comfortable affluence in its well-kept gardens and traditional Dutch design. A young African woman answered his knock and after a short time returned to say that Mr Isaacs would meet him in the garden. Saul was escorted through the house with its lingering scent of strong tobacco, leather and exotic herbs. At the rear, he found Mr Isaacs bent over, pruning a native shrub with secateurs.

'Who are you, young man?' he asked bluntly in excellent English without turning to greet his visitor.

'Private Saul Rosenblum, sir,' the Queenslander answered with his slouch hat in his hand. 'I am a friend of your daughter. We met in Bloemfontein.'

The older man ceased pruning his shrub and straightened to turn so he could fully appraise the soldier standing in his garden. Isaacs was tall and his face reflected a quiet intelligence. Although his hair was thinning it had not lost its

175

colour and he wore a three-piece striped suit with a gold chain running into the fob pocket of his trousers.

'You have a Jewish name,' Isaacs stated, now mildly curious. 'I had friends in London by the name of Rosenblum. A wealthy and respected merchant. Are you related to them by any chance?'

'Doubt it, Mr Isaacs. I'm from the Colony of Queensland. Not many of us Rosenblums out my way. But I do have an uncle who came from England as a convict many years ago. His name was Solomon Cohen. Did you know him?'

Isaacs smiled at the tall young man wearing the dusty uniform of his enemy. The young colonial had a quick intelligence and a gentle sense of humour.

'I am afraid not, Mr Rosenblum, and I must apologise for my lack of manners to one who is a friend of my daughter. I should offer you something to drink as I suspect, from the look of you, your march on our town has been a somewhat trying ordeal. A cool drink possibly?'

'I won't say no to a drink. I'd kill for a beer if you have any.'

'That I do.'

Isaacs called to the African servant to fetch two bottles of English beer and gestured for Saul to take a seat on the back verandah of the house.

'I suppose that you have come to inquire about my daughter?' the older man asked carefully as they sipped on the ale. 'As you are a friend of hers.'

'I am, Mr Isaacs. When I last spoke to her she said she was intending to return to Pretoria, to be with you.'

'When did you last see my daughter?' Isaacs asked softly.

'About four weeks ago. But I guess she is still in Bloemfontein if she is not here.'

'She is not in Bloemfontein, Mr Rosenblum,' Isaacs stated quietly. 'Nor is she in Pretoria.'

Saul felt a terrible shadow fall on him. It chilled his soul with a crippling uncertainty. 'Could she be elsewhere?' he asked weakly.

'No,' Isaacs answered with a slump of his shoulders. 'She could not be anywhere else.'

'How can you be sure? Couldn't she be visiting friends or something?' Saul asked with a rising note of concern in his voice. 'Maybe she has gone back to Bloemfontein.'

'No. I wish that were so but I know in my heart that something has happened to my beloved Karen. I cannot tell you why I know this, Mr Rosenblum. Some things it is better that you do not know.'

'What things? What shouldn't I know about your daughter?'

'To tell you might involve more than you could understand,' Isaacs said, looking away into the shadows of the garden. 'Are you in love with my daughter?'

'I am, Mr Isaacs. Karen would often tell me about you and the plans you have of going to Palestine when the war is over. She wanted me to come with you.'

'Then she loved you very much,' he sighed sadly. 'You must be a man of great honour to have earned my daughter's love.'

Saul bowed his head. 'She has to be alive,' he said in a firm voice, attempting to convince himself. 'I cannot believe anything could have happened to her. There are no reasons why any harm could come to her. She wasn't fighting in this war like her brothers.'

'Maybe you should know the truth,' the older man said quietly. 'I think under the circumstances I must trust you, even if you are an enemy. My daughter was fighting for the Boer cause in her own way. She was to deliver a consignment of diamonds to me here in Pretoria. Her mission was vital for our war effort against the British invaders.'

Saul sat stunned. The woman whom he had loved with

his whole body and soul was an enemy agent working against him!

Isaacs saw Saul's expression of utter shock and disbelief. He had not really known the enigmatic young woman who was his daughter as much as he thought. He reached over and grasped Saul on the arm.

'Sadly, love does not recognise political agendas. It is an emotional weakness of human kind,' he said sympathetically.

Saul remained silent staring out at the garden. A tiny bird flitted from flower to flower seeking the nectar of the buds with its long beak.

'I . . .' He shook his head and found that he could not reply. He was choked with a turmoil of emotion.

Isaacs let go his arm and the two men sat in silence, contemplating the terrible tragedy that most likely had occurred.

'I should go, Mr Isaacs,' Saul finally said as he rose from his chair and picked up the rifle by his side. 'I have to return to my squadron before they find me missing.'

'Go with God, young man. Maybe we will meet in better times.'

Saul took the hand offered to him. 'I hope so,' he replied in a choked voice. He turned on his heel to leave the house, fighting his fears. He could not accept that the woman he loved could be dead. And yet her father had.

In a daze he stumbled back to the campsite of the Queenslanders. No, Karen was just missing. She would turn up somewhere.

Two days later his burning hope would be shattered. The message came to him at his squadron camp via Mr Isaac's African servant. She had walked to the camp and sought out the soldier she had met two days earlier with the verbal message carefully memorised.

Saul received curious glances from his comrades when she called to him in the lines where he was combing down his horse. She drew him aside and he listened carefully to her instructions.

Saul waited until dark and last post was bugled, signalling lights out in the rows of white tents. He knew the layout of the lines and the positions of sentries and was able to slip past them.

He walked in the night along a narrow, faintly marked wagon trail until he came to the *kopje* the servant girl had described. It stood out against the night sky like a stubby, broken finger pointing at the stars. He was unarmed as he had been instructed and felt very vulnerable away from the heavily guarded perimeter of his own forces. This was Boer country where the commandos were far from beaten, despite the fall of their capital.

'Halt, Englisher!' a guttural voice came out of the dark. 'Hands up.'

Saul obeyed and prayed that this was the man with whom he was to make his rendezvous. If not, he had walked into a trap and become not only guilty of deserting his post, but also of surrendering to the enemy.

'Private Saul Rosenblum, of the Queensland Mounted Infantry,' he called out and stood with his hands in the air.

A figure rose on the skyline about fifty yards from him. 'You are alone?' the figure called back.

Saul could see the shape of a rifle in the man's hands pointed at him. 'I'm alone. I've come to meet Field Kornet Isaacs.'

The figure disappeared below the skyline and in a short time reappeared beside him. Saul could see that he was a big, bearded man about his own age. The rifle was no longer pointed at him so he dropped his hands.

'I am Field Kornet David Isaacs,' the man said gruffly with a trace of an Afrikaans accent. 'My father has told me you are a man of honour. If this is true, I have something that should interest you. Come. We will go up to the *kopje* and have some Cape brandy together.'

Saul followed him up the hill where he was startled to find four other heavily armed men sitting and watching the track. Karen's brother was obviously a cautious man. They hardly gave Saul a glance but peered intently into the night, alert to roving patrols of colonial troopers.

Field Kornet David Isaacs produced a bottle of the fiery liquid and took a swig before passing it to Saul, who politely followed his host's example. They both sat down amongst the rocks to prevent being silhouetted against the night sky.

'My sister is dead,' the Boer commander said bluntly. 'She was murdered by one of our people – and one of yours.'

'How do you know?' Saul froze, still holding the bottle which Isaacs took from him.

'Our agents in Bloemfontein informed us that a man called Bronkhurst had fallen under suspicion for his activities with the British. He was brought to us and questioned when he returned from a patrol with a *rooinek* sergeant. He was reluctant to talk so he was left to me personally,' the big Boer officer said with a quiet vehemence that left Saul in no doubt as to how Bronkhurst had been questioned. 'After a while he told me the truth about my sister, and how she had died. He said that the Englisher sergeant had killed her against his wishes. But I knew he was lying.'

'Where is Bronkhurst now?' Saul asked.

The Boer commander flashed him a savage smile. 'He is hyena food. An eye for an eye. I killed him myself.'

'Where is Karen?' Saul asked quietly, his expression stricken with pain and sorrow.

Her brother turned to stare south in the direction of Pretoria. 'Another commando found her body on the *veldt*. They buried what was left of her,' he added bitterly, taking a long swig from the bottle.

A silence fell between the two men. Finally Saul spoke. 'I was told by your father's darkie girl that you wanted my help.'

Isaacs turned to stare, contemplating the Australian trooper before replying. 'You and I are enemies in this war, Rosenblum. But we shared a love for my sister. I believe that love . . . how is it that you say . . . transcends even this war. My sister was murdered, not killed like we expect to die as soldiers. Bronkhurst gave me the name and unit of the English sergeant who was with him when she was murdered. I have . . . as you say . . . executed one of our own for that murder. Now you must execute one of yours to avenge her death. Can you do that?' he asked, leaning forward and staring into Saul's eyes with an intensity as hot as fire. 'Can you deliver justice for her murder?'

Saul kept his unwavering stare. 'What is his name?' he replied and the field kornet nodded as he passed the bottle to him.

'Sergeant Temple. He is with the Third London Yeomanry now occupying Pretoria. He is the man you must kill.'

'Then it will be done. I swear this to you on my love for your sister.'

'I believe you, Englisher.'

'I'm not a bloody Englisher,' Saul growled. 'I'm an Australian.'

'Then why are you fighting us, *Uitlander*? This is not your war. You are fighting for Cecil Rhodes and men like him. Not for anything else.'

Saul stared at the brother of the woman he had loved.

'I'm fighting just to stay alive when your bloody pompoms and artillery blast us. I'm fighting now just to get out of here and go home. Does that answer your question?'

The big Jewish Boer nodded and rose to his feet. 'Ja. I understand. It is just a pity that one day we might meet again on the battlefield where you will have to kill me – or I kill you. Then one day the war is over and all the politicians shake hands at some conference. Except you and I are not around to do the same. That is war.' He extended his hand to Saul and added sadly. 'Goodbye, my friend. I hope in God's name we never meet again in this war.'

Saul took the offered hand and their grips were firm. 'So do I. I hope you and your father live to see your sister's wishes of you going to Palestine one day come true. It meant a lot to her.'

The two men parted and Saul watched the small party of Boers disappear down the side of the *kopje*. He listened to the regular pounding of horses' hooves as they galloped away into the night and then made his way back to his squadron.

As he trudged along the bullock wagon track his thoughts were only on one subject: how to find and kill the man who had murdered Karen. That was the easy part. How to get away with the execution was another matter.

Major Patrick Duffy returned the guard's salute at the entrance to Lord Roberts' Pretoria headquarters. He stepped inside the building that had once housed the Boer seat of government and was met by the famed colonel's aide, a young captain sporting a waxed moustache and the diffident manners of one used to dealing with British aristocracy. The captain eyed the big colonial major with some disdain until his eyes fell on the ribands he wore on the left side of his tunic. The major might be a colonial but the decorations indicated his extensive service to Her Majesty.

'Colonel Hay Williams will see you in just a moment, sir,' he said in the accent of an Oxford graduate. 'He is rather busy at the moment.'

Patrick nodded and stood with his hands behind his back as the captain disappeared into a room that had a wooden plaque with the title *Orderly Room* over the door. He did not have to wait long before the captain ducked back and led him to another door marked with the colonel's name. The captain knocked lightly and a voice boomed to enter.

The white painted room contained a large desk, hat stand and fireplace over which a leopard skin and crossed assegais – the short, stabbing spear of the Zulu warrior – were displayed. The colonel grunted his welcome when Patrick saluted and indicated a chair in the corner of the room. Patrick sat as the colonel continued to browse through a report which Patrick recognised as his own, submitted to the headquarters. Finally he closed the papers and stared hard at the colonial major.

'I have read the report that you have submitted, Major Duffy, on this fellow Rosenblum and his actions at the Modder, some weeks back,' he said in an intimidating manner that made Patrick aware all was not well. 'And frankly, I find the circumstances of the report rather bizarre.'

Patrick frowned. He could not find anything bizarre in being snatched from certain death or imprisonment. 'What do you find bizarre, sir, if I may ask?' he questioned, puzzled.

'Well, the fact that you – as the officer being rescued – should recommend this man for the award of the Victoria Cross. I have no other precedent in this war for such a procedure.'

'I will grant you, sir, that the circumstances were unusual in that I made the recommendation, but Private Rosenblum's actions, in returning into a hail of enemy fire at great risk to his own life, more than warrants such a recommendation. Courage is courage under any circumstances.'

'That may it be,' the English colonel said with a distant expression on his face, 'but the second point I would like to make is that we do not have any report on this man's character from his commanding officer. The man is obviously err . . . of the Jewish faith . . . and we all know what these people are like.'

So that was it, Patrick thought savagely. The bloody British colonel was a bigot. The rest of his lame excuses were just a means to thwart the recommendation.

'Yes, sir, Private Rosenblum is of Jewish extraction but then wasn't Mr Disraeli, the Earl of Beaconsfield, also?' he retorted, knowing full well that the colonel would squirm under the comparison. The famous English prime minister of only twenty years past had done much to make the British Empire what it was.

'Err, I believe that is correct, Major Duffy,' the colonel replied reluctantly. 'But he was not a colonial Jew. He was a man who understood what was expected of him, as a gentleman in society.'

'Private Rosenblum is a soldier of the Queen, sir, and as such a volunteer prepared to lay down his life in the interests of the Empire. I should say that counts for something in society.'

Patrick could see that his quietly pointed argument was

upsetting the English colonel. Williams' face was now red with suppressed rage at such impudence from an upstart colonial major.

'I believe you are attached as a special services officer to Colonel De Lisle's staff, Major Duffy.'

'That is correct, sir,' Patrick replied, wondering why the colonel had asked.

'Then you would know how many men are recommended for decorations. Far too many to give every one of them the VC. I personally feel that under the circumstances recommending *this* Private Rosenblum for the highest award the Queen can bestow is not within the guidelines. As such, I will not be forwarding your report to Lord Roberts with my concurrence on this matter.'

Patrick stared at the pompous colonel with undisguised contempt. 'I will strongly object if you do so, sir,' Patrick fumed. 'The soldier has displayed the highest standards of bravery in the face of the enemy and that cannot be pushed under the carpet because you have a dislike for Jewish people.'

'Careful in what you say, Major Duffy,' the colonel said menacingly. 'You might overstep your mark.'

'Well, sir,' Patrick said as he rose from his chair and saluted his superior officer, 'if this is all we have to talk about, I suggest that I leave and not waste your valuable time.'

On that note Patrick marched himself out of the colonel's office, closing the door behind him. The captain who had ushered him into the colonel's office gave him a quizzical look as he brushed past. From the savage expression on the big colonial officer's face, all had not gone well.

Patrick strode down the street passing the Afrikaner women, out shopping in their long dark dresses and bonnets. The matter was not finalised as far as he was concerned.

185

Saul Rosenblum had earned some recognition for his out-standing courage. He would get a character report for the colonel from Saul's commanding officer and he would chase up the young lieutenant who had provided covering fire that day with his Maxim machine gun. A fellow officer's corroboration had to count. He could play their bureaucratic game if that is what it took.

NINETEEN

Locating the English sergeant who had murdered Karen was not difficult. A few discreet inquiries and Saul had marked his man.

Now Saul stood in the shadows of the night listening to the tinkle of a piano and the raucous laughter of drunken men and women coming from the building opposite. He waited until the dusty street was deserted before he made his move to cross.

Taking a deep breath, and with his head down, Saul walked quickly to the yard of the house frequented by the English sergeant when he was on leave, as he was tonight. The front room was packed with customers who paid for the grog and the services of the two ladies in the age-old tradition of camp followers.

The British occupation headquarters had been slow to react to demands by the staunchly religious members of the Afrikaner church for the proprietor to be flogged out of town and his two employees branded with the mark of the scarlet woman. Instead, the military rulers had established a roving patrol of military police to ensure that the rowdiness was discreetly kept on the outskirts of town.

Saul had carefully reconnoitred. Now familiar with the house and the movements of the military police, he chose a night when most soldiers had been confined to their respective lines. Only senior non-commissioned officers were able to visit this house of ill repute tonight.

He made his way along the side of the house as unobtrusively as possible but still bumped into an inebriated Canadian sergeant, urinating into the bushes. The Canadian greeted Saul with the bonhomie of the drunk. Saul mumbled his greeting lest his Australian accent be detected and kept his head down, remaining in the shadows as best he could. Then he was in the spacious, bushy backyard amongst the heady scent of gum trees.

Saul glanced around to ensure that he was alone before stepping back into the darkest corner. Now it was only a matter of waiting and hoping luck would bring his man to him.

Two hours and around fifteen visits to the backyard by men with full bladders passed before Saul saw his man step out to relieve himself against a tree. He was alone. The Queenslander felt his heart pounding. The hand wrapped around the handle of his sword bayonet felt clammy. He wiped it before taking a firmer grip.

The sergeant was swaying on his feet as he hosed down the trunk of a tree, whistling in a tuneless way that Saul found strangely irritating. The Englishman was almost as big as himself and his back was to the light of the house behind him. Saul knew it was too risky to approach him where he presently stood, he would need to lure him into the darkness from where he watched.

'Hey, Sergeant,' he called softly. 'You want a clean Dutch girl?'

The English soldier stopped rocking on his feet and peered suspiciously in the direction of the voice. 'Who the bloody 'ell is that?' he questioned, buttoning his fly. 'Where you callin' from?'

'Over here, Sergeant. I can't show myself or the bloody military police might cop me again.'

The sergeant staggered a few feet towards Saul. 'What are you talkin' about?' the sergeant queried and his inebriation seemed to fall away. 'What's this about a Dutchie girl?'

'I know where you can get one of the ladies here whose husband is out with the commandos. She's bloody lonely and said she wanted to meet a fine soldier like yerself.'

'Show yourself,' the sergeant commanded. 'I know you're one of those bloody colonial Australians. I can tell from ya voice.'

Saul felt his nerve slipping. The sergeant did not appear as if he would come any closer unless Saul stepped out of the shadows. He was about fifteen feet away but still illuminated by the dim light cast from the windows and doorway of the house. He could easily be seen from inside the house by anyone who should look out.

'I told you, I can't show myself.'

'How come you don't want 'er then?' the sergeant asked.

Saul had to think quickly. 'I already had her. Decided I could make a quid or two on the side.'

The sergeant suddenly grinned with a leer. 'Yeah. You

bloody Australians would sell ya own mothers for a quid. About ya standard.'

He stumbled forward to meet the man who would profit from some poor, lonely Boer wife and bumped up against him. Immediately Saul lashed out with one hand to grab the man by the throat so that he could not scream. The Queenslander's hands were as strong as a vice from years of hard work and the English sergeant's eyes bulged with fright at the sudden, disabling attack.

'The Dutch girl's name was Karen Isaacs,' Saul hissed into the petrified man's face. 'I believe you knew her once, didn't you, you murdering bastard.'

The sergeant's bulging eyes seemed to flicker with recognition at the mention of Karen's name – and he also knew death when he saw its face. With all the strength he could muster he attempted to bring up his arms to grip Saul's hand on his throat.

Lightning fast, Saul brought the long bayonet in an upward swing to tear through the sergeant's diaphragm just under his ribcage. At the same time he foot-swept the Englishman so that he fell backwards dragging the Queenslander down on top of him. The force of their fall caused the deadly bayonet to thrust even deeper into the lung cavity and penetrate the heart.

Saul held his hand over the dying man's mouth to prevent him crying out. As he held him down on the ground their eyes locked for just a short moment. The sergeant's lungs collapsed as Saul tore the bayonet from them and stood up. He was shaking but still in control of his wits.

Quickly he wiped the long blade on the sergeant's tunic, slid it back into its scabbard and took a grip on the dead man's ankles. With a grunt he dragged the body into the shadows. It would be some time before the sun came up – or before those in the house noticed the sergeant missing. Either way he had time to get away and back to his own lines.

It was the mixed-blood proprietor who found the body in the early hours of the morning and informed the military authorities. Not long afterwards, he left town with his girls, suspecting that some outraged Afrikaner had taken the law into his own hands instead of letting God do his work.

But the investigating military authorities were familiar with the distinctive wound a British bayonet makes on its victim and strongly suspected that the sergeant had been murdered by a soldier of the occupying force. They were determined to find out who had carried out the killing and were fortunate that a Canadian corporal had noticed a stranger push past him and disappear into the shadows of the backyard. All he could remember of the man was that he wore the uniform of an Australian mounted infantry-man, but that at least narrowed the search down. Should they find their man and he was proven guilty there could only be one sentence appropriate for a murder on active service – death by firing squad.

TWENTY

Young Alexander Macintosh was in heaven. At least that was how it felt waking up each morning at Glen View. The silence of the night, broken only by the distant lowing of cattle or a night bird calling across the plains, took on the sounds of activity of a big homestead coming to life at piccaninny dawn: the Chinese cook in the kitchen clattering pots and pans as he prepared breakfast for the boss and his missus, the Aboriginal stockmen's soft laughter and easy banter as they saddled horses in the yards across from the house, and the constant slamming of the gauze door on the back verandah as the domestic staff came and went. Above all, Alexander could hear the sweet sounds of the bush birds, the butcher bird's melodic call to the magpie's lazy warble. For the youngest son of Major Patrick Duffy the almost primitive sounds and sights, so alien to those he had known in the sophistication of his Sydney life, were ones he did not ever want to forget. He felt strangely at home, as if he had discovered where he truly belonged.

And Mr O'Flynn with the black leather eye patch had proved as exciting and mysterious as any character Alex had read about in all the Boy's Own stories.

When he first met Mr O'Flynn in Sydney Alex had been frightened by the man who towered over him like some huge bear, with his broad shoulders and powerful arms. And yet when he was finally able to stare up into the single grey eye he saw only a supreme gentleness, despite the gruff, deep voice.

George, his brother, had spoken ill of Mr O'Flynn behind his back. He said that the man was most probably a former convict, an Irish papist, one of those known around Sydney as an old lag. Alex suspected that secretly his brother was frightened of the big Irishman.

Fenella's reaction was even more puzzling. She had said little in his presence when they were introduced to him in the drawing room, but her frown had concealed her awe. There was something about the stranger that she felt was familiar, although she was mystified as to how or what that could be.

When Lady Enid had introduced him as a dear friend of her father, fresh from the war in South Africa, Fenella had immediately sensed the love the man seemed to have for them even though he was a total stranger to their lives. She sensed an almost paternal love, the affection that she missed so much from her own father, still fighting in a war across the sea. Had the big man moved to put his arms around her she would have willingly allowed him to do so. And perhaps then all the pain she was feeling for the absence of her mother as well would have flowed in a torrent of tears.

As Lady Enid informed Alex that he was going to

accompany Mr O'Flynn to their Queensland property of Glen View the boy's reactions were mixed. He had never travelled further from Sydney than visiting the town of Bathurst once with his father. Now he was going to the other end of the country with this big, mysterious man whom he hardly knew. Why Lady Enid, a stickler for him not missing classes at his expensive school in Sydney, had suddenly allowed him to be sent away was all a worrying mystery to him.

But when the day came and he stood on the wharf waiting to board a coastal steamer for Rockhampton via Brisbane, all such anxiety disappeared in his excitement at the adventure ahead of him. Although he had felt tearful on the carriage trip to the harbour Alex forced himself to retain a calm composure. Mr O'Flynn had growled something about women not being able to help themselves when it came to shedding tears at farewells and Alex did not want Mr O'Flynn to think he was a sissy.

From Rockhampton they travelled by Cobb & Co coach across the hills and down onto the plains to Glen View, way west of the coastal town. The days travelling, the changing landscape and interesting people they met, made the journey an adventure in its own right. Always, Mr O'Flynn proved to be caring, and informative about everything Alex asked questions of, although he spoke very little about himself. Alex had enjoyed every day of their travels although he missed his sister and his great-grandmother. But he did not miss his brother and felt a strange independence he had not known before.

Mr O'Flynn seemed to get on with the many people they met. He appeared equally comfortable talking to the wealthy squatter they met on the ship as he was chatting with the stockmen on the streets of Rockhampton. Alex's cloistered life had rarely brought him into the world of the working class and he was surprised to find that they were people he could relate to. So long as he did not attempt to point out that he was born of wealth, the strangers would treat him as a young man in his own right when he showed an interest in their lives.

When Michael spent time conversing with him, Alex was able to learn much about the mysterious man. Mr O'Flynn had fought in many wars but he would not say why he had. He said that he had never married and yet once, when they were on the steamer and he had drunk a lot of rum, he said that he had loved a girl, and had a son to her. It was a shocking disclosure for Alex who had a strong sense of morality from his staunch Protestant upbringing.

Only once had the young boy felt his awe for Mr O'Flynn turn to fear. An offhand remark by Alex about a man being 'a mere tradesman' caused Michael to turn on him and snarl, 'No-one in this world is a mere anything, boy. I have seen so-called gentlemen turn to water when the chips were down. And I have seen men and women, who your world looks down on, give their lives for the likes of those who did not deserve to be born. Always remember that a man's spirit, his courage and goodness, cannot be measured by Macintosh standards.' And yet the fear turned to understanding and Alex had bowed his head in shame for his own misconceived words.

This was the fifth day Alex had spent on the sprawling family property managed by Duncan Cameron. He liked Mr Cameron's wife, Mary, who was serene in the face of any of the crises that rose from time to time around the homestead. Whether it be Matilda, the mother of the young stockman Nerambura Duffy, breaking a valued piece of china when she was cleaning, or one of the stockmen being

195

brought in by his mates with a broken arm, she handled each situation calmly and competently. Alex knew she had children who attended a boarding school in Townsville and she treated him as if he was one of her own sons.

Alex missed the gentle touch of a woman in his life and often, in the long hot hours of the night, would find himself crying quietly when he thought of his own mother far away in Ireland. She wrote often but her letters did not say when she would be reunited with them. She never mentioned his father in her letters and the mystery of what had happened between his parents left the boy with a sinking heart, although he never let go of a small flame of hope that one day his family would be united again.

In the absence of Mr O'Flynn, Nerambura Duffy had spent the previous day attempting to teach Alex to ride. Alex liked Nerambura. The shy young man was patient with him and he looked forward to his lessons in the saddling yard with the little roan mare especially selected for him.

Michael had spent the previous day with Duncan Cameron on a ride to one of the outlying parts of the property to supervise a cattle muster. He had returned that evening and for the first time met Alex's cousin Helen and her husband Karl, who had been visiting Balaclava station adjoining Glen View. Even the young boy had been struck by his older cousin's beauty. She was admittedly very old, probably in her thirties, but her emerald eyes sparkled when she laughed. Not that she seemed to laugh very often, except when Mr O'Flynn engaged her in conversation over the great wooden table in the homestead's spacious dining room. Her husband was ten years younger than his wife and had very blond hair that was cut short. His pale blue eyes always looked as if he carried the woes of the world on his shoulders. Alex had learned that he was a Lutheran missionary and a very educated man in something called anthropology which he had studied in Berlin. Although the beautiful woman with the slender neck and long jet black hair piled on her head was a cousin, she was more of a stranger to Alex than the big Irishman. He had grown used to the gruff man with the eye patch and felt comfortable in his company.

Alex stretched then swung sideways and dropped his feet to the floor. He heard the approaching footsteps before the door to his room was flung open.

'Breakfast is ready, boy,' Michael boomed cheerfully. 'Get your clothes on and join us before the sun is up.'

Alex dressed quickly in the working clothes belonging to one of her sons, who was about the same size as himself, that Mrs Cameron had set aside for him. When Alex joined Mr O'Flynn in the kitchen a plate of steak and eggs was plonked in front of him by the surly Chinese cook who muttered under his breath in his language. The boy was stunned when Mr O'Flynn replied in kind, but not half so shocked as the cook whose eyes flew open, as did his mouth. Michael grinned across the table.

'Do you speak Chinese, Mr O'Flynn?' Alex asked with awe.

'Enough to tell old Wing Lee to mind his business and stop giving advice to the son of the owner of Glen View.'

'Did you learn to speak Chinese in a war?' the boy asked, mouth agape.

'Sort of,' Michael replied as he lit the end of a long thin cigar. 'Not the kind of war you would understand. There were only a couple of us fighting it.'

'Who was the other man?'

197

Michael drew on the cigar contentedly before he answered, thick smoke hovering in a blue cloud around his head.

'An Englishman called Horace Brown. A very brave man who saved my life once – but died doing so.'

'Oh, that is sad,' Alex said with genuine sympathy for the man who was just a name to him. 'He must have been a nice man.'

Michael's laughter rolled through the kitchen and he leant forward to slap his grandson on the shoulder. 'He was one of the greatest rogues I ever had the misfortune to meet,' he said, continuing to laugh. 'But that was a long time ago and old Horace is probably plotting with Saint Peter to keep the Germans out of heaven.'

Alex did not understand Mr O'Flynn's last remark so he cut into the fried steak and dunked it in the yolk of an egg.

After breakfast, Michael led two horses to the house, one the little roan mare Alex had been learning to ride the day before. 'Get on,' he ordered. Alex struggled into the saddle. 'Just let her do all the work, young Alex,' Michael said as he mounted his own horse with the ease of a man who had spent years in the saddle. 'We are going for a ride today to visit a very special place.'

'Where?'

'You will find out when we get there,' Michael replied. 'It's not too far from here.'

Alex felt very grown-up astride his mount, riding in the brigalow scrub behind Mr O'Flynn. They passed a group of stockmen off to their left who were searching for cattle amongst the prickly dry trees. After a while the boy became aware of a low range of ancient hills appearing above the scrub. Mr O'Flynn did not seem as interested but searched about the shimmering, stunted trees for something else.

Finally he reined his horse to a halt and helped Alex, whose first long ride was leaving him feeling just a little stiff off his mount.

'We have found what we have been looking for,' Michael said as he wiped his brow with the back of his hand. 'Over there.'

Alex followed his gesture to a clearing where a big, old gum tree grew. He saw nothing other than the endless scrub beyond and was disappointed. He had hoped they might have gone to the hills to explore them.

Michael strode across the clearing with Alex in tow and halted to gaze down at three piles of stones amongst the straggly clumps of grass growing out of the crumbly red earth. Michael crouched on his haunches and removed his hat.

'Here is a part of your heritage, Alexander,' Michael said softly. 'Here is buried one of your great-grandfathers, Patrick Duffy, for whom your own father was named. And beside him is Nerambura's father, Peter Duffy, who was the son of a very famous man called Tom Duffy, your great uncle.'

'Why was he famous, Mr O'Flynn?' the boy asked.

Michael smiled sadly. 'He was what the traps called a bushranger, and he rode with a Darambal warrior called Wallarie. Between them, the two men roamed from here to the Gulf of Carpentaria and were the scourge of your great-grandfather, old Sir Donald Macintosh.'

'You mean Grandmama's husband?' Alex asked, open mouthed.

'Yeah, Lady Enid's husband who Wallarie was supposed to have killed a long time ago. Speared him, just as he speared young Angus Macintosh, way back in the sixties.'

'Why?'

Michael frowned at the boy's innocent question. 'The

Native Mounted Police came and killed all Wallarie's people not far from here. Wallarie blamed your great-grandfather for the slaughter of his people.'

'Did you know the people buried here?'

'Yes, I did,' Michael answered with a sigh but did not elaborate.

He could not tell his grandson that the bushranger Tom Duffy had been his brother, and that the big Irish bullocky, Patrick, had been his father. It was better for the moment that he remain in the boy's eyes a friend and nothing more. Alex turned his attention to the third pile of stones.

'Who is buried in the third grave, Mr O'Flynn?'

'Just a blackfella who was Patrick Duffy's friend,' Michael replied as if Old Billy had not really existed. 'I don't remember his name.'

'Are there any wild blackfellows here now?'

'Not anymore. The last was Wallarie but he would have to be dead by now. He would be older than me if he was alive and that is pretty old for a blackfella.'

Alex stared at the three piles of stones, stunned to learn that he was related to a bushranger and that his new friend, the mixed-blood stockman Nerambura Duffy, was also a distant relative.

'Father never told us about the people here,' Alex said in an awed voice. 'He never spoke about his father either.'

'Didn't he,' Michael growled softly. 'Well, you know about your great-grandfather now. He was a remarkable man who came to this land to dig for gold at Ballarat and ended up murdered here.'

'Who murdered him?' the boy asked aghast.

'A low bastard by the name of Mort. Morrison Mort. But he's long dead now. In the end cannibals got him up around the Palmer track.'

Alex shuddered. The thought of cannibals disturbed him. He had read of their cooking pots and how they put missionaries in them.

The Irishman fell silent, then stood and placed his hat on his head, resting his hand on the young boy's shoulder. 'Always remember their names, boy. Your blood is not only that of the Macintoshes. In your veins flows the blood of some grand Irishmen.'

'But they were probably papists,' Alex replied, horrified.

'That they were,' Michael replied. 'And religion means nothing to the goodness and courage in a man. Never judge a man by the church he prays in. Accept all men as they accept you. You never know, one day your life might rely on someone who does not believe in the things you do. And now, I suppose, I should take you to see the graves of old Sir Donald and his son Angus, back at the homestead,' Michael sighed. 'Though God knows, I only do that for the sake of Lady Enid.'

Without thinking, Michael took his grandson's hand and walked with him back to their horses grazing in the shade of the trees on the other side of the clearing. But the boy was aware of his hand in the Irishman's and felt secure for the first time since his father and mother had gone away. He wished above all else in his life that Mr O'Flynn could be a part of his family too.

TWENTY-ONE

Dinner was a pleasant affair in the spacious dining room: corned silverside, potato and canned peas with a side dish of Indian pickles and fried onion. Afterwards Mary Cameron retired with Helen von Fellmann to one end of the long verandah while the men – Helen's husband Karl, Duncan Cameron and Michael – sat at the other and chatted idly on subjects near and dear to a cattleman's heart: the price of beef, the weather and troubles with Aboriginal stockmen going walkabout with their families.

Alexander had been sent off to bed after dinner which he ate in the kitchen with the Chinese cook. Eventually, Duncan excused himself and also retired for the night, leaving the Lutheran pastor and Michael alone to sip on the claret provided by the manager of Glen View for his special guests. Duncan's letter from Lady Enid had clearly instructed that only the best would be good enough for her grand-daughter Helen and her husband, and for his Irish guest, Mr Michael O'Flynn.

Karl stared up at the myriad stars in the clear night sky. The bite of the sun was gone from the plains and the moths had come to hover around a lantern that cast a dim yellow light in the night. Karl's command of the English language was not as good as that of his pretty wife, not surprising as she had spent the first half of her life living in Sydney before travelling to Germany to complete her education.

'I wonder why you have not told your grandson who you really are,' Karl said quietly in his native tongue. 'My father has spoken a lot about you, Mr Duffy.'

Michael's expression did not register his surprise at the German missionary's knowledge of his true identity.

'I have my reasons, Pastor,' he replied calmly in fluent German as he sat on the steps of the verandah puffing on a cigar. 'It is my son's place to tell Alexander who I am, not mine, and I hope that he will do so when he returns from the war.'

'That makes sense,' the missionary said, quietly reverting to English. 'My father has told me much about you, Herr Duffy. He has said that you are the most dangerous man he has ever known.'

'Second most,' Michael snorted with mirth. 'Old Horace Brown was far more dangerous than me.'

'Ah yes, Herr Brown. My father said he was truly a dangerous man to the Kaiser's interests in this part of the world. He has much respect for him.'

'*Had*, Pastor,' Michael corrected. 'Horace is now in the past tense.'

'Yes . . . had,' the missionary reflected. 'So you saw action in South Africa, Herr Duffy?'

'I would prefer that you call me O'Flynn, Pastor,' Michael

203

replied. 'And I would appreciate your silence on the matter of who I am.'

'I will respect your wishes, Mr O'Flynn,' Karl replied. 'Not even my wife knows that you are the father of her half-brother.'

'How did you know?' Michael asked, taking a sip of his claret between puffs of his cigar.

The pastor smiled. 'You have used the name of O'Flynn before, according to my father. And how many Irishmen in Australia have your scars and one eye? No, I knew you had to be my father's legendary opponent. And as it is, he speaks very highly of you, Mr O'Flynn. I suspect that you are one of his last true friends, even if he did try to kill you once.'

Michael grinned. 'And how is the count?' he asked with a wry smile. 'And your beautiful mother, the countess?'

'They are well,' Karl replied with an enigmatic smile. 'I suspect my mother misses the company of her cousin, Fiona. Sadly my wife has never come to terms with what once occurred between her mother and mine,' Karl continued as the smile faded.

'You do not seem to judge people,' Michael said. 'That seems rather unusual for a man of the cloth.'

'No, Mr O'Flynn, my role in life is to save souls – not judge what only God should.'

'Then you are a rather unusual man and, I have to say, nothing like your father.'

'No, I am not like my father,' Karl reflected. 'But my brother is very much like my father. Hans follows the path of war. I fear that he has joined the sabre rattlers who desire a confrontation with Britain. He and my father are hoping that the war in South Africa will provide an excuse for the Kaiser to declare war on his cousins in England.'

'Not likely while Britannia rules the waves,' Michael said.

Karl cast him a curious look. 'It is unusual for a man with your Irish background to support the British. Did not your own father fight the British army at the Eureka Stockade?'

'You have a point, Pastor. But you forget some men are mercenary when it comes to war. I guess I was just one of them. The British paid well.'

'So you have left behind the ideals of your family?' Karl queried.

Michael frowned. He had never really thought about his life, other than that it had been marked by a series of wars from New Zealand to Africa. 'Irishmen just like a good fight, I suppose,' Michael finally answered with a short laugh. 'Doesn't matter about the cause.'

'I believe you have a relative, Father Martin Duffy, who still believes in causes.'

Michael stared hard at the Lutheran pastor. 'How did you know about that?' he asked with a hard edge in his voice.

The German glanced away before answering. 'Maybe I have said too much. Some things said are better forgotten.'

'I heard Father Duffy was recruiting for the Boers in South Africa,' Michael said quietly. 'Is he in communication with the German government?'

'It is inevitable that he speak to Germany,' Karl replied. 'He sees us as natural allies in this war of liberation against the oppression of the English. He feels that war will eventually come to Europe and that we will see Germany pitted against England. In that case, he also sees the Irish rising with German assistance against the British army. We are natural allies.'

'What do you personally think?'

'I think that while such men exist they give fuel to foolish German aspirations amongst the warmongerers. It will not take much to light the fire for what I see as a terrible war. We have used science to develop weapons far beyond our control. To unleash such weapons of science spells the certain death of a whole generation of young men. I suppose you could call me a pacifist, Mr O'Flynn. A man not in any way like you, or my father.'

Michael stared at Karl for some time before nodding in agreement. The young man belonged to a new generation. 'For the sake of us all,' Michael said quietly, 'I hope that such men as Father Duffy cease in their cause or are thwarted in some way from fuelling such a slaughter.'

'Amen,' the young missionary said quietly and Michael understood his prayer when he reflected on the murderous campaigns of the American Civil War: trenches, machine guns, barbed wire, quick-firing artillery guns and the communications to ensure maximum concentration of death at any given point on the battlefield.

Karl spoke again. 'I shall bid you a good evening and retire for the night. Tomorrow will be a long day as my wife and I will be leaving.'

'I thought that you had come here to set up a mission station,' Michael said in surprise. 'Surely you have not done that already.'

'Your son and Lady Macintosh will not allow us to use a part of Glen View for such matters,' he replied sadly.

'Ah yes, I think I know why,' the Irishman answered softly. 'But it is something I would not expect you to understand, Pastor.'

'The curse that you all believe in,' Karl replied. Michael shot him a look of surprise. 'Oh, I know all about your beliefs. My wife almost believes in the curse herself. But fortunately she has come to realise that pagan religions are based on superstition. There is only one God, and He is not the evil avenging spirit of the Aboriginal people of this land. Their beliefs are nothing more than animistic traditions.'

'Well, I'm not exactly a practising Christian,' Michael said with a wry smile. 'So my mind is a little more open to other people's beliefs. Even primitive blackfella ideas about curses.'

Karl von Fellmann frowned at the Irishman's mocking tone. What was it about this vast and seemingly desolate land that drove otherwise rational people to such heretical beliefs?

Karl and his wife did not commence their journey to Sydney the next day. Helen sat in the dining room with her hands in her lap, her husband standing beside her, listening to Michael relate the extraordinary events of that morning.

'Nerambura Duffy says the old warrior, Wallarie, is still alive,' Michael said, seeing the expression of hope on Helen's face as she reached out to grasp her husband's hand. 'He says he knows where he might be.'

'Where, Mr O'Flynn?' Helen asked leaning forward in her excitement.

'Young Nerambura says the old blackfella has gone walk-about up north towards Burketown. Left a few months back.'

'We must find him,' Helen said glancing up at her husband. 'If we find him and bring him back to Glen View, my grandmother will honour the promise to grant us land for our work amongst the Aboriginal people.'

'Wallarie is the man who killed your grandfather and your uncle,' Michael cautioned. 'In the end, Lady Macintosh might not be so keen to have him back, considering the damage he has done to your family.'

'But what do you think, Mr O'Flynn?' Karl asked point-edly. 'From your own experiences?'

Michael realised that Karl was deferring to his real

identity without letting on to his wife. 'I think we should find Wallarie,' he answered. 'I think he is the key to many mysteries that require answers – rational or otherwise.'

'I agree,' Karl answered, holding Michael's gaze. 'My wife and I should speak to Nerambura Duffy and ascertain Wallarie's whereabouts.'

'Not so easy,' Michael warned. 'Nerambura reckons the old warrior would be pretty wary even if you find him. Nerambura and I will come with you in the search. It's pretty wild country out there.'

Karl felt his wife squeeze his hand. It was clear she agreed. 'I cannot see any problem with your suggestion if that is your wish, Mr O'Flynn,' he said. 'I am sure Mr Cameron will provide us with what we need.'

'I'm sure he will,' Michael agreed. 'There is one other thing.'

'What is that?' Karl asked.

'Young Alexander will travel with us in our search for Wallarie.'

TWENTY-TWO

Away from the intensity of campaigning, the thousands of soldiers camped in and around the pretty little town tended to get themselves into trouble as they sought ways of relieving the boredom of camp life. But murder was going beyond the usual drunken brawls that brought the wrath of the ever-vigilant British military police down on trouble-makers. Being appointed to assist the military police in their investigation was not an assignment that Patrick welcomed. Colonel Hay Williams had suggested his appointment to the investigation, knowing full well that the Australian major would lose his popularity with the colonial troopers if he were forced to ask intrusive questions in a murder investigation. Under the terms of reference presented to him by a coldly smiling Colonel Hay Williams at the Pretoria head-quarters, Patrick was appointed to coordinate questioning of soldiers from the Queensland contingents.

One of the worst aspects of the occupation of Pretoria for Major Patrick Duffy was the mountain of paperwork he found himself buried under. Patrick now sat in his tent with papers scattered on his camp bed. He had been looking forward to a relaxed evening with his fellow officers in the mess but the investigation had stopped that pleasant interlude. He had before him the names of four soldiers who had been absent the night the British sergeant had been stabbed to death. Four men who had been reported missing from their lines without leave approved – and one name on the list particularly disturbed him: Private Saul Rosenblum.

Patrick frowned as he stared at the list. Rosenblum was a soldier with an impeccable record of service and a man whose courage under fire had earned him a recommendation of a gallantry medal. No, Saul Rosenblum may have been absent that night, but he could not have possibly killed the English sergeant.

But he felt a twinge of guilt for what he knew was a personal bias. Was it because he owed the soldier his life? Would he betray the very spirit of his commission as an officer if he turned a blind eye to one particular soldier in the investigation? Patrick sighed and shuffled the papers. His doubts were unfounded, he told himself. Private Rosenblum would have an explanation for his whereabouts on the night of the murder and that would end the matter.

The following morning all four of the Queenslanders on Patrick's list were marched by the company sergeant major to the orderly room, set up in a deserted farmhouse just outside Pretoria.

Patrick sat behind a battered kitchen table serving as an office desk and listened to the CSM bark his commands to the four soldiers outside before marching into the orderly room. There was a crashing halt of boots on the wooden

210

floor followed by a salute that made his arm appear to be sprung steel.

'Soldiers present and correct, sah!' the CSM bellowed as if he were still on the parade ground.

Patrick returned the salute. 'Very good, Sergeant Major. You can stand the men at ease outside and send in the first soldier.'

'Very good, sah,' the CSM barked, saluting, and made an about turn and marched out of the office.

'Private Hinton. Look smart, man. On the double. Report to Major Duffy.'

In turn Patrick questioned three troopers at length as to their whereabouts on the night of the murder. All were already facing a military charge of being absent without leave, but they were eager to cooperate when they learned that the major's inquiries were in relation to a murder investigation, and each was able to provide witnesses to his whereabouts.

But Saul Rosenblum, the last to be questioned, could only say that he had gone for a walk that night, with no alibi as to his exact whereabouts. That did not mean the Queenslander was guilty, Patrick reassured himself. It just simply meant he did not have an alibi. And the Canadian corporal only had a fleeting glimpse of the soldier who had brushed past him in the night. All he had been sure of was that the soldier wore the uniform of a Queensland mounted infantryman, and he could even have been wrong about that.

Saul stood to attention in front of the desk and stared at a fly on the wall behind Patrick's head.

'Did you ever meet a Sergeant Temple, of the yeomanry?' Patrick asked quietly.

'No, sir,' Saul replied without blinking. He had not met the dead English sergeant before he killed him!

A silence followed and Patrick scanned the face of the soldier. He appeared calm and confident. 'Private Rosenblum, you are the only man I have questioned who does not seem to have an alibi as to where you were on the evening Sergeant Temple was murdered. As such, I will be forced to submit your name to the military police for further interrogation on the matter. But believe me when I tell you that I am reluctant to do so. I can only reassure myself that you could have no reason to kill a man you had never met before.'

'I understand, sir,' Saul replied, knowing full well that the major meant his words. 'I have nothing to hide.'

'Very good, Private Rosenblum. I would like to take this opportunity to thank you for coming back for me at the Modder River. You risked your life under the most perilous conditions that day without any thought for your own. I would like you to know that I made recommendation in my despatches for official recognition of your courageous actions.'

'Thank you, boss,' Saul said with a sad smile. 'But that wasn't necessary. I just did what any other of the blokes would have done for you.

After dismissing Saul, Patrick returned to Lord Roberts' headquarters to report to Colonel Hay Williams, confident that Saul Rosenblum had nothing to do with the murder. But his confidence was soon to be shattered by an overheard conversation in the officers' mess that evening. Patrick would wish he had spent the evening elsewhere.

As officers are prone to do, Captain Garling of the yeomanry company was discussing his late platoon sergeant – the deceased Sergeant Temple – with a fellow captain from another yeomanry unit. Patrick had been sitting in a comfortable chair, reading a three-week-old copy of the

Times, sipping a whisky and soda. It was the mention of the dead sergeant's name that had attracted his attention and the fact that Captain Garling had expressed his relief at no longer having the troublesome man in his company.

Patrick placed the English paper on a cane table beside his chair. 'Captain Garling, I could not help overhearing you say you are relieved that the late Sergeant Temple is no longer in your company. Why is that?'

The captain appeared ill at ease at having been caught out. 'I would prefer not to discuss the matter, sir,' he replied defensively. 'It is simply a matter pertaining to an incident that occurred some weeks ago.'

'I do not wish to pry into matters concerning the good order and discipline of your command, Captain Garling,' Patrick said from where he sat. 'But I have been assigned to the investigation of your sergeant's apparent murder. Anything you may tell me would only relate to assisting in the case.'

Frowning, the captain clutched his gin and tonic. 'Well, I suppose in the interests of solving the murder I could tell you. The rumour amongst the ranks is that Sergeant Temple was killed by a Boer in the uniform of one of the colonial troops.'

'Why would they think that?' Patrick asked, although the practice of Boer commandos using captured British army uniforms in such a way was not uncommon. 'What reason would a Boer have for risking his life and going after Sergeant Temple in a town garrisoned by so many of his enemy?'

'It appears that Sergeant Temple, in company with some Afrikaner, was responsible for the death of a Boer girl out on the *veldt*. Mind you, she apparently killed two good soldiers of mine and they supposedly had no choice but to kill her in their own defence. But we have since learned that she was the sister of a Boer field kornet, a particularly dangerous man who rides with De la Rey. The rumour amongst my men is that he had Sergeant Temple killed.'

'You were saying that you were relieved to have Sergeant Temple out of your command,' Patrick repeated. 'Why was that?'

The English captain's unease returned. 'I'm afraid his story about the incident with the Boer girl left a lot of questions unanswered when we had the bodies of the two soldiers disinterred for a proper burial in Pretoria. We found that one of the soldiers had been shot through the head as if executed. We know from the gun that killed them that the girl could not have done it. I was about to question Sergeant Temple on the discrepancy, which he had not mentioned in his report, when the sergeant himself was killed.'

'What about the Afrikaner who was with Sergeant Temple? Has he been questioned?'

'A bit difficult,' Garling replied. 'It seems that his own kind executed him not long after the incident according to the intelligence chaps. They seemed to know a fair bit about the matter. Even knew the name of the girl. Seems she slipped through their fingers at Bloemfontein carrying something rather important for Pretoria. They are not quite sure what it was but considering her connections, my guess is that it was information on our dispositions. Apparently she was something of an enigma, a Dutch born Jew educated in England and working for the Boers.'

The description of the dead girl sent a cold fear through Patrick. Very few of the Queenslanders did not know where Saul Rosenblum went on his time away from the lines in Bloemfontein. They had in fact helped cover for him on occasions so that he could rendezvous with the pretty dark-eyed girl. Needless to say, Patrick had heard the rumours of Saul's affair. He did not want to ask the next question.

'Was the dead girl's name Karen Isaacs?' he asked softly.

The English captain cast him a quizzical look. 'Did you know her, sir?'

'No. Just knew of her,' Patrick answered with a sick feeling churning his stomach.

Saul Rosenblum had killed the English yeomanry sergeant! His motive was simple. Revenge for the death of the woman he loved. Would he do no less if something had happened to Catherine?

'Are you all right, sir?' the captain asked as he stared at the stricken expression on the colonial major's face. 'Not a touch of that damned enteric fever by any chance?'

Patrick shook his head. 'No. Thank you for the information, Captain Garling.' He rose from his chair. 'If you will excuse me, gentlemen, I have an early start in the morning.'

They nodded and watched the major leave the mess after bidding good evening to the president of the mess committee as protocol dictated.

'Funny chap, that Major Duffy,' Garling commented to the other yeomanry captain. 'A colonial.'

As Patrick walked back to his tent his thoughts were in turmoil. He had a duty as an officer to report all he had learned, albeit inadvertently, to the investigating police. Saul Rosenblum had a strong motive for killing the English sergeant. It was all circumstantial but solid enough to have him arrested. Military justice was harsh and should he be found guilty he would surely be executed. By the time Patrick had reached his tent he had made his decision. It was a matter of honour, though the decision did not rest well with him. But fate, and a tenacious Boer commander,

General Botha, intervened in any decision Major Patrick Duffy might have to make. He was summoned to attend an important operations briefing first thing in the morning. The matter of Saul Rosenblum would not be a priority this day.

TWENTY-THREE

Lord Roberts' concern at the growing concentration of Botha's army east of Pretoria had prompted him to counter the threat. He feared the Natal Boers being pushed ahead of Buller's columns would unite to pose a formidable threat to Pretoria itself but his tactic of engaging the centre of the Boer army whilst outflanking it had been anticipated by the wily Botha. Roberts, however, was not to know this at the time he sent his depleted army forth from Pretoria to engage his enemy.

Major Duffy was assigned to the New South Wales Mounted Infantry and the secondment did not rest easy with him even though he personally knew many of the officers and soldiers of the unit. He had grown used to riding with his Queenslanders and the change in the order of battle left him with an ill foreboding, superstitious as such feelings were. It was as if he had lost his talisman. But the assignment to Colonel De Lisle's mounted column was heartening in one aspect; he respected the astute commander's ability to react quickly to all opportunities that presented themselves on the battlefield.

They had rode out of Pretoria to a range of hills shaped like a horseshoe called the Tiger Poort Range. Here they bivouacked in the shadow of Diamond Hill, watching the British infantry make a determined assault on the heavily defended plateau. But the British infantry came under intense fire from the Transvaalers and by nightfall they had captured little ground for heavy losses. In his usual brilliant style, Colonel De Lisle spotted a key position to the battle in a *kopje* at the south-eastern end of the plateau. It was time to commit his colonial mounted infantry to the battle for Diamond Hill.

Patrick sat in the grass resting his horse and chatting with his men. He had known many of them as an officer back in Sydney and they were glad to see him. His feeling of unease began to dissipate. It was mid-afternoon when the order came down to the New South Welshmen that it was their turn to attack with the West Australians in support.

The senior NCOs strode amongst the waiting troopers with directions to check the girths on their saddles. One of them, a sergeant who had worked for a Macintosh company in Sydney, saw Patrick tightening his saddle strap and stopped. 'You coming with us, sir?' he asked curiously.

'Sergeant Higgins, isn't it?' Patrick quizzed.

'Yes, sir,' the sergeant answered, pleased to be recognised. 'It is. I used to work for you at the shipping office in Bligh Street, sir.'

'I remember,' Patrick smiled. 'You did a bloody good job then and now I expect you will do even better.'

The sergeant could not help but beam at the praise.

'It will be good to have you with us, sir,' he replied and thrust out his hand as a civilian would, forgetting for the moment they were a long way from the shipping offices of Macintosh & Company.

Patrick took the hand. 'Good luck, Sergeant Higgins.'

'And you too, sir,' he replied.

'By the way, Sergeant,' Patrick said with a grin as he swung himself easily into the saddle. 'Remind me to give you a raise when we get back to Sydney.'

The sergeant returned the grin and waved as Patrick trotted over to join a young officer assembling his squadron of men. He was casually briefing them on their objective, as if explaining a nice place to picnic: a farm set amongst a stand of gum trees at the end of a broad, rolling, grass covered plain dotted with ant nests. There they were to dismount to advance on foot.

The order was given to mount and three hundred and fifty infantrymen on horseback were deployed on command to a spacing of fifty yards. Patrick experienced the usual tension of all soldiers before an action but felt a strange calm descend once the order was given to advance.

The horsemen trotted into their lines then quickly broke into a gallop, making for the farm near the Boer-occupied hill. Behind the galloping horsemen the pompom guns opened fire at the entrenched Boers to give the horsemen support in their attack.

Patrick leant forward along the neck of his mount as the long lines of colonial horsemen charged forward, the exhilaration of the traditional cavalry charge upon him as any fears were absorbed in the wild ride.

The initial thunder of hooves was drowned by the rapid crash of the pompoms from behind, firing over their heads. To his front, Patrick could see the objective and wondered at first whether there were any enemy occupying the position. But the dust that began to sprout in front of the charging line of colonial horsemen soon confirmed that they had come under withering rifle and artillery fire which rained down on them from the heights of the plateau. Luck intervened when the long range Boer artillery suddenly shifted their aim to a herd of cattle away on the plain, mistaking them for horses, and under the barrage, the terrified animals ran about wildly as the shrapnel tore them apart.

Then they were on their first objective, the farmhouse and its surrounding outbuildings. The order to dismount brought the New South Welshmen tumbling out of their saddles with their carbines.

Patrick carried a Lee Metford as well as his service revolver, snatching a bandolier of rounds from around the neck of his horse before he joined the colonial troopers. De Lisle had wisely sent the pompom guns forward to take up a position behind a low-set stone fence. From there they could continue to provide covering fire to the troops who would now advance on foot in extended order, a spacing of thirty yards between each man.

Gazing across to the final objective, Patrick felt a cold fear for what was ahead: a steep, bare escarpment covered only by thin, straw-like grass. Beyond the escarpment he could see other stony terraces, rising like giant steps to the top where the Boers were well entrenched behind their stone built sangers.

The dismounted infantry advanced in their frontal attack, scrambling up the rocky slopes which would give some protection until they came to the final terrace where the Boer met them with unrelenting fire.

As he struggled alongside the younger troopers, Patrick

felt as though his lungs were on fire. Occasionally he stopped to snap off a shot at the little stone fort sangers from where the Boers poured their fire upon the advancing infantry.

The gunfire had reached a crescendo with the explosions of the deadly pompom shells adding to the hell around him. Men screamed curses or died with strangled cries of despair as bullets ricocheted and the ground was churned with splintering stone and metal from spent rounds. Amidst the death and dying on the slopes just below the crest of the plateau, the order was given to fix bayonets and make the final charge to sweep the Boer position clear.

The almost impersonal charge across the plain had now brought the enemy close enough to make the war very personal. Patrick was not carrying a bayonet but rose to join the tough colonial troopers. He would use his rifle like a club to dislodge the entrenched enemy. It was like Tel-el-Kebir and McNeill's Zareba all over again when men met in close-quarter fighting in a killing frenzy. Wooden rifle butts against steel knives, men's fists and feet against those of his enemy. There would be personal and vicious deaths where a man would see into the eyes of his foe as a long bayonet was driven into his chest, throat or stomach.

A wild yell went up from the troopers who surged forward with their deadly bayonets extended like primitive spears on the ends of their rifles. The sight of the long lines of enemy infantrymen sprinting the last yards towards them caused the Boer riflemen to break, fleeing their entrenched positions in the last light of the day, but not leaving their wounded behind.

Patrick found himself swept up in the adrenalin-powered charge and was roaring the slogans he had learned many years earlier as a young officer commanding the tough

Scots soldiers. He did not hear the incoming whistling shell that exploded into the earth behind him. For Major Patrick Duffy the war was over and he would not share the victory of the New South Welshmen as they swept the hill clear of enemy resistance.

Patrick was not aware how badly he had been wounded. He was mercifully unconscious as the four troopers carried him in a blanket down the hill and back to the farmhouse where the wagons of the medical corps waited to transport the wounded of both sides back to Pretoria. When Patrick finally regained his senses, he wished he was still in that blissful place of darkness where the terrible pain could not reach him. With each jarring bump of the mule-drawn medical wagon, his shrapnel torn body arched in agony, but his moans of pain were lost in the many cries of badly wounded soldiers who lay beside him. He could not see the extent of his injuries but sensed he had taken the full brunt of the explosion. In the dark night the wagon slammed into a pothole and slewed sideways. The soldier lying beside him tumbled onto Patrick who cried out in agony.

'You'll be all right, sir.' A gentle voice came to him out of the dark as a hand touched his face. 'I'll get him off yer. Looks like the poor blighter is dead anyway.' True to his word the dead man was hauled away but the agonising pain remained with Patrick from the numerous shrapnel wounds. 'Not too far to go before we have you in a hospital at Pretoria,' the gentle voice continued reassuringly. 'Got good people there.'

Patrick gritted his teeth, embarrassed by his protests of pain. He was an officer and as such expected to bear his torment in silence. But despite such thoughts he still reached out his hand to seek the hand of the disembodied voice and was rewarded with a firm grip. 'Where have I been hit?' Patrick asked, his voice weak from loss of blood. 'I'm thirsty,' he added. 'So bloody thirsty.'

'Can't give yer any water, sir,' the medic said sadly. 'Yer got some shrapnel in the belly as well as in the chest, arm and legs. Water's no good fer a gut wound.'

'How bad?' Patrick asked.

'Seen worse an' seen the same men up and walkin' in a few weeks,' the medic answered. 'With any luck your wounds might get you a trip to London and out of this war.'

The driver berated his mules into greater exertions to pull the ambulance wagon free of the pothole. As the jarring caused further waves of agony to sweep over Patrick, his involuntary cry of pain died away into silence. Once again he had entered into the darkness whose gateway opened into the world of the dead. Major Patrick Duffy was not sure which way he should go.

TWENTY-FOUR

Thousands of miles east on another continent, Michael Duffy, alias Michael O'Flynn, sat astride his horse and stared across a shimmering plain. He glanced up at the angle of the sun and calculated it must be around noon then dropped his searching gaze back to the horizon. The distant tree line was barely visible but he knew from experience that it marked a waterway. Behind him, a pair of horses hauled the wagon and its two passengers with Nerambura Duffy at the reins, the young stockman's horse following on a lead.

Behind the open wagon rode young Alexander Macintosh on the roan that had been purchased for him by Michael. His riding had improved considerably on the trek west across the dusty plains. It had been over a week since they had departed Glen View station and Nerambura had guided their way almost instinctively.

'We camp up ahead about two to three hours away,'

Michael said over his shoulder. 'Seems as good as any place to spend the night. I'll ride on and check it out.'

With a sharp dig in his mount's flanks he broke his horse into a trot. Three hours later the wagon reached the distant shimmering tree line to find a virtual oasis of coolabah trees overhanging a series of cool, clear waterholes and rocky pools. The river was wide but the Dry season had caused the level to drop to a fordable passage just a couple of hundred yards upstream. Michael already had a campfire burning in a ring of river stones and his hobbled horse grazed under the shade of the river trees.

'It is a beautiful place, Mr O'Flynn,' Helen exclaimed from the wagon's seat. 'You have chosen well. But are there any crocodiles in the river?' she asked apprehensively.

'Too far inland for crocs,' Michael answered with a grin. 'Just the bloody mosquitoes you have to worry about here at night. Big enough to suck a croc dry.'

Karl von Fellmann eased himself from the back of the wagon and stretched with a groan of relief before assisting his wife down. The journey in the rear of the hard sprung wooden wagon had not been pleasant and every muscle cried out.

Alexander's eyes were wide with wonder at the beauty of the wild river that flowed through the plains, dry for hundreds of miles around. It was the biggest they had seen in their days on the trek. 'Are there fish in the river, Mr O'Flynn?' he asked with boyish excitement.

'Should be. I hear they have a particularly good eating fish out here called a barramundi. You'll get a chance to see if you can catch us one or two.'

The boy's face beamed with pleasure. 'I know how to fish,' Alex said enthusiastically. ' My father took us fishing once at Manly when we stayed there.'

'A nice little cottage by the sea,' the Irishman sighed.

'Have you been to our place at Manly?' the boy asked, wondering how Mr O'Flynn might know of the Macintosh seaside resort.

'A long, long time before you were born,' Michael reflected sadly and the boy sensed wisely that he should not ask any more questions.

Setting up the camp did not take long. It had become a practised routine over the days on the journey: a canvas sheet was spread under the wagon for Michael, Alex and Nerambura and a short distance away a small canvas tent was set up for the pastor and his wife. The von Fellmanns used camp stretchers to sleep on whilst the others slept on the canvas sheet, using saddles for pillows. Coarse blankets kept them warm against the chill of the western plains nights although the days had proved to be hot.

Michael and Nerambura headed to the river to collect firewood, to keep the campfire burning throughout the night. As they approached its banks the young stockman from Glen View frowned. 'Big mob of blackfellas up along the river, boss,' he said, crouching to examine the faintly discernible tracks at the river's edge.

Michael peered at the prints. His years in Africa hunting lions had also honed his skills in tracking.

'How many do you reckon?' he asked.

'Mebbe thirty,' Nerambura replied. 'Mebbe they bin see Wallarie.'

Michael nodded. 'Maybe we should have a talk to them.'

Then the matter was put aside as the two men went about their task of fetching timber before returning to the camp where Alex was assisting his aunt set out the cooking pots.

Alex liked his father's half sister. As she had lived most of her life in Germany he had known little of her until now and was only vaguely aware of the odd circumstances of his relationship to the woman. He knew that his grandmother Fiona White was both the mother to his own father and to the very pretty lady who was his aunt. Other than that nothing much had been explained to him. It was a subject that was as good as taboo in the family.

Michael explained to Karl von Fellmann what he and Nerambura had found on the river and the Lutheran pastor appeared pleased.

'I will go and meet them,' Karl said. 'I have not as yet had the opportunity to meet with the wandering Aboriginals of this country.'

'Not a real good idea, Pastor,' Michael cautioned. 'These people don't always take to white men. It's not that long ago we were hunting them down and shooting them as vermin. The tribes up this way have a reputation for armed resistance.'

'I can take Nerambura with me, Mr O'Flynn,' von Fellmann replied, 'if you will stay and provide my wife with protection at the camp.'

Michael frowned as he pondered on the pastor's request. He respected the young man, and more than likely he would come to no harm. Perhaps this was an ideal time to show his grandson how to catch one of the big, silver scaled fish he had heard so much about from the Palmer River bushmen years earlier.

'I suppose you will be safe with Nerambura. But they're a fair way upriver – looks like you can expect to camp overnight with them.'

'That is not a problem. I would like to have the opportunity to examine them in their natural setting. I studied their culture at the Berlin University but this is the first time I have had the opportunity to see for myself how they live.'

'Well, you can take my horse,' Michael said. 'And Nerambura can take my revolver as insurance.'

The pastor smiled. 'Thank you, Mr O'Flynn. I know that God will protect us but I am sure Mr Samuel Colt will be good to have as a friend here on earth.'

Michael smiled. 'That he will,' he replied and turned on his heel to saddle his horse for the pastor.

Within ten minutes Nerambura and Karl von Fellmann rode away, following the line of big trees that ran along the edge of the river. The sun was high enough above the horizon to provide them with good light in their search for the nomadic tribesmen.

When the cooking pots had been set out and all was ready for the evening meal, Michael excused himself to take Alex to a promising bend on the river where a huge tree had collapsed and settled in the shallows. The old bushmen had told him that the barramundi liked to lurk in the tangles of such trees and could be coaxed out with a little patience. Michael soon had Alex set up on the trunk dangling their handlines into the cool, clear water that eddied around the submerged limbs of the tree. The boy sat with an expression of eager anticipation on his face, hardly registering Michael's instruction to stay put while he returned to the campsite for some lines he had decided to set overnight.

When Michael reached the camp he was surprised to see that it was deserted. They had left Helen alone but Michael had done so with little fear for her safety. This was not a country where predatory animals stalked as in Africa and the most dangerous animal in Australia was man himself. He picked up the Martini Henry rifle he had left propped against the wheel of the wagon and went in search of her. His first guess to look downriver proved correct.

As Michael stood high on the bank amongst the shadows of the trees, Helen waded naked in a shallow of the river, the water swirling around her knees. Her long dress and pantaloons lay on a big rock in the river nearby and Helen stood oblivious to his presence amongst the trees. Michael did not feel as if he was intruding, his artist's eye seeing only beauty in the sight of the young woman relishing the freedom that the wild river country gave her. She stood transfixed as if the rest of the world did not exist, the silence broken only by the gently gurgling water and the warble of bush birds. Overhead a flock of cockatoos screeched their noisy call as they swirled in a white cloud and Helen glanced up, her long raven hair falling as a soft tumble to her waist.

Michael drew a cigar from his shirt pocket and lit the end, blowing hazy clouds of grey smoke into the still, late afternoon air as Helen let herself down into the water slowly, allowing its gentle massage to wash away the dust and sweat of the trek. The water caught her long hair sweeping it straight. The sun was losing its bite.

Rising quietly from where he crouched, Michael padded back into the trees. As he walked back up the river he could hear Alex shouting excitedly, obviously struggling with his first big catch.

'It will get away,' Alex cried in desperation as the heavy line ran through his hands.

Michael placed the rifle on the ground and stripped down to his trousers. He slid into the water with his knife and felt with his hands for the line. When he found it he followed the line through the tangle until his hand touched the scales of the big fish. It jerked away from him but was caught up on the hook. Taking a breath Michael dropped below the surface, feeling for the wide mouth of the fish. It was a beauty!

Alex watched anxiously. Michael exploded to the surface bringing the fish up with him. The young boy could not restrain himself from jumping up and down in excitement as Michael hauled himself up the bank, dragging the fish with him. It flipped and flopped at Alex's feet and was as long as the Irishman's arm, a big, fat fish for the cooking fire.

Michael caught his breath, his shoulders heaving. 'You got him, boy,' he said with a grin. 'Now you have to learn how to cook him.'

When they returned to the camp Helen was dressed and combing her long hair. She greeted them with surprise when she saw the huge fish dangling between them. Alexander's fixed grin beamed his pride in the catch.

'A change of diet,' Michael said as he dropped the fish on the ground in front of her. 'Alex is going to cook it for us.'

Their eyes met and Helen wondered at the strange smile on the Irishman's face. She felt a sudden twinge of guilt for her wanton delight in the river and glanced away lest he read her thoughts. There was something about the big man that disturbed her in a way she could not understand. He stood bare-chested to dry off and she could see the scars on his body that marked the violence of his life. She knew very little about Michael O'Flynn except what she had heard from her husband: that he had been a mercenary soldier most of his life and had fought in many wars around the world. When Helen had initially learned that he had been a soldier of fortune she had been horrified, but her husband had been strangely defensive.

But now it was not his violent past that intrigued the

young woman so much as his gentle presence and artistic nature. He would often sit in the saddle or around the campfire and sketch a scene with the stub of an old pencil. He carried his many sketches in a battered leather satchel but did not volunteer to show his work.

Michael gutted the big fish and placed it in the coals of the fire while Alex, squatting beside him, watched with acute interest. Helen prepared the damper bread as Michael had shown her at the commencement of the trek. She had grown to like the crusty bread fresh from the heavy, cast iron camp oven and with the fish that Michael dragged from the fire the meal was superb. She could not remember ever tasting fish as delicious and delicate before. The white flesh seemed to melt in the mouth as she picked at it with her fork.

By the time they had finished eating the stars were rising in the sky. Michael lit a kerosene lamp to give them more light. Alex wanted to sit up and enjoy the night but Michael growled that he should make his bed under the wagon and get some sleep. The boy knew not to argue. When he was comfortable Michael tucked him in. 'Proud of how you didn't lose the fish today,' he said gruffly, patting him affectionately on the shoulder. 'I think I made a good choice in teaming up with you, young Master Macintosh.'

Alex smiled in delight at the praise from the big Irishman and had an impulsive urge to reach up and hug him. But he restrained himself as he knew men did not show emotion like women.

'Thank you, Mr O'Flynn,' Alex replied seriously. 'I wish today would never end.'

'It won't,' Michael said. 'These kinds of days always stay in your memory, no matter what happens. They are good things to fall back on when things get tough. Always remember that, boy.'

Alex nodded. 'I always will, Mr O'Flynn. I will always remember you no matter what happens.'

Michael glanced away. 'I'm not dead yet,' he said with a choked laugh. 'And don't forget to say those damned Protestant prayers Lady Enid is so fond of before you go to sleep.'

Michael rose and was about to walk away when Alex called out to him softly.

'Mr O'Flynn?'

Michael paused. 'Yes, boy?'

'Will you ever forget me?'

'Only if you don't get to sleep,' Michael growled gently and walked back to the fire to join Helen who had prepared two mugs of coffee. Michael found a cigar and lit the end from a burning twig. He sat down on a log, sighing with contentment at the nicotine rush the cigar brought on, and looked over to where Helen sat on the opposite side of the fire sipping her coffee. Her hair was clean and dry and reflected the fire's dancing lights. Michael reached for his battered leather satchel and pulled out a sheet of heavy paper. Bending his head he sketched in silence by the light of the lantern. His face appeared so young and contented as the graphite scratched away at the paper.

When Michael was satisfied he passed his sketch across to Helen with one of the enigmatic smiles she had grown used to. She gasped, almost dropping her mug of coffee when she saw what he had sketched. It was a likeness of her standing full breasted in the river that afternoon, but with little angels around her head.

'I was not spying on you, Mrs Fellmann,' Michael said softly before she could comment. 'I was worried when I returned to the camp and you were not there so I went looking. When I found you in the river I felt that I should not intrude on your privacy. But,' he continued with a broad smile, 'as an artist, I could not resist the impulse to sketch what I remembered of an Australian bush nymph in her natural setting.'

Helen slowly looked up at him, blushing, her emerald eyes a turmoil of emotion. Helen knew that she should be angry at his brazen drawing and yet at the same time she felt flattered by his artistic capturing of a beautiful and serene moment in her life. 'I have seen something like this before,' she said quietly. 'It was a sketch my mother treasured above all the jewellery my father gave her. A sketch of her drawn by her lover a long time ago.'

Michael glanced down at the fire. 'A strange coincidence, Mrs Fellmann,' he replied unconvincingly.

But Helen persisted. 'My mother loved that man very much, but lost him to war,' she continued softly as she gazed across the fire. 'She never spoke of him to me and all that I have learned was from my Aunt Penelope. Even Aunt Penelope once admitted to loving this mysterious man at one stage in her life. All that I knew of him was that his name was Michael Duffy and that he was an Irishman – just like you, Mr O'Flynn.'

'That was a long time ago,' Michael replied sadly as he stared back into her eyes. 'Fate was never very kind to your mother and I.'

'Did you love my mother, Mr Duffy?'

Michael bowed his head and poked at the fire with a stick. 'We were young. I had plans for us to go to America where we could be together away from the restrictions of colonial society. I had planned to be a painter but instead of a paintbrush I ended up spending a lifetime carrying a gun. Many times I would think of your mother and many nights I would cry for what was lost in our lives. But you can only cry so much,' he added bitterly. 'After a while I stopped mourning the loss of a love that was never possible. And that was it.'

'Poor Mr Duffy,' Helen said with a sigh. 'So much pain in my mother's life, and yours. I used to feel ashamed of my mother's unnatural love for Aunt Penelope but as I have grown older I think I understand how such a thing could be.'

'Their love was a lot stronger than most that I have known,' Michael said. 'Your mother and Penelope were linked by events that came into all our lives after the dispersal on Glen View. Never be ashamed of a love that is not yours.'

Helen stared down at the sketch in her hand. 'It is truly beautiful and I will always treasure it. But I do not think my husband would understand, so this will remain a secret between us.'

'Like the other secrets you keep from your husband,' Michael said.

Startled, Helen glanced up at him. Her eyes were wide with questions and amazement. 'What do you know of me that you could make such a statement?'

He puffed at the cigar and returned her gaze. 'That you have a deep sensuality that you do not share with your husband.'

Her mouth fell open. 'What makes you say such a thing?' she asked in a frozen heartbeat.

'A lifetime of living on the edge. Maybe it's just an artist's instinct to attempt to capture on the easel that which is the person's soul. Watching you this afternoon I could see that you felt free amidst the beauty of this special place.'

'I . . . ' She hesitated and looked away, embarrassed by the Irishman's acute perceptiveness. Glancing back, she saw him appraising her with a frankness that was not intrusive. She wondered at the thoughts he seemed to release in her mind. 'I have never known a man to speak as you do, Mr Duffy,' Helen finally said. 'It is as if you can see into places no-one else has before.'

'Ah, but I can because I am old enough to be your father, young lady,' Michael said with the wisp of a sad smile. 'Or maybe because for a short while I touched the soul of your mother, and you are very much like her.'

Helen found herself staring at his hands. They were the hands of a man who she suspected had killed many times and yet clearly they were also capable of touching a woman's body with the gentlest of caresses. They were strong hands.

'You are a most unusual man,' Helen said. 'You are everything my Aunt Penelope described – extremely dangerous to both men and women.'

Michael smiled at her summation of his character. 'But not to you, Helen,' he said as he stood and stretched. 'I will bid you a goodnight.'

She watched him stride away from the light of the fire and could not help but admire the way he moved with the grace of a giant hunting cat.

By mid-morning the next day Karl and Nerambura returned. Karl's expression reflected his pleasure at finally having met with the people he had been sent by God to minister in the years ahead. The tribesmen had proved to be hospitable and curious at the appearance of the white man amongst them. A gentle people, Karl said. A gentle people in need of his God to save their eternal souls from the damnation of ignorance.

Nerambura said very little. They were not Darambal people and thus not worthy of consideration. His was the pride of his people and when he did speak it was to Michael to tell him that the visit had proved fruitful. The people of the tribe had told him by way of signs that a great sorcerer had passed their way. But he had not stopped with them as they were afraid of his powers.

To Michael it sounded as if they were on the right track in their search for Wallarie. He gave the order to break camp and continue across the plains. Ahead was the frontier town of Cloncurry where they would stop for supplies. Then they would push on to a place south of the killing grounds where many years earlier Wallarie had faced with spear and battle axe the rifles and pistols of the Native Mounted Police, a place where the echoes of an ancient curse rolled in the mineral rich hills of the now-dispersed Kalkadoon warriors.

TWENTY-FIVE

Fenella Macintosh stared at the envelope addressed to her that was lying on a silver salver. Lady Enid smiled at the young girl's obvious surprise and delight.

'Young Mr Duffy has finally corresponded it seems,' Enid said from her chair at the long polished cedar table sipping a cup of tea. 'It seems that he must be in good health to do so. The letter arrived yesterday whilst you were at school,' Enid continued with a smile. 'I would suggest that you open it, young lady.'

Fenella could not tear her eyes away from the crumpled envelope and was almost too frightened to open it.

'I will, Lady Enid,' Fenella responded as she picked up the envelope and allowed herself to feel the paper in the palm of her hand. It was as if she was actually feeling the touch of the young man's hand on hers. 'I shall read the letter in my room.'

With that she skipped away leaving her great-grandmother alone in the dining room to reflect on the world she now knew in her old age: young people falling in love and a grandson away at a war. Enid had long learned that human nature was not guided by logic as much as it was by passion. The young Queenslander who wrote to her great grand-daughter was just such a creature of passion. To leave his mother and a good life to run away to a war defied logic. But that had also been the essential difference between the blood of the Irish Duffys and the Anglo-Scots Macintoshes. Her own family had been ruled more by cold-blooded logic, whereas the Duffys allowed their feelings to guide the events of their lives. The mixing of the two bloods in her grandson's veins had produced a remarkable man in Patrick. He had proved himself more than simply capable of guiding the family's vast fortune into the twentieth century; he had taken the enterprises forward into a bigger and brighter future. And yet he still put physical and moral courage above all that was purely mercenary. He was both a man of passion and pragmatism and in his children she could see those same qualities.

Her thoughts were directed to the youngest, Alexander, and the letter that she had received from Mary Cameron of Glen View station informing her of the group's trek west in search of the old Aboriginal warrior, Wallarie. Enid's first reaction to the news that her great-grandson had gone on the arduous journey was apprehension. But she had quickly reassured herself that he was with Patrick's father who she knew would never allow his own grandson to be exposed to danger. In fact, the more she thought about the trek in search of the old Aborigine, the more it seemed all a part of the greater scheme of things.

Enid had always realised that it would take something

akin to the patronage of a man like Michael Duffy to teach the shy boy that he was capable of holding his own in the Macintosh empire, rather than being completely dominated by his older brother, George. If anyone could teach Alexander it had to be Michael, who had survived almost impossible odds to eventually return to Australia. With a twinge of remorse Enid remembered the years past when she had seen him as an enemy to be crushed. It was strange how time could change situations and now that very same man could be instrumental to the Macintosh future.

Enid sighed and stared at the tea leaves in the bottom of her cup. There were people who said they could read the future in such leaves. But all Enid could see was an indefinable mess . . . a bit like the future. Was the Aboriginal man who had killed her eldest son and her husband somewhere in the leaves? She doubted that they would find him. He was more myth than real. She had heard all the stories of the legendary, elusive Darambal man who had become a part of the folklore of the frontier. Michael Duffy and his expedition were chasing nothing more than a ghost. But what if he was still alive . . . ?

The thought caused her to shiver, as if the window had been left open and a cold draught from the wet, cold winter's day outside was seeking her out. Could any such meeting resolve the guilt of the family? Could a reconciliation with the old Aborigine – the last of his tribe – take away the terrible curse that had haunted her for forty years? The intangible force had caused so much anguish between her daughter and herself, apart from any other troubles.

In the privacy of her room, Fenella sat at a writing table and slit the envelope carefully with an ornate, brass letter opener. With great care she slid the stained pages free, vaguely aware that she was holding her breath and unfolding the pages as if expecting them to suddenly fly away. She let out her breath and began to read the bold writing that was in pencil. The letter was addressed from a place called Bulawayo and was eight weeks old. Before reading any further, she took an atlas from a shelf on the writing desk and turned to a map of Africa. Fenella had followed the war from newspaper accounts and the names of places such as Ladysmith, Kimberley and Mafeking were as well known to her as the suburbs of Sydney. But Bulawayo was a mystery. Her finger traced a line north to the place on the map marked Rhodesia. She frowned. It was a strange place to write from as the war was further south in the Orange Free State and the Transvaal. But at least Matthew was not in the centre of the fighting like her father. His last letter to them had been posted seven weeks earlier from Pretoria.

She placed the atlas to one side and began to read.

My Dear Miss Macintosh,

I have not written before as I was afraid that you might have forgotten me. I have not forgotten you . . .

'Silly boy,' she muttered with a wistful smile. 'How could I forget you?'

. . . Well, as you can see I am in Rhodesia. Our ship arrived in Cape Town in April and we all thought that we would disembark and go to the front but the ship was rerouted to Beira in Portuguese East Africa where we finally disembarked. The Portuguese were very good to us. The officers were welcomed with a tennis party, afternoon tea and a ball at night at Government House. I was a little homesick I must admit when I saw all the gum trees lining the streets and the houses were like the corrugated houses I have seen in Queensland. We were camped outside of the town in a place that we worked out must have been a swamp in

the wet season. The heat, flies and mosquitoes were extremely bad. A lot of the men have gone down with fever. At night some of the New Zealanders, Canadians and our own men would go into town. It did not matter to them whether they had been granted leave or not. I am afraid their antics in town were somewhat boisterous.

We were not long in Beira before we were put on a train to travel to Marandellas about three hundred and eighty miles away. The journey slow but exciting. The land changed very much as we rose up into the mountains. I saw hippopotamus, monkeys in the jungle and one of the boys shot a buck from the train. We had to sit on tarpaulins on the floors of the railway trucks and stops were frequent for firewood for the engine. Sometimes we had to get out and walk so that the engine could get the carriages up steep slopes while the Kaffirs pulled on ropes at the front. I did not mind walking those times as we were able to explore the jungle and sample the wild fruits. There were many beautiful flowers in the jungle and they reminded me of you . . .

As Fenella lingered on his words she let out a deep sigh. If only she could once again look into those serious grey eyes of Matthew Duffy. She pressed the letter to her breast as if she could embrace him.

. . . Finally we reached Marandellas which was at the top of the highlands. The country was different there. A bit like the country west of Townsville with its stunted trees and grassy plains. We constructed a base camp with the help of Mashona Kaffirs there. We built native style huts out of wattle and red mud with thatched roofs. Each hut to house fifteen men.

Sadly many of our horses died from a disease the veterinary surgeon called Blue Tongue. It seems they caught the disease on the train trip up to the highlands. A lot of my mates went down with malaria.

Finally we got the order to ride to Bulawayo as part of the

Rhodesian Field Force. We were very eager to get away and go south as the rumour was we would be used in the relief of Mafeking. I have made a lot of friends with the Canadians who are fine chaps.

So here I am in Bulawayo and I am ashamed to say that all the time in Africa I have not seen any action. Many of the chaps are saying that the war will all be over by the time we get out of Rhodesia. Others are saying that the Boer might try and attack Bulawayo and we will be the only thing between him and our defeat. I do not think I am brave but I know I must face battle one day to see for myself who I am when things get tough.

I often think about you and how you came to the parade when we left from Sydney. I remember how pretty you looked and hope that one day we will meet again. I feel very bad about having lied to my mother about what I have done. I pray that she is well and not missing me too much. Soon I will write to her and tell her the truth of where I am.

There is not much else to write about so I shall close for now and will write when we leave Bulawayo. I have just heard that Mafeking has been relieved by Colonel Mahon's column. He had a lot of Queenslanders in his force and I wonder how things might have been for me if I had been able to join the Queenslanders instead of the Citizen Bushmen's Rifles in Sydney. I might have been in the relief of Mafeking.

Yours Sincerely,

Trooper M. Duffy.

When she had finished reading, Fenella re-read those passages where Matthew had broken away from a dialogue of travel to refer to her in romantic terms. The other girls at her school for young ladies of good breeding could not understand her obsession with following the newspaper accounts of the distant war. Fenella could not tell them of the young man barely older than herself who had enlisted to go away to fight. She had not even confided in Emily Newmarch, her best friend. Now that the letter had arrived she considered sharing her romance with Matthew Duffy. But a disturbing thought dampened her impulse. How could she explain the fact that Matthew was a Roman Catholic – a papist? Some boundaries could never be crossed and Matthew was on one side of one of those boundaries, she on the other.

Even as Fenella carefully folded the letter, Matthew lay under a blanket, shivering uncontrollably from the bitter cold of an African winter night. The fragments of slate-like rock that made up the surface of the small domed plateau bit into his back as he stared up at the shreds of clouds scudding across the southern sky. His teeth chattered and all he wanted was to see the sun rise and take away the miserable chill from his body. Matthew had travelled thousands of miles from his home to partake in the great crusade for Queen Victoria only to find himself standing guard over a great pile of bully beef tins and sacks of flour. But the depot was strategically situated on the main road between the towns of Zeerust and Rustenberg and had telegraphic communication with Zeerust. Not that the communication helped the soldiers' lives much. No mail had arrived in over six weeks from the outside world. To add to his woes, Matthew had met up once again with Saul Rosenblum, who had seen action with the Queenslanders while Matthew had been in transit from Sydney to this godforsaken place named Elands River in the Western Transvaal.

Their surprise meeting had not been comfortable. Saul still felt guilty at not having better prevented the young man from enlisting, while Matthew feared that the

Queenslander might reveal his unlawful enlistment. Both had been tasked to draw water for the supply depot, an area covering six acres on top of the almost flat mound adjoining the river. The water was drawn half a mile upstream at a crossing known as Vlakfontein Drift, covered by two small outposts where trenches had been dug to provide shelter for the troops stationed on the hills. The soldiers had exchanged a few cold words of greeting beside the water carts but little else was said.

Saul had arrived at the supply depot with a contingent of Queenslanders two weeks earlier, Matthew a week before that. Saul had been hoping to see more action against the Boer commandos further south, but instead was detached to guard the small mountain of supplies at the Elands River crossing. And the way things were going all hopes of seeing action seemed to be fading.

The bitterly cold nights came and went on the river plain and the monotony of the piquet duty on the bags of flour and tins of meat was broken by the occasional skirmish with enemy patrols. But Matthew had not even been with the patrols at the time they made contact with their adversaries. He could only sit around the cooking fires at night and listen enviously to those who told with elation of such skirmishes. It was as if God had known of his unlawful enlistment and was either punishing him – or protecting him – from battle. How could he ever return to Australia knowing that he had not seen any real action?

Matthew sighed as the first rays of the rising sun brought a soft glow to the darkness on the eastern horizon. At least the chill would soon go from his body and he could once again think about another letter he might write to Miss Fenella Macintosh, somehow disguising the monotony of his far from glorious war against the Boer commandos.

244

He had been able to post a letter just after leaving Rhodesia, telling Fenella of his new posting. He hoped that she would receive it soon. He could hear the mules, horses and oxen stirring on the slopes of the plateau as they too sensed the coming of the dawn.

Matthew rose stiffly to his feet and stretched with a shiver, blinking away the soreness from his eyes brought on by lack of sleep. He had stood piquet duty the evening before and a shift early that morning. For now all he had on his mind, gazing around the field depot of wagons and tired, cursing men was breakfast and a mug of steaming tea to warm his insides. Already the detail whose task it was to take the wagons to the river crossing half a mile away to draw water had lumbered out. Matthew guessed it was about six-thirty as he bent to pick up his rifle and blanket, about the same time that he might have been sitting down at home to a breakfast of hot, milky coffee and bacon and eggs with buttered toast.

He was straightening when an eruption of rifle and machine gun fire drifted to him from the southern outposts overlooking the river crossing.

'Stand to . . . stand to.'

The young soldier glanced desperately around the plateau. Men were running in all directions where seconds before they had been dragging themselves to find a campfire for breakfast. Others stood casting about as Matthew did, attempting to ascertain the threat.

Then he heard the unfamiliar sound, a soft, ominous whistling in the early morning sunlight. The noise seemed to be coming towards him and he did not know what to do. Had he been as experienced as Private Saul Rosenblum he might have flung himself to the ground and waited for the whistle to end, praying for deliverance.

The earth-shattering explosion of the well-aimed artillery shell landed square in the centre of the plateau and flung him from his feet. Almost simultaneously, a deadly hail of bullets and exploding shells raked the stony ground with pieces of hot iron. The outpost of Elands River was totally surrounded. From four sides the outgunned and outnumbered defenders came under a furious barrage that would rain down seventeen hundred high explosive shells in the first day alone.

Trooper Matthew Duffy crawled on his belly to a nearby shallow trench. He could hear men and animals screaming as their bodies were torn apart. Matthew's innocent wish for adventure in war had finally come to pass but right now he felt none of the romance he once imagined, only a petrifying fear.

The defenders of the backwater of Elands River did not know it then but they were about to carve out a small piece of bloody military history against one of the greatest of Boer commanders, General De la Rey. All Trooper Matthew Duffy knew was that he had wet his pants. It was not a glorious beginning to his war.

TWENTY-SIX

The incoming artillery and rifle fire was relentless, sweeping the plateau with fragments of iron and nickel death. The terrified mules and horses on the exposed slope of the plateau adjoining the river were blasted with high explosive, ripping them apart and spilling their blood in red rivers of their own.

A horse with its front legs blasted away stumbled on its stumps into the shallow trench that Matthew had managed to crawl into. He glanced up in horror as the big horse crashed down beside him, thrashing wildly in its agony until a stream of bullets from an enemy Maxim machine gun walked a spouting path up the slope and mercifully into the body of the horse. The rapid thwacks of the bullets hitting the beast made the terrified young trooper acutely aware that, had the big animal not stumbled into the trench, then it would have been his body absorbing the stream of bullets.

With a shrill whinny, the horse died. Unwisely, Matthew raised his head to glance over the body of the dead animal to see where the Maxim was firing from.

'Get yer bloody head down, you stupid bastard,' he heard a voice scream at him over the deafening crash of fire.

Matthew ducked his head just as an artillery round exploded in front of the trench, shredding the horse's carcass with shrapnel.

'Bloody bad enough yer here at all,' the voice continued beside him.

Matthew turned, ashen-faced, to stare with wide eyes at Saul Rosenblum hugging the ground in the trench.

'I don't want to die,' Matthew blurted. 'I didn't know it was like this.'

'None of us did,' Saul growled. 'If we'd known, we wouldn't have volunteered.'

'Are we going to die?' Matthew asked as he crawled closer to the older soldier who now reached out, gripping Matthew by the shoulder.

'If we keep our heads down only a direct hit will kill us,' Saul reassured. 'Just stick with me, young fella.'

Matthew nodded dumbly as he stared into the eyes of the Queenslander. Across his shoulder he could see other troopers sprawled on the ground; he heard the muttered prayers of some, and the curses of others. But worse was the screaming of men badly wounded, lying on the exposed ground, caught in the open by the first shells and bullets that had raked the plateau.

The two Australians lay in the trench facing each other until Saul eased himself to a position at the lip. He lay his rifle on the edge and scanned the ground in front of the distant hills. Matthew followed his lead, not knowing why Saul was risking exposure to the shrapnel and bullets that still filled the air.

Then Saul's rifle bucked as he fired off a shot at something in the distance. 'Got him!' he exclaimed.

Matthew squinted into the distance and just caught sight of a figure falling into the long grass out of sight.

'The bastards will try to use the bombardment to get their snipers in close,' Saul said as he eased back the bolt of his rifle, ejecting the spent cartridge and slamming it forward to chamber a fresh round from the magazine.

All along the trench, other colonial soldiers were also spotting Boer marksmen who were attempting to use the heavy shelling to close for sniper positions. Matthew caught a movement from the corner of his eye and swung the foresight of his rifle on the distant, tiny figure running in a low crouch towards the plateau. He felt his heart pounding as he realised that the tiny figure was a living man and he flicked off the safety catch and took a deep breath. The figure was still running towards them but had not attempted to zigzag. Matthew calculated that he was about four hundred yards out and a strange calmness came over him. With a conscious effort he exhaled slowly until the foresight, rear aperture and running figure all came into line. As his world shrank to all that was in his rifle sights, he squeezed the trigger until the butt of his rifle bit into his shoulder. The figure in the foresight disappeared and Matthew felt a sickening wave of horror sweep over him when he saw the man down on his knees gripping his stomach. In his mind he could hear the badly wounded soldier's screams of despair and pain. 'Oh God, forgive me,' the young soldier mumbled, the impact of what he had just done hitting him as surely as a Boer bullet.

'Finish him off!' Saul yelled in his ear. 'Finish him off before he goes to ground.'

Matthew reacted to the order by re-sighting on the

kneeling man and pulling the trigger. But nothing happened. He had forgotten to rechamber a fresh round. Beside him Saul's rifle jumped as he fired off a well-aimed shot and Matthew saw the wounded man's head snap back. He seemed to sit on his heels for a long time before slowly toppling on his side.

All through the day they returned fire until the Boer marksmen finally desisted, contenting themselves with raining bullets onto the defending Australians and Rhodesians on the exposed plateau. When night came the exhausted defenders noticed with relief that the shelling had tapered off, although the incoming rifle fire continued spasmodically.

A young lieutenant moved along the trench in a low crouch, issuing orders to reinforce the defences, although he hardly needed to. Soldiers used their initiative, piling up cases of tinned meat and sacks of flour in front of their trenches as well as digging into the thin soil to remove the slabs of slate and reinforce the trench system. The white flour bags were smeared with mud to make them less conspicuous to the Boer artillery in the hills.

In some places, wagons within the encampment were dismantled and the parts used to build earth packed roofs over the trenches. From all over the plateau men dug furiously with bayonets, shovels and their hands to bury themselves as deeply as possible in the life-saving earth. Picks, in short supply, were hired from their owners for the princely sum of three pounds for half an hour's use. But the equivalent of a week's wages meant little to men who faced the possibility of death within hours.

The three ambulance wagons that had been brought in with Saul's contingent of Queenslanders were used as a field hospital, located at the centre of the defensive position on the plateau where a low sanger of slate helped shield against bullets and shrapnel. A double wall of biscuit tins, with a tarpaulin sheet as a sun cover, helped build up the field hospital. The only army doctor attached to the outpost, Captain Duka, worked on the wounded, conducting surgery with the occasional stray bullet thudding into the biscuit tins around his head with a whack. The Australian medic's first patient was a trooper whose right leg had been torn off by an exploding artillery round. He would have many more patients before the siege ended.

Near dawn of the second day, an exhausted Matthew Duffy propped his back against the wall of the now much deeper trench. Beside him, Saul gnawed listlessly on a hard army biscuit. Matthew hardly noticed the bitter cold or the periodic crack of the bullets that still came in the night to seek out unlucky victims. 'It's Sunday the fifth of August,' Matthew said.

'So what's important about that?' Saul asked as he swallowed the last of the biscuit and reached for his pipe.

'My mother's birthday.'

'By all rights you should have been home with her,' Saul replied with a note of disapproval. 'Not here in this place.' He tamped down a plug of dark tobacco into the battered bowl of the pipe with his thumb. 'Does she know you are here?' he asked as he lit the pipe.

'I wrote her a letter before we rode out of Bulawayo. That was about five weeks ago. I suppose she does by now.'

'Shit! Your mother is going to blame me for you signing up,' Saul groaned. 'I doubt that she will be too willing to give me a job on the Balaclava run when we get back.'

'I wrote to her that you tried to stop me joining in

251

Brisbane,' Matthew said quietly. 'It's just kind of ironic that we ended together in this place.'

A silence fell between them, punctuated by the steady crack of incoming bullets. Finally Matthew spoke. 'You think Carrington will relieve us soon?' he asked.

It had been a little over twenty-four hours since they sat around the campfires celebrating the news that General Carrington, with a sizeable force of one thousand men, six field guns and four pompoms, was on his way from the town of Zeerust to the Elands River outpost. There had been singing in a camp concert and their voices had echoed in the surrounding hills. But now the songs were gone and only the moans of the wounded echoed in the night.

'If he can get through we'll be all right,' Saul offered as he puffed on his pipe. 'But . . . ' He trailed away.

'You don't think he will get through?'

'I know the Boers,' the Queenslander answered dully. 'They'll be expecting Carrington's column and will have planned an ambush. The Boers are tough bastards and know this country like the back of their hands. I don't like Carrington's chances.'

'Which means you don't like our chances,' Matthew added softly. 'I never thought I'd die like this.'

'Yer not dead yet,' Saul said. 'We only have to keep the Dutchmen off this hill. It's as simple as that.'

'You think we can do it?'

Saul did not answer but picked up his rifle and slid back the bolt. It was time to clean the weapon which he knew was the only thing between the defenders and certain death if Carrington was ambushed. Soon the dawn would be upon them and the enemy artillery observers would have a clear view of the outpost under the African sun. Then the shelling would commence and they would lay helpless in their hastily reinforced trenches. The situation was not looking good. They were trapped. For the young Jewish stockman from Queensland death was of little consequence. He had lost the most precious thing in his life, murdered by a soldier from the British army. But Matthew cared very much about living, as his love was waiting for him in faraway Sydney.

When the dawn came colonial officers at the outpost watched helplessly with field glasses as the Boer scouts returning along the road from Zeerust marked the road with ranges for enemy marksmen. All the indicators confirmed Private Rosenblum's worst fears. There was nothing the defenders trapped at the outpost could do to warn Carrington's relief force.

That day they watched the scouts from Carrington's force driven back a mere two miles from the outpost by the well-placed Boer marksmen. They huddled in the trenches as the enemy artillery poured shells into their six acres of the stony mound. In a sad twist of fortune the British General Baden Powell set out to reinforce Carrington's column, but as he approached the Elands River outpost the sound of fading gunfire brought him to the conclusion that the Australian and Rhodesian colonials defending the stockpile of supplies were fighting a lost battle.

He turned back in the belief that no British unit could possibly withstand the Boer artillery and superior numbers of enemy soldiers besieging the outpost. His decision left the defenders on their own, with no hope of assistance.

The Elands River commander, Lieutenant Colonel Hore, was faced with two options: to fight to the last man and die; or surrender to General De la Rey. Five days later the erroneous news was cabled to the world that the defenders of the besieged outpost had surrendered.

As Fenella Macintosh read the news in the *Sydney Morning Herald*, she paled and her hands shook. Matthew's last letter had stated that he had been sent to guard the crossings at some place called Elands River.

TWENTY-SEVEN

From Kate Tracy's verandah, the young woman watched the sun set over the bush west of Townsville. Her long dark hair coiled into a pile on her head under a fashionable straw hat, Sarah James displayed an exotic new beauty in an ancient land. In her early thirties, part Irish and part Darambal, her marriage to the former officer of the Queensland Native Mounted Police had produced five equally beautiful children. Gordon James now worked as one of Kate Tracy's depot managers in Rockhampton and the lifelong love Sarah and Gordon had for each other had transcended even the awesome power of the avenging spirits of the Nerambura ancients.

Although baptised a Catholic, Sarah had always been haunted by a spirituality much older than Christianity. Her inexplicably deeper feelings for the world around her could not be explained by her knowledge of the catechism, drummed into her by the good nuns when she was at school. A dream was never just a dream. It was an echo of her Darambal blood. And it was a dream that had brought her north on a coastal steamer from her husband and children in Rockhampton to meet with her Aunt Kate.

Sarah gazed across the bush at the sinking sun and felt its warm spirit give her temporary solace. Her fixed attention on the horizon, which glowed from end to end with its orange and mauve mantle, was distracted by the clatter of a horse-drawn gig along the track that led up to the sprawling timber house. Kate's return from her office in town would not this time bring the joyous reunion that normally marked their meetings. The deeply troubled expression on Sarah's face, and the haunted look behind her dark eyes, gave words to her uncharacteristic silence.

'You have seen him,' Kate said as she embraced the niece who was more like a daughter to her. 'He has come to you.'

Sarah did not need to question her aunt; she too had the ability to see into that world beyond the understanding of men.

'The old Nerambura man of the cave,' Kate continued. 'The same old man who came to me so many years ago with feathers and paint daubed to his body to tell me things I still do not understand.'

Sarah held her aunt. 'His name is Kondola,' she whispered. 'And he came to me six nights ago. First as an eagle, then he turned into a man. I knew then that I must come to you because only you would understand.'

'It is death,' Kate said with a sobbing sigh. 'He has come to tell us that it is not all over. That the spirits of your

256

mother's people are not at peace even after forty years. I know, because he has also come to me.'

'But he will not say who is to die, Aunt Kate. Or even why.'

Kate drew away from Sarah and slumped onto the cane chair where she had so often sat in the evenings, enjoying the cool peace that the setting of the sun brought to the tropics. Kate instinctively glanced at the chair where Matthew had so often sat in her company on those happy occasions. She could not bring herself to even consider that the curse had fallen on her only child. Child? He was thousands of miles away fighting in a war. Her nephew's letter had arrived a fortnight earlier, and since then she had cabled frantic telegrams to Victoria Barracks in Sydney to ascertain her son's situation. The return telegrams had assured her that they would look into his enlistment and take steps to have him returned to Australia.

And then she had received a letter from Matthew. He had written begging her forgiveness for any pain that he may have caused her by running away to join up. But he had also clearly expressed his burning desire to see action at any cost. As if to reassure his mother, he wrote sorrowfully of his being sent to some supply depot at an outpost on the Elands River. He had hoped for detachment to one of the fighting columns pursuing the Boer commandos on the *veldt* but had been posted to a location well behind the front lines. But the letter had arrived two days after the newspapers heralded the news of the terrible battle and subsequent annihilation of the surrendering colonial defenders at the Elands River outpost. Kate had prayed that her son might have been taken a prisoner rather than killed or wounded in the fighting. But the old warrior Kondola had come to her the same night that she had read her son's letter and told her that a death was close. And now her niece stood on the verandah grim faced, confirming that which she would not admit to even herself.

Despite what had been reported in the press, the Australians and Rhodesians defending the isolated outpost at Elands River had not surrendered. The besieging Boers had been reinforced and their numbers now swelled to around three thousand experienced fighters under the command of the brilliant guerilla commander, De la Rey.

On the second day of the siege, the Boers had moved their artillery guns to within two thousand yards of the fortified mound but the deadly accuracy of the defenders' rifle fire had driven them back.

Lieutenant Annat, a Queenslander, had led a patrol of twenty-five men against one of the Boer pompom gun emplacements. They had crawled through the long grass to within two hundred yards of the gun and its crew and opened up with rifle fire. The Boer crew were forced back and only kept their gun when a Boer fighter crawled forward to attach a rope so it could be retrieved.

Later in the siege, the brave lieutenant was killed when an incoming, twelve-pounder artillery shell exploded at his feet. Draped with a Union Jack, his men carried his shattered body to a burial site just outside the defences and buried him at midnight.

After long, exasperating days attempting to crush the Australian and Rhodesian defence, the gallant Boer general sent one of his officers under a flag of truce to offer the stubborn defenders generous terms of surrender. But the British commander of the colonials declined, stating that his men would cut his throat if he accepted. As hopeless as the situation appeared, the defenders had chosen certain death to a man rather than give up the tiny hill. No relief was in sight and the world had accepted that no force, outnumbered and outgunned as Colonel Hore's colonial force was, could withstand the superiority of the battle-experienced Boer commandos.

Under cover of night, Trooper Matthew Duffy was sent with a reinforcement party of New South Welshmen to a small *kopje* south of the main defence. The outpost was commanded by Captain Butters, a Rhodesian veteran of the Matabele Wars, and there Matthew sheltered in a trench. When the sun rose, Matthew experienced a day of screaming and whistling Boer artillery shells pounding the small *kopje* as the Boer general turned his attention to neutralising the outpost which guarded the water supply for the defenders.

Matthew had aged. The shine of his youthful eyes was gone and they were now dull and haunted. It was only a matter of time before one of the exploding shells claimed his body and smashed his flesh into a pulp of bloody meat, or a sniper's bullet shattered his head and forever put out the faint light that remained behind the haunted eyes. He had lived with an unrelenting fear of death for over a week: the petrifying distinctive whistling of the incoming shells followed by the concussive blast of the explosions renting the earth around him seemed to tear through his body to his soul. The constant sound of the giant doors to hell slamming caused him to huddle in the earth at the bottom of his trench shivering uncontrollably. He did not have the option to say he had enough.

Matthew was trapped in hell and it was only a matter of time before the devil came for him. He was only fifteen but felt as if he had lived for fifty years.

Just on dusk, when the bombardment lifted, the Boers came in waves against the southern outpost. Matthew felt a strange relief to see his enemy coming forward. Now he had a chance to hit back. He leant against the packed low wall alongside eighty other colonials with their rifles tucked into their shoulders, and calmly adjusted his rifle sights to fifty yards as Captain Butters' cool orders passed down the line. And at fifty yards Matthew could hear the Boer commanders bellowing orders to their men as they struggled on. Matthew selected a target: a burgher who, Matthew noticed, was barefooted and wearing little more than rags. Matthew wondered whether, if the Boer killed him, he would take his boots. But he figured they would be too small for the Dutchman.

'Fire!'

The order was given and Matthew squeezed the trigger. The Dutchman pitched forward and the single Maxim of the defenders opened up to rake the advancing lines. The well-aimed volleys tore holes in the ranks of the advancing enemy, adding to the carnage on the slope.

Matthew fired rapidly, working the bolt on his rifle without conscious thought. He paused only to reload the empty magazine as he crouched below the wall, before resuming his position at the breastworks to pour fire into the rapidly thinning ranks of the attacking Boers. He was hardly aware that the enemy was retreating down the hill when the order came to cease fire. He slumped to the bottom of the trench with his back against the wall and placed his rifle between his knees. The barrel was too hot to touch and Matthew's ears rang painfully. He felt his body trembling and his hands shook so badly that he doubted he could reload his magazine.

The next day the Boers came again.

But this time they used the old Matabele ruse of driving

sheep and goats before them in an attempt to fool the defenders. It did not work. Captain Butters knew the trick and once again Matthew worked the bolt of his rifle as he poured rounds into both the flock of animals and the ranks of enemy. And, once again, the defenders of Captain Butters' tiny knoll held out against overwhelming odds.

The siege of Elands River was entering its second week but all that meant for young Matthew was that he was still alive to kill more Dutchmen. He had changed in ways that would never allow him to go back to his youth. Nor would he ever again be completely at ease with those who had not known the savage fury of battle. In the few moments of snatched sleep between guard duty and standing to at the breastworks, fevered and fitful dreams echoed with screams. Sometimes the screams woke him and a hand on his shoulder – and a gentle, gruff word – told him that the screams were his. At those times he would shake off the trembling and try to think about a beauty that lay beyond the shattered land around him. He would withdraw into a place where he was once again sitting on the verandah at his mother's Townsville house enjoying a sunset. Or he would remember the gentle touch of the beautiful Fenella Macintosh, the feeling of her hand in his as they walked side by side up the flower-strewn path from the harbour's edge to her home. If he tried hard enough, Matthew could smell her sweet perfume amongst the acrid stench of cordite and lyddite.

TWENTY-EIGHT

Swinging himself into the saddle, Nerambura Duffy waved back to the wagon. Karl and Helen returned the gesture while young Alexander, holding one hand over his eyes against the glare of the rising sun over the red plains also waved.

Nerambura had informed Michael and the others over the campfire the previous evening that he would bypass Cloncurry to ride north into the Godkin Range. Michael had not questioned why he had made his decision to ride on in search of Wallarie; he had long accepted that the young man might have a good idea where he might find the wily old warrior.

When Nerambura was a shimmering silhouette on the horizon of the termite nest plain, Michael gazed west. The strange, rugged outcrops of ancient rocks jutted into the azure sky. 'The 'curry's just west of here,' he said. 'According to my reckoning, we should reach it in a few hours.' He folded a map and placed it inside his shirt.

Just after noon they reached the tiny township that lay among the stony outcrops. As unimpressive as it was, the town of timber and corrugated iron was a vital oasis on the vast expanse of brigalow plains. It provided the services that made life bearable for parched and weary travellers on the frontier.

The first service that the Irishman sought was a hotel to provide Helen and her husband with the more refined pleasures of civilisation: a hot bath, clean sheets on a soft bed, and a meal not cooked in the ashes of a campfire. Michael had been prepared to press on but he had sensed that a night in town would be a blessing for the von Fellmanns. They were not bush people, although they were trying hard to be so.

The wagon stopped in front of a low-set building with a wide verandah at the front. A motley crew of bearded stockmen and scrawny dogs sprawled, eyeing the newcomers, especially Helen, with some interest. The pastor helped Helen down from the wagon and Michael hitched his horse to a rail in front of a hotel.

'Wait here,' Michael said. 'I'll go and see if they have any rooms for us.'

Michael was able to secure a room for von Fellmann and his wife and a couple of beds on the verandah at the rear of the hotel for himself and young Alex. But when he returned to inform his small party of his success he walked into trouble. A young, partially inebriated stockman was facing down the pastor in the dusty street. Helen and Alex stood ashen faced, watching the confrontation unfold.

'A bloody sausage eater!' the tough-looking stockman spat as the pastor attempted to step back, hands raised to ward off the belligerent man.

'What's the trouble here?' Michael asked mildly with a faint smile on his face, stepping between the two unequally matched men.

The stockman turned on Michael. 'You're the fella who rode in with these German bastards,' he snarled as he sized up Michael. 'You on the side of these bastards giving aid to the bloody Dutchmen over in South Africa against our mates?'

'On the first count, you are right,' Michael said calmly. 'I rode in with the pastor and his wife. But on the second, I think we need clarification, boyo.'

'What's this clarification yer talkin' about?' the stockman asked suspiciously as he glanced at his mates on the verandah who were watching with some amusement.

'What I mean by clarification is this,' Michael replied as he swung a left hook into the young stockman's stomach. The stockman gasped and fell to his knees with his eyes bulging. He gripped his stomach, desperately seeking air. The blow that had connected was harder than that from any horse that had ever kicked him. A low gasp of surprise rose from those who watched. 'That's what clarification means.'

'Get up and give 'im a thrashin', Jacko,' a voice called angrily from the verandah. 'Don't let the old bastard do yer. It was a lucky punch.'

The young stockman's face was a mask of rage as he caught his breath and glowered up at the man standing over him with a faint smile on his face. Taking a breath, the stockman lurched to his feet and with a roar swung at Michael who easily parried the wildly thrown punch, stepping inside to deliver a barrage of well-aimed punches to the man's face and midriff. Michael was once again the champion bare knuckle fighter of Redfern's backstreets. His

264

skills had been used many times in his violent life. Although the younger man stood as tall as Michael, and was as broad in the shoulders, he was no match for years of accumulated experience.

The smile was gone from Michael's face now as he waded into the stockman who reeled under the systematically delivered blows. The spectators watched with breathless awe as Michael turned the face of the district's champion brawler into a bloody mess. With a broken nose and swollen eyes, all the stockman could do was retreat. He desperately attempted to block the punches that came with blurring speed. Finally, he crashed on the verandah at the feet of his mates, who stepped back to avoid spilling their beers.

Michael paused with his fists half raised to see if the young stockman was foolish enough to attempt to rise. He did not, but lay on the verandah, doubled up in his pain.

'Anyone else here need clarification?' Michael asked, glaring around at the faces of the bearded spectators. 'Anyone here think I was just lucky?'

'Not us, mate,' one of the men mumbled, still awed by the stranger's skill with his fists. 'Haven't seen anything like that around here for a long time.' Michael smiled and unexpectedly held out his hand to the young man on the verandah. 'You okay, young fella?' he inquired gently.

The young man spat a glob of blood from where one of his few remaining teeth had been, and tried to smile. 'Bloody tooth was giving me trouble anyway,' he said as he accepted the hand of friendship. 'For an old man you hit like a bloody kicking horse. Maybe even harder.'

'I'll shout you and your mates to a round in the hotel and we will forget what happened here.'

The stockman frowned as he was helped to his feet and rubbed his jaw.

'Yer a strange one, mate,' he said. 'But yer all right. I think I'll buy you a beer. Yer the first bloke who ever put me down around here.' The tension was gone and he slapped Michael on the back. 'Me name's Jacko, an' these are me mates.'

Helen was still transfixed by the sudden unleashing of violence that had occurred. One second two men appeared to be intent on killing each other and the next they were the best of friends, slapping each other on the back. She shifted her gaze to Michael's face, unmarked by the fight, and again thought her Aunt Penelope may have been right. Fighter, painter, poet – and lover. To date she had only seen a gentle, sensitive man old enough to be her father, but she remembered how he had in fact been her mother's lover and was the father of her half-brother, Patrick Duffy. Now she found herself wondering at his skills as a lover and felt guilt surge through her body. He was extremely dangerous to women, she reminded herself, despite his age. But he was also a man who had seen much violence in his life. Not all his scars, she suspected, were physical.

Michael turned from the verandah with a smile and, as if reading her thoughts, winked. 'You will find a nice room waiting for you inside. And I wouldn't mind if you looked after young Alex for me while I go and have a drink with the boys.'

Helen nodded, speechless.

The word quickly spread around the little frontier town of Jacko's defeat at the fists of the one-eyed stranger. And the word spread to the publican's wife, a pretty woman in her mid-forties with flaming red hair and milky pale skin. Between rounds in the busy afternoon swill of the hotel's public bar, she was able to engage the stranger in light conversation. She could not help being entranced by his easygoing charm and slow smile. Here was a gentleman, rare in the rough back country of Queensland.

Michael was not slow to see the signs. The publican's wife was more than just interested in him as another patron of the hotel. There was something in her eyes and the way her hand lingered on his when she served him a tot of rum. It was only a matter of waiting for the cloak of night to arrive to see if he would taste more than the alcohol the hotel had to offer.

While his wife took Alex for a walk to see the few shops in the town, Karl decided to remain in the tiny hotel room to make notes on his meeting with the Aborigines he had encountered east of Cloncurry. Helen did not mind and Alex proved to be good company, although his recounting the way Mr O'Flynn had beaten the younger stockman did become repetitive.

'He was so fast, Aunt Helen, and when he hit the other man . . . I wonder if Mr O'Flynn could teach me to fight like that?'

She smiled and tolerated his excited prattle. 'Fighting is not good, Alexander,' she replied gently. 'It is not God's way.'

'Yes, but if Mr O'Flynn had not hit the other man then he would have hurt the pastor. And he might have hurt you and me.'

'I'm sure your Uncle Karl would have talked the man out of hurting us. Your uncle is a very learned man of books and knows many things.'

'But he does not know how to fight like Mr O'Flynn,' the boy replied somewhat tactlessly as he walked beside his aunt along the dusty street. 'Sometimes books are no good out here.'

Helen had to agree with the boy's observations. This was a strange and hostile land where values were measured according to a tough, dogged spirit of survival – not the works of philosophers writing from the comfort of civilisation. As she walked she was hardly aware of the dusty streets and the frontier town's shops. Her thoughts were in turmoil as she fought her rising feelings. Although she was desperately attempting to quash her desire for Michael, she could not help wondering what it would be like to just once in her life feel his body become part of hers.

When Helen and Alex finally returned to the hotel mid-afternoon, Michael Duffy was leading the bar in a round of Irish songs. Helen went to her room where she found her husband busy at his notes. She sat on the bed and watched him scribbling in his journal, feeling a desperate need for physical release. But she knew her pious husband was immune from such carnal cravings so she lay back on the bed and allowed him to continue with his work. She soon fell asleep, waking only when it was time to join him and the others for a meal in the hotel's dining room.

TWENTY-NINE

Michael was not at dinner and nor was he still drinking in the public bar. Helen did not really know why she should be concerned except that she and Karl needed him to guide them into the Godkin Ranges north of Cloncurry the next day. She was annoyed that he should disappear for the evening. He would be of no use if he turned up drunk or hungover.

She had little appetite for the plate of badly cooked steak on the cracked china plate and complained peevishly to the young girl who served the meal. But, a growing boy with a big appetite, Alex did not mind the overcooked meat and mushy vegetables. The journey was turning his puppy fat into muscle and his fair skin was now tanned. He bore little resemblance to the pallid, timid boy who lived overlooking Sydney's magnificent harbour.

Karl was preoccupied but still found the stifling heat had

taken much of his appetite. He would have preferred a plate of venison accompanied by a goblet of crisp, chilled Rhine wine, but such luxuries were things of his father's home in Prussia. The best he could get here was a dirty tumbler of lukewarm gin. He glanced up at his wife when she snapped at the waitress, a girl of barely fourteen wearing a grubby dress that looked as if it had not been changed in many dinner sittings. 'Hush, my wife,' he said gently in German. 'The young lady is not the cook of this meal before us.'

The girl stood aside and curled her lip with contempt for the churlish foreigners.

'Where is your cook?' Helen asked angrily. 'I would like to send this back to the kitchen.'

'Dunno,' the girl answered with a sneer. 'Probably some-where with that big Irishman, for all I know. Old Arthur's doin' the cookin.'

Helen stared at the girl in bewilderment. 'With the cook!'

'Yeah, probably. She's 'ad her eye on him all arvo. Just hope Mr Crofton don't find out or 'e will give her a real thrashin'. 'E's the publican.'

'But you know,' Helen argued. 'Why should the innkeeper not also know?'

The girl gave Helen a curious look.

''E an' his missus don' get on. Don't think 'e cares so long as she keeps to 'erself what she does,' the brazen waitress replied with an understanding far beyond her tender years.

Helen dropped her line of inquiry and pushed her plate aside.

The tinned peaches that followed the main course proved to be somewhat more appetising. Karl commented that they should stock up on tinned fruit from the local store before they set out on the next leg of their search but

Helen paid him little heed. Her thoughts were focused on Michael's betrayal. Betrayal of what? The question echoed in her mind as they left the dining room and headed for their beds, the drunken merriment of the raucous frontiersmen carrying with them to their stuffy room.

Alexander found his stretcher on the verandah and was soon being entertained by an old prospector who regaled the young boy with stories of his life. Commanche Jack had an American accent and a face that bore the scars of his escapades. Alex listened, enthralled by Jack's adventures fighting Indians on the American frontier.

When Alex told him that he was travelling to the Godkin Ranges the next day the old man sighed. 'Used to be big blackfellas up there a few years ago,' he said, scratching at the sweat under his grey beard. 'Big warriors called Kalka-doon, amongst the finest and bravest of the fightin' men I ever fought. That was back in '84 when we trapped 'em on a hill, but theys wouldn't surrender an' died to a man. Wes just kept shootin' until theys was no more standin' up to fight anymore. All gone now an' that's the pity of it.' He bowed his head as if remembering another time in his life. 'You remember old Commanche Jack, young fella, when you go ridin' in the Godkins. Remember those big heathens who stood and died like real men out there.'

Alex nodded. The gruff old American told stories the likes of which he had only read about back home, so far from this noisy verandah. How could he forget Commanche Jack? Before Alex knew it, he was dozing.

Sleep did not come so easily to Helen. She lay beside her husband in the big, sagging double bed. The noise from the bar continued, accentuated by the tinkling crash of a glass. This was followed by the heightened voices of men locked in an argument, which in turn gave way to the sounds of a scuffle and the voices of men swearing as they slugged it out in a fight. Suddenly she missed the serenity of the nights spent on the plains by a campfire listening to the soft sounds of the bush, the swish of birds in flight or the sweet song of a nearby creek, broken occasionally by the splash of a big fish rising from the water. Helen sat up and felt the perspiration run in rivulets between her breasts.

'You cannot sleep?' Karl asked. 'It is very hot.'

'No, I cannot sleep, Karl,' she answered, placing her feet on the wooden floor and proceeding to gather her dress from a sideboard. 'I think I shall go for a short walk. Perhaps that will help tire me.'

Her husband cast a concerned look in the semi-darkness of the room. A light from the hallway filtered under the door and from the fanlight above it. 'Do you think that is wise at this time of night? The men around here are rough and unpredictable.'

Helen touched her husband's face with her long fingers. 'They may be rough and unpredictable,' she said gently, 'but I do not fear them as much as I fear not being able to sleep.'

Karl watched her dress. He sensed that she had things on her mind. Maybe it would be better if she went for a short walk.

Helen made her way down the hall and out through the back door of the hotel where she found herself in the backyard, bordered by the horse stables. She did not really have a clue where she would go but knew she had to get away from the confines of the hotel room. Or was it that she had to get away from Karl? She had never really questioned their marriage until she had set out on this journey across Queensland's vast plains. She had always accepted her husband as an intelligent, kind and sensible man who had professed his need for her. She had also come to accept that

272

they could not have children, though it was never certain which one of them was barren. Their lives had settled into a comfortable routine in Germany and the most exciting thing Karl had ever suggested was this: to travel to the country of her birth and undertake missionary work and his academic studies of Aboriginal people. She had agreed to his dream as the thought of a change in their lives promised something. But what? Nothing had really changed in her life, Helen reflected. Her gentle, educated husband had simply been transplanted in terms of geography alone.

Helen crossed the yard with the intention of strolling out into the street to take in the night air, away from the smell of horses, when she suddenly froze at the sound that came from the stables. There was no mistaking Michael's deep voice. Nor was there any mistake in comprehending what was occurring. Helen felt her face flush at the unmistakable sounds of a woman in ecstasy. The young girl had been right!

Helen's curiosity was overwhelming. Cautiously she made her way across the yard and keeping to the shadows she slipped through the open door of the stables. She sank back against the wall, her eyes sweeping the darkness until she saw movement. She felt her breath coming in small gasps as if she were suffocating. Even in the dark she was aware that the undulating shape was that of a naked woman straddled across a man lying back against a pile of horse rugs. The woman's long hair flowed over her shoulders and down her naked back. Michael's hands were on her breasts as she moved her hips slowly and rhythmically, moaning softly in her pleasure. Helen could not tear herself away. So now she was witnessing the pleasure the Irishman could bring to a woman in ways that did not bide by God's laws. As her eyes adjusted to the darkness, Helen became aware of Michael staring back at her.

In guilty terror, Helen spun on her heel and ran from the stables out onto the dark street. Slumping finally in a vacant yard across from the hotel, she found herself weeping uncontrollably. She huddled on the dry earth, staring up at the brilliance of the star-studded sky until she felt she was suitably in control of her emotions. Then she stood, brushed herself down, and walked unsteadily back to the yard. Michael was sitting on the step of the hotel's back verandah smoking. Beside him was a bottle of cheap rum. Helen felt her heart pounding in panic. He was barring the way to her room. She hesitated for just a moment before walking towards him.

'Good evening, Helen,' Michael said softly as he took a long puff on his cigar. 'I was worried that what you saw might upset you.'

'Why should it, Mr Duffy?' Helen asked defiantly. 'I saw only animals in their natural state.'

Michael chuckled softly and took a swig from the bottle.

'I've been called worse,' Michael said with a sigh. 'But not by a woman as pretty as you.'

'I expect you have been called many things worse. Murderer, mercenary, cad.'

'Cad, now there's a word I wasn't expecting,' Michael replied as he stared up at her with a smile. 'But it is pretty mild compared to murderer.'

'Well, you are, aren't you?' Helen spat contemptuously.

Michael looked away for a moment, avoiding her angry stare. 'It depends whose side you were on when I did the killing,' he replied with an edge of pain and bitterness in his voice. 'To the British, I was a necessity. Albeit one that they kept quiet about. To Mr Abe Lincoln I was a hero. He even gave me a medal to show how he valued my services to the Union way back then. But that was before you were born

274

anyway, so I suppose it doesn't count. And I should not forget your own family, Helen. To your grandmother, Lady Macintosh, my services a quarter of a century ago up along the Palmer River settled a matter of vengeance for your Uncle David's death.'

Helen sensed the pain in his reflections and felt guilty for her accusing words. 'I'm sorry,' she said quietly. 'I don't know why I said those things to you. I suppose it's just that you once loved my mother, and that seeing you in the stables with that woman felt like a betrayal to her memory.'

'To her memory,' Michael said, staring into her eyes, 'or to your feelings? But you have nothing to fear from me,' he continued. 'You are the daughter of a woman I once loved very much.' He took a long swig from the bottle and rose to his feet. Helen felt his hand touch her cheek and brush back a wisp of her hair from her face. 'God knows that I want you more than anything else on earth right now,' he said in a tight breath.

Tender feelings mixed with yearning welled up in Helen. She placed her hand over his and pressed it into her skin, as if attempting to absorb his very soul.

'If only we had met in another lifetime, Mr Duffy,' Helen said with a strangled sob. 'If only God had granted us another life to live away from your past and my present. Perhaps then, everything would have been different.'

Dropping his hand abruptly, Helen brushed past Michael to the room she shared with her husband.

Michael drained the bottle before staggering to his bed on the verandah. He could not change the past. In the morning the sun would once again rise over the plains. He was to yet meet with the mystical old warrior who held the answers to so many of the terrible events that had haunted the two families for so many years. He had a job to do.

THIRTY

Under cover of the bitterly cold night, Captain Butters sent the wounded back to the main defensive position with the water cart detail. Among them was Trooper Matthew Duffy. He was able to walk. The piece of jagged shrapnel had ripped through the fleshy part of his side and, other than an ugly open wound, had not damaged any vital organs.

Matthew trudged slowly with his rifle slung over his shoulder. The small column of soldiers was winding its way north towards the once insignificant rocky mound that was now as important to each of them as any geographical feature on earth. Matthew reflected on how lucky he was to be alive, despite his wound. Another few inches to one side and the shrapnel might have disembowelled him. He had lost a lot of blood, as the soaked wad of bandages strapped to his side testified. But it had all happened so haphazardly that Matthew hardly remembered the explosion.

One minute he had been lying face down behind the sanger of rocks as the shells came raining down and the next moment he felt as if he had been kicked in the side by a giant wearing a red hot boot. Matthew did not remember screaming but he must have. A fellow soldier had leapt to hold him down as he had attempted to stand. To do so would have meant certain death as the deadly sprays of shrapnel sought out anything alive above ground level.

When the bleeding was stemmed Matthew had lain on his back and watched a hawk circling above the battlefield in the blue sky. He had wished that he was that hawk and could fly from this terrible place of carnage. The little water that could be spared was given to him and although the pain was excruciating, he slipped into a blissful state of unconsciousness until the night came when he was ordered to join the others making their way back to the field hospital.

As Matthew and the rest of the walking wounded passed through the picquets manning the outer trenches, they were assailed by the stench of decomposition. Dead horses, mules and oxen littered the slopes from the first day of the siege. The unpleasant stink of their own unwashed bodies was hardly noticeable to the soldiers anymore.

At the hospital, a bullet riddled wagon behind walls of tinned meat and bags of flour, the doctor examined Matthew's wound and changed the dressing. At his own insistence Matthew was given permission to man the defences. The doctor, however, was concerned about infection and gave the young soldier strict orders to report each day to have the dressing changed.

Matthew groped his way through the jumble of trenches and flour bag defences until he found the Queenslanders' section. Whispered directions from shadowy shapes in the dark led Matthew to the end of the trench where he found

Saul Rosenblum dozing with his back against the wall. Saul snapped out of his troubled sleep when he heard Matthew's voice call to him.

'Yer still alive,' Saul answered with obvious relief. 'I heard you Whalers took on the Dutchmen over on Captain Butters' hill a couple of days ago and . . . ' He ceased speaking once Matthew was close enough for him to see him in the dark. 'You been hit. How bad is it?'

'Not bad,' Matthew answered as he eased himself down into the trench. 'A bit of shrap in the side but it went clean through and left me with only a bit of a cut.'

'Looks like more than a bit of a cut to me,' Saul said peering at the wad of dressings. 'Looks like the shrap left a bloody big hole in you.'

'I'll live,' Matthew replied with a nonchalant shrug. 'How have things been in this part of the world?'

'Same old thing every day. The Dutchmen shell us. And when they are not shelling us their bloody snipers make life hell. Some of the night raiding parties have had a bit of luck though. A few of the boys brought back some fresh-baked bread they got from a farmhouse over there,' Saul said indicating with his rifle out into the dark. 'Got the bloody sniper who was using the farmhouse too.'

'I heard a rumour that one of the boys went out on his own accord, a couple of nights ago, and not only settled a matter with a sniper but also found fifty sovereigns in his pockets.'

Saul flashed a grimy unshaven grin at the young man. 'Yeah. That's true. Lucky bastard. Not a bad effort for a night's work in any job. Sure beats wrestling all day under a hot sun with some cranky scrub bull back home.'

'I suppose you could say the army is teaching us a lot of useful things,' Matthew said with a grin. 'Except civilians would hang us if we did the same back home.'

Saul laughed softly. He has shaped up to be a bloody good soldier, he thought, with admiration for the way Matthew was handling himself under fire. A bond had formed between the two men that would never be broken in their lives. Age and social differences between them meant nothing anymore. Under their unwashed skins and rags for uniforms they were brothers.

A bullet cracked close by. Instinctively, both men flinched and Matthew felt the tic at the corner of his eye return. His nerves were stretched to breaking point.

'There's a bloody Dutchman about eight hundred yards in front of our positions who works us over every day,' Saul said in a grim voice. 'He's a cunning bastard, uses the long grass as cover. I reckon he has dug a series of shallow hides in the night and is able to move from one to another on his belly whenever we think we've got his position fixed after he fires. If he is still there in the morning, I'm going out after him tomorrow night. The bastard is starting to get to me.'

Matthew frowned. 'Sounds like you aren't looking for permission to go out.'

'I wouldn't get it if I asked,' Saul growled. 'But I'm going anyway. He got Frank just before last light so I intend to even the score.'

Matthew knew that he would say nothing, even if he did not agree with his friend's plan to take on the sniper. Loyalty was everything under the present conditions.

'I'll go with you.'

'Not with that wound,' Saul retorted. 'Your job is to cover for me if questions get asked.'

'I'll do that,' Matthew said. 'Just be bloody careful.'

'And don't start swearing, young Matthew,' Saul remonstrated with a grin. 'Yer not old enough yet to start swearing.'

'When am I old enough to start swearing?'

'When yer old enough to start shavin'.'

Both men laughed at the idiocy of the situation. They were into the second week of the siege and the Boers had reinforced their numbers, pinning the colonial defenders on all sides. Although the English military command had written them off as either captured or killed, the stubborn Australian and Rhodesian troops were too proud to admit defeat. At home, bushfire, drought and flood could not crush their spirits or drive them from the land. The Boer were just another force to overcome. They still had their rifles and when the bullets ran out they had their bayonets – so long as the tattered British Union Jack fluttered defiantly over the mound.

Saul waited until near midnight before leaving the trench. With his rifle cradled in his arms, he crawled slowly on his belly through the long dry tussocks of grass until he was far enough out from his own position that the sounds of the men in the defences were muffled. The night was bitterly cold and dark clouds scudded across the night sky, threatening a deluge of cold lashing rain before dawn. For once Saul would welcome the rain to cover his movements.

He paused after what he calculated was around five hundred yards distance and was aware that he could hear the guttural voices of Boer picquets manning posts on the forward edge of their lines. He listened carefully to pinpoint their locations. He would have to avoid them at all costs if he were to achieve his aim of neutralising the sniper.

When Saul was satisfied he had a clear path he continued to creep forward. The sound that he had hoped to hear came to him: the soft snoring of a man totally oblivious to the danger he was in. Saul inched further.

The Boer sniper lay asleep on his back in a shallow trench barely a foot deep and similar to the other such trenches Saul had discovered as he had moved forward. The sleeping man's weapon lay beside him and Saul recognised the clean lines of a Mannlicher hunting rifle, no doubt a donation from the Imperial German government to aid in killing British soldiers.

Very carefully, Saul slid his bayonet from its scabbard and crawled the last inches with his hand wrapped around the wooden handle. As he watched the man's face, Saul found himself wondering if he had a wife and family. Momentarily, he hesitated, realising that his hands were shaking. He forced the thoughts from his mind and plunged the blade into the man's chest with his right hand, groping for the man's mouth with his left. The knife hit the cartilage between the ribs in the centre of the chest but Saul used his wiry strength to force it through until it came out the man's back. The body under him arched and kicked as the dying man attempted to free himself from the agonising pain that had come to his dreams. He thrashed about with Saul's weight holding him down until he suddenly went limp and a soft sigh escaped from between Saul's fingers.

With great difficulty the Queensland soldier removed the bayonet and wiped it on the grass beside the trench. He could feel the stickiness of the other man's blood on the front of his tattered shirt, its warm and pungent scent clogging Saul's nose. Saul felt the bile in his stomach rise at what he had done to a fellow human but reminded himself that the dead sniper had killed his mates. After a few moments, Saul was surprised to feel nothing for the man he had just killed and quickly searched through the man's pockets. He found nothing of value.

Saul removed the sniper's rifle bolt and rendered it useless. From a water bottle beside the dead man he took a long swig, keeping his own bottle full. Water was as precious as bullets. Satisfied that he had completed his task, the Queensland trooper began to crawl back to his own lines.

About a hundred yards further on a new course, Saul heard a soft moaning. He paused and recognised that the sounds uttered in Afrikaans were agonised pleas for water. Saul's first instinct was to disregard the wounded man, but the voice sounded very young and Saul was drawn to a slight Boer, barely older than Matthew. The boy had been shot through the chest and had been a long time left out on the *veldt*. Saul wondered how the boy had survived so long with such a mortal wound. The floppy hat beside him looked too big for him, as did the trousers and shirt he wore. They were obviously the clothes of a man older than himself but all that had been available to provide the young boy with a uniform. Saul knelt beside the dying boy who gazed up at him through eyes already dimmed with impending death.

'Here, young fella. Try and sip this,' Saul said gently as he dribbled water from his canteen into the boy's mouth. 'Just take sips.'

The boy tried to focus on the softly spoken angel who had come to him on the battlefield but he did not understand the language of angels and began to cry. Between his tears, the words came as a desperate plea and Saul realised that he was begging for his mother. The boy gripped Saul's hand as if attempting to stave off the ominous shadows all around him.

Saul felt uneasy. He was deep inside the Boer controlled territory and knew that he should leave the boy to die alone and get back to the safety of his own lines before the sun rose. But the boy continued to weep and babble in Afrikaans, and the little of the language Saul had picked up on the campaign made him realise that the boy was talking about his family.

As a mother would, Saul cradled the dying boy's head in his lap and stroked the beardless face with gentle soothing sounds. Soon Saul found himself crying silently, tears splashing down his unshaven, dirty face. Saul cried for his own mother, long buried under the old pepper tree she had planted as a sapling on the Jerusalem property, and he cried for the wasted lives killed in a war he no longer believed in. Saul cried for the loss of the beautiful young Dutch girl barely older than the boy cradled in his arms. It was all so pointless.

Just before the sun rose the boy died peacefully. And then the Boers took Saul prisoner. They were not rough with him when they realised what the Queenslander had done for the young soldier they had been searching for in the dark. But they took Saul's boots anyway.

THIRTY-ONE

Under the August sun of central-west Queensland, an eagle soared high in the pale blue sky. Below it an open wagon trundled slowly along a rough bush track. Ahead of the wagon were two horses upon which rode a man and a young boy. They were riding north and followed a low line of hills where once the feared Kalkadoon warriors had lived and died. Winding through the range was a river named after the famed German explorer Leichhardt who had disappeared somewhere in Queensland's interior with his expedition.

Michael Duffy scanned the western horizon which was dominated by the low hills with their sparse covering of scrubby trees. Satisfied that he had brought them to the point where they should head west, he turned in the saddle to call back to the wagon.

'We go that way towards the hills,' he said. 'That will put us on the river before nightfall to make camp.'

Karl von Fellmann nodded and pulled down on the reins to turn the wagon.

Michael had a feeling they would find Nerambura Duffy in the hills. If so, it would be along the life-giving river that wound its way through the ancient, eroded landscape.

The rifle butt bit painfully into young Alexander's shoulder. The sound of the shot rolled around the hills with its haunting memories of another time when the guns had spat death into the ranks of the Kalkadoon warriors.

'Squeeze. Let the gun go off without thinking about the recoil,' Michael said as he sat beside Alex. 'Let the rifle become an extension of your mind and body.'

Alex was still smarting from the powerful recoil of the big Winchester repeating rifle.

'It hurts, Mr O'Flynn,' he said in a small voice.

'Not as much as whatever the bullet hits,' Michael chuckled. 'And don't forget to chamber another round as soon as you have fired. That sort of mistake could cost you the second between being alive and being dead.'

Obediently the young boy lowered the lever under the rifle and forced it up, chambering a second round.

'Now do as I have told you and take your time. Don't flinch, and forget everything except what you have in your sights.'

Alex listened carefully for he was convinced the man sitting beside him knew almost everything. So far he had taught him to ride and live in the bush, things he had never dreamed he would learn in his lifetime although he knew his own father had the skills. Mr O'Flynn was tough and understanding like his father, and yet gentle and sensitive like his mother.

'See that small tree on the other side of the waterhole, about fifty yards out? See if you can hit the branch on the left hand side.'

Alex adjusted his posture and levelled the rear and foresights so they lined up. He took a breath and let it release slowly from his lungs. When the breath was gone and his body was perfectly still, he squeezed the trigger. The gun barked and the branch cracked and fell.

'Good,' Michael grunted and took a cigar from his pocket. 'Now prove to me that your shot was not just lucky. Shoot at the point where the limb is hanging.'

The boy fired again but the limb remained dangling from the tree.

'Close,' Michael grunted. 'Your shot was a few inches off. But I think that's enough for now. You can practise later. Maybe you will get us a wallaby for tonight's cooking pot like you got the fish before Cloncurry.'

Alex beamed at the praise and lowered the rifle. 'How many men have you shot, Mr O'Flynn?'

Michael stared across the placid waterhole ringed by stately gum trees. 'Too many,' he said softly. 'Maybe not all bad men either.'

Alex frowned and tried to digest the strange answer. But war was beyond his comprehension except for the wood-block reproductions he had seen of Queen Victoria's gallant soldiers standing bravely against the hordes of savages that they fought in the many colonial wars.

'Do you think Father will . . . '

He hesitated and Michael glanced down at him.

'Yes, Alex. Your father will be home soon. He's a Duffy, and Duffys are bloody hard to kill, believe me.'

'I do, Mr O'Flynn,' Alex answered in a trembling voice. The rifle in his hands and its terrible power had summoned the fears he harboured for his father fighting in a war so far away.

Michael put his hand on the young man's shoulder. 'He is due to return just after Christmas and that is only a few months away. Off you go now, back to the pastor and your aunt, and help them with the camp.'

The boy struggled to his feet and passed the rifle to Michael who remained sitting, watching his grandson walk away from him through the trees until he was out of sight. His thoughts were far away and dwelled on nothing in particular except the beauty of the land that he felt he wanted to capture on canvas.

'I have never seen you appear so much at peace,' Helen's voice said from behind him.

'Places like these are sanctuaries God put aside for the soul,' Michael replied.

'May I invade your sanctuary?' Helen asked, sitting down beside him without waiting for an answer. 'I must confess, I was watching you teach your grandson to shoot.'

'If you had been a lioness hunting, then I might have been dead by now,' Michael said with a slow smile. 'I must be getting too old to be out in the bush.'

'There are no lions in this country. Just a tiger that roams Tasmania.'

'Maybe there is a lioness in this country,' Michael said teasingly. 'And maybe she is sitting beside me now.'

Helen laughed.

'And that lioness has the sweetest of roars,' Michael continued.

'Ah, Michael, your words belie the tough soldier and lion hunter that I know you once were. Your words are like the beautiful strokes of your hand on the canvas.'

Michael turned to face Helen, aware of her gentle touch

on his arm. He could see the same deep, beautiful green eyes of Fiona in the young woman and behind the eyes the same sensual appreciation of life. 'Shouldn't you be with your husband?' Michael asked, as if attempting to remind them both that their meeting alone was not altogether safe.

'Karl has gone exploring up the river. He thinks he might find some traces of the native habitation that was once here. He said he would not be back until sunset.'

Michael continued to gaze into Helen's eyes, noticing that they had grown wide and her lips slightly agape. 'I think we should return to camp,' he said. 'Otherwise I may do something I would regret.'

'You know that I want you,' Helen whispered. 'God knows why I should want you so desperately but I do.'

Michael smiled sadly and touched her face with his hand. 'You are as beautiful as I remember your mother,' he said.

Helen ignored his words and suddenly clung to Michael, her lips seeking his. Michael felt her kiss and the sweet taste of her mouth. She held him with a desperation born of desire but Michael gripped her shoulders, forcing her away from him.

'This is not right,' he said softly and she thought she could see pity in his eyes.

'I don't care about anything except being with you,' Helen said as tears of pain and rejection welled in her eyes. 'We could be together.'

Still holding her shoulders, Michael took a deep breath. 'I am no saint,' he said. 'I have done many things I am not proud of and if you and I went beyond friendship, you would end up hating yourself.'

'Do you not want me?' Helen pleaded. 'Am I not desirable?'

'You are one of the most beautiful women I have ever met,' Michael replied gently. 'But some things can never be.'

288

Helen jerked away and stood back to glare at the Irishman with the pain of rejection in her eyes. She turned and stumbled back to the camp, leaving Michael remaining beside the river, deeply troubled by what had occurred. He should have known better, he cursed himself. He shook his head and walked back to the campsite where Helen sat by the wagon, staring vacantly at the bush. Michael wanted to say or do something to heal her pain but sensed anything he attempted would only aggravate the situation.

THIRTY-TWO

The fire raged along the plains of the Elands River outpost, crackling with long fingers that chased the billowing clouds of smoke and obliterated the afternoon sky. Matthew was unconcerned as he watched. The grass fire had been lit by the Boers in an attempt to burn the defenders off the small hill, but Colonel Hore had anticipated the enemy's tactic and earlier counter-burned the *veldt* to a distance of a hundred yards in front of his lines.

It was the tenth day of the siege and still there was no hope of being relieved. Matthew scratched at his chest and thought fleetingly about a bath. His uniform was in tatters and the wound in his side throbbed and itched. The doctor who changed the dressings each day had frowned when he examined it, fearful of infection. But the soldier was young and his wound was fighting putrefaction.

Saul Rosenblum was still missing after two days, and

questions had been asked. But all the men denied any knowledge of his whereabouts, even though most knew what he had set out to do.

General De la Rey had sent one of his officers under a flag of truce to organise the return of two wounded South Australian prisoners, Lieutenants Collins and Douglas. A Cape cart was organised to go out and bring them back from the Boer lines and when the Boers were questioned during the truce about the missing Queensland soldier they adamantly denied that he was among any prisoners taken.

Finally Saul Rosenblum had his name ticked off as missing in action in the squadron roll book and the matter was closed. For now, all that mattered to the survivors at the beleaguered outpost was that they stay alive just another day. Already they had almost eighty killed or wounded in their ranks and the depletion of men was starting to tell.

Matthew saw the telltale flashes from the big Boer artillery guns ranged against them from ridges either side of the river. He did not have to shout the warning as the bleary eyes of the other defenders also picked up on the muzzle blasts of the big guns. Those in exposed places above ground scuttled for the shelter of the trenches, now reinforced against the exploding rounds.

Matthew lay low and waited with fatalistic patience for the rounds to land. He was surprised when only three shells exploded and a long silence followed. It was as if the Boer gunners were simply going through the motions of letting the defenders know they were still out there. Or was it that the Boers were running out of artillery rounds? But the Mauser fire continued all day, making life miserable for the already physically and mentally exhausted Australian and Rhodesian defenders.

Through a rare stroke of luck, an African messenger,

despatched by General De la Rey to take a message to his fellow commando General De Wet, was captured by a mounted patrol scouting ahead of General Kitchener's advancing column. The British general had been pursuing the wily Boer commander for some weeks and had been unsuccessful in his chase of the highly mobile commando. But the contents of the captured dispatch stunned him more than the frustration of the unsuccessful pursuit. The outpost at Elands River had not been captured or destroyed. In the message, General De la Rey was asking his fellow general to join him in an attempt to finally crush the stubborn colonials.

Acting on this new intelligence, Kitchener did not hesitate. New orders were quickly issued and the weary column changed route to march the fifty miles to the beleaguered garrison at Elands River.

On the twelfth day the defenders rose to fight another day. But no incoming shots were returned in response to their probing volleys of rifle fire. The defenders had fought them to a standstill and when De la Rey learned through his own intelligence sources that the British were sending a large force to relieve the colonials, he chose to withdraw.

When the first of Kitchener's relieving column of twenty-five thousand men rode into the outpost – now resembling a giant garbage dump, littered with smashed cases once containing meat and jam – the defenders cheered.

All except Trooper Matthew Duffy. As the myriad new campfires flickered in the night, Matthew lay among the wounded in a deathly fever. His wound had turned septic and he was suddenly very close to dying.

Amongst the relieving force was a British colonel who was

normally attached to staff duties at headquarters, preferring his lot there to duties in the field. He walked amongst the defenders who scarcely gave him a second look. But if the defenders did not pay him much heed, he did them. He stopped and quietly asked questions about a certain Queensland Bushman by the name of Saul Rosenblum. In his pocket, Colonel Hays Williams carried a piece of paper. It was a warrant duly sworn for the arrest of the colonial soldier on a charge of murder of one British sergeant.

The British colonel was bitterly disappointed when he was informed by the man's commanding officer that Private Rosenblum was officially listed as missing in action. As the Boers had denied taking him prisoner, then his body must be somewhere out on the *veldt*, bloated and rotting under the African sun. But a thorough search of the area did not find his corpse amongst those retrieved.

With this information Colonel Hays Williams could not accept that the man was dead. The British officer suspected strongly that the wanted man had deserted and he determined to find him one way or the other. When he did, the colonial would be punished to the full extent of the law. Rosenblum would stand before a firing squad and pay for his deeds.

Colonel Hays Williams was right in one respect. Private Saul Rosenblum was well and truly alive, riding with the commando and no longer wearing the uniform of an Australian Bushman. Saul had swapped his uniform for the garb of the enemy: the floppy hat, crumpled shirt and trousers of a Boer farmer.

He rode in silence alongside Field Kornet Isaacs of De la Rey's commando as they slipped away from the advancing army under the command of Kitchener. Saul's thoughts were mixed as he rode; he was leaving behind his countrymen, who would now call him a traitor, and riding into an uncertain future. He had given his word that he would no longer take up arms against the Boers, and indeed it was his former enemy who had most certainly saved his life from a British firing squad.

On the morning Saul was taken prisoner he had been marched barefooted before a bear of a man. Mutual recognition dawned on both their faces at the meeting and the grim-faced Isaacs had called for a bottle of Cape brandy whilst he spoke in private with the captured Queenslander.

They had walked a short distance from the lines of wagons and bivouacs of the tough Boer fighters who stared with curiosity at the enemy soldier. For reasons known only to their commander, Isaacs had given orders that the Australian was to be shown courtesy. When they were out of hearing of his men, Isaacs offered the bottle to Saul who took a deep gulp of the fiery liquid. It helped chase away his weariness and the feeling of despair at being captured so easily.

'I was told how you stayed with the boy, my friend,' the Dutchman said gruffly but without hostility. 'You could have left him to die and got away.'

Saul let the fiery fumes waft through his weary body and shrugged. 'He was only a boy.'

'He was a soldier. Like many of the other young men you see around here who have yet to feel the sprouting of a man's beard on their chins.'

Saul could see that those without beards were indeed mere boys – some younger than Matthew Duffy. 'Yeah, well I stayed, and here I am.'

'It is for the best,' the big Dutchman said quietly. 'Your capture may have saved your life.'

Saul blinked as he passed the bottle back to the enemy commander. His eyes felt puffy and as if sand had been rubbed into them. 'What does that mean?' Saul asked with a frown and the Dutchman levelled his gaze.

'Had you survived our siege of your outpost, then you would have been arrested for murder, by the Englanders.'

'What!'

'The British have evidence that you killed the pig who was responsible for my sister's death.'

'How do you know this?'

'Some weeks ago we captured a dispatch being sent to Elands. Amongst the papers was a message to have you brought in under guard to Pretoria to answer a charge of murder. It seems that they are very sure of your guilt. So, should we hand you back to your Colonel Hore, as we already have with two of your countrymen, you will surely be arrested should you survive our siege.'

Saul reached for the bottle and took another swig to settle the fear in his stomach. 'What are you going to do with me then?'

'That is your choice,' the Dutchman replied. 'But, should you give me your parole to cease fighting us, I will make arrangements for you to escape British justice.'

Saul looked away, staring across at a line of hills. It was kind of funny seeing the sweating backs of the Boer gunners toiling at the guns when he had only ever faced the flashes of their muzzles before. He had never felt so trapped. Always there had been options to get him out of danger but this time he had only one.

'You have my parole,' Saul answered without turning to the Boer officer. 'What happens next?'

Isaacs placed his broad hand on the Queenslander's shoulder. 'I think you have the right to know that the

English woman my sister was staying with said she thought Karen was pregnant.'

Saul gasped. He had not suspected!

'I do not expect you to fight beside us, my friend,' Isaacs continued gently. 'But I do expect you to carry out a favour, in return for the help I will give you to disappear from Africa. It is a very personal favour which will take you a long way from this country to another life. But by accepting my request, you will never be able to go back to your own land. This you must understand.'

'I will do whatever you ask, so long as it does not require me to fight against my mates.'

The Dutchman smiled sadly. 'No, it will not require such a thing. But it will require great sacrifice.'

As Isaacs outlined his conditions, Saul listened in stunned silence. But when Isaacs had finished Saul agreed to the proposal. At least it was an alternative to being shot by his own side for murder.

Field Kornet Isaacs issued instructions to his men that the Australian prisoner did not officially exist amongst the captured, and as Saul rode north with the commando he realised that he was now a man without a country. There was no way back.

On a hill overlooking a sluggish series of waterholes in Queensland's north-west, an old man sat cross-legged staring into the flames of the small fire made to roast the goanna he had speared. His long grey beard reached to his chest and his body revealed the scars of his initiation as well as those inflicted by the whiteman's bullets.

Wallarie, the feared warrior and former bushranger who had once rode with the notorious Irishman Tom Duffy, poked at the fat body of the lizard in the fire. It sizzled with a delicious aroma that filled the nostrils of the hungry man. He had trekked countless days and nights in his life across the length and breadth of the inland plains and this day was just the end of one long trek and the beginning of another. But he knew his next journey was possibly his last.

Wallarie did not know who were coming to meet him, but the spirits had visited him in his sleep and told him that they were coming into the hills of the Kalkadoon. And when they came to him, something important to the long dead people of the Nerambura clan would happen. Was it that she who would one day save the memory of his spirit people was with them? The spirits of his people who spoke to him in the silence of the night did not tell him these things. But Wallarie did know that while one among the travellers was under the protection of the sacred hill of the Nerambura clan, death would visit another of those now entering the empty lands of the Kalkadoon.

THIRTY-THREE

The warm tropical surf swirling around Saul Rosenblum's bare legs felt good as he stood looking out over the Indian Ocean, brooding about the future. David Isaacs had delivered him to the Portuguese harbour town of Lourenco Marques in East Africa, having detached both of them from the main commando to more easily elude British patrols. On arrival, Saul had found himself in a world as alien as he could ever know, a place of mixed races from India, Europe and Africa.

Saul's first meal in the neutral territory of spicy *peri peri* chicken had come as a shock. Until now the only spicy condiment he had known was English mustard but the subtle taste of the Portuguese food was a delight to his palate. He had shared the meal with Jakob Isaacs and his son David in an Indian eating house where the scents of Asia and Africa blended in a heady mix of unusual aromas. Over the meal David had explained to Saul his task: escorting his father to the Ottoman-ruled province of Palestine. As Jakob Isaacs would be carrying a small fortune in uncut diamonds, Saul was to ensure that harm did not come to the Jewish man on his secret mission to the ancient land.

Neither Jakob nor David ever mentioned Karen's name in Saul's presence. Saul had wondered why but let the matter alone. Maybe it was a way of shielding themselves from the terrible pain of grief, he thought, as he too tried to forget that she would never again tease him about his forgotten ancestral roots, or cling to him after they had made love.

But standing in the surf that swished with a gentle hiss on the hot sands, he found her fresh in his memories and recalled her plans to take him with her to Palestine when the war was over to start a new life. Saul wiped away the tears flowing down his sun-tanned cheeks. To remember the pain of the past achieved nothing. He would go with Jakob Isaacs to the land he had heard his father talk about if for no other reason than to honour the memory of the only woman he had ever loved as well as that of his father.

The next day he and Jakob were scheduled to depart the Portuguese town on an American cargo ship steaming for Egypt. From there they would travel to Palestine and a future he could not really imagine.

As Saul waded back to the beach to collect his boots and walk barefooted along the sand back to the town, he wondered what Palestine was like. Would it have anything in common with the sweeping flat lands he had so much loved but could never return to? Within weeks he would find out.

Trooper Matthew Duffy stood to attention inside the tent, and stared directly ahead at the heat shimmering through the white canvas wall behind the officer.

'I am pleased to see that you have fully recovered from your wound, Trooper Duffy,' Major Glenn said from behind his folding field desk.

Matthew noted uneasily that the major's tone was not altogether friendly and sensed that his order to parade before his squadron commander was not to congratulate him on his role at Elands River. By now Matthew was sensitive to the subtle nuances of military life and the summons – gruffly relayed by the squadron sergeant major – had tipped him off that all was not well. Besides, the squadron sergeant major had personally escorted him to the tent, and was waiting outside like a wolf.

'Or should I say Trooper Tracy,' Major Glenn drawled, as if enjoying the delivery of his news.

'Ah, it's like this, sir,' Matthew replied, stumbling over his words, his face burning with fear, and a sick feeling in his stomach.

Major Glenn stared directly into Matthew's eyes and for a moment Matthew thought he saw a flash of humour.

'A relative of yours, I believe, sent me a despatch before he was wounded,' the major said. 'Major Duffy informs me that you ran away from your home in Queensland and enlisted under-age with us in Sydney. You do, of course, realise the gravity of such an offence, Trooper.'

'Yes, sir. I . . . ' Matthew was still at a loss for words and continued to stare bleakly ahead.

The major glanced down at a pile of papers. 'Under all other circumstances I know I should report this matter to higher command. You would be charged under the Queen's regulations. During active service such a matter is regarded very seriously and has dire consequences. But, considering how you conducted yourself during the siege, and the fact that Major Duffy is a man I know and greatly admire, I am going to bend the rules for you.'

A great sense of relief flooded Matthew. He was only too aware of the gravity of such a military charge in the field. He had often wondered whether he would be found out and concluded gloomily that it would probably only be a matter of time. Under the circumstances, Matthew knew that he must remain silent unless asked to speak by his officer commanding.

'I am going to place your name on the list of men to be returned to Australia because of their wounds,' the major continued. 'And when you reach Sydney, you will be honourably discharged from the unit. When you are discharged you will return to Queensland – or any other place – and you will not tell anyone how you got past our recruiters. Is that clear, Trooper Duffy?'

'Yes, sir,' Matthew gulped with relief. 'I just want to thank you . . . '

The major raised his hand to silence him. 'Don't thank me, Trooper. Thank Major Duffy, if you ever get the opportunity, which at the moment is not looking good.'

'How is Major Duffy, sir?' Matthew asked.

'Last I heard, they sent him back to England. His wounds are pretty severe and there is a chance he won't make it.'

Matthew bowed his head, wishing now he had got to know his cousin better. He must have been a remarkable man to have seen so many terrible campaigns for the Queen in the years past. Matthew's own brief taste of war had revealed that hell was not a place you went to after death. It was in the technology of mass destruction he had experienced under artillery and machine gun fire.

'That's all, Trooper Duffy,' the major said, dismissing the young man. 'But in parting I would like to add, off the record, that you were to be mentioned in despatches for your part in the siege. Needless to say, that will not occur now, considering all the matters before me. But at least you know that your service was recognised where it counts.'

'Thank you, sir,' Matthew said as he threw his finest salute, before about turning and marching out of the tent into the formidable presence of the gruff squadron sergeant major, whose impeccably waxed moustache glistened under the African sun.

'Trooper Duffy,' he bawled, 'get your kit together and report to the orderly room, immediately.'

'Yes, sah,' Matthew replied with a grin.

'And wipe that smile off your face, Trooper,' the sergeant major growled. 'Just because yer going home a wounded 'ero to impress all the girlies, that's no reason to smile.'

'No, sah,' Matthew replied, attempting to wipe away the smile.

'Besides,' the burly sergeant major added with his own unexpected smile, 'I think yer mother will have a word or two about you running away to serve Her Majesty in savage Africa. Yer got a letter from her.'

For a moment Matthew was stunned. He took the envelope handed to him by the grinning man.

'Despite everything, Trooper Duffy, you did a man's job,' the sergeant major added. 'Yer made us bloody proud of yer back there at Elands. Hope yer mother knows that.'

Matthew glanced up from the envelope. Suddenly he felt a loss he could not explain. He was going home and yet he felt so lonely. Matthew realised just how much the men he had served with meant to him. They were closer than any brother he might have had. Even the aloof sergeant major, who had made his life hell from time to time in the name of military discipline, was special.

'Thank you, sir,' Matthew replied. 'Thank you for everything.'

The tough professional soldier turned from the young trooper and marched away. He was a good kid, he thought. Would make a bloody good soldier when he was old enough to enlist.

Colonel Hays Williams took the general salute from the smartly turned out sentries at Lord Kitchener's headquarters. Inside the cool shade of the spacious stone building he walked briskly to the department of the provost marshall, a slim leather briefcase dangling from his left hand. As yet Trooper Saul Rosenblum may not have been located but inside the briefcase Colonel Hays Williams had the sealed and stamped papers for his arrest on a charge of murder. There was no statute of limitations on murder and, the colonel had consoled himself, the man could not hide forever from the long arm of British military justice, no matter where he might go. If only that damned colonial Major Duffy had done his job and apprehended the man then he would not have been subjected to chasing the papers required to legitimise the arrest. Nevertheless, he would get him in the end. It was only a matter of time.

THIRTY-FOUR

The dust rose in a small cloud and hung over the shimmering plains of scrub.

'What is it, Mr O'Flynn?' Alex asked.

'My guess is that it's a big mob of cattle being driven south.' Michael turned in the saddle to glance back at the sulky. 'Looks like we might have some company,' he shouted to Karl and Helen.

Nerambura kicked his horse forward and joined Michael and Alex. 'Maybe we get some meat,' Nerambura said hopefully. 'Boss man might have some to spare.'

'Good idea,' Michael agreed. 'See how we go when we meet up.'

It was near sundown when the motionless cloud hovering on the horizon took on the lowing sound of cattle and the strong smell of their presence. It was indeed a cattle drive and the Aboriginal and European stockmen rode at its edges, keeping the herd together as it moved slowly south for the greener pastures of New South Wales.

Michael broke away from his small party and rode towards the stockmen to identify their boss. He was directed to a man about his own age who rode a fine roan horse.

'Michael O'Flynn,' he called. The leading stockman stared at him curiously. 'You the boss?'

'Yeah. Bill Smithers is the name,' he replied from the saddle. 'Where you headed?'

'Going north,' Michael replied. 'Wondering if you had any spare beef.'

The weather-beaten face of Bill Smithers broke into a slow smile. 'Got a mob here of about two thousand beasts, but none to spare. If you are looking for a bit of fresh meat, we passed an old scrub bull up the track, about ten miles back near a waterhole. If you can find him he might give you a meal.'

'My thanks, Mr Smithers,' Michael said as the great herd passed him by. 'Good luck with the drive.'

Smithers gave Michael a nod and watched the big man with the eye patch wheel away to trot towards a travel battered sulky. When Smithers squinted against the glare of the setting sun he could see what appeared to be a woman and man seated on it, and a young boy with an Aboriginal man astride horses. A bit of a curiosity so far from any township, Bill Smithers thought as he patted his pockets for his pipe. But the one-eyed man, O'Flynn, seemed fairly capable, he concluded. Just something about him.

Michael rejoined his party. 'They don't have any beef to spare,' he said as he dismounted. 'But we will make our camp here and tomorrow head up the track to a waterhole to camp.'

Alex remained in the saddle, watching the great herd passing by. He wondered if Glen View had as many cattle and hoped that one day he might have the opportunity to muster on a cattle drive.

'C'mon, young Alex,' Michael said. 'Time to help set up camp.'

Alex was reluctant to take his eyes off the slowly moving herd but obeyed Michael's request as he would that of his father.

That night Alex snuggled under a warm blanket and stared up at the night sky. There was a weak moon and the stars stood out as sharply as glistening pieces of glass. Alex could hear the murmur of the adults' voices from the campfire nearby and the distant howling of a dingo. Although they had partaken of canned bully beef and biscuits for the evening meal, Mr O'Flynn had said that they would be eating fresh meat on the morrow. What was more exciting was that he'd promised to take him on the hunt for the scrub bull he had been told about. Alex sighed. How could life be any better than this? He did not care if they never found the old Aboriginal warrior Nerambura Duffy had told him so much about, despite being enthralled by the stories. The search could go on forever as far as Alex was concerned. Sydney and its crowded life were another world, one that he did not miss.

From time to time he thought about Fenella and Lady Enid but he definitely did not yearn for the company of George. Alex shuddered at the recollection of his older brother's bullying. George's reign of terror against him had been subtle, punching or pinching him when there were no witnesses and threatening him with further pain if he attempted to complain. But worse was the deriding of his achievements. Alex had come to believe that he could do nothing important in his life – until now. Mr O'Flynn had taught him many things on the trek across the vast plains of the west, even how to box.

After the violent incident in Cloncurry, Alex had tentatively approached Michael and asked him if he would teach him to fight. Michael had stared hard at the young boy and for a moment Alex regretted his request. But Michael broke into a broad smile and placed his arm around Alexander's shoulder.

'Learning to fight is a bit of a family tradition,' Michael had said. 'I only wish I had old Max Braun here to properly teach you.'

Alex stared up at Michael. 'Who is Max Braun?'

'A wonderful man who taught not only me how to fight but also your father.'

'Does my father know how to box?' Alex asked with a note of awe.

'Your father was once the champion of the bloody British army,' Michael replied proudly. 'But he was never as good as me,' he added mischievously. 'So I will teach you the finer points of fisticuffs.'

At first Alex shied away from the apparent violence of the art of boxing but Michael was patient. 'Always remember,' he said, 'that if you are feeling pain from your opponent, so is he when you hit him. It's just a matter of standing your ground until the other bloke realises that you are not going to give in – even if you are losing.'

Alex thought about the words; they made sense. Soon he was displaying a natural aptitude that made Michael nod his head and smile. Albeit reluctantly, Alex agreed to fight Nerambura, who had been instructed not to show any mercy to his smaller opponent.

Against the horrified protests of Helen, Michael drew a large square in the red earth and the two squared up in the improvised ring. Nerambura was a good head taller but both were about the same weight. On Michael's command the fight began with a flurry of fists.

Alex lost after a knockdown but was surprised that he had not felt fear as he had imagined he might. Nerambura helped him to his feet as Helen rushed forward with a clean hand-kerchief to stem the flow of blood pouring from Alexander's nose, berating Michael for allowing the fight to continue.

'He will be all right,' Michael chuckled as he stood back. 'He doesn't need mollycoddling.'

'Your own grandson,' Helen snapped savagely at Michael as she held the cloth to Alexander's face. 'How could you stand by and see your own flesh and blood hurt in such a brutal manner?'

Michael paled as Alex turned to stare quizzically at him, confused by Helen's slip. Mr O'Flynn was not his grand-father, so why would Aunt Helen make such a mistake? There was a dark frown on Michael's face as he turned to Helen, who now appeared flustered.

'I think that is enough boxing lessons for the day,' he said, patting Alex on the head. 'Time we did some work.'

Michael walked away, leaving Alex with Nerambura who appeared to be evasive when Alex questioned him about the strange statement.

'Don't know,' Nerambura mumbled and he too walked away, leaving the confused boy alone.

Lying under the southern sky, Alex singled out a star and made a wish before drifting into sleep. He wished that Helen's words could have been true and that he would wake up in the morning and learn that the man who had taught him so much and with such love and understanding was indeed his grandfather.

By the fire Michael sat against his saddle. Helen and Karl sat side by side drinking coffee from enamel mugs chipped by age, and Nerambura stared into the flickering flames. Since Cloncurry, a tension had crept into the party of travellers. It was not tangible but was apparent in the noticeable aloofness Karl displayed towards his wife.

'I think we should turn back,' Karl said, breaking the silence. 'I do not think that we will find Wallarie. The land is just too big.'

'Maybe you are right,' Michael said. 'I have a feeling old Wallarie just doesn't want to be found.'

'We have come so far,' Helen protested. 'I feel that we should go on.'

Michael looked to Nerambura.

'Wallarie will come to us when he is ready,' Nerambura answered softly as he gazed into the flames. 'He knows we are looking for him.'

'But how could that be?' Karl asked. 'He does not even know we exist.'

'Wallarie knows,' Nerambura answered, and added nothing more. How could he explain to this man with his Christian god that Wallarie's insights were older than anything the white man knew?

'We turn back tomorrow,' Michael stated.

Karl nodded but Helen remained silent. She felt an emptiness as deep as the land they were travelling through was wide. The fruitless journey had become very much like her own life and she did not have the strength to argue that they should go on.

'Tomorrow I will take Nerambura and young Alex to

309

find that scrub bull for some fresh meat,' Michael said as he stood and stretched. 'At least we can mark the search with a couple of decent steaks.'

Helen watched Michael heave his saddle over his shoulder and make his way into the night. She still smarted from his rejection of her offered love. Very few words had passed between them since Cloncurry and Helen sensed that Karl must suspect that her heart was not with him.

The old bull was where Nerambura calculated it would be. He picked up its tracks late the following afternoon not far from the sandy creek bed with its precious supply of slime-covered water. The bull stood on the plain watching them through rheumy eyes as the trio gazed at him from astride their mounts.

'Need to get closer,' Michael said quietly. 'Don't want him to bolt if he hears the shot and I miss.'

'I can ride around him to stop him getting away,' Nerambura offered. 'Push him in your direction.'

'Good idea,' Michael responded as he eased himself from the saddle and reached for the rifle in its bucket strapped to the horse. 'You take Alex with you.'

Alex looked down at Michael with a pleading expression. 'Can I stay with you, Mr O'Flynn?'

Michael manipulated the bolt of the rifle so that a round was chambered. 'Bit risky,' he grunted. 'I will be on foot and you never know what these old scrubbers will do if they are wounded. He's been the king out here for a while, by the look of him, and he won't want to give up his crown too easily.'

Nerambura reached for the reins of Michael's horse and started to lead it away. Alex reluctantly followed, glancing back at Michael one last time, hoping that he would change his mind. But the big man was standing alone, the rifle casually in his hands, without any sign of countermanding his direction.

Michael kept his eye on the bull, which held its head high as it continued to watch with suspicion the man now alone and afoot. The animal swung its head to catch sight of the two humans riding slowly around him and gave a snort of irritation that his enemy should divide into two parts. He lowered his head with its sharp horns, tail swishing from side to side to brush away the myriad flies that made his life miserable. Then he turned and began to break into a slow run.

Michael groaned when he saw the bull turning. It was a long shot but he would try anyway. He threw the rifle up to his shoulder and steadied the foresight on the bull. The rifle bucked as the heavy bullet left the barrel and Michael was pleased to see the bull flinch. He had aimed at the half exposed flank and forequarter, his goal to at least wound the bull and slow its escape. At close range he could finish it off.

The bull felt the projectile slam into the muscle at the top of his shoulder and swerved at the unexpected, stinging wound. Turning to identify what had caused the pain, the bull saw a man and boy riding hard at him across the plain. With a savage snort, the animal spun and turned away from the horsemen.

Alex felt the thrill of the charge. He leant forward in the saddle, yelling at the top of his lungs to stop the hunted animal escaping their encirclement and was pleased to see that he and Nerambura had succeeded. The bull was now charging towards Michael who stood calmly with the rifle at his shoulder.

Michael smiled to himself as he lined the approaching

target in his sights. At close range the .303 round would bring the bull down with one shot and tonight they would be eating the choice bits barbecued over the campfire.

Alex watched the charging animal heading straight for Mr O'Flynn. He began to feel a rising dread but fought the feeling, knowing that the man who stood facing the charging bull was only waiting for the right moment to fire.

The enraged bull was almost on him and Michael squeezed the trigger. He heard the click of the firing pin hit the centre base of the chambered round. But that is all. Instantly he realised that he had a misfire. Without taking the rifle from his shoulder Michael slammed open the breach to eject the faulty round and chamber another from the magazine.

Alex wanted to scream. Why hadn't Mr O'Flynn fired by now? And then to Alexander's horror the impossible happened. He saw Michael flung in the air on the horns of the wounded bull.

Michael knew that the situation was hopeless. The bull was on him before he could fire again. He had left it all too late this time and a tip of horn tore through his stomach, entering his chest as the animal raised its great head to hurl him in the air. Michael crashed to the earth as the bull swerved to return and finish him off. He lay on the red earth, bleeding profusely from his wound and vaguely aware that a horse was between him and the bull which was returning to charge again.

'No, no!' a voice screamed and Michael knew it was Alex.

The bull hesitated for a moment, gauging who it should attack but losing precious seconds which allowed Nerambura to leap from his horse and scoop up the rifle Michael had dropped. With the calm expertise of the bushman Nerambura stepped over Michael and fired. The bull felt the impact of the bullet and dropped to its knees before slumping to the ground.

'Mr O'Flynn!' Alex cried as he slid from his mount to kneel beside Michael. 'Don't die, please don't die! I will go and get help.'

Michael gritted his teeth to ease the terrible pain that swamped him in a continuous wave of red haze. 'Don't waste your time, Alex,' he managed to whisper. 'It's all over this time.'

Michael was able to focus on Nerambura who stood impassively over him. From the expression in Nerambura's dark eyes, Michael knew his fate was confirmed. 'Get Alex back to camp,' Michael said hoarsely despite his racking pain. 'Nothing you can do for me now.'

Nerambura nodded and took Alex by the shoulder but the boy shrugged off Nerambura's attempt to force him away from the dying man. 'I will never leave you,' he sobbed. 'I will stay with you, Mr O'Flynn.'

Michael tried to smile at his grandson's concern. 'Never forget that you have the blood of the Duffys in your veins, young Alex,' he said with a strangled gasp and grimaced. 'I will never forget you.'

Slowly, Michael's eyes closed as Alex desperately clutched his hand.

'He is dead,' Nerambura stated bluntly. 'We go back to camp and get some shovels to bury him.'

'I will stay with him until you get back,' Alex replied between short sobs.

He knew Nerambura was right about Mr O'Flynn being dead because he no longer breathed or responded to his touch. But Alex could not let go. Never before had he experienced so much pain – not even when Nerambura had given him a bloody nose in their fight. But this was a different kind of pain. He thought it would literally break his heart.

'It's good that you stay,' Nerambura said softly behind Alex. 'This man was your father's father.'

From where he knelt beside Michael's body Alex turned sharply to Nerambura. 'What do you mean?' he asked. 'Is Mr O'Flynn really my grandfather?'

'Mr Duffy didn't want you to know,' Nerambura said gently. 'I don't know why. But his real name is Michael Duffy and he is your father's father. Maybe Mrs Fellmann can tell you better. She knows.'

Nerambura turned to walk to his horse, leaving Alex alone with a turmoil of thoughts and the body of Michael Duffy. His wish the night before had come true. Mr O'Flynn was his grandfather.

Alex remained with his grandfather's body whilst Nerambura rode back to fetch Karl and Helen. Within a couple of hours, just as the sun was disappearing below the flat horizon, the three returned.

They buried Michael by the light of a lantern and Karl uttered prayers for the dead over the earthen mound that marked the grave of the man who had been born on Irish soil but who now lay under the sod of the Queensland colony. Each mourned in their own way for the loss, but none felt Michael Duffy's passing as badly as Alex, who sobbed uncontrollably until Helen took him aside and laid his head on her breast. She soothed him with the pieces of the story that she knew of Michael's dangerous life and her words brought some comfort to the boy.

As she related the life of the man who had fathered Alexander's own father, Helen pondered what might have been at the end of this journey with Michael Duffy. Could fate have finally opened his eyes to her love for him, despite the age difference?

When the sun rose over the plains the next day Nerambura took command of the party. He would lead them back to Glen View. When they departed mid-morning, all that remained to mark Michael Duffy's resting place was the nearby carcass of the old bull, now a meal for the great wedge-tailed eagle circling overhead, and a mound of red earth marked with a crude wooden cross.

In time, only the scattered and dry bones of the old bull would mark the site as the winds of the arid lands eroded the heaped earth. But when the rains came with the summer storms, wildflowers would sprout in the soil and a sweet perfumed scent would waft in the Outback air.

BIRTH OF
A NATION

1901

THIRTY-FIVE

Sydney, New South Wales
Australia
February 1901

My Beloved Patrick,
The time that you are away from us is almost too hard to
bear . . .

Patrick Duffy glanced at the date on the letter from his grandmother, Lady Enid Macintosh, and realised that it had taken two months for it to reach him in England. He shifted a little closer to the great open fireplace in the country house outside London and continued to read.

. . . Much has happened since you left us for South Africa and
that terrible war, which, I am overjoyed to read, Lord Roberts has
proclaimed is over . . .

Patrick pulled a pained expression at his grandmother's

statement. He well knew that the war was far from over, as Roberts had prematurely declared on his return to London. During his long convalescence Patrick had received occasional letters from fellow colonial officers stating the war was entering a new and sinister phase which involved the rounding up of all Boer women and children and placing them in concentration camps to break the spirit of the rebel farmers. The underlying theme of the letters had been the disgust many of the colonial soldiers had felt at carrying out this task: burning the farms to the ground, killing the livestock, and herding frightened women and children to the newly established camps. To Australians, many from farming backgrounds themselves, this new phase of war did not sit well. No, the war was far from over – just different.

. . . I pray for your speedy return to your loving family although it may be overshadowed by your father's tragic death. Helen told me she wrote to you last month to inform you of the circumstances surrounding the unfortunate incident but feels your father has found peace in a better place.

Patrick paused in his reading of the fine copperplate hand. Was it inevitable that his tough father should die in such bizarre circumstances when he had survived so many wars and intrigues? Patrick had not been able to cry when he received the news from Helen. His father had been almost a stranger to him, but maybe his loss would be more keenly felt when Patrick's own time drew near.

Patrick had even received a letter of condolence from Baron Manfred von Fellmann in Prussia. The old German aristocrat and former adversary of Horace Brown and Michael Duffy expressed his great admiration for a fellow warrior from a past era that few could now truly appreciate.

. . . Helen is still in Queensland with her husband attempting to make contact with a colleague in the Lutheran Church, Pastor Otto Werner, and his mission station. It appears that Wallarie may still be alive and in occasional contact with Pastor Werner. If so, Helen and Karl hope to make contact with the Darambal man. I have promised that if they can prove that Wallarie is alive then they may have title to a part of Glen View to establish their own mission.

To find Wallarie had become some sort of crusade, Patrick reflected with a frown. What did they expect to achieve? Forgiveness for the violence that his grandfather had brought almost forty years earlier to an obscure clan of people?

. . . Alexander has returned to us and it appears that he formed a deep bond with your father. He still mourns for his loss but is a very different young man now. I am afraid he gave George a thorough thrashing only a short time after he returned over a matter he would not discuss with me. George no longer attempts to tease Alexander. When the matter of the fight was reported to me by the servants, I did ask Alexander in private where he had learned to stand up for himself and the name of Max Braun came up. I thought you would like to know that your old German friend's spirit is still alive in the Irish side of your family . . .

For the first time, Patrick smiled. He suspected that his grandmother's superficially objective account of his sons' clash carried a certain amount of satisfaction. And his smile did not fade when he re-read her words about Max Braun. Was she stiffly acknowledging the good in the Irish side of his blood, just a little? This was not the Lady Enid he thought he knew so well.

. . . It is a shame that you have missed the celebrations to mark our colonies coming under one flag as a new nation in the Empire. I am pleased to see those idiotic trade tariffs dropped between the

321

colonies. They were an obstruction to our trade for the Macintosh companies as you well know, but it is a strange feeling to think that we are all now one nation, although we all accept that England will always be our Mother.

The Federation of Australia had also affected Patrick's career in the army. He was no longer a member of a colonial unit but part of the Australian army, though he doubted the colonial soldiers from Queensland and New South Wales he had served with would be quick to identify with the new army model. They had gone to war with regiments that had fought hard to earn battle honours and the idea of these honours being absorbed by one nation was not easy to accept.

Patrick continued to read the long letter. It contained snippets about life back in Sydney as well as mention of mutual friends. The letter had been written at the height of the Southern Hemisphere summer and now Australia was moving into winter. In England, the cold sleet and wet winds would soon be replaced with a massive revival of life in the fields and hedgerows with the coming of spring.

. . . Your adoring grandmother, Lady Enid.

With a sigh Patrick placed the carefully folded letter back in its envelope and gazed into the gentle flicker of the flames.

'You have a visitor, Major Duffy,' a voice said behind him.

'Who is it, Davies?' Patrick asked the manservant.

'A Captain Thorncroft from Australia, sir,' Davies replied with just a hint of distaste in his voice, no doubt due to this reminder of the new nation of former convicts.

'Arthur!' Patrick exclaimed softly. 'Send him in, man,' he commanded.

'Very well, sir,' Davies replied. He reappeared a short time later with Arthur in tow.

Patrick rose from the great leather chair to greet his old friend with a warm handshake.

'You are looking very well, Patrick,' Arthur said as he stood back to appraise him. 'The suit is just a little loose but I suppose you have lost some weight since the surgeons extracted all that German iron from you.'

'It is good to see a familiar face,' Patrick smiled. 'I did not expect to see you until I returned to Sydney.'

'Have you forgotten,' Arthur laughed, 'that the Macintosh empire is paying to send me on a fact finding mission around the world?'

'Ah, yes, to find out more about moving pictures. How is your enterprise going?'

'I could lie and say that I have been busy exploring the technical world of moving pictures,' Arthur replied with a grin. 'Or I could also tell you that I have been having a very good time doing so.'

'Rather the truth, old boy,' Patrick said, realising as he spoke that his convalescence in the Macintosh country house in England had transferred some English ways onto him, even down to his manner of speech.

'Well, I heard that you were back from South Africa, albeit under rather brutal circumstances, and I decided that part of your recovery would depend on my contacts,' Arthur said. 'So as part of my commission I have come to fetch you back to London for some entertainment befitting a warrior of the Queen.'

'I think I am up to that now,' Patrick replied. 'It has been a long time since I sought the company of others. Since I came here all I have really done is sit by this fire and brood about the future.'

'And what are your plans?' Arthur asked.

'I don't really know,' Patrick replied, glancing back at the flames in the hearth. 'The medical board has passed me as fit to remain with the army but what I hear coming out of South Africa disturbs me. I think I might be at odds with Kitchener in the way he is pursuing the war.'

'Met Kitchener once,' Arthur reflected. 'It was back in the Sudan and I didn't like the man. A cold fish, who I sensed had aspirations beyond his breeding.'

'You have to give him credit for how he handled that campaign,' Patrick defended. 'But I don't think he has the ability to handle this one. We are fighting a new kind of war, in a new century.'

Arthur broke into a broad smile to distract his friend from gloomy recollections. 'Well, what about the trip down to London? I have a rather pleasant surprise waiting for you if you get yourself ready. You could say that the money your companies pay me to conduct research brings some rewards in the world of opera. Ah, but don't expect me to tell you more, Major Duffy,' Arthur continued when he noticed the quizzical expression on Patrick's face. 'You will have to meet her yourself.'

'Catherine?' Patrick asked hopefully, although he knew his wife had nothing to do with opera apart from occasionally attending a performance.

A dark expression clouded Arthur's face and Patrick knew he was wrong. 'I am afraid not,' Arthur replied. 'But someone who has shown a great interest in meeting you. It seems that she has rather a lot in common with your family.'

Patrick sighed at his friend's love of intrigue. But he would go to London in company with Arthur. It would be a break from the confines of the Macintosh residence in a country throwing off the last cold blankets of winter.

~

Father Eamon O'Brien met his visitor with some reservation. Despite the fact that he was a fellow priest, although not wearing the cassock, Eamon still knew who he was. Father Martin Duffy already had a dark reputation in the village for political intrigue rather than a devotion to his religion. But that was the way with the Jesuits, Eamon thought, as he ushered the Australian priest into the presbytery.

'God bless you, Father O'Brien,' Martin said as he shook off the bitter cold of the grey day. 'It is good to finally make your acquaintance.'

Eamon hoped that the edge of annoyance he felt did not show. The Jesuit had been in the village on other occasions without the courtesy of stopping by the church to introduce himself. He noticed that his visitor was similar in many ways to Patrick Duffy except that he was not as solidly built, his leanness giving him the illusion of height.

'I believe you are Patrick Duffy's cousin,' Eamon said.

'I am,' Martin replied as he rubbed his hands in front of the iron stove. 'We grew up together in Sydney many years ago. For the first part of my life I thought Patrick was my brother.'

'We are all brothers,' Eamon replied.

His sarcasm was not missed by Martin. 'I gather that you do not approve of me,' Martin said turning his back to Eamon. 'But you were educated by the English, I believe, and that may explain your antagonism towards the cause I fight for.'

'I was born in England,' Eamon bridled, 'but I was ordained in Rome and my loyalties are to the Church, not politics.'

'Justice for the oppressed is God's work,' Martin said, turning to face Eamon. 'But I do not expect a parish priest to understand that.'

For a second Eamon felt the sting of his patronising comment. 'Pride is a sin,' he replied. 'It is something that I try to avoid. But putting our differences aside, Father Duffy, I am curious as to why you should finally make your presence in the village known to me.'

'I have not declared my presence in the past so as to avoid involving your name in the cause to free Ireland from the English,' Martin replied. 'I can assure you, it was not prompted by any intended discourtesy.'

Eamon was taken slightly aback by the explanation and softened his demeanour towards the Australian priest. He had made a point of not getting involved in the ever-present issue of the English occupation of Ireland and was never truly sure whether it was because he had been born in England, or because he felt his mission tended towards the religious rather than secular matters of the parish.

'I accept your explanation,' Eamon replied in a conciliatory tone, 'and can offer you a fine drop of Irish whisky to help warm the soul.'

Martin smiled for the first time and Eamon was reminded again of Patrick Duffy. He fetched the bottle and both men sat at the battered wooden table in the warmth of the presbytery kitchen.

When the tumblers were filled Martin raised his glass. 'To a free Ireland,' he toasted.

Eamon raised his glass. 'God bless her.'

'I have come to see you,' Martin said after a generous sip, 'because I know that you are well acquainted with my cousin's wife, Catherine Duffy.'

'Catherine and I had a mutual interest in archaeology,' Eamon replied guardedly. 'But sadly, we have had little contact since her . . . condition. She has isolated herself at the Fitzgerald manor and sees no-one. But what is your interest in Patrick's wife?'

Martin did not answer immediately but stared at the table for a short time, gathering his carefully chosen words. 'Despite Patrick's and my estrangement over the years, he will always be like the brother I first thought I had. I learned of Catherine's pregnancy some time ago and feel that I owe it to Patrick to try to help.'

Eamon stared into Martin's eyes but could not see any guile in his explanation. 'You have some knowledge of her dilemma?' he asked.

'I know that the baby cannot be Patrick's,' Martin replied. 'I also know that my cousin was badly wounded in the fighting in South Africa last year.'

'If I must say so,' Eamon said quietly, 'I find it strange that you should show your concern considering that I know of your activities to recruit the village men to go to South Africa and fight the English.'

'That is not personal,' Martin replied, taking a long swallow of the whisky. 'Patrick is still my flesh and blood – and that is personal.'

'So what do you propose?'

'I thought that I might pay Catherine a visit,' Martin said. 'If nothing else, offer her my counsel in her difficult time.'

Eamon pondered the proposal. He had attempted to make contact with Catherine but she had turned him away each time. The dig had been abandoned and the stone altar reburied. He had warned Catherine that only evil could come of it, his religious beliefs overriding his logical scientific approach to the dig once they had uncovered the mysterious stone.

'If you can help Catherine in any way,' Eamon finally said, 'then I would be grateful. She is a lost soul and I fear her baby's soul will be also lost if she does not get help.'

'Who is the father?' Martin asked.

'Catherine is under the delusion that Satan is the father but I strongly suspect that it is a Mr Brett Norris who now owns the Fitzgerald manor. He does not live there anymore, but I have heard he will soon return to visit Catherine.'

At the mention of Brett Norris's name, Martin frowned. He knew of the man whose enterprises were substantial suppliers of arms and munitions to the British army.

'How advanced is she in her pregnancy?' he asked.

'I suspect a good nine months already,' Martin replied. 'You will need to see her as soon as possible if you are going to do any good.'

Father Martin Duffy rose from the table. 'Thank you for your hospitality, Father O'Brien,' he said.

'If you wish lodgings for the night you are welcome to stay here,' Eamon offered.

'I have lodgings,' Martin smiled. 'But your offer is appreciated. I think it would be wise for me to leave. My visit to you may have been noted by any English informants in the village, although I doubt even they would be out on a night like this.'

As Eamon accompanied Martin to the door, he noted with a frown that the Jesuit priest was joined by a shadowy figure as he stepped into the night. For a man of God, it was strange that the Australian priest put his faith in the powers of a bodyguard, Eamon thought as the sleet and dark took the two men from his sight.

THIRTY-SIX

Next to Sydney, London was Patrick's most loved metropolis. And now it offered so much in the way of distraction from his insular brooding on the war wounds he had received. The army surgeons had removed all the shrapnel, leaving his chest, legs and arms forever marked. But the thin scar from a small shard of shrapnel that had sheared along his jaw was the only outward indication that he had been wounded.

Arthur had rented a small but comfortable set of rooms not far from London's strip of vaudeville houses. He had already made his contacts amongst the entrepreneurs who were exploiting the moving picture technology to make money from London's masses.

Inside his lodgings Arthur showed Patrick to his tiny room, apologising for the cramped accommodation. Patrick only smiled and reminded his friend it was far more comfortable than the conditions they lived under back in '85 in the Sudan campaign.

That night they dressed for the opera. The renowned antipodean diva Miss Deborah Cohen was performing arias from Bizet. Arthur had obtained the tickets through his contacts in the world of theatre and he grinned at Patrick's surprise at his enterprise, 'I believe Miss Cohen is your Aunt Kate's god-daughter,' Arthur said. 'I thought that you might like to meet her.'

'You can do that?' Patrick asked with just a touch of awe.

'Certainly, old chap,' Arthur said, puffing out his chest in mock importance. 'A fringe benefit of moving in the circles of the rich and famous.'

That evening as they sat in a box overlooking the stage, Miss Deborah Cohen's voice proved as entrancing as her reputation suggested. With the discipline of a regimental sergeant major, she controlled the notes to extract the clearest and most beautiful effect from them. Although Patrick was not a great lover of opera he found Deborah's performance exceptional. Or did his attraction to her promise a small link to a sun-drenched country far away where his family resided?

When the performance was over and the well-dressed patrons filtered out to attend parties in the city, Arthur took Patrick's elbow and guided him to a hansom cab. 'We have an invitation to drinks with Miss Cohen,' Arthur said. 'Just another service provided by the Macintosh money wisely used to employ my exceptional services.'

'Miss Cohen,' Arthur said formally, 'may I introduce you to Major Patrick Duffy, from Sydney.'

Patrick stood a little self-consciously amongst the well-dressed crowd in the swank hotel foyer.

'Major Duffy,' Deborah said sweetly as she offered her gloved hand. 'I already know everything about you from your wonderful Aunt Kate.'

Patrick took her hand, aware that her dark eyes were watching him with more than a passing interest. She was relatively tall and the shimmering black dress she wore accentuated her graceful curves. The famed opera singer's luxurious, jet-black hair was piled high on her head, and in every way Patrick had imagined she was indeed beautiful.

Patrick already knew that she was just slightly younger than he, as Kate had often mentioned her god-daughter in letters. Kate was as proud of Deborah's ascent to international fame as if Deborah had been her real daughter.

'Not everything, I hope,' Patrick replied lamely. 'There is a lot that even I would rather forget.'

'Kate has told me that you are very much like your father,' Deborah continued, and suddenly checked herself. 'Oh, I am sorry,' she said apologetically. 'Kate wrote to tell me of your father's passing last year.'

'There is no need to apologise,' Patrick offered. 'My father led a remarkable life, and died in a way I think he would have preferred to the onset of illness or old age.'

'Ahem!' Arthur coughed. 'I thought that before you two got into a reminiscence of the past that we should steal away from here and retire to a place less public.'

Patrick glanced at Arthur with a puzzled look but received a wink in return.

'Oh, yes,' Deborah said, reluctantly releasing Patrick's hand. 'Dinner.'

'Dinner?' Patrick was puzzled. 'What dinner?'

'The three of us are scheduled to dine at the Savoy,' Deborah said with a soft laugh. 'Perhaps Arthur has not told you of our long acquaintance from the past. We first met when I was struggling to achieve recognition and it was Arthur who helped open the doors for a poor colonial lass, such as myself, to enter the world of European aristocracy.'

'I did not know,' Patrick said, staring at Arthur with a new respect for the man's less lauded achievements.

'I kind of found myself as an agent after I was discharged in '86,' Arthur said. 'Then one day this skinny young thing from the barbaric wilds of Queensland knocked on my door. She claimed that she could sing . . . and here she is.'

Deborah took Arthur's elbow with a gentle squeeze of affection. 'Arthur had faith in me, and I do not forget who my real friends are.'

'I must tend my apologies,' Arthur said in a more serious tone as he flipped open the cover of his gold fob watch and noted the time. 'I have an appointment with an American from New York concerning some new photographic equipment being manufactured over there. But the reservations have been made and a cab awaits to rescue you from your adoring but possibly overwhelming public, Deborah.'

'You are right, Arthur,' Deborah said and excused herself to address the gathering of patrons of the arts. After a short and breezy speech, she took Patrick's arm and they followed the doorman to a cab waiting outside.

As Patrick sat beside Deborah, for just a moment he felt at a loss for words. Here he was in the company of one of the most admired and talented women in the world – and yet he did not know what to say. As if sensing his awkwardness, Deborah astutely opened the conversation by asking Patrick about his grandmother and his children, a subject Patrick was able to speak on at length and with warmth. Since Deborah did not ask him about Catherine, he suspected that she already knew of his wife's estrangement from him.

When they arrived at the hotel the staff received Deborah as if she were royalty and once again Patrick felt just a little out of place, not for anything that Deborah did, but for the way she was courted by strangers who vied to kiss her hand. As it was, the coy looks he caught from one or two pretty young ladies told a surprised Patrick that they found the mysterious man escorting the famed Miss Deborah Cohen attractive in his own right.

They were seated in a private alcove away from the gawking diners attempting to catch a glimpse of the opera diva. An elegantly dressed waiter hovered at the table to take their order which Deborah delivered in a manner which indicated that she was naturally born to a life of fame and fortune.

The soft flicker of the candlelight in the alcove accentu-ated the depth of her dark brown eyes and Patrick felt an uneasy twinge of guilt for the desire that this woman had awoken in him. Between courses, Patrick turned Deborah's conversation on herself and she appeared flattered, relating anecdotes of her life touring the world. Patrick laughed, grateful for this wonderful diversion from thoughts of the future – or darker reflections on Catherine's absence from his life. For that he felt even more guilty.

But as the evening moved along, Deborah seemed to become aware of something missing from the conversation. 'Major Duffy, you have spoken so little of your remarkable life,' she said. 'You have tricked me into speaking about my own and I have prattled on incessantly about matters of little consequence to the state of the world. You are a man who has truly lived and yet you remain so modestly silent about yourself.'

'You know,' Patrick said disarmingly, 'you have the most beautiful eyes.'

As Deborah glanced away Patrick thought he saw a flush rise under the golden hue of her olive skin. 'I do not mean to flatter you or attempt to win your affections,' he continued hastily when he saw her reaction. 'There is just something quite bewitching about them.'

Leaning towards him, Deborah said softly, 'I know about your sadness. Kate wrote to me of how your wife left you for another. I am very sorry but I must say that your wife must be the most foolish woman ever born, to leave a man such as yourself.'

'You do not know what I am really like,' Patrick responded, looking down. 'I think that I made the mistakes that forced Catherine from my life. It is not she who is completely at fault but I.'

'I know a lot more about you than you might imagine,' Deborah said. 'I have followed your life through the years via Kate's letters. It was as if I was with you from that terrible time you were listed as missing in action in the Sudan, to when you were wounded in South Africa, last year. And all the time that I read about you over the years I drew a picture of a rather remarkable man.'

Patrick was humbled by the intently delivered words of this beautiful woman. He sensed a genuinely caring woman with an infinite capacity to give love without asking anything in return.

'Miss Cohen —'

'Please call me Deborah,' she said cutting him short. 'May I call you Patrick?'

'I would feel more at ease if you did,' Patrick replied. 'In a sense, you have been very much part of my extended family. It is just that now we have finally met.'

'I know that it is extremely brazen of me to suggest that we meet again,' Deborah said softly. 'But I would like the opportunity to learn more about the man who has until now only existed in Kate's prose.' Noticing the slightly confused expression on Patrick's face, she hurriedly added, 'Oh, please do not misconstrue my intentions. But it would be nice to have the company and conversation of a fellow colonial when I am surrounded by men who only want to claim my affections. With you, I feel that you are an honourable and genuine man, and in my world that is a rare thing.'

'I would be honoured to see you again,' Patrick said. 'In fact, you could visit my place in the country for the weekend, if that is possible?'

'I would be delighted,' Deborah answered sweetly. 'Shall we say this weekend? I am free, if you are?'

'I am and will look forward to sharing a walk with you, weather permitting.'

When Patrick departed from the hotel late that evening he did so in a gloomy confusion of thoughts. He had never expected to meet a woman such as Deborah Cohen, one who had the ability to turn his world upside down.

'Bloody imbecile,' Patrick muttered to himself as he waited for the doorman to hail a Hansom cab on the busy street.

He was angry at the attraction he felt towards Deborah and suffered a terrible guilt for the fact that he still loved his estranged wife. But no harm could come from a weekend in the country, he consoled himself. It would be good to have some company in the empty old mansion far from the crowded city.

Deborah stood in her plush hotel room wearing only a tight corset. She too felt confusion for what had unexpectedly transpired between them over dinner. Or was it that she had always wanted to meet the man whose life she had followed in Kate's letters?

'Silly girl,' she sighed as she ran her hand down her stomach. Patrick Duffy was not one of the royal princes she had bedded in the past, nor was he a man of European sophistication. So why should she find him so desirable?

Deborah struggled from the corset to slip on an ankle length flannel nightgown. No, Patrick was not the kind of man she should ever have any romantic thoughts about. After all, she could have any man she wanted. She attempted to dismiss him from her thoughts. But the more she tried to do so the more he returned in a way that was disconcerting. She had fleeting images of his head buried between her breasts and his strong hands forcing her legs apart as she lay beneath him. The more she attempted to rationalise her relationship with Patrick, the more she wanted him.

Deborah slipped under the thick eiderdown to sleep. It did not surprise her that Patrick came so easily to her dreams that night.

THIRTY-SEVEN

A feeling of despair at the desolation of the Holy Land greeted Saul Rosenblum. It was not the land of milk and honey of his father's nostalgic words for a land he had never even visited. Instead he found a miserable landscape where barely a tree flourished in a terrain of rock and dust shimmering under a baking sun. He and Jakob Isaacs were travelling by donkey to the newly established *moshava* in the Ottoman territory of Sanjak Jerusalem. The *moshava* was a privately owned farm village inhabited by Jewish European men and women seeking to turn the seemingly barren lands into self-sufficient hamlets. But, as Jakob had explained on their journey south from the old city of Jerusalem, the immigrants were not farmers and they were only able to survive thanks to the financial support from the great European banker Baron Edmund de Rothschild.

But the support came at a price. The baron insisted

on placing his representatives in the *moshavas*, to make decisions on just about every aspect of community life. The settlers found themselves in opposition to many of the decisions, and Jakob had explained how the diamonds he had exchanged for cash would go a long way towards making the *moshava* he had adopted self-sufficient.

Saul had learned much about Palestine from Jakob on their sea voyage from Portuguese Africa. He knew that Jakob had attended a congress in Basel, Switzerland, four years earlier to hear a Jewish Viennese journalist speak about the idea of Zionism. Jakob had been inspired by the words of Theodor Herzl whose aim was to establish a permanent homeland for the dispossessed people of the Hebrew faith who were persecuted across Europe and beyond. Eretz Israel was proclaimed and now Jakob told Saul optimistically that they were the small vanguard for the millions of Jewish people, first scattered two thousand years earlier by the Romans. They would unite in the land of Abraham.

Unmoved, Saul had listened to Jakob's impassioned recounting of history and current politics. Only the memory of Karen – and the knowledge that he was wanted by the British authorities – had caused him to travel to this land, so foreign from what he had known in the past. What was familiar was the unforgiving nature of the land for the settler. Alongside his father, Saul had experienced the taming of a tough land and Jakob had pointed out that such a venture would be very little different to what lay ahead. In no uncertain terms, Saul had explained to Jakob that he intended to eventually make his way back to Australia, to Queensland. The vast former colony, now a state in the Commonwealth of Australia, was considered by Saul to be big enough to provide him with anonymity. Palestine was not his land; it was merely a place to stay for a few months before finding a berth on a ship steaming to the Pacific.

Jakob had acknowledged Saul's plan with a knowing nod, muttering something in Yiddish Saul did not understand. With the matter settled Saul added, 'I am not even a real Jew. My mother was what you call a gentile.'

Jakob pondered the young man's declaration. 'My daughter loved you,' he said. 'She wrote to me about you and said that you were destined to be like Gideon, a warrior fighting for the chosen people. My daughter was like her mother, and her mother wisely chose her husband.'

Saul reflected on Jakob's words and wondered if he would ever understand the Jewish jewel trader's logic. But a gentle bond had formed between them, and Saul sighed.

'A bitterly cold winter will come to these lands soon enough,' Jakob said as they rounded a bend on the stony track to look down on a shallow arid valley with a small stone village at its centre. 'And when winter comes we will need the funds I have obtained to get us through.' He brought his donkey to a stop. 'Ah, there it is,' Jakob continued. 'My *moshava* – and your new home, Saul.'

Saul gazed down at the distant village surrounded by fields wilting under the sun. It did not look very impressive.

'Do they speak English?' Saul asked hopefully. The local languages seemed impossible to learn.

'English, Russian, Austrian, Slovakian and everything else, even a little Hebrew. But mostly Yiddish. Maybe you should learn Yiddish.'

'Thought so,' Saul mumbled. 'Nothing comes easy around here and I bet Yiddish has to be the toughest language of the lot.'

Within a couple of hours the two men arrived at the village to be met by a giant bear of a man with a huge black beard. He greeted Jakob with a crushing hug that lifted him off his feet.

'Saul,' Jakob said when he had disengaged himself. 'I would like you to meet my very good friend Ivan Putkin. He was once a Cossack in the Tsar's army.'

Ivan turned his attention to Saul as he stood by his donkey. 'Is good to eat you,' he said with a crushing handshake.

'I think the word is "meet",' Jakob said with a chuckle. 'Ivan is still learning English.'

'Hope so,' Saul said from the corner of his mouth. 'Because he looks like he could eat the donkey and me in one sitting.'

'Da, meet you,' Ivan echoed as he realised his mistake. 'You fight Africa for English?' he asked.

'Fight for Queensland, not bloody England,' Saul quickly countered.

'One day we talk battles,' Ivan said throwing his huge arms around Jakob and Saul's shoulders and leading them across a dusty courtyard to a substantial stone building. Saul could see only a handful of older men and women and children in the village, guessing rightly that the younger adults were working. Saul had first noticed the fields, scraggly olive groves and vineyards beyond the little township as he and Jakob descended the winding narrow and rough track.

When Saul was introduced to the older men of the village, they seemed impressed as Jakob extolled Saul's farming experience in far-off Australia.

'But I know cattle – not crops,' Saul growled when Jakob explained what he had been telling the men in Yiddish. 'I don't know the first thing about bloody olive trees or cereal crops.'

'But you must know something about animal husbandry,' Jakob argued. 'We do have goats.'

'Goats! We shoot them as pests in Queensland. Damned

things strip the land of everything worth eating for the stock.'

'Here they give us milk, cheese and meat,' Jakob said, offended. 'And an animal is an animal.'

'I think you chose the wrong person to come with you,' Saul replied. 'I'm sorry that I can't be of much help.'

'Karen chose you,' Jakob pointed out quietly. 'And I think she chose wisely. God has a plan for you, which only He knows.'

Saul shrugged and stared at the men sitting around the crude wooden table watching him with some expectation. 'I'll have a look around and see what I can do,' Saul finally conceded. 'Maybe there is something – but no promises.'

'Good,' Jakob said and turned to the grim-faced men to explain that the young man who had accompanied him on his journey knew all about goat husbandry. They smiled and raised small cups of thick, black coffee to toast Saul's acceptance into their struggling community.

Saul was billeted in a one-roomed stone house with Ivan as the Russian could speak enough English to explain the workings of the community. The following day he was taken on a tour of the *moshava*. The two men walked the dusty and almost silent lands to the top of a craggy rise overlooking a depression of reedy swamps.

'We get this land from Arabs,' Ivan said as they surveyed the large tract of swamp. 'Land no good to Arab, so he sell to us.'

'Not much you can do with a swamp,' Saul agreed. 'But it would be good land if you could drain it.'

'How we drain?' Ivan growled. 'I think Jakob not so smart buy this land.'

'Back home we find that where gum trees grow they just naturally drain swamps. You blokes ought to be planting a few around here. It looks like the climate will take to gums okay.'

'What is gum trees?' Ivan asked, scratching at his beard.

'I think you call them eucalyptus trees, or something,' Saul answered, staring down at the swamp. 'Kind of miss them a lot,' he added wistfully.

'Maybe you talk to Jakob about this thing,' Ivan suggested. 'Maybe Jakob know about gum tree.'

'Maybe,' Saul mused.

After a midday meal of bread, goat cheese and green olives the two men continued the tour. It was sundown by the time they finally returned and Saul first saw the population of the village gathered. In the short time he had been in the community he had only fleeting glimpses of the younger men and women going and returning to the fields. But this time they were gathered around a bonfire at the edge of the village.

'What's going on?' Saul asked Ivan.

'What you say, celebration. First baby born in settlement. People happy.'

'Good enough,' Saul smiled. 'You don't happen to celebrate with beer, do you?' he asked hopefully.

'No beer,' Ivan responded. 'Vodka and wine.'

'That'll do,' Saul sighed. 'Better than a poke in the eye with a blunt stick.'

Ivan glanced sideways at the Australian. He presumed poking people in the eye with a stick was something they did where Saul came from. It didn't sound like a good pastime – not as good as drinking copious quantities of vodka.

Ivan generously shared his supply of precious Russian vodka with Saul that night as the young men and women sang and danced by the flickering light of the bonfire. It was rather subdued compared to similar gatherings Saul remembered from his past. On the rare occasions that the stockmen came together in his part of the world it usually ended up in a drunken brawl.

Saul sat with Ivan, admiring the graceful movements of the young women in their long, peasant-style skirts. One girl stood out from the rest. Unlike the majority with their olive-hued skin, dark eyes and hair, this girl had striking blue eyes, fair skin and blonde hair. Saul was entranced by her swaying movements as she linked arms with the other girls to dance in a graceful circle around the bonfire.

'Who is that girl by the fire?' Saul asked Ivan. 'The one with hair the colour of the desert.'

Ivan blinked and turned to see at who Saul was pointing. He squinted and then frowned. 'That is Anna, she is what you say, sister of mine.'

Saul looked with surprise at the huge man beside him. 'Your sister!'

'Da, little sister,' Ivan confirmed.

Saul was wise enough not to point out that the graceful young girl looked nothing like her brother.

'All boy chase Anna,' Ivan continued. 'I break neck of boy chase Anna,' the big Russian grunted.

Wisely, Saul did not pursue any questions about the bewitching girl who stood in the shadows of the fire. Ivan swigged from the almost empty bottle before passing it to Saul, his new friend's question already forgotten.

'Time we dance,' Ivan said lumbering to his feet unsteadily. 'All dance,' he repeated, hauling Saul up and partly dragging him to the circle where Saul found himself beside Anna. Ivan said something to his sister and she laughed softly as she took Saul's hand. Her eyes levelled on his and Saul registered a strange feeling he thought had died forever with Karen.

'I am Anna,' she said slowly as she smiled up at Saul. The sound of her voice was as sweet as the scent of the gum trees Saul so much missed.

Saul learned that Anna was Ivan's only living relative. Their family had escaped Tsarist Russia after a pogrom against their village, but Ivan's parents had died on the terrible trek across the seemingly unending Russian steppes to Europe.

Prior to the pogrom, Ivan had been a cavalryman in the Cossacks until he was revealed to be a Jew, although he had never felt religiously committed to his parents' beliefs. Most of his friends had been the Orthodox Christian boys of the village who respected Ivan for his physical size and strength. He had eventually left the village in search of adventure and had joined a Cossack regiment stationed at St Petersburg. He had been happy as a soldier for the Tsar until his past caught up with him and he had been forced to choose between burning predominantly Jewish villages or deserting. He chose the latter after a troop of Cossacks forced his family out of their home and it was he who organised the exodus of the survivors to seek a new home in America. But he did not get that far. His aged parents had died in the snow, and when they reached Budapest in the Austro–Hungarian Empire, he and his sister had heard the rumours of a new land being forged in Palestine for the scattered people of David and Abraham.

Anna was now sixteen and had at first been confused by the war waged against her village in Russia. She was after all more Russian in appearance than Jewish, but this did not matter to the villagers she thought she knew. They had turned on her family as if they had been complete strangers. So she had left her homeland with mixed feelings.

'You like me,' Ivan would often tell Saul during a bout of

drinking. 'You soldier, not farmer. I get you job working for me,' he added and continued to talk about his past. Sometimes he would tell Saul a little about his beautiful sister and Saul would listen to every scrap of information. Then Ivan would burst into a sad folk song, tears running unashamedly down his weather-beaten cheeks into his bushy beard. When that time came, Saul would ease himself from Ivan's company to allow him to mourn privately for what was lost.

The strong bond forming between the two men was reinforced when Jakob came to Saul to suggest that he might be better employed working with Ivan to provide an armed guard for the village. Armed with an old French military carbine, Ivan currently worked alone, patrolling the *moshava*'s perimeter on horseback. There had been incidences of theft in the past as well as harassment by gangs of roving men from a nearby Arab village, although nothing of great consequence.

But Jakob still worried. With only three old rifles, two pistols and a limited supply of rounds, the settlers were vulnerable to any organised attack should the nearby Arabs choose to retake the land they had purchased from them. To date they had only sneered at the European Jews who had come with aspirations to make the worthless land fruitful. They had sold the new settlers the swamps and rocky fields and left them to learn that Allah had ordained the land to be barren. But slowly the settlers were actually redeeming what the Arabs considered worthless, and now their sneers were changing to expressions of greed.

'There will be a time when they turn on us,' Jakob had warned at the meetings of the *moshava* council. 'A time when we will have to defend ourselves.'

'But we are not soldiers,' many had argued. 'The Ottomans will protect us.'

'The Ottomans are Muslim,' Jakob cautioned. 'They will be like the Europeans, and turn a blind eye, as the French have with Captain Dreyfuss.'

The situation kept Jakob awake at nights. He had an idea but it would require money and the right men to carry it out. Saul Rosenblum came to mind.

Saul had taken to the often boring and lonely task of patrolling the hills and valleys between the *moshava* and the surrounding scattered villages of the Palestinian Arabs. Astride a horse and with a rifle at his hip, Saul felt he had at last a meaningful role in the community. He was a soldier and knew his job. Sometimes he would be accompanied by Ivan and in the distance the Arab goat herders would watch the armed men on horseback. It was a tiny show of strength but it seemed to be working. The incidences of theft and harassment ceased.

On night patrols Saul sometimes took up a position close to the Arab village and observed how they went about their routine. He would look for signs of any parties of armed men leaving the village or anything else that might indicate that a threat was emerging. But nothing unusual happened and Saul often had time to sit under the desert stars gazing into the night. It was little different, he reflected, to the life he had left behind in South Africa as a soldier.

Between patrols, Saul would find excuses to seek out Anna's company. He would go to the fields where the young men and women removed stones from the fields before ploughing and was able to engage Anna in conversation while working alongside her. During the midday meal break they would sit in the shade of a scraggly olive tree and talk. Anna displayed an interest in the land of Saul's birth. The other young men and women would cast knowing looks in their direction, the girls giggling while the boys smirked. But these were the only times they had the opportunity to be together as at night Anna would remain in the company of the village girls and Saul mostly with Ivan, whose fractured English was increasingly tolerable the more vodka he consumed.

A month after Saul had been living in the *moshava* a letter arrived via a tortuous route from Africa to inform Jakob Isaacs that his remaining son, David, had been killed in the fighting in South Africa. Jakob's mourning was private and when he reappeared to the villagers he seemed a bent and beaten man.

'I have nothing,' he told Saul who went to offer comfort. 'God has asked more of me than he did of Abraham.'

'The people need you,' Saul said, watching the bowed head of the man he had grown to know as if he had been his own father.

Jakob was a quiet and decisive figure who the *moshava* leaders had come to rely on for his organisational skills. After a discussion with Saul, Jakob had ordered the eucalypt seedlings and when they arrived in the village Saul had supervised their planting in the swampland. They were thriving and every day Saul would observe their progress. When the sun and wind were right, he could actually get a whiff of the distinct scent that reminded him of home.

Saul found life hard but pleasant as he worked to establish this tiny foothold in the Holy Land for a dispossessed people. Anna had shown no romantic interest in him and Saul sometimes felt that he may as well have been her older brother. But he was patient. Sooner or later the girl would

347

grow to understand that his feelings for her were as strong as any he had ever experienced before. Saul had fallen in love with this sweet, golden-haired angel from the steppes of Russia. All she had to do was recognise his love to give his life meaning once again.

THIRTY-EIGHT

With the weekend drawing close, Patrick found that he was experiencing an almost youthful apprehension about the unknown. Deborah was expected on the Friday night and Patrick had briefed Davies and his wife, who was Patrick's cook, to prepare for her visit.

'Very good, sir,' Davies had replied and went about airing the guest's room.

Mrs Davies had pedalled to the village to purchase something special for the weekend and was quick to inform the butcher that none other than the famous Miss Deborah Cohen would be staying.

When Friday arrived, Patrick returned from a vigorous walk to be met by a familiar face waiting for him in the drawing room. It was not Deborah.

'John! What a pleasant surprise, after all this time,' Patrick said to the uniformed man standing by the fire. 'I thought you were still in Sydney.'

Colonel John Hughes stepped forward to take the offered hand.

'Got back a fortnight ago, old chap,' Colonel Hughes said with a broad smile. 'Heard you were staying up at the family estate and decided to pop in while I was in this part of the world. Your man was kind enough to let me in to wait for you.'

'I hope he offered you a drink,' Patrick said as he moved to the warmth of the fire to rub his hands.

'As a matter of fact he did,' Colonel Hughes replied. 'But I thought it would be awfully rude to have one without you. I am sorry that I did not send my card ahead, but I ran out of time and decided to fall on your colonial lack of formality by just dropping in.'

'Why is it that I sense you are not here just to say hello?' Patrick asked.

The officer shifted just slightly. 'I hope that we have the opportunity to do a little fly fishing on my estate after I finish my current assignment with the intelligence chappies,' Colonel Hughes said. 'But you are right, Patrick, I need to solicit your assistance in an ongoing matter we originally discussed in Sydney.'

'It's Martin, isn't it?'

'I am afraid so. It seems that he is now linked to a group of Irish killers planning to assassinate a British subject of some importance to the war effort.'

'How do you know all this?' Patrick queried.

The colonel could see that the man he had soldiered with in the Sudan was attempting to hide his annoyance.

'The police have informants amongst the Irish population of Liverpool and they passed on the information to us.

But I cannot tell you any more than that, old chap. I know you will understand, being a commissioned officer in His Majesty's army.'

'I am an officer in the Australian army nowadays,' Patrick said with a wry smile, 'or haven't they told you yet that the colonies federated to become a nation?'

'Just a mere formality,' John Hughes returned with his own smile. 'You will always look to Mother England for your foreign affairs.'

'No doubt, John. But what of Martin?'

'As far as I know he is in Ireland and in contact with some rather shifty locals from the village of your ancestors,' Colonel Hughes said, as if delivering a briefing. 'I was hoping that you might once again find a reason to pop over and visit the old sod.'

'I haven't been back since '86,' Patrick said wearily. 'It is not a place with fond memories for me anymore.'

'I heard,' John Hughes said gently. 'I'm sorry, old chap. You have not heard from your wife then?'

'No,' Patrick said moving away from the warmth of the fire. 'Not even when I was wounded.'

'I know what I am asking may bring you into contact with your wife,' Hughes said sympathetically. 'But we are both soldiers for the Empire and what I can tell you is that contacting your cousin is no less important than the surrender of one of those damned elusive Boer generals. We need you to persuade him that we are onto his every move and if he knows what is good for his Church's reputation he should desist.'

'Why don't you get someone else to tell him?' Patrick asked. 'Why me?'

'Not as easy as it seems,' the colonel coughed. 'Martin too is as elusive as De la Rey himself out there on the African *veldt*. I suspect that he would reveal himself to you out of a sense of family.'

'You know I will do it,' Patrick conceded. 'Because I suspect that if I don't something untoward might happen to him.'

Hughes did not answer but turned to look at the flames in the open hearth. Patrick knew he was right. He and Martin had shared so much as young boys, growing up in the loving environment of his Aunt Bridget and Uncle Frank's hotel in Sydney. Patrick had always stood up for his once gentle and scholarly cousin against bullies. But this time the perceived bully was the whole British Empire.

'Ahem!'

Both men turned to the door where Davies stood discreetly.

'Miss Cohen has arrived, Major Duffy,' he said. 'Shall I show her in?'

'Miss Deborah Cohen?' Colonel Hughes asked with a raised eyebrow.

'You should know, John,' Patrick said with an edge of disapproval in his voice. 'I have no doubt that the army has been keeping my life under scrutiny since I am related to a Fenian.'

'Not I, Patrick,' the colonel said as he reached for his cap and swagger stick on the mantelpiece. 'We have been friends for too long. But there are those who might. When this dreadful matter is out of the way you and I shall do that spot of fly fishing. Davies can show me the way out. You are a lucky man, old chap.'

Patrick felt himself blushing. But part of the flush was caused by the thought that John Hughes was first and foremost a soldier for the Empire rather than a loyal friend. Patrick knew that he was indeed suspected by those in

Protestant London of harbouring papist loyalties. Ancient sectarian animosities had not died with the new century.

He heard muffled voices from outside the room and realised that the colonel had introduced himself to Deborah in passing. Gathering his composure, Patrick turned as Deborah swept into the drawing room as a queen would into her court.

'Patrick, it is so good to see you,' she said. 'I had the brief pleasure of meeting Colonel Hughes. What a charming man. Will he be visiting again this weekend?'

'I am afraid not,' Patrick said with as much sincerity as he could muster. 'The colonel has to return to London.'

Deborah removed the feather-adorned hat from her head with the flourish of an actress and dropped it on a chair. There was something slightly unsophisticated about the gesture that Patrick liked. Perhaps it was a reminder of his less than formal colonial roots. 'I am delighted to have you as my guest,' he said. 'I will have Davies show you your room, and when you are ready, we can sit for dinner.'

'Is something wrong?' Deborah asked, moving closer to Patrick. 'Did Colonel Hughes bring you disturbing news of some kind?'

'Oh, I am sorry,' Patrick quickly replied. 'It was just a military matter of no real consequence,' he lied, 'but it is forgotten now that you have brought some brightness to this house. One could say a little bit of that Queensland sunshine I vaguely remember from my visits north.'

Deborah laughed lightly at Patrick's clumsy attempt to divert her question. 'Major Patrick Duffy, I strongly suspect that the heart of a poet beats in your chest as strongly as the drums of your regiment.'

'Now who is being melodramatic?' Patrick asked with a broad smile.

Deborah's very presence seemed to make the rest of the world and its intrigues grind to a halt. For the moment the colonel's ominous visit was already forgotten. Patrick knew he was under Deborah's spell. Her company and conversation felt so natural and yet he was acutely aware of his sworn vow of fidelity. He was a man who lived by a code of honour as binding as the oath of allegiance he had sworn as an officer to the Crown. He had never questioned this even when Catherine had betrayed her oath of loyalty in marriage.

The lilt of Deborah's voice blended seductively with the fine food and excellent French wine of the evening. Why had he so quickly invited this beautiful woman to share the weekend with him, Patrick wondered, unconsciously turning his glass to reflect the candlelight in the blood red wine of his crystal goblet.

'You are in a faraway place, Patrick.'

'I'm sorry,' Patrick apologised, noticing that Deborah was watching him with a curious smile. 'I did not mean to be so rude.'

'A penny for your thoughts,' Deborah said.

Patrick found that his attention was on the swell of her breasts just above the daring black dress she wore so well. He was also guiltily aware of how darkly red her lips were.

'I was just wondering why I wanted your company so much, and how I have been like a schoolboy waiting for the report. Kind of nervous but with an anticipation of doing well.'

'I must confess that I have had little sleep thinking about my visit,' Deborah said in a husky voice. 'I don't know what it is, but all the idle chatter we have indulged ourselves in before dinner has been like marking time.'

'It is wrong, I know,' Patrick said with an expression of

anguish. 'But I have wanted you even from the moment I first saw you at the opera, and yet I know it is wrong to just want someone if it is not based on love.'

'Do you know, Patrick, that is the very quality I admire about you above all other men I have known in my world. You have a beautiful simplicity in your approach to life. I suppose I came here hoping that you might take me to your bed and yet I think I should have known better. You are a man who would rather die than betray all that we women secretly hold most sacred.'

'And what is that?' Patrick asked.

'What we most desire is for a man to put us on a pedestal to the exclusion of every other female. I am no different. I have always tried to convince myself that I am a libertine, but through the years I have rejected offers of marriage from some of the most eligible men in Europe because I fear that they have too ready an access to other women. I want a man who will love me to the total exclusion of any other.'

'That I cannot do,' Patrick said softly. 'I have a wife, and although she may have chosen to disregard her vows of obedience and fidelity, I cannot.'

Deborah glanced away. She hoped that the disappointment in her face would not show. She had also felt the attraction from the moment they had met in the hotel foyer. Admiration for a man's sense of honour was one thing, she thought bitterly, but wanting to feel him possess her with his body and soul was another.

'Do you know what I am looking forward to this weekend?' she said brightly, surprising Patrick with her sudden change in mood. 'I think I would like to stroll down to the village and buy a big bag of fish and chips. We could find a pretty paddock and sit under one of those English oak trees and eat them.'

Patrick found that he was smiling despite the disappoint-ment he sensed in Deborah. If only she knew just how tough it was for him. Maybe his father would have handled the situation in a different manner, he mused. From what he had heard of his reputation with the ladies, Miss Deborah Cohen would not have made it through the entrée before he had her bedded. But he was not his father.

'Davies tells me that they have a good fish and chip shop in the village. Weather permitting, tomorrow we shall partake of England's national dish down by the brook that runs through the estate.'

The weekend was truly memorable, if largely for the fact that when they parted on Sunday afternoon it was with regret for what might have been.

Patrick waved and watched until the little horse-drawn cart was out of sight around a bend in the lane leading from the house, then sighed and walked back to the house. Nei-ther had mentioned ever seeing the other again. Maybe it was for the best, Patrick consoled himself. After all, the army medical board had passed him fit for active service and he had his covert mission to Ireland, a land that did not wel-come those wearing the King's commission.

But as Deborah watched the gentle English countryside pass by her she intuitively knew that one day Patrick Duffy would be hers. For now she would be patient and allow Patrick's life to run its course. When they would be together, Deborah did not know.

THIRTY-NINE

With his head down and dressed in the garb of an Irish working man, Father Martin Duffy drew no attention as he stood aside to let a platoon of English soldiers march past him along the narrow road leading from the Fitzgerald manor beyond the village. Extra patrols had been mounted on orders from London. There were rumours that the Irish Fenians were planning something and a show of force just might quell any ideas to raise arms against the occupiers of the ancient Celtic lands.

Martin even tipped his hat at the soldiers with their rifles sloped at the shoulder. When they were gone, he continued his walk to the house, passing the strange man-made hill before arriving at the ivy covered mansion. As was his habit in these troubled times, he stopped and scanned the building and could see that the house had fallen into the first stages of disrepair, a sure sign of an absentee landlord.

When Martin knocked on the door he was met by the housekeeper, who asked what his business at Mr Norris's house was. He asked politely if she would deliver a letter to the mistress of the house and the old woman gave him a curious look.

'Yer not from around these parts,' she commented.

Martin only smiled in reply and remained patiently by the door as it was closed to him. Hands in his pockets, he stamped his feet against the cold until a good time later the housekeeper returned to open the door.

'Yer can come in,' she said. 'Mrs Duffy will see you.'

Martin followed the broadly proportioned woman to a room lined with bookcases. It was stuffed in every corner with papers, books and the occasional work of the taxidermist, a swooping owl or falcon with wings outstretched.

'Father Duffy,' Catherine said in a tired voice as she clumsily attempted to rise from a wooden swivel chair. 'We have never met but I have heard of you from my husband.'

Martin motioned for her not to rise. He could clearly see that Patrick's wife was in the last weeks of her pregnancy, the swelling very obvious under the peasant-style skirt she wore. She appeared tired and pasty-faced, as if the library had been her permanent home during the confinement.

Martin engaged Catherine in small conversation for some minutes, talking about the weather. But Catherine sensed that Patrick's cousin had not come to merely engage in trivial chitchat and have a cup of tea. She could see it in the tenseness of his body posture and the fact that he was not dressed in the traditional garb of a priest.

'May I call you Catherine?' he finally asked politely. 'I was informed by Eamon that you might be in need of some spiritual solace,' Martin lied. 'He has confided in me of his concern for your welfare and I hoped out of my respect for Patrick that I might be of some comfort.'

'What comfort do I need?' Catherine flared. 'As you can see, I am with a bastard child born of the devil, and nature will run its course. Given time, I shall bear more of the devil's brood when he comes to me from the hill.'

Martin could clearly see that Catherine was under a strain that was unhinging her mind, a wild look flashing briefly in her eyes then dying, to be replaced by despair. She needed more than he could offer.

'Catherine, I would like you to allow the doctor to visit.'

'I don't need a doctor,' Catherine spat. 'I need . . . '

Her words tapered away and she turned to hide the tears rolling down her cheeks.

'What do you need?' Martin said as he crossed the room to stand beside her and take her hand.

She did not resist his gesture. Catherine bowed her head, rocking her body as the sobs came in waves. She would not answer Martin's question. What – or who – she wanted would not want her, now that she carried this thing in her body. In her mind she was convinced that she was forever lost and life no longer had any meaning.

'Talk to me,' Martin said gently. 'I might be a priest but I think I can help.'

Catherine ceased rocking and looked up at the man standing over her. 'Can you get Patrick to forgive me, and love me again as we did when we met?'

'I can contact Patrick,' Martin said quietly. 'I could tell him that you would like to see him. I know my cousin, he is a compassionate man and, I think, very understanding.'

'How could any man be understanding of a foolish woman who has left her family in another country to pursue her own selfish dreams? How could any man accept the thing I carry which is not his?'

Martin stared at the bookcase covering one wall, jammed with old volumes. He wished that he could find within them an answer that did not sound condescending. He had long excommunicated himself from the Church by his political activities. The director general of the Jesuit order had sent a summons for him to return to Rome to explain himself and he had broken his priestly vow of obedience in defying that summons. Martin was too immersed in the murky waters of rebellious intrigue to ever explain the actions that were seen as running contrary to his role as a priest.

He had come to the Fitzgerald house with a more sinister intention, but seeing the plight of the wife of the man he most missed from his life had for a moment made him feel more like a priest.

'Catherine, you are in need of help although you may deny this,' he said gently, holding her hand. 'I know that you are acquainted with the landlord, Mr Brett Norris. If I contact him he may be of assistance.'

'Brett has not visited since I told him of my condition,' Catherine said. 'Nor do I ever wish to see him again. I know of the many women in his life.'

'Where do I contact him?' Martin persisted.

Catherine wiped her face with the back of her sleeve. 'He has written to say that he will be returning to the house to settle some business affairs,' Catherine replied calmly. 'But I doubt that he will want to see the bastard he has sired with the help of the devil.'

'Do you know which day he will be in the village?' Martin asked, trying not to sound too intense.

'It is here,' Catherine said with an edge of annoyance in her voice. 'In the letter.'

360

She shuffled through the litter of papers on the desk and handed a neatly folded page to the priest. Martin scanned the words couched in a cold and formal prose until he found the date of the absentee landlord's return. He glanced up at Catherine who was staring ahead at the bookcase and sensed that her mind was no longer in the room.

'Thank you,' Martin said placing the folded letter on the desk. 'I will attempt to make contact with Patrick and –'

Catherine seized his hand with a vice-like grip that startled Martin.

'Please, do not tell him anything,' she asked in desperation. 'I beg you on your word of honour as a priest not to tell Patrick about me. I have plans to . . . '

She suddenly tapered away again, releasing her strong grip.

'What plans?' Martin asked in alarm. 'I hope you are not planning anything foolish, like taking your life. You should know such an act is a mortal sin in the eyes of God.'

'I am not a Catholic,' Catherine said with a bitter laugh. 'I can't go to hell for what I do not believe. Swear to me that you will not tell Patrick.'

Martin stared down at Catherine. Her once beautiful eyes spoke her plea. 'I will not tell Patrick,' he said gently.

As Martin left the manor to return to his safe house in the village, he trudged the pretty country lane bathed in late afternoon sunlight and wondered bleakly about the salvation of his own soul.

It was an unlikely combination of men for a committee of such importance: a schoolteacher, a publican, two peat diggers and a priest. Martin sat at the head of the table in the upstairs room of O'Riley's public house with his back to the wall. It was an old habit he had acquired from years of warily watching doors to see who would come through: friend or foe.

The meeting had been convened as a result of Martin's trip to the old Fitzgerald manor and the men in the smoky room looked to the priest for a report.

'Norris will be coming at the end of next month,' Martin said without any preamble. 'His . . . ' Martin hesitated. What did he call Catherine Duffy? 'His mistress has confirmed his arrival, with a letter I was able to read.'

'The bloody British have increased the patrols in the county,' O'Riley muttered. He was a balding man in the latter part of middle age but no less effective as a rebel in the cause to oust the English. 'It might be that they have wind of our activities.'

'Not likely,' a young and bespectacled man said from the end of the table. He was a schoolteacher, an efficient organiser and a learned man who had the role of intelligence officer in the cadre. 'My information points to a show of strength, nothing more.'

'How do we do it?' one of the peat diggers asked, slouching by the door to guard against a possible raid by the English controlled authorities.

'We ambush him,' Martin said. 'Where and how I will brief you when I have a bit more information from Mrs Duffy.'

'Catherine Duffy is a relative of sorts to you, Father,' the schoolteacher stated. 'Does that cause you any problems in this matter?'

Martin turned to the schoolteacher. 'Personal matters are a secondary to what must be done to free Ireland,' he responded. 'Tonight was the first time I had ever laid eyes on the woman.'

'But she is the wife of your cousin,' the schoolteacher persisted. 'I have heard it said that you and he were pretty close back in the colonies.'

'I have not seen my cousin Patrick in years,' Martin answered defensively. 'I doubt that, considering the way our lives have gone, an officer of the King's army would be shouting me a drink in Mr O'Riley's pub these days. No, what has to be done is all that matters right now. Norris is a big wheel in the British armaments industry and the Brits need to see that we can take the war to them when and where we decide. His death should shake up a few others in London.'

The schoolteacher bowed his head in recognition of the priest's commitment to the cause, although he and the others hardly considered Father Martin Duffy as a priest anymore. Martin may as well have been defrocked as far as they were concerned. His involvement in their cause had been a point of resentment to many who had believed priests might speak out on political matters but not act. Indeed, at first the Australian had simply crusaded with words to enlist the young men of the county to fight against the British in South Africa. Now he was planning an assassination.

'There is nothing more to discuss for the moment except to commit ourselves to the elimination of Norris when he returns to the county,' Martin concluded. 'We will keep in touch.'

The committee members nodded, chairs scraping as they rose to adjourn to the bar. Only Martin remained to reflect on what had occurred. He had sanctioned the killing of a man. Despite everything less than priestly about his life, he took a small black book from his pocket to read the prayers that were compulsory to a priest. He knew of priests who broke the vow of chastity on a regular basis but still performed as men of God. Was fighting for the freedom of a people any less noble?

When he had completed the prayers of his office, Martin slipped the missal back into his pocket and stared at the wallpaper peeling at one edge of the small, airless room. He tried to picture Patrick's face, remembering him as a young man, and Martin's lips broke into a brief smile. It had been Patrick who had forced him into the calling of the priest, he thought ruefully, to placate the Jesuits of St Ignatius when they were caught stealing the altar wine. How strange that his choice of vocation had brought him to Ireland and the village of his ancestors.

FORTY

'What you see?' Ivan asked from atop his horse. 'Little ants?'

Saul knelt in the dust and stared at the marks that only his trained eyes could read. 'Not sure as yet,' Saul said as he slowly scanned the surrounding plateaux. Ivan scratched at his beard and gazed off into the distant blue sky. A few fluffy white clouds sat on the horizon and somewhere he could hear the distant screech of a falcon searching the desert for prey.

'I see nothing,' Ivan frowned as his friend remained dismounted and examined the earth around them. 'No footprints. I not know how you see these things.'

'You weren't trained to track by the world's best,' Saul said quietly as the marks began to talk to him. Barely discernible as they were to his trained eye, they still told a story. He felt old Terituba, wherever he was, would be proud of his protégé's skill.

'Who teach you?' Ivan scoffed. 'There is nothing there.'

'An old blackfella taught me,' Saul said. 'But you wouldn't need tracking skills in Russia,' he continued with a cheeky grin. 'Blokes as big as you leave bloody big footprints in the snow.'

'Not always snow in Russia,' Ivan sighed. 'Sometimes so many flowers in summer that you go blind looking.'

Finally Saul raised his eyes and peered across the arid valley below. 'We have to be careful,' he said. 'There is a party of at least eight Arabs out there around a half day away and from what I can see they have at least three rifles between them.'

Ivan stared at Saul as he rose from the dust to remount his horse. 'You make joke,' Ivan said disbelievingly. 'You not tell all this from earth.'

Saul swung himself into the saddle and looked at the big Russian. 'Given time I could tell you what they ate for breakfast.'

Ivan shook his head and muttered in Russian. Saul guessed that it was not a compliment but ignored his friend's disbelief. The faint outlines of footprints gave Saul an idea of how many and roughly how old. The imprint of rifle butts as the roving party stopped to rest also told him of the arms they carried. And from the current state of the weather and the direction of the tracks he could discern just how long ago and where they were going. It was not something learned overnight and he knew that a tracker's skill depended on gut sense as much as observation.

Ivan followed Saul silently along a narrow trail to the bottom of the valley until Saul raised his hand and gave the signal to dismount. Without a word he moved forward to a good observation point, Ivan following. With the skills of seasoned soldiers both men lay on a rocky outcrop and carefully scanned the gorge ahead. Ivan gasped. There were eight men sitting in the shade of the gorge eating dates. Between them he counted five rifles and two ancient muskets. Ivan glanced across at Saul with sudden respect.

They watched the party for half an hour and when they were satisfied that the nomads were moving away from the *moshava* the two men made their way cautiously back to their mounts.

'How did you know, my friend?' Ivan asked, shaking his great shaggy head. 'It was as you say.'

'You would have to ask Terituba,' Saul said with a broad grin.

'Who this Terituba?' Ivan asked.

'Told you before,' Saul sighed as he swung himself into the saddle. 'An old and wise Kalkadoon blackfella.'

Ivan just shook his head and followed Saul.

The matter was reported to Jakob and the *moshava* committee when they returned the following morning.

'Do you think they were a bandit gang or Arab villagers?' Jakob asked.

'Villagers,' Saul replied without hesitation. 'I've seen their tracks before around here.'

Jakob looked to Ivan for confirmation but the Russian shrugged. 'I say Saul right,' he replied. 'Don't know how, but he right.'

Jakob accepted Ivan's confirmation. The two men were a good team and inspired a sense of security in the small community.

'We will stay on our guard,' he said with a wave of his hand. 'I would like to talk to you, Saul,' he added as the men prepared to withdraw from the meeting.

Ivan glanced back as he left the meeting room but Saul looked at him blankly. The Russian was followed by the village leaders, leaving Jakob and Saul alone.

Jakob gestured for Saul to take a seat.

'I feel that it is very important to train and equip our young people against the possibility of an attack from the Arabs,' Jakob said.

'Ivan and I can train them all right,' Saul said. 'But we don't have any guns or ammunition.'

Jakob steepled his fingers and gazed tensely through the doorway at the blaze of pale blue sky. 'I know where we can purchase a good supply of rifles and ammunition,' he said. 'But I am not an expert and I will need you to advise me on what we need.'

'That is not a problem,' Saul said casually. 'Where will you buy the arms?'

'England.'

After discussing the details of the weapons enterprise, Saul bid Jakob a good day and left. He had only one task now and walked to the fields to find Anna. But when he arrived he saw her in the company of Aaron Herzog.

Saul scowled. The young man had arrived from Austria a month earlier and been accepted into the community to work alongside the *moshava* members. He had been a religious student in Vienna and hoped to be a rabbi one day. Anna seemed drawn to the serious young man from the day he had arrived, and although she still spoke with Saul he sensed a distance had come between them.

He watched the couple laughing and talking, oblivious to his presence at the edge of the field. He did not like the newcomer, not only for the fact that he had won Anna's attention but also for his sanctimonious demeanour. Privately, the elders of the community had lauded the new-comer as a possible leader. He had, after all, a great knowledge of the Torah and was educated. This land needed men of God and Aaron was such a person.

Saul turned and walked back to the village with a heavy heart. When he was back at the house the expression on his face told his disappointment. Ivan had always known of Saul's feelings for his beautiful sister.

'You went to fields,' Ivan grunted as Saul flung himself on his simple plank bunk with its mattress of clean straw. 'Herzog was there.'

Saul did not answer but lay on his back staring at the ceiling.

'My sister is young and silly,' Ivan continued but said nothing more, having made his point.

For the following week Saul had little opportunity to see Anna. She was constantly in the company of the newcomer and Saul carried his pain with him on his constant patrols.

When he and Ivan returned from a patrol in the early morning they both noticed a distinct change in the atmosphere of the village. People were gathered together – some of the women weeping – and the faces that they saw from atop their mounts glared up at them with a mixture of fear and accusation.

Jakob hurried to meet them. 'They came in the night,' he said breathlessly. 'They took three of the girls.'

'Anna?' Ivan gasped, as if sensing something dark and evil.

Jakob glanced away, confirming the Russian's fear. Ivan looked desperately to Saul who had paled at the news.

'The bastards must have been bloody lucky, or they had our movements noted,' Saul said. It would not be hard to observe the coming and going of a mere two-man security force. 'How long ago?' Saul asked.

'Three, maybe four hours,' Jakob answered.

Saul wheeled his horse away towards the women's quarters. He now had to trust in everything Terituba had taught him.

The raiders had not bothered to conceal their tracks. Saul examined the footprints carefully, now as familiar to him as if he knew the men who left them. 'Same mob,' Saul muttered so only Ivan could hear him. 'That means we are outnumbered and outgunned when we catch up with them.'

'Da,' Ivan said. 'But maybe we surprise them,' he added hopefully.

'That's all we've got,' Saul said looking up to a rise beyond the village.

It was in that direction the raiders had gone and Saul knew the hill was in line with the local Arab village. He did not want to think about the fate of the three girls. All he wanted to think about was tracking the men, finding them and killing as many as they could with their limited arsenal. Without a word he spurred his horse forward.

The trail had been easy to follow. The only problem the two men had was riding onto the raiding party without alerting them, so they moved cautiously between geographical features and dismounted before each rise in the terrain, creeping forward on foot with their rifles ready.

Just on sunset they were dismounting before a small ridge when Ivan heard the muffled laughter. He cautioned Saul and, keeping low, they crawled to the rise. Lying on their stomachs, both men peered over the summit to a gorge below.

Ivan gagged at what they saw and Saul realised that he would have to restrain the Russian from mounting a single-man attack on the raiding party below. Sickened as he was, Saul knew that there was nothing they could do to help the three young women whose naked, torn bodies lay spread-eagled on their backs in the dust. Eight men stood around them. Blood spread in a pattern around each of the girl's heads indicated that their throats had been cut.

Saul held his hand firmly on Ivan's back and could feel

his trembling. 'We will kill them all,' he hissed to the Russian. 'We will kill them – as they killed Anna.'

Ivan did not reply and Saul knew he was sobbing silently for the loss of his little sister. All Saul could feel for now was a terrible burning desire to kill the men who had brought this atrocity into their lives. To achieve his aim he would have to remain calm and patient. He and Ivan were out-numbered and outgunned. But they had surprise and the motivation of vengeance on their side.

They remained on top of the hill and watched with a burning but controlled rage as the raiding party casually went about setting up camp for the night. In that time Saul observed and differentiated each of the party of raiders. Two were just boys probably, no older than twelve. This did not soften Saul's hatred. If they lived, they would be even worse in their later years, he justified to himself. They had been blooded by their elders and did not appear to be unduly disturbed by what they had done to the *moshava* girls.

When the night came they waited until the campfire burned to a gentle glow. A guard of one man had been left to keep watch but in time he appeared to doze by the fire.

Saul and Ivan made their way down the slope, guided by the fire until they were in the camp. Saul worked his way around to the dozing guard, one of the young boys, until he was on him with his knife. The boy came awake with a start when he realised that the shadow was not imaginary but terrifyingly real. But it was too late for him to react. Saul's finely honed knife sliced his throat from ear to ear as he held his hand over the guard's mouth to pre-vent him from screaming. Saul gripped his slight body until his struggles ceased and noticed that a man sleeping nearby was stirring.

Saul dropped the body and pounced on the second man

before he could rise. Again he struck with lethal professionalism, hoisting the befuddled man to his feet so that he could wrap his arm around his head and slice the exposed throat. The dying man tried to scream but drowned in his own blood.

Ivan had himself despatched two men quickly by snapping their necks before they could awake. But the slightly noisy presence of the two intruders awakened the remaining raiders and Saul kicked brushwood into the fire. Flaring, it illuminated the campsite. Only three men and one boy remained alive. They scrabbled to grab hold of their weapons but hesitated when they realised that they were looking down the barrel of Ivan's rifle.

'You will tie them up,' Saul declared. 'And in the morning finish the job.'

Ivan frowned. He was not sure what Saul planned – he was ready to finish the killing now. But he complied and sat back with Saul to wait for the dawn.

The sun was just rising above the silent hills when Saul stirred. The bound men looked with fear upon the terrible spectre of their comrades.

'Untie the boy,' Saul said softly to Ivan.

When the boy was released he stood unsteadily, watching with his dark eyes like a desert rabbit waiting for the hawk to swoop.

'Hold him so that he cannot run away,' Saul commanded and Ivan seized his arms.

The boy screamed, causing the three other prisoners to wail pleas for the boy and themselves. Saul drew his knife and walked past the terrified boy to the three remaining men, still tightly bound. With a deft movement, he cut each man's throat before they could plea once more for mercy.

Even Ivan was struck dumb by the merciless efficiency of

Saul, who he had never really considered a cold-blooded killer.

'You can let the boy go now,' Saul said turning from the now twitching men, bleeding away their lives in the sand. 'He can go back to his village and tell the story of what will happen to any man who should dare touch another woman of the *moshava*.'

At first the boy stood petrified but an angry shout from Ivan sent him stumbling on his way. As the boy ran over the rise and out of sight, Saul wiped the blade on the leg of his trousers.

'You will need to bring the horses down,' he said and Ivan looked from him to the three young women, their naked bodies still in the open.

Saul walked over to them. Tears flowed and he attempted to wipe them away with the sleeve of his shirt. He remained at his vigil until Ivan returned, leading the two horses down the slope.

With great tenderness Saul lifted two of the young women over his horse and left Anna to be lifted by her brother. As they led their horses back to the village Saul felt nothing. Two women he had loved had died. He was sure that God did not belong to his Jewish ancestors any more than He belonged to the Christians. From now on he would be God and bring death to any who dared interfere with the villagers. Jakob would acquire the tools and he would use them. Anna had trusted in his skills as a soldier but now she too was dead, a bloody corpse draped over her brother's horse.

FORTY-ONE

The Irish village of Patrick's ancestors had changed very little in the fifteen years or so since he had last visited. He stood outside the public house with its quaint shingle and noted that the hotel still belonged to Bernard O'Riley. One or two passing villagers stared at Patrick with expressions of curiosity mixed with puzzlement: had they not seen this face before?

Patrick hefted his battered valise and strode into the hotel's public bar. The publican, O'Riley, stared at Patrick, recognition slowly dawning.

'Captain Duffy, would it be?' he asked.

Patrick was surprised to be remembered after so many years. 'Major Duffy, now,' Patrick responded. 'I was wondering if you had any accommodation, Mr O'Riley?'

O'Riley glanced along the counter at the faces of the

men who had turned to observe the outsider seeking bed and board. 'For how long?' he asked.

'Not sure – but I will pay you a week in advance,' Patrick said, dropping his bag on the floor.

'That will be fine,' O'Riley said and came out from behind the bar to escort Patrick to a room upstairs. With formalities completed the publican closed the door behind him, returning to his duties in the bar.

'You know that man, Bernie?' one of the patrons asked.

'He's Catherine Fitzgerald's husband,' O'Riley replied, wiping down the counter. 'An officer with the British army.'

The patron scowled and the peat digger sitting beside him looked directly at the publican with a meaningful expression of contempt. As if reading his thoughts Bernard O'Riley said, 'Major Duffy is named for the big man himself, Patrick, who fought the British in the Colony of Victoria at the Eureka Stockade.'

'Then his grandson is a bloody traitor to his people,' the peat digger spat, 'if he wears the uniform of our enemies.'

'Don't be going and thinking bad thoughts, Sean,' O'Riley cautioned. 'He is also blood kin to Father Martin.'

'Then it will make it worse for the priest,' the man countered, 'having a traitor as a blood relative.'

O'Riley felt uneasy. Sean O'Donohue was a wild one, unpredictable and hot blooded with a deep and burning hate for anything to do with the British. The potato famine still reverberated in every Irish village and hamlet. O'Donohue's ancestors had been decimated by the death brought on by starvation and while he lived he had sworn to kill as many of the perceived collaborators of the British as he could.

The Irish publican left Sean O'Donohue to brood. This

was a matter that warranted a discussion with the council, the peat digger considered. A Duffy or not, the man was well and truly part of the English establishment and his sudden appearance in the tiny village suspicious.

Patrick knew whom he would first visit and was perceptive enough to sense the animosity his stay in the village had generated. It was in the looks of hostility he received when he walked the cobbled streets, and the silence that met his arrival wherever people were gathered. Even when he stopped a villager to make innocuous small talk, he was answered with curt replies.

At least he knew of one person who would not cut him short, and when he rapped on the door of the presbytery he was indeed greeted warmly by Father Eamon O'Brien, who ushered him inside with words of welcome.

'Patrick, it has been a long time,' Eamon said as he pulled out a chair for him at the table in the kitchen. 'How long must it be?'

'Not since I resigned my commission back after the Suakin campaign. Must be fifteen years.'

'So much has happened in your life since then, I have heard,' Eamon said as he automatically sought out the bottle of whisky. 'Even that you have renounced the true faith in favour of your grandmother's Protestant beliefs.'

Patrick smiled as he took the tumbler. 'I think you know me well enough to know that I never really had much interest in any religion in the first place. My conversion to my grandmother's religion was little more than a matter of politics – not belief.'

Eamon took a seat at the table and sighed. 'Ah, yes, you and your father were never ones to grace the portals of the Holy Mother Church.' He raised his glass to Patrick. 'But it is good to see that you are alive, and looking well.'

Patrick acknowledged the salute with his own. 'And it is good to see a friendly face in the home of my illustrious, if not rebellious, ancestors.'

'I gather that you have been availed of the people's mood then,' Eamon observed.

'That I have,' Patrick replied. 'I get the feeling that my stay here is not exactly welcomed.'

'You must realise that my parishioners see you as part of the British army and therefore an enemy. I think that it is worse for you because the word has got around already that you are descended from Patrick Duffy, whose feats fighting in this county against the English have not been forgotten. I think you can understand their reaction to your involvement with the very enemies your grandfather fought.'

'Could you perhaps let it slip,' Patrick said leaning forward, 'at your next mass that I am not with the British, but with the Australian army. I am not English – I'm Australian.'

Eamon grinned. 'I just might do that,' he said. 'But I cannot guarantee it will do any good. It seems that there is something sinister going on around here at the moment. The people are highly suspicious of all outsiders – especially those of a military nature.'

'I am only here to seek my wife. Nothing else.'

At the mention of Catherine, Eamon frowned. He wondered how much Patrick knew about Catherine and her present circumstances. It seemed every time they met, regardless of years intervening, it would be he who would inform the grandson of Patrick Duffy of bad news.

'Then you have heard?' Eamon asked carefully.

Now it was Patrick's turn to frown. 'Heard what?'

'That Catherine gave birth last week to a baby boy.' All colour drained from Patrick's face and for a moment the priest feared that the man opposite him might collapse.

377

'I regret to say,' Eamon continued, 'that the poor child did not live for very long. It was sickly and died before I was able to give last rites. Fortunately Father Duffy did that, despite protests from Catherine.'

'Martin?' Patrick whispered. 'Father Martin Duffy of the Jesuit order?'

'I know of his relationship to you, Patrick,' Eamon said gently. 'Maybe it was a good thing that it was he who delivered the little one's soul into the hands of God.'

'You know it was not mine,' Patrick said in a strangled voice. 'I did not even know that my wife was expecting a child.'

Please, God, why me, Eamon questioned. Why is it me who always seems to be telling this good man terrible news? 'I am sorry for the loss of an innocent baby's life,' he said. 'But it was God's will and –'

'God be damned! It was the work of Mr Brett Norris – not God.'

Eamon could see the cold rage smouldering behind the grey eyes of the man who had known so much pain in his life.

'What will you do, Patrick?' he asked gently.

'I don't know,' Patrick replied, staring at a space beyond the room. 'I really have no idea.'

'You know that you can always talk to me,' Eamon offered. 'And I think that Catherine may need you in her time of pain and grief.'

Patrick's expression of betrayal suddenly took on a look of savage anger. 'She has the man she chose over me to look after her,' Patrick replied. 'I will have nothing to do with her ever again.'

Eamon did not reply. He knew Catherine well enough to see the change that had come over her soon after she arrived back in Ireland and sensed that she had realised her mistake. Eamon found himself in sympathy with Catherine, whose soul was lost to the mystical world of the Old Ones of the Celtic past. Pride was a terrible sin, he thought. It kept apart two people who should be together. But Patrick Duffy was not a man who could be lectured to. He was a man who must find his own answers to save his soul.

Patrick left the presbytery in a daze of pain. He had come to renew his friendship with the Irish priest and covertly glean information from him about his cousin Martin's whereabouts. Instead he had been informed that Catherine had borne the child of a man he hated more than any enemy he had ever faced on a battlefield. In coming to Ireland he had not been sure whether he would see Catherine. He had resigned himself to the idea that it was she who must seek him out. At least now he knew that his wife, who he had admitted to himself he had not stopped loving, was forever lost to him. Her heart belonged to another.

From a presbytery window Eamon watched Patrick trudge away into the late afternoon. The priest brooded on the presence of the former British officer whose blood was so powerfully a part of the very soil the man walked upon.

Eamon sighed for the pain of this tiny country that was also his own, despite his English education. Sometimes it seemed as though the Old Ones had never gone from the land, that they merely lived in the dark shadows and moon-lit nights and forever cast their nefarious spells on those whose lives they controlled from the lakes, groves and rocky hills of the emerald green land. Maybe Saint Patrick had been astute to weave Christianity into the old beliefs, rather than attempt to convert the people with an imposed Romanised religion. But perhaps sometimes the Old Ones reached out from their shadowy places and sought

Christian souls, as the Druids had made human sacrifices to placate the Celtic gods.

Eamon shuddered. He sensed that a drama was being played out as old as the people themselves. This was an Irish pagan ritual of blood, lust, intrigue and revenge, not something belonging to a Christian world of written laws and civilised attitudes.

FORTY-TWO

The bellowing cattle trudged through the spindly scrub, raising a low, red cloud of dust that permeated the skin of the stockmen. Matthew Duffy rode listlessly at the edge of the great herd of Balaclava's beasts, pondering on the vagaries of his young life. He had experienced the horror of war on a continent on the other side of the Indian Ocean, fallen in love with the daughter of the legendary Major Patrick Duffy and returned to a mother both overjoyed and furious. But mostly his mother had just been grateful for his safe return, although Matthew found her love just a little smothering after months of living alongside the tough men of the mounted infantry. It had been his suggestion that he spend time at their property to get his thoughts together and decide on the course of his life. Kate had reluctantly consented and Matthew packed his old army kitbag to travel inland from Townsville to the Balaclava station his mother owned adjacent to the Macintosh property of Glen View.

As the herd meandered its way south to the greener pastures of New South Wales, Matthew had a lot of time to reflect on life. He still smarted from his failure to see Fenella. Her great-grandmother, Lady Enid Macintosh, had forbidden any contact between them.

When Matthew's real identity had been exposed Lady Enid had paled. There was no way whilst she breathed that a papist would have anything to do with her only great grand-daughter. Lady Enid had written to Kate to express her view that the couple were far too young to have any liaison.

Kate had read the letter and smiled grimly. She knew exactly what her old adversary really meant, but Kate had agreed with the aristocratic woman's opinion. Very little of good had come from contact between the two families.

Kate had met her son at the wharf when his ship had arrived in Sydney and after the tears and hugs a fiery scene occurred where Matthew was forbidden to make contact with Fenella. Matthew was at a disadvantage on account of his running away in the first place. But he loved this strong woman who had sacrificed so much for his future and reluctantly agreed to abide by his mother's wishes.

But now, out on the hot and dusty plains of central Queensland, he was re-assessing his life.

'Hey, Duff, get your head out of yer ass and round up those stragglers,' a voice called to him across the tramp of plodding cattle.

Matthew had answered to Duffy for so long and wore the name with such pride during his months in South Africa that he had broached his mother with the idea of officially adopting her maiden name.

At first she had resisted, as if the division in names might herald a split between mother and son. Tracy was the name of a fine man who had achieved so much in his life. But Matthew pointed out that he had never really known his father. So they compromised and Matthew adopted his father's family name as his second Christian name. From now on he would be Matthew Tracy Duffy – or just Duff to those who liked him.

Matthew snapped from his daydreaming and glanced around. He saw Texas Slim wheeling away on his horse and noticed that three of the stock had drifted away from the herd. Texas Slim was an American who had been employed by Kate because of his knowledge of cattle from his home country. He was a dashing young man of flamboyant dress who had served with American expeditionary forces in the Spanish American War in Cuba in '98. Bringing with him an American know-how at a time when Kate was in need of new ideas, he'd been appointed head stockman at the Balaclava property. At first his position was resented by the older men, but they grudgingly conceded the Yank had some experience and talent. Better still, he was a firm, fair and friendly boss. He was also a superb horseman and great favourite with the ladies and had befriended the son of his employer when he learned of the young man's record as a mounted infantryman in South Africa. Theirs was a friendship of those who knew the camaraderie of fighting men and many nights on the track had passed in long conversations around the campfire discussing the life of a soldier. Although ten years lay between the two men, war had bridged the gap between them.

Matthew spurred his tough stock horse into a canter to head off the renegade cattle. Within a short time they were back with the herd and their heads pointed south. For the

moment Matthew's thoughts were occupied with anticipation of the end of the day and a good meal. His mother
would have been pleased to know that her son was getting
on with his life. But she would have been less pleased to
know of the plan that was already forming in Matthew's
head for the end of the muster.

FORTY-THREE

Fenella Macintosh had not taken kindly to Lady Enid's command that she was to have no more contact with Matthew Duffy. She stamped her foot and tossed her head defiantly. 'I am a young woman now, Lady Enid,' she said. 'I do not think it is fair that you should make such decisions for me.'

'There is much more to this matter, young lady, than I could ever explain,' Enid said calmly. 'One day you will understand, but for now you will obey me.'

But Fenella crossed her arms and assumed a stance that told her great-grandmother she was not prepared to listen. How could Lady Enid know what it was like to be in love, she huffed. She was after all an old woman without the capacity for passion.

'I wish you were dead,' Fenella said as she stamped her foot again and stormed to the door.

Enid frowned as Fenella slammed the door of the library and rushed away to her room. So defiant, Enid sighed. Not like Patrick's own mother, Fiona, at her age.

For a moment she felt her heartbeat flutter and experienced a short period of giddiness. Enid gripped her breast and breathed slowly to steady herself. The family doctor had warned that she must remain calm at all times. He had detected an irregular heartbeat. Enid closed her eyes and sat quietly behind her great polished wooden desk in the soft shadows of the late afternoon.

So much over the years had occurred in this room, she thought in her pain. It had been a place primarily of sadness. The confrontation with Fenella reminded her of the time so many years earlier she had confronted her own daughter about her illicit liaisons with a young Irishman, Michael Duffy. The event had left them estranged for many years and the pain of separation between mother and daughter was not easily cured by their eventual reconciliation. Too many valuable years had been lost to them both.

The shadows were lengthening in the room, creeping unstoppably from under the draped window which overlooked the gravel driveway. Enid's eyes opened on the display of Aboriginal weapons mounted beside the floor-to-ceiling bookcases – the spears, shields and boomerangs of a long dispersed clan of people once known as the Darambal tribe.

For a second she imagined that a shadow had materialised in the corner of the room and she shifted her gaze to catch it. Had it merely been the gentle flapping of the drapes in the late afternoon breeze? For a moment it had appeared to have a greater substance than a mere shadow. She stared hard at the corner of the library and a grim smile set on her fragile face, still smooth and without wrinkles after so many years of life.

'You have finally come,' she whispered as the pain tightened, vice-like inside her breast. 'After all these years I am now able to gaze upon your face and speak to you in person of the terrible sin we did to your people.'

Then Enid was at peace once more as the shadow smiled upon her.

An hour later the maid Betsy went to the library to inform Lady Enid that supper would be served in the dining room. She knocked unobtrusively and called to her mistress. There was no answer and Betsy tentatively opened the door.

She found Lady Enid sitting in her chair and thought that she might be asleep, such was the peaceful smile on her wan face. But as Betsy stared she saw no sign of breathing and closed the door behind her as she went to call the family doctor.

It was Fenella who experienced the most pain as the gravediggers shovelled the earth over the coffin. She had been the last person to see the grand old lady alive. Had their forceful argument caused her death? Her last ill-chosen words haunted the young woman who stood beside the grave, Alexander's hand gripping hers as she swiped away the tears with her free hand.

Very few had attended the funeral. Lady Enid's true friends were long dead but one or two prominent people in commerce and finance were present out of respect for the formidable lady who had once ruled a great financial empire. Fine words of praise for her considerable achievements were intoned at the service in the church she loved so much.

'It wasn't your fault,' Alexander whispered gently to his older sister. 'Lady Enid was really old.'

'How do you know how I feel?' Fenella snapped under her breath, immediately regretting her terseness.

'Because I felt the same way when our grandfather was killed up in Queensland,' Alex replied sadly. 'I felt it was my fault because I couldn't stop the bull killing him.'

Fenella turned to her brother who was now rapidly catching up to her in height. She saw in his eyes a terrible sadness for a memory not all that long past. Alex had returned to his family a different person and, in his own quiet ways, seemed much wiser than his tender years. He no longer backed down in the face of George's bullying, for a start. In fact, it seemed that George now feared his younger brother.

'I am sorry,' Fenella said as she squeezed her brother's hand in reassurance. 'You're right, Lady Enid was very old.'

The mourners were trickling back to their coaches and buggies leaving only Alex and Fenella by the grave. The man shovelling the earth had retired to the shade of a tree to take a swig of water. Although it was heavily overcast, the heat rose from the earth, promising a wild storm by the end of day, not uncommon in Sydney.

'You have never spoken much about your trip away,' Fenella said as they turned to walk back to the coach and the stern nanny waiting for them.

'There were lots of wonderful things that happened,' Alex replied quietly. 'And Mr . . . ' He paused. It was hard adjusting to the name of the man who had taught him so much about life. 'Our grandfather . . . '

Alex choked on the words and Fenella did not press him. Perhaps one day he would speak more about the man who, from the moment she had laid eyes on him, she had sensed was very important in their lives. Not that her feelings made any sense until she learned of the Irishman's true identity. For Michael Duffy reminded her of no-one more than her own father, and she missed him so much.

When they reached the coach George was waiting for them with a bored expression on his face. He was still a good half-head taller than Alex but his larger size was no protection anymore against Alexander's anger and fists.

'The old . . .' George was about to comment on his great-grandmother's passing when he noticed the cold fire in Alexander's eyes, anticipating a derogatory remark. George was wise enough not to utter another word and they climbed into the open coach drawn by four grey horses.

As the coach trundled back to the mansion by the harbour, Fenella found her thoughts drifting again to the young man she had known all too briefly prior to his leaving to fight in South Africa.

For George Macintosh, his thoughts were on his inheritance. Now that Lady Enid was gone, his father would no doubt inherit the huge fortune left in the estate. And as the eldest he was next in line. What he could do with so much money! He could indulge himself in excesses he had only dreamed of.

Alex caught the look on George's face as he sat facing his brother in the coach but controlled the urge to wipe away the smirk and whatever evil lurked behind the cold grey eyes. Alexander was now old enough to understand that some people – like his brother – are just born bad.

The cattle drive was over and Matthew stood in the dusty street of the New South Wales town of Moree waiting

389

patiently for Texas Slim to settle with the stock and station agents. The discovery of artesian water in the district had prompted Kate to invest in land, and her venture had paid off. No matter how bad a drought hit Queensland, she could have her stock driven to her property in northern New South Wales to be watered and, if need be, fed on fodder.

'Well, young Matt,' Texas Slim said as he strode across the street with his saddle slung over his shoulder. 'What next?'

'How is it that you decided to come over here?' Matthew asked unexpectedly as they stood in the shimmering heat of the tiny frontier town. Randolph Gates, alias Texas Slim, was a man he had come to admire. The tall, easygoing American embodied all the qualities of the friends he had left behind in South Africa – and at the same time was a bit exotic, maybe even like his own father had once been.

Randolph looked at Matthew with a quizzical expression on his smoothly shaved and tanned face. 'Kind of funny question to ask after all this time we have been on the trail together, pardner.'

'I was just wondering,' Matthew replied. 'You see, my father was a Yank. My mother told me he came out to the goldfields at Ballarat in the '50s and got himself into the big fight against the British at the Eureka Stockade. I was just wondering how come you decided to come over here.'

The smile on the American's face slowly turned to a frown. 'I was a bit restless after being with the Rough Riders in Cuba. Got back home and saw the advertisement in a farming almanac for a man to work in the Australian Colony of Queensland. It sounded interesting and satisfied my need to see a bit more of the world. So here I am. Anything else?'

Matthew shook his head and fell into step as they made their way to the hotel for a cold beer. Although Matthew was legally under the age to drink, all the men who knew him vouched for him. Somewhere in his life Matthew had lost his youth and catapulted himself into manhood.

Drinking in company with the stockmen and being prepared to stand up in a fight against any man came naturally to Matthew, much to the despair of his mother. To Kate he would always be the little boy who she had nursed in sickness and cuddled. But she also saw in her son the father he had never known. He had a spirit of fierce independence and adventure. All she could do now was to stand quietly in the shadows of his life and be there for him. His life was that of the traveller in the lonely places of the great plains; he might see the life-giving rains fall as a storm in the distance, and hurry his journey to catch the refreshing, momentary coolness of the water, only to see it move away. To chase the storm was often a waste of time, as it would always remain tantalisingly ahead of the traveller. Matthew was the desert storm of her life – just as his father had been.

'So what are your plans?' Texas repeated.

'Thought I might stick with you for a while,' Matthew answered as they entered the coolness of the hotel's main bar to be met by the rest of the stockmen who had made the drive to Moree.

'Well, pardner,' Texas drawled, 'I have some leave due according to the boss, your ma, and I intend on seeing the bright lights of Sydney before returning to Balaclava.'

'Thought the same thing myself,' Matthew grinned.

'You are going to be in a heap of trouble with Miss Kate,' Texas frowned. 'She gave me the impression that you were to head back to Townsville as soon as the drive was over.'

'I will,' Matthew said. 'As soon as I take my leave in Sydney.'

Texas shook his head and pushed his way towards the bar.

'Just make sure that you tell Miss Kate that I had nothing to do with you going to Sydney – or I will be looking for another job.'

Matthew thrust out his hand. 'Promise,' he said as he gripped the American's hand. 'Going to Sydney was all my own idea. So, when do we leave?'

Texas groaned as a glass of foaming brown beer was placed before each man. As Matthew raised his glass he had a fleeting memory of a time that now seemed so long ago when he had gone south from Townsville with Saul Rosenblum to enlist. He raised his beer and muttered, 'To you, Saul, old mate, wherever you are.'

Matthew had never believed that Saul had been killed at Elands River. Maybe captured, and if so he would eventually one day return to Queensland. But not killed.

When Matthew awoke next day, still dressed, he had trouble putting together the time between his first beer and the sun rising over him as he lay on his bed on the hotel verandah. From the soreness of his knuckles and the blood on his face, he strongly suspected that he had been involved in a fight. He groaned as the shadow of Texas fell over him.

'Time to go, pardner,' Texas said with a broad grin. 'Daylight's awasting and Sydney's acalling.'

FORTY-FOUR

No matter how much Patrick attempted to persuade himself that Catherine no longer existed in his life, the memories of happier times haunted him. He lay on his bed in the small hotel room and stared at the ceiling. There he could see a young and happy woman who had followed him halfway across the world to express her love, and from that love had come three children. The remembrance of a passionate time when there seemed no possibility of it ever ending caused Patrick to squeeze his eyes shut, as if the act could make the painful memories go away.

He had attempted to justify to himself that the only reason he had travelled to Ireland was his mission to make contact with Martin, but he knew that was a lie. He had come to see his estranged wife and try to resolve their seemingly impossible situation. Only then would he be able to get on with his life.

Patrick had made his decision and it was time to do something about it. The small revolver lay on the bed next to Patrick's shaving kit. He picked it up and carefully loaded the .32 calibre bullets in the chambers. Not a powerful weapon, he reflected, but still a gun that could kill at close range.

He pocketed the revolver and left his room to walk through the bar of O'Riley's, aware that the patrons had fallen into silence at his presence. But he bid them a good day despite their sullen hostility.

Patrick stepped onto the cold and bleak narrow street. Hunched against the drizzling rain, he set off with a soldier's walk towards the edge of town but became immediately aware of a man who emerged from the shadows to dog his footsteps. Patrick felt the reassuring butt of the pistol in his pocket.

The night was falling when he reached the old Fitzgerald mansion and Patrick stood uncertainly outside the house. He could see a light shining through a window upstairs and then stepped forward to knock. It was some minutes before the door opened to reveal Catherine's gaunt face. She stood with a stricken expression staring at her husband.

'It is good to see you, Catherine,' Patrick said gently.

'You should come in,' his estranged wife said, 'or you will freeze to death.'

Patrick glanced over his shoulder as he stepped inside. He could not see the man who had followed him but knew that he was most probably waiting and watching from the gathering cloak of night.

Inside, Patrick felt awkward. Catherine had changed – but so had he. It had been over two years since he had last seen her and time had taken its toll on her beautiful vitality.

'Why did you come?' Catherine asked as they stood facing each other in the dark foyer.

Despite the dim light he could clearly see that she was on

the verge of breaking down. 'You are my wife and I love you,' Patrick simply replied. 'I have come to take you home with me.'

Catherine spun away and took a couple of steps into the house. 'It is not as easy as that,' she said, anguished. 'Too much has happened for us ever to be together again.'

'I know about the child,' Patrick said quietly. 'That is all past and I know that our children need you with them – as do I.'

'But do you, Patrick? Do you really need me by your side again?'

Patrick felt the weariness. He had been betrayed but somehow he could not stop loving the woman who had fled their marriage with another man. Despite all that he had experienced in his life – war and the loss of loved ones – his love for Catherine was the one constant that would not leave him.

'I need you,' he replied. 'I have never stopped loving you. I don't know why that is, but I do know that I still love you regardless of all that has happened.'

Patrick's words stabbed Catherine as sharply as any dagger. The guilt of her passion for Brett Norris was still very much a part of her life.

'You cannot say that when you don't really know me,' she answered in a strangled voice. 'You have never really known me. To you, I was just something in your life – like a pretty ornament – not truly the person to share your life.'

Patrick went to protest but Catherine already knew what he would say. She held up her hand but could not bring herself to look into his eyes. To do so would have weakened her resolve. From the moment she had heard the stories from her housekeeper of his arrival in the village she knew it was inevitable that he would call on her.

'It would be better that you leave the house and return to Sydney,' she continued. 'We are different people, Patrick, you and I.'

'The children?' he protested.

'The children are better off without a mother as evil as I.'

'You are not evil,' Patrick said, advancing towards his wife. 'How could you say that?'

Catherine turned to look into his emerald eyes. 'I am either evil – or I am going mad,' she said sadly. 'Either way, you and the children are better off without me.'

'I believe neither,' Patrick said seizing Catherine by the shoulders. 'You are my beautiful wife and mother of my children. I love you, Catherine, and want you . . . no, need you back in my life, to make me a complete man again. Please don't shut me out. We have shared too much together.'

Catherine stared up into her husband's eyes and saw the depth of love in his soul. She felt a terrible wave of pity for him and broke down in tears. Patrick drew her to him and wrapped his arms about her head and shoulders as she sobbed against his chest. He gently stroked her thick mane of red hair, now prematurely streaked with grey, and Catherine felt his love envelop her. It was both gentle and strong.

'Oh, Patrick,' she said in a muffled voice as she clung to him, 'I wish I could give you what you want but I cannot. I need time to think.'

Patrick held his wife at arm's length and kissed her on the forehead. 'I think I understand,' he said. 'I will be leaving the village in four days. I will come back to fetch you away from here and take you with me to Sydney.'

Catherine wiped at the tears with her hand and tried to smile for Patrick's sake. 'I promise you that I will think on what you have said.'

'Then, I will be back,' Patrick said. 'And when I return we shall depart Ireland.'

Reluctantly Patrick left the house, recognising that his wife needed time to consider. But walking away from the house was the hardest thing he had ever done in his life. Every instinct told him to stay with her and prove his feelings. He was hardly aware of the man following him.

From an upstairs window Catherine strained to see Patrick as he vanished into the night. Her heart ached to see him disappear from her life. She fell to her knees and sobbed for the loss of her soul. There was so much that she wanted to tell the man who seemed to love her without reservation. If only life could be so simple, she thought in her despair. And that she could turn back time. But Brett Norris was expected within days and that was an issue she had not resolved.

Catherine lay huddled in a corner of the hall and listened to the rain beating a mournful tune on the window pane. For a brief moment she thought about Patrick trudging back to the village, cold and wet, and the thought touched her in a way that only exacerbated her despair. What if this loving and gentle man should catch a cold and sicken to the point of death? What else would her children have in their lives?

Sean O'Donohue was angry when the man he had been following disappeared on entering the outskirts of the town. 'Bastard!' he swore, and continued into the narrow, deserted streets of the village. At least he knew where Major Duffy was staying. No doubt he was heading back to the warmth of his hotel room.

Suddenly an arm wrapped around his throat and he was wrenched off his feet.

'Don't try anything, laddie,' a voice hissed in his ear as Sean felt the painful thrust of a gun's barrel in his ribs. 'I have stalked men far more dangerous than you and most of them are dead now.'

'You've got the wrong man, mister,' Sean protested. 'I was just out for a walk.'

'No fool goes out for a walk on a night like this unless he has important business,' Patrick growled. 'So I would be wanting an answer as to why you were following me, or you just might disappear forever – and that is a promise.'

'I think you know why,' Sean said through gritted teeth as the gun bit deeper into his ribs. 'You are a Brit, and any Brit in these parts attracts interest.'

'You're wrong about that,' Patrick said quietly. 'I am an officer in the Australian army, not the British army – but I don't expect someone as bog stupid as you to even know where Australia is.'

'I know where Australia is,' Sean replied angrily. 'It's the place the Brits sent all their convicts.'

Patrick released his grip and Sean massaged his throat.

'You can turn around,' Patrick said.

Sean turned to face the man who had materialised out of the night to ambush him so easily. He had a sudden, grudging respect for the grandson of the legendary Patrick Duffy who had caused the occupying British army so much trouble in the county over a half century before. But this made his grandson no less a traitor in the Irish rebel's eyes as Duffy had faithfully served the Queen for many years.

'Am I free to go?' Sean asked in a surly voice and Patrick nodded.

As he was leaving Sean clearly heard the Australian's

softly delivered warning. 'Don't be going out to the Fitz-gerald house again. Or I will personally hunt you down and kill you.'

Sean believed every word Major Duffy said.

'Oh, and by the way,' Patrick called to the back of the retreating man. 'If you happen to come across Father Martin Duffy, please give him my regards, and tell him that his cousin Patrick would like to meet with him.'

Sean knew the Australian's relationship to the renegade Jesuit. He would pass on the message.

O'Riley was behind the bar when Sean entered from the cold night. He could see the angry scowl on the young peat digger's face. 'Top of the evening to you, Sean,' the publican greeted cheerily. 'And what would the dark look be for on such a grand evening?'

Sean stepped up to the bar. 'Have you seen the priest?' he snarled, ignoring O'Riley's cheerfulness.

'He's around,' O'Riley shrugged as he polished a tumbler with a clean cloth. 'Would you be wantin' to see him?'

'Just tell him that his traitorous cousin asked after him.'

O'Riley leant across the bar. 'You talk to Major Duffy tonight?' he asked quietly.

'You could say that,' Sean answered. 'But the next time we meet, Major Duffy will be a dead man, you can bet on that as a sure thing.'

The publican frowned. He could see the fire of hate burn-ing in the fanatical young man's eyes and felt uneasy. No-one had sanctioned the execution of the Australian. After all, there were many in the new country who sym-pathised with the Irish plight. Many of Irish ancestry had indeed fled to the Australian colonies – or been transported.

These were now the people they needed to protest from foreign shores against British occupation of Ireland. Major Duffy may have once fought for the Queen, but so too had many loyal Irishmen, seeking a way out of soul-destroying poverty by enlisting under the colours of the Union Jack.

'Don't be goin' and doing anything rash,' the publican hissed. 'Major Duffy's grandfather was the big man here, as well as in the Australian colonies.'

'Did you know that Major Duffy turned Protestant?' Sean replied. 'Maybe that should tell you something about his loyalty to his blood.'

O'Riley did not know about Patrick's conversion and the news came as a shock. If what the young peat digger said was true, then a shadow was indeed cast on Major Duffy's kinship to the values of his ancestors. Was it that he had gone over to the British in every way? And if he was seeking out his cousin, Father Martin Duffy, for what reason? O'Riley felt a dread he could not comprehend. Whatever it was, the Australian's presence in the village bode no good. Maybe young Sean was right. Maybe the major should become a legitimate target.

Father Eamon O'Brien closed the door to the confessional box, leaving behind the world of sins mortal and venial. The church was empty as penitents had intoned their Hail Marys and Our Fathers and left for hearth or pub.

The priest sighed and wondered how much whisky was left in the bottle in the kitchen cupboard of the presbytery. The burden of the knowledge he carried was weighing like a millstone around his neck. In many ways he wished Father Martin Duffy had taken the confessions this day.

Eamon genuflected before kneeling at the altar to pray

for guidance. God did not speak to him but at least praying gave him time to reflect on what he could do to save a life, without defiling the sanctity of the confessional. His parishioner had confessed to a sin yet to be committed and Eamon had argued vehemently that confession would in no way absolve the man from his sins if he went ahead.

How could he tell his friend Patrick Duffy that he had been marked for execution? Maybe a warning was not strictly a breach of the sanctity of the confessional. He would not, after all, be breaking his sacred oath.

Eamon crossed himself and rose, glancing up at the depiction of the agonised figure of Jesus on the cross. How could men still condone murder with absolution through religion? For Father O'Brien, his faith was one of love and forgiveness – not hatred and politics.

FORTY-FIVE

Saul Rosenblum sat quietly by the swamp, gazing at the young eucalypt saplings. How well they were growing, he mused. They had taken to the ancient lands of Moses and Abraham as if they were always meant to be a part of the ongoing story of the chosen people.

Since the arrival of the arms supply from Europe, Saul had gained a reputation as a hard man. The young people of the *moshava* both admired and feared him as he went about training them in the use of the few rifles they had acquired. He and Ivan's search for the missing girls and the bloody end to that story were well known to all, but only the newcomer, Aaron Herzog, had expressed his disapproval of the way Saul and Ivan had handled the situation to the leaders of the *moshava*.

'It is not God's way to kill on the Sabbath,' he had stated. When his criticism was related to Saul he was only held back by the giant Russian from going to the pious man and thrashing him within an inch of his life.

'It is not the thoughts of the others,' Ivan had soothed. 'But I fear his kind will try one day to control us after we have tamed this land.'

To find peace Saul would often ride to this swamp which the eucalypt roots were struggling to strangle so that the land could be tilled for agriculture.

'Jakob wants to see you,' Ivan said from behind him. 'He says we have visitors.'

Saul rose from the earth and waved an acknowledgement to his friend astride his horse. 'I will head up and see him now,' he answered.

When Saul rode back to the little village he noticed a group of well-dressed Europeans – both men and women – standing around a column of horses and pack donkeys. From the amount of stores packed on the donkeys Saul immediately concluded that it was some kind of expedition.

Jakob hurried to meet Saul, who dismounted and gazed around curiously. 'We have guests, Saul,' Jakob said. 'A party from England who are interested in searching for ancient ruins in this area.'

Saul made a closer appraisal of the English, two women and three men. The women were of middle age and dressed in long white skirts and blouses, now dusty brown after the long trip from the coast. The men were dressed in the attire of English gentlemen abroad: pith helmets and walking clothes more at home on the slopes of the Swiss Alps.

'I would like you to meet the leader of the archaeological expedition,' Jakob said, guiding Saul to a tall, aristocratic looking man of military bearing. 'Colonel Hays Williams, I would like to introduce you to Mr Saul Rosenblum.'

403

Saul extended his hand to the Englishman. 'Pleased to make your acquaintance,' Saul said.

The expression on the colonel's face seemed to change to one of puzzlement.

'From your accent, you sound like a colonial,' he replied. 'You wouldn't by any chance have served in South Africa with the Queensland Mounted Infantry?'

Suddenly Saul felt as if the hot day had turned bitterly cold. Alarm signals flashed in the Australian's mind.

''Fraid not, Colonel,' Saul replied, trying hard to conceal his nervousness.

Jakob immediately sensed some tension in the situation and broke in. 'Saul has come to us from Australia,' he said. 'You must have him mixed up with someone else.'

The colonel glanced at Jakob with an expression of disbelief. 'The man I am referring to is a wanted man of the lowest kind, a traitor and murderer.'

Jakob held the man's glare. 'That is not Saul then,' he said calmly. 'Saul is a man who grows trees.'

Hays Williams turned his attention to Saul.

'So what can we do for you, Colonel?' Saul asked calmly.

Hays Williams did not answer immediately, as if considering something. It was an uncomfortable silence.

'I am on leave with some friends,' the colonel finally answered. 'We were hoping that your people might know of some promising areas for us to search for ruins. My colleagues are from the British Museum. They're authorities in the culture of the Holy Land.'

'We'll help you as much as possible,' Jakob said, 'but I'm afraid we do not know of any ruins in our area. Have you inquired with our Arab neighbours?'

'We have,' Hays Williams replied. 'They could not help us.'

'You are welcome to stay,' Jakob offered. 'We have accommodation to suit your needs.'

'Thank you,' the colonel said. 'We will take up your offer, and perhaps Mr Rosenblum can tell me a bit about growing trees.'

Saul scowled inwardly at the Englishman's sarcasm. It was obvious that the British officer was not convinced. Of all the places in the world, this English colonel – whoever he was – had to end up here. But what should he do? The first thought that crossed Saul's mind was to simply kill the colonel at a convenient time. But that would attract international attention. The Ottoman Empire was on reasonably friendly terms with Britain so would undoubtedly pursue the matter. At least he was not on soil under British jurisdiction. Saul was thankful for that.

The colonel turned his back and strode to join his party while Jakob and Saul watched him go.

'I could never have guessed,' Jakob said, letting out a held breath. 'I am sorry, Saul.'

'No matter,' Saul shrugged. 'There is nothing the bastard can prove while I am here. And even if he does, I doubt there is anything he can do.'

Jakob glanced at the former soldier and could see a deep concern written on his face. As nonchalant as Saul wished to appear, he could not hide his feelings altogether.

'Be very careful, my young friend,' Jakob warned. 'I do not like that man and I fear he may make mischief.'

'He can try,' Saul said as he walked away to join Ivan.

'You look unwell,' the Russian said when Saul joined him. 'Do you know our visitors?'

'The English colonel seems to think that he knows me,' Saul said glancing back at the archaeological party. 'I wish I knew how.'

'Is there something you have done?' Ivan asked bluntly and Saul stared contemplatively at his friend.

'Back in South Africa I killed a man,' he said.

'I know,' Ivan replied with just the trace of a grim smile on his bearded face. 'Jakob told me about the man who had defiled his daughter.' Saul shook his head at the Russian, who continued, 'Not much is secret here, my friend. You were right in what you did.'

The following day Saul gathered his small army of seven young men and three young women to continue their training in the use of the Enfield rifle, a weapon Saul was familiar with from his service with the mounted infantry. The lesson was held at the edge of the village on a rifle range he and Ivan had constructed.

'Not like that,' Saul bellowed at one of his trainees who gingerly held the brass butt of the rifle to her shoulder as if it would bite. 'Tuck it in and then relax.'

Ivan translated the order into German as some of the recent immigrants did not understand English. But it was unnecessary in the case of one young girl from Austria. Her name was Elsa and her widower father had chosen to leave the country of his birth after hearing the inspiring words of the newly formed Zionist organisation in Europe. However, he had died of a fever months earlier in Jerusalem where Elsa had learned of Jakob Isaac's community. With the last of the money she and her father had between them she had made her way south. Although the people had welcomed her into their village she still grieved both for the loss of her family and of the country she had left behind. Palestine had proved to be a barren land, a place of hardships she could never have imagined. If she had, then she would not have followed her father's dream to immigrate to the Promised Land.

And now Saul towered over her with a dark scowl on his face. He did not consider her gender a defence against his wrath when it came to weapons handling.

'Learn to make the rifle a part of your body if you want to survive in this country,' he continued in a softer but menacing tone.

Elsa's bottom lip quivered as she fought back tears of humiliation. She was a pretty girl with brown curly hair to her shoulders and dark eyes. Elsa had never experienced such harsh words from a man and dared not look up.

'You seem to have a good grasp of firearms drill for a man who plants trees,' the voice of Colonel Hays Williams said from the edge of the buildings.

Saul swung in his direction and saw the tight smile on the man's face. 'We all learn to defend ourselves here, Colonel.'

The Englishman turned away to disappear behind the building, leaving Saul feeling uneasy. The man was arrogant and very sure of himself, which was unsettling. Saul turned his attention back to his trainee who was staring up at him, her big, brown eyes sending a sudden surge of sorrow through Saul. God willing that she would never experience what Anna had in her last moment alive, he thought. The memory of the Russian beauty he had once yearned for spurred Saul back to his task of being the hard man. Pity was something he could no longer afford if he was to keep his promise to Jakob, that no other man or woman of the *moshava* would fall victim to raiders. Nor would he ever allow himself to get close to a woman again. To do so seemed to be a death warrant for her.

～

Two days passed and the English archaeologists enjoyed the hospitality of the *moshava*. Saul kept out of the colonel's way and counted the days till his parting. He even volunteered for extra patrols of the perimeter to ensure that he was able to avoid meeting with him.

After a night of sleeping out in the arid lands Saul rose to blink away the sleep from his eyes and prepare for the day. Nothing worth noting had occurred on the Arab side of the valley to suggest a possible retaliatory raid, although Saul had observed strangers coming to the Arab village. But after the strangers departed all would be quiet again.

He shook his bedroll and secured it to the saddle. His hobbled horse was grazing a short distance away just below the ridge Saul had selected for his bivouac. He flung his saddle over his shoulder and hefted his rifle to walk to the horse but suddenly froze. In front of him was a very faint but distinctly European-style imprint of a boot – and not his.

'I would not make any rash moves, Trooper Rosenblum,' the voice said from his right. 'I am a crack shot and could have killed you as you slept.'

'You have no authority here, Colonel,' Saul said casually, but knowing he was at a great disadvantage. 'This is Ottoman territory.'

'I am aware of that. As much as I am sure that you must be one and the same as a certain Trooper Saul Rosenblum, wanted on a warrant for the murder of an English non commissioned officer. I always had a strong feeling that you were not killed at Elands River. Your sort are like rats leaving a sinking ship.'

'I didn't desert,' Saul replied angrily. 'I was captured.'

'Desertion will be added to the charges when I take you back to face British justice,' the colonel said as he advanced on his prisoner.

'I can't see how that will happen when here you have no bloody right to arrest me.'

'It's either that – or I carry out a summary execution here and now.'

Saul smiled. 'That you will never do because, if nothing else, you are English and pride yourself on the fairness of English justice. I have to give you bloody pommies that much credit.'

Saul slowly lowered the saddle and turned to face the colonel full on, still holding his rifle but making no attempt to raise it. From the expression of self-doubt on the colonel's face, Saul could see that he had touched a nerve with the Englishman.

'Did you kill that sergeant?' the colonel asked, his revolver unwavering.

'Yeah, I killed him,' Saul said defiantly. 'After he killed an innocent girl. And I would do so again under the circumstances.'

'Then you readily confess to your crime, Trooper,' Hays Williams said. 'I am surprised that you would considering the position you are in.'

'Are you married, Colonel?' Saul asked.

'I am,' the Englishman replied stiffly. 'Your point, Trooper?'

'What would you do to the man who killed your wife if you knew he could go free for the murder?'

Hays Williams frowned. 'That is irrelevant,' he replied.

'Well, I did what I knew was right, and killed the man who murdered the woman I loved. So you had better execute me now, because I am never leaving this land alive.'

The colonel raised the pistol level with Saul's head and aimed. The Australian stood stock still, staring defiantly into the Englishman's eyes as if daring him to fire. With his thumb, Hays Williams cocked the pistol.

The sun was rising as a great yellow ball over the ancient, arid lands of Saul's distant ancestors. If this was where it was to end then he was ready.

Slowly, Hays Williams lowered the pistol and carefully eased off the hammer. 'You are right about our sense of justice, Trooper Rosenblum,' he said. 'But I can promise one thing – so long as I live I will do everything in my power to bring you before a military court.'

Saul felt terribly weak. He had faced his firing squad and expected to be shot. He watched the colonel stride away stiff backed to disappear behind the ridge.

Very slowly, Saul bent to pick up his saddle. Was it that the threat of death no longer concerned him, he wondered as he continued his walk to his horse. It was a terrifying thought. Saul sensed that he had not seen the last of Colonel Hays Williams. He did not appear to be a man to utter idle threats. But when and how they would meet again was beyond Saul's control.

FORTY-SIX

When news of the death of Lady Enid Macintosh reached Karl and Helen von Fellmann in Queensland, they immediately packed their few possessions and took a ship from Brisbane to Sydney where Helen, as Patrick's half-sister, assumed the role of the mistress of the house.

Alex was pleased to be reunited with his Aunt Helen and Uncle Karl who he could talk to about the trek they had undertaken in search of the legendary Wallarie. But sadness tinged their recollections whenever the conversations touched on Alexander's grandfather, Michael Duffy.

Over afternoon tea served in the garden, Fenella listened intently to the conversation, and sighed for the fact that she had not been granted the privilege of travelling with her grandfather. 'Oh, why can't women live like men do?' she blurted.

'Times are changing,' Helen said, sipping at a cream-laced coffee served in a delicate china cup. 'I believe that in our own lifetime women will live to enjoy the rights men take for granted.'

Karl tried not to smirk and glanced at Alex who frowned. His sister had some strange ideas and so too did his aunt, he thought.

'What do you intend to do with your life when you come of age?' Helen asked her niece.

Fenella's pretty face broke into a beaming smile. 'I am going to be an actress and travel the world,' she replied, eliciting a disapproving frown from her uncle.

'Nice young ladies do not aspire to become actresses,' he said. 'You should be considering seeking the hand of a good, God-fearing young man with expectations.'

Fenella's bright expression faded. 'The only young man I would have considered went away to South Africa,' she sighed, 'and when he returned, Lady Enid forbade me to see him again.'

'She means Matthew Duffy,' Alex said tactlessly.

'I am sure Lady Enid had her reasons,' Helen consoled her niece. 'No doubt you will meet again if it's meant to be. You know,' Helen continued, 'we met Matthew's mother after we returned from visiting Pastor Otto Werner and his wife Caroline on their mission station west of Townsville. Mrs Tracy is a wonderful woman who has achieved more in her lifetime than most men could in ten.'

'Father has talked of his Aunt Kate,' Fenella said. 'Matthew must be like his mother then.'

'Or his father,' Karl reminded. 'Men are more likely to be like their fathers. It is a well-known fact of nature.'

Both Fenella and Helen raised their eyes to the heavens. Each tacitly decided at that moment that they liked each other. For Fenella, her Aunt Helen was another woman she could talk to in the absence of her own mother. And in Fenella, Helen saw the girl she hoped her own daughter might be like – if that was ever possible. She could only pray so. Meanwhile, Helen hoped that she would be able to spend a lot more time with her niece.

Only Karl and Helen attended the legal offices of the Macintosh companies to hear the reading of the will. A bald-headed solicitor with bushy mutton chop sideburns sat behind his impressive desk of polished mahogany. He adjusted the spectacles perched at the tip of his nose and, with a cough to clear his throat, commenced to read the document containing the last wishes of Lady Enid Macintosh nee White, who had been born in England and died in Sydney.

The lawyer droned on through the usual legal preamble and read out the expected beneficiaries of her estates. Naturally she left the bulk of her estate to her beloved grandson, Patrick Duffy, and his heirs. Miscellaneous items were left to favoured members of her staff but towards the end both Helen and Karl sat up with a start.

'... and a portion of Glen View as surveyed in a plan lodged with my solicitors as a title deed is to be bequeathed to my grand-daughter Helen von Fellmann to be used for the purposes of the Lutheran Church to bring God to the remaining native peoples of the Glen View region. This land is to be utilised as a mission station so long as seen fit by the Lutheran Church and administered by my grand-daughter Helen with the provision that the Aboriginal known as Wallarie returns to Glen View, of his God-given free will, within a year and a day of my demise. If this does not occur

413

then the land is to remain as part of Glen View. To my . . . '

Helen did not hear the remaining bestowments. Her mind was in a whirl. Her grandmother had finally recognised that she should do something for the Aboriginal people the family had dispossessed so many years earlier.

Outside the office on the city street busy with buggies and lumbering drays, Helen and Karl discussed the repercussions of the land grant. They finally had a home from where they could do God's work amongst the native people. Lady Enid Macintosh had recognised the need to reconcile with the ghosts that haunted Glen View. It was now up to Helen and Karl to find Wallarie and bring him home.

Pastor Otto Werner, who they had met in northern Queensland, had not been much help in locating the man who had once saved his and his wife's lives a quarter of a century earlier. So how would they find Wallarie where all others had failed, including the old warrior's former nemesis, the Queensland Native Police? Helen sensed that to fail in their search for Wallarie would have repercussions beyond merely losing the valuable Glen View land. An uncomfortable and superstitious thought, flying in the face of her Christian beliefs, made Helen think that the curse that seemed to dog her family might continue if they failed.

Lady Enid had left a quaint little sandstone cottage on the northern side of the harbour near the village of Manly to Fenella. A kookaburra brayed its welcome from a great gum tree in the backyard and the wisp of salty air made the place feel festive. Helen stood beside the young woman gazing at the overgrowth of plants around the house.

'It is really mine?' Fenella asked in an awed voice.

'It certainly is,' Helen reassured. 'I remember this place from when I was even younger than you. Sometimes my mother would bring your Aunt Dorothy and I here to get away from Sydney. An old man was the caretaker. I think he used to be a convict and he would catch fish and net ducks for our suppers.'

'Oh, I want to see inside,' Fenella exclaimed in her excitement.

She had loved the grand old lady, despite her aloofness. And by way of her will she had demonstrated her eternal love for her great grand-daughter in the magnificent gift of this house.

Helen led Fenella up the stairs onto the shaky wooden verandah and opened the door with the key left in Enid's desk. The place had a musty smell but otherwise seemed in good repair as a caretaker had maintained the holiday house since Helen had last visited as a little girl. As Helen opened some drapes to allow the sunlight to flood in, she could hear Fenella excitedly moving from room to room.

'Can we stay tonight, Aunt Helen?' Fenella asked breath-lessly as if she had been running.

Helen patted her niece affectionately on the head. 'I have come prepared for such an occasion in anticipation of your wishes,' she said with a warm smile. 'Go back to the carriage and tell Henry he can bring in our supplies while you and I tidy the cottage. Henry can prepare a fire in the stove while you and I sweep and dust.'

For once Fenella did not object to domestic chores. This was, after all, her house. A magical place. A place she could call *her* home, despite it being a lot less grand than the mansion she had grown up in.

The coachman staggered under the piles of boxes to be deposited in the living room and grumbled as he went to work chopping wood for the stove. He was a man skilled with horses, not a mere navvy. But when the work was complete Helen rewarded him with a bottle of beer and he bid the two ladies goodnight before returning to the city.

Both women rolled up their sleeves and went about restoring the house. By last light they were sufficiently satisfied that the place was habitable.

'I do not know how to cook,' Fenella confessed.

'Fortunately I do, young lady,' Helen smiled. 'One learns a lot when one is married to a missionary.'

They ate a meal of cold corned beef and boiled potatoes with garden peas by candlelight. Not as elaborate as the fare Fenella was used to, yet it somehow tasted better than any meal she could remember. They followed with mugs of sugared black tea taken on the verandah, where they slumped in a couple of old cane chairs found in a bedroom.

The evening was balmy and Fenella felt very content. This was her adventure and for the moment all her cares were gone. But suddenly she remembered something she had found which had intrigued her. While cleaning in the master bedroom she came across an old leather satchel behind a bureau. Upon opening it she found inside a mysterious sheet of paper. Now she would ask her Aunt Helen if she knew anything about the sketch that had been in the satchel. Although the drawing was very faded and frayed by time, the face stood out on the thick paper. Fenella passed the sketch to Helen who drew the candle close to examine the stiffened sheet.

'Is that a picture of you, Aunt Helen?' Fenella asked as Helen strained to read the faint words on the page. The face of the young woman depicted was surrounded by tiny fluttering angels. 'It looks so much like you but I imagine it was done a long time ago,' Fenella continued.

Helen read aloud the words: *May the angels protect you – forever.* At the bottom of the page Helen could vaguely make out the artist's name and a date: *Michael Duffy, 186—.* It could be 1862 or 63, she mused. Tears welled in her eyes and soon became a gentle sobbing.

Fenella reached over to touch her aunt's hand. 'What is the matter, Aunt Helen?' she asked. 'Is it the picture?'

Helen nodded and gazed away as if searching for something: a mother she no longer had, and a man she had known who had once loved her mother. If only they might suddenly appear from the night shadows, hand in hand, to walk into this house together.

She glanced at her niece and saw an expression of grief. 'I will feel better in a short time,' Helen said reassuringly. 'The picture is of my mother when she was not much older than you are now. The man who made this beautiful drawing was your grandfather, Michael Duffy. I think he loved my mother very much.'

'Lady Enid never spoke about my grandmother,' Fenella said. 'I always felt that something terrible must have happened, before I was born. I always wanted to know more about her . . . ' Fenella tapered away as she considered her relationship with Aunt Helen. 'My grandfather was in love with your mother,' Fenella breathed, captivated by the idea which was both terribly romantic and sad.

Helen's tears were replaced with a gentle laugh and she impulsively hugged Fenella to her. 'We certainly have a colourful family and I think it is time that I told you as much as I know.'

Fenella's mouth was agape. Helen told the young woman all that had never been spoken of by Lady Enid Macintosh as the evening turned into a dark night full of sparkling stars. It was near midnight and the last of the candle flickered as Helen tucked her niece into bed, bidding her a goodnight.

Fenella lay between the fresh sheets and stared at the dark ceiling. She had learned that her grandfather Michael Duffy had once killed a man in Sydney and was wanted by the police so he escaped from Australia. That he had become a soldier of fortune and roamed the world fighting in wars and being wounded many times. That her own father finally met his father in Africa before she was born. And Fenella learned that her father had Irish papist relatives who were well known in Sydney's social and political circles. This had shocked Fenella who had grown up under her stern great-grandmother's suspicion of those who belonged to the Church of Rome. One of her distant relatives was in fact a priest who had grown up with her father in Redfern before he had come to live with Lady Enid.

So much learned in one night that Fenella's mind raced, initially defying the need to sleep. When sleep did finally come, she dreamed that something was watching her from the corner of the dark room. Not something tangible, but rather a strong presence that woke her in fright. It took a lot of courage to slip past the shadowy figure in the corner and go to her aunt's room where she woke Helen before climbing in beside her.

'I think there are ghosts in the house,' Fenella explained in a strained voice. 'Can I stay with you tonight?'

Helen tried not to laugh at the young woman's over-active imagination and pulled up the sheets to cover them both.

'If there are ghosts in the house then they will be friendly ones,' Helen said, sleepily. 'I think the ghost might be

Michael Duffy come to find my mother and look after you.'

Fenella was not convinced but the reassuring presence of her aunt brought an untroubled sleep.

The weekend passed all too quickly for Fenella. When the two women were satisfied that the cottage was restored to a comfortable state, they took walks to the little village of Manly bounded by the harbour and the Pacific Ocean. In the township they drank tea at cafes and strolled along the yellow sands of the beach, exploring the rockpools and inlets covered with tough native bushes.

It was a time of peace – except for the second night when Fenella imagined an old Aboriginal warrior was standing in the corner of the room watching her. She did not know why she should see such a spectre. She had never even seen a native before, but he appeared so real for the brief moments before fading from her sight. It was unnerving and once again Fenella had rushed to her aunt who chided her over active imagination.

In the last hours of her stay at the cottage, Fenella took a walk along the great stretch of sand that was the Manly beach. It was a wonderfully balmy day with little white puffs of clouds floating serenely above. She removed her shoes and skipped between the lapping waves that rushed onto the sands before retreating back to the blue seas.

As she walked, Fenella thought about her mother and father. Their absence from her life was something she had learned to cope with but she could not deny the pain of missing them. She would give anything to have them back. To feel her father's strong arms wrapped protectively around her as if she were still a little girl and to hear the gentle Irish lilt of her mother's voice discussing things that only women understood. Finding the old sketch of Helen's mother, Fiona White, herself a Macintosh before marriage, had caused her to experience a yearning for that thing called love – any kind of love in her life.

She stood at the edge of the water deep in thought as she looked out to sea. Her parasol was tilted against the sun and her other hand hitched up her long skirt to her knees. A steam ship offshore blew smoke that trailed as a thin plume in the calm air.

'Fenella?'

Fenella turned to see a young man striding towards her. 'Matthew!' she exclaimed. 'What are you doing here?'

Matthew stopped a few paces away. He was dressed in a white shirt with the sleeves rolled up and a pair of dark trousers. A coat was hooked over his shoulder by his thumb and he wore a smart hat.

'I came down to Sydney with a mate for a short spell,' Matthew answered awkwardly. 'I went to your house and was told about Lady Enid. Your uncle told me that you were over in Manly at the family's retreat for a while. So, I got directions and decided I would come over and see you. I am sorry to hear the news of your grandmother's death.'

'I am so pleased to see you, Matthew,' Fenella said, her heart beating in her breast like a sledge-hammer. 'I treasured every word in the letters you wrote to me.'

Matthew hung his head and shuffled his feet. 'I wanted to see you, despite what my mother and Lady Enid said, that we would be cursed if we ever saw each other again.'

Fenella frowned. She had heard the stories from Lady Enid of how an Aboriginal curse had come on the family as well as that of Matthew's family.

'Do you really believe that we are cursed?' she asked. 'Because I think that is silly.'

Matthew gazed at the beautiful young woman and shook his head. 'I know that curses are just made up stories but . . .' He trailed away. He was uncertain. The stories of the Glen View curse had been related to him by his own mother. She was renowned as a sensible woman and yet she firmly believed in the curse. 'I don't know,' he concluded, contradicting his first answer.

'Well, what are you going to do?' Fenella asked. 'Are you going to leave again without calling on me at my father's house?'

'When I was in Africa I used to dream about you every night,' Matthew said shyly. 'I missed you very much, although we had hardly seen each other before I left. I still want to see you but I have things to do before that can happen.'

'What things?' Fenella sniffed.

'I don't know exactly. Maybe the war changed things. All I know is that I have this feeling that the time is not right for us. It's as if I have to go out and do many things.'

Fenella felt her heart crush. Matthew was so different to the boy she had first met. He now looked and acted many years older than the person who had written letters from the battlefields of South Africa. She knew that she had lost him.

Matthew could see the pain in her face and now wished he had not searched for her. He desperately wanted to reach out and hold her, to take away the pain he knew that his declaration had caused. But he was out of his depth in such matters of the heart and reacted in the only way he knew.

'I think I should go,' he mumbled. 'Texas Slim is waiting for me back in Sydney and I will miss the ferry if I don't leave now.'

Fenella stared at him defiantly, refusing to let her hurt spill over into tears. She was a Macintosh, and as such pride was a virtue, not a sin.

'I hope you find that which you seek,' she said, controlling the quaver in her voice. 'And thank you for at least paying me the courtesy of personally delivering your message.'

Matthew did not know how to react so he held out his hand as he would to a man. 'I will bid you a good day, Miss Macintosh, and hope that we meet again some day.'

Fenella stared at him. He dropped his hand self-consciously and walked unsteadily away.

When he was almost swallowed by the crowds of strolling couples promenading on the Corso, Fenella's tears came. She stumbled home to Helen who immediately saw her distress. With soothing words, Helen stroked her niece's long hair as she would that of a child.

Matthew and Texas Slim painted the town red until their money and welcome at the hotel ran out. It was time to catch a steam train heading north for Queensland and get back to mustering cattle.

At night on the train Matthew stared from the window of the carriage, feeling an emptiness in his soul for what had eventuated on the beach at Manly only days before. He had been torn between his desire for Fenella and the yearning to be free to seek what life held for him. Whatever it was, he knew he must find it alone, and when he did, maybe things could be different between him and Fenella. Only time would tell.

FORTY-SEVEN

The cadre gathered: the publican, schoolteacher, peat digger and priest. This time the meeting was held in the house of a sympathiser, the rebels careful to avoid being seen together too often in the one location at one time. Idle talk of such matters might be heard in the wrong places.

As always, a guard was set to observe if any British soldiers or local police might be patrolling the area around the tenement house and nearby streets. But the mood was already tense tonight. This time the talk would go beyond treason.

'You are sure of the arrival of Norris?' O'Riley asked the schoolteacher, who nodded. 'Then Sean will carry out his mission.'

'What about the major?' Sean asked from his usual position by a door. 'If the opportunity arises.'

Father Martin Duffy swung on him. 'Major Duffy is not

with the British,' he said. 'He is an Australian and killing him would be counter-productive to our cause.'

'You say that because he is your cousin,' Sean sneered. 'I have never thought that you were committed to freeing Ireland. It's easy for you priests when things get tough. You leave the rest of us to face the bloody British.'

Martin was aware of a ripple through the room at the young peat digger's words. 'I have sacrificed more than you will ever know,' Martin replied quietly. 'Enough to put me beyond all hope of eternal salvation.'

Martin did not elaborate as to how his activities had filtered back to the Vatican and the superior of the Jesuit order. He was now a defrocked priest – excommunicated by the Pope himself. But he had known it was inevitable that this would happen. He understood through the teachings of his Church that he was born with original sin but he also knew that he was born with the freedom to make his choices in life.

'What do you say to Sean?' O'Riley asked.

'That killing Major Duffy would be a grave mistake,' Martin explained. 'Despite Patrick's past as a soldier for the Crown, his grandfather was the big man himself, Patrick Duffy, who led the British in a merry dance in these parts early in the last century. Patrick was a hero to the Irish in Australia when he stood with Peter Lalor at the Eureka Stockade back in '54. How do you think my fellow Irishmen in Australia would feel about the killing of Patrick Duffy's grandson by us here? You don't think we would lose credibility for the cause of freedom?'

Martin could see the frown on the schoolteacher's face and knew his argument had hit home.

'Martin might have a point,' the schoolteacher agreed. 'I vote that we leave the major alone.'

'Me too,' O'Riley conceded and looked to Sean. 'And you also will leave Major Duffy out of this. The man is a customer of mine and pays well.' This brought a smile to both the schoolteacher and Martin. 'Then it is agreed,' the publican said. 'We only kill Norris and the major is left unharmed.'

Sean scowled and stormed from the room. Despite O'Riley's instructions, as far as he was concerned the major was a traitor deserving a traitor's fate. He would kill Norris as planned but he would also hunt down Duffy.

Martin watched the impetuous young killer leave and had no doubt that Patrick was still in grave danger. The peat digger's reputation for utter ruthlessness in his crusade to spread terror amongst the occupiers of Ireland was well known. He had killed a magistrate in front of his family only a year earlier and gloated whenever he recounted the assassination. 'You should have seen the look on the bastard's face when he knew he was going to die,' Sean had chortled. 'But better was the look on the bastard's wife's face . . .'

Some men were born bad and the cause of freedom gave them the justification to kill when, under other circumstances, they would have done so for the sheer thrill of taking a life, Martin reflected. Sean was a born killer.

Patrick sat at the edge of his bed in O'Riley's hotel holding the pistol in his hand. The publican had taken him aside in a corridor upstairs when he returned from his early morning stroll from the village down to the beach.

'I have a message from Father Duffy,' O'Riley had said. 'He has told me that he would like to meet with you at the hill near the Fitzgerald manor just after midday.'

Patrick had always suspected that the publican had links with the rebels in the county and viewed his message with suspicion. But it might be genuine and he had a need to meet again with the cousin who had once been as close as a brother.

Patrick knew they had both changed much in the intervening years and they were now on opposing sides. Patrick no longer considered that he had any loyalty to his grandfather's crusade to free Ireland. He was an Australian who had once sworn allegiance to the Crown as a commissioned officer of the British army. And even now that he was a member of the Australian army, his sworn allegiance was still to the British.

As for Martin, Patrick knew that his cousin was acting against all that Patrick had sworn on his life to protect. They were nothing more than soldiers in opposing armies, when all was considered.

Patrick placed the pistol in his pocket before leaving the room to make the rendezvous with whoever might be waiting for him. He was pleased to see that the weather had broken to reveal a pale, blue sky, but there was no break from the cold wind that whipped the green fields and grey sea on the horizon. He stopped at the base of the ancient burial mound and warily scanned the surrounding countryside with a soldier's eye. The hill was a good place to lay in wait for a target. It was high ground and a natural choice for an ambush. But even as he spied out the hill he could see a figure standing at the top. Although they had been many years apart, Patrick recognised his cousin dressed in the garb of a civilian.

Martin raised his hand and disappeared beyond the rim of the small hill. Patrick slipped the revolver from his pocket and commenced his ascent. If it was an ambush, then he was ready.

When he reached the top he noticed that the hill he had

first climbed over sixteen years earlier had been disturbed with picks and shovels.

Martin was sitting on a rock. 'You came,' he said with just a trace of surprise.

'You asked,' Patrick replied, the revolver hanging at his side.

'It is good to see you again,' Martin said. He rose from the rock to cross the short distance to his cousin. 'You look well considering what I heard of your wounds in South Africa.'

They stood facing each other almost as if they were total strangers, suspicion filling the gap between them.

'You know why I came,' Patrick said, breaking the awkward silence. 'I have a message to warn you that if you continue in your activities against the Crown then you will lose your protection as a man of the cloth and be treated as any other traitor would be.'

'I am no longer a priest in the Holy Mother Church,' Martin said bitterly. 'I was excommunicated.'

Patrick was taken aback by the revelation. He could never imagine his cousin as anything other than a man of God. He had always been the religious one.

'I am sorry for that, Marty,' Patrick said, hardly noticing how he had slipped into the familiar use of his cousin's name. 'Bit of a bad break for you.'

Martin smiled for the first time in their meeting. 'It was you who made me promise to be a bloody priest when we were at school and we got caught stealing the altar wine. Do you remember?'

Patrick was puzzled for a moment but then suddenly recalled the incident. He broke into a broad smile. 'Yes, and I remember well that it was I who ended up being caned to save your scrawny neck.'

Time dissolved. Once again they were a couple of wild

427

young boys playing in Fraser's paddock under the old gum tree.

'It is truly good to see you again,' Martin repeated.

Patrick stepped forward to embrace his cousin in a hug. 'You little bastard,' he said. 'You are still causing me grief after all these years.'

Martin stepped back from the embrace and gazed sadly at his cousin. 'I am sorry that it has come to this, Patrick,' he said. 'But we can never go back to the past and be the boys we were. I cannot give up my cause to free Ireland. All I can hope is that you respect my reasons in the name of the family and its history to free this country from the British.'

'You are an Australian,' Patrick pleaded. 'What goes on in the old country has nothing to do with us.'

'An Irishman is someone who has been scattered to the far-flung parts of the world because of what the British have done to us over the centuries. I wonder how they would react if we Irish had invaded their land and under pain of death and imprisonment forbade them to speak English, practise their religion and eventually allow a famine to starve them to death. You don't think they would fight back against us?'

Patrick could not refute Martin's point of view. He knew that Britain was occupying a land they had no political right to. But he also knew that many in Britain would be more than happy to see the end of the Irish question. It was only a matter of extracting England from the troublesome country in a dignified and logical way. For this reason Patrick knew where his loyalties lay, and they were not with armed insurrection. 'Your recruiting of Irishmen to fight on the Boer side in South Africa put mine and many other Australian lives in jeopardy,' he countered. 'That had nothing to do with freeing Ireland.'

Martin turned to stare at the grey sea beyond the fields. 'Pat, anywhere we can cause the British to feel our resistance is acceptable. We have no great love for those stiff-necked, bigoted Dutchmen. Just their cause of resisting colonialism.'

'I see that you and I will never be able to reconcile our differences,' Patrick said quietly, suddenly remembering the pistol in his hand. It reminded him of his mission on behalf of Colonel Hughes and the Crown.

'I always suspected that your purpose in coming to Ireland was more than just to see Catherine,' Martin said. 'I imagine that your meeting with my old adversary Colonel Hughes at your place in England has something to do with you coming to see me here today.' Martin smiled grimly at Patrick's surprise. 'You must know that we have friends in places you would never suspect.'

'But only . . . ' Patrick stopped himself. He was about to reveal a name that he prayed could have nothing to do with Martin's intelligence gathering.

'But only Deborah Cohen, you were about to say,' Martin finished for him. 'No, you were not betrayed by her, if that is what you are thinking, but one close to her. Your Colonel Hughes and I have been adversaries for a long time, although we have never met.'

Patrick did not know what to believe. He was quickly learning that this covert world of intelligence he had unwittingly fallen into was a dirty place of lies, treachery and shadows.

'And I know that you have instructions to stop my activities,' Martin continued calmly. 'In whatever way it takes. Persuasion is your first option. The gun in your hand, the second.'

At the mention of the pistol, Patrick self-consciously

raised the gun as if he did not know why he had it in his hand. 'I will not resort to the second option,' Patrick said quietly. 'Maybe others will – but not I. We were once as brothers and I could not have the blood of a brother on my conscience, despite my sworn oath to the Crown.'

'I didn't think you would,' Martin said. 'If I'd thought you would kill me I would never have come here alone.'

Patrick was taken aback by his cousin's pragmatic reasoning. There was a hardness in the man he had never known existed. Martin was a long way from the shy and rather meek boy Patrick had protected with his fists against the bullying of others at school.

'I doubt that we will ever meet again, Patrick,' Martin said sadly. 'But in parting I just want to warn you to stay away from Catherine if Norris is at the mansion. Under no circumstances go there.'

'What do you mean?' Patrick asked with a puzzled frown. 'What do you mean not go near my wife?'

'Only until a certain matter has been resolved,' Martin replied. 'I cannot tell you any more than that and what I have already told you could brand me as a traitor to the cause. Just stay away for the next three days.'

'Stop talking in riddles!' Patrick exploded and took a step towards the former priest. 'Is Catherine in any danger?'

Martin did not reply but turned and walked away. Patrick was left alone on the hill. A cold, biting wind swept up from the dark sea, whispering and moaning. It carried a message of dread and Patrick knew that before he left Ireland he would once again see blood running as red rivers in his life. Maybe it would be his, he thought, as he watched the figure of his cousin walking across the fields back towards the village.

FORTY-EIGHT

The stockmen's quarters at the Glen View homestead was the only home Nerambura Duffy really knew. He had been raised there by his mother, Matilda, who worked as both nanny and cook for the station manager's family. In many ways Glen View was the only home he had ever wanted. He felt as one with the endless horizons and the brigalow scrub plains that surrounded the property.

On this evening the sun was a gentle orange and sitting just above the sparse, stunted trees when Nerambura rode into the dusty yard between the sprawling homestead and stockyards. He had been on boundary riding duties for the last two weeks, patrolling the newly established fence line that marked the neighbouring Balaclava station and kept the respective stock from mixing. A rivalry existed between the two great properties and the Glen View manager considered Balaclava cattle inferior to his imported breeds.

The young stockman swung wearily from the saddle and led his horse to the yards to drink from the water trough.

'Nerambura.'

He looked up to see his mother hurrying across the yard to him.

'He has come,' Matilda said when she reached her son. 'He wants to see you.'

Nerambura did not have to ask who she meant. It could only be one person.

'Where?' he asked.

'Wallarie says over on Balaclava near where the water-holes are. He says he wants to see you before the morning.'

Nerambura groaned inwardly at the old Aboriginal warrior's demand. He had ridden many miles in the last few weeks and had been looking forward to his mother's cooking and catching up with the other stockmen. But he was also aware that as an initiated man he must obey the command of an elder.

When his horse had taken her fill he unsaddled her and threw his saddle on a fresh mount. He tightened the straps wearily before swinging himself astride and setting out into the gathering darkness. Whatever the meeting was about must be important, Nerambura thought, as he let his mount pick her way through the scrub. Wallarie had come to his mother in a dream and the young stockman did not doubt what his mother had seen for one moment. Visions, he once heard the white missus from Glen View call them.

It was near sunrise when Nerambura finally saw the dying embers of a fire by the waterholes of Balaclava station. He dismounted and approached cautiously, not wanting to startle Wallarie, a man who had survived so long by remaining alert. Nerambura did not want to be mistaken for an unwelcome visitor. To do so risked one of the deadly twelve-foot barbed spears finding him as a target.

Weeks after the meeting between Wallarie and Nerambura Duffy, a telegram arrived at the Macintosh residence in Sydney. It had come by a tortuous route. Karl read the telegram addressed to him and his wife.

'Helen!' he called. 'I have news of Wallarie.' He hurried along the hallway to the parlour where his wife sat sewing a small tapestry of a religious scene. 'We are to pack and travel north.'

Helen paused in her work. 'Who has sent the telegram?' she asked.

Karl glanced at the paper in his hand. 'It is from Kate Tracy in Townsville.'

'Patrick's aunt,' Helen reflected. 'I wonder why she should inform us?'

Karl frowned. 'I do not know, but she asks us to go to Glen View as soon as we can.'

Helen placed the half-finished tapestry aside and closed the little ornate basket containing her selection of needles. 'Then we shall do so. I will speak to the children's nanny while you make arrangements for us to take a ship to Queensland.'

Karl nodded and carefully folded the slip of paper. It said very little other than that Wallarie had been found and that they were to return to the station.

The pastor was not the only one mystified. Kate Tracy had received the news in a letter sent to her by the young stock-man who she knew was a distant relative. The words were

433

barely literate but the message clear. She too was to go to Glen View.

When Ivan was overdue from a patrol Saul Rosenblum went searching for him. The circling carrion birds in the clear blue sky led the Australian to a gully where he found the bodies of both Ivan and his horse.

Saul slid his rifle from the bucket strapped to his saddle and quickly scanned the surrounding hills for danger. He saw none and dismounted to go to the fly-covered corpses. He knelt beside the big Russian. Ivan's pale, naked body blended with the dusty earth, the myriad stab and slash wounds a testimony to how hard he had fought his attackers in a deadly hand-to-hand battle.

Saul slowly shook his head as he sat back on his heels. Most of the ugly cuts appeared to be mutilations inflicted on Ivan after death. Had the Arab villagers returned to inflict them as an act of revenge? Or was the killing of Ivan a prelude to something else?

Saul stood up and walked away from the body of his friend. The sun was already causing it to blacken and bloat. Ivan had not been dead for very long and Saul's knowledge told him that his friend had probably been ambushed just before dawn. It appeared that he had been on the move before first light when attacked. There was no sign of his campsite in the immediate area. From past experience, Saul knew something must have caused Ivan to break camp earlier than he normally did.

To corroborate the theory that was developing in his mind, Saul used all he knew of tracking to sweep the area. Finally he found what he was looking for. Saul squatted by the tracks. Ivan had been riding back to the *moshava* in a hurry. It appeared that he had met a party of between ten and fifteen men when he had attempted to take a short trail through the gully, generally avoided because it was an ideal site for an ambush.

Saul rose from the tracks and walked back to the site of the ambush. The black splashes of blood leading away indicated that Ivan had wounded his ambushers, who had chosen to use cutting weapons rather than firearms to bring him down. Saul frowned as a terrible thought occurred to him. The ambushers did not want to use firearms so as not to alert anyone who might be in the area. This was a carefully planned action.

Saul followed the faint blood trail away from the site and before long stumbled on two dead men. They were Arab villagers and had died from knife wounds, most likely inflicted by Ivan in a vicious hand-to-hand fight. The bodies had been laid out with some respect; it was this that confirmed Saul's worst fears. The two dead men had been left because the ambushers intended to return and carry them back to the village after they had completed their mission.

Saul took a few paces back to scan the earth leading to the *moshava*. He needed no other sign than the scores of footprints he saw to send him racing back to his mount. Maybe a hundred or more Arabs were moving into position to attack the unsuspecting village. His people were vastly outnumbered and a massacre was sure to occur unless he was able to get back and warn them.

Saul dug his spurs into the mount. Time would be measured in minutes rather than hours if the tiny settlement was to survive. He rode hard and just before noon reached the vineyards of the *moshava*.

'Get everyone back to the settlement,' he yelled from the

saddle to the young men and women working amongst the grapevines. 'Now!'

Two of the men he had trained had their rifles and responded immediately, herding the vineyard workers away without questioning his command. Saul spurred his horse on to ride to the fields to pass on the same message. When he was satisfied that he had warned as many as possible he rode his lathered mount into the scattering of stone buildings, reining in at the community's meeting hall where he was met by Jakob.

'What is it?' Jakob asked, his face creased with concern. 'Has something happened?'

'Ivan is dead,' Saul answered in a flat voice. 'The bastards ambushed him in a gully east of here, about an hour's ride away.'

Jakob's face paled. 'We should go and fetch his body.'

'If we do, then we will most probably share his fate,' Saul said. 'I am certain that they are going to hit us in the next few hours. Probably during the night, if I know their tactics well enough.'

'If what you say is true, I should call a meeting with the council and decide what we should do,' Jakob said in a distant voice. 'I must hurry.'

Holding the reins of his horse, Saul led her to the stables. His warning had brought the settlement to life and rifles appeared in the hands of the small but efficient fighting force he and Ivan had readied. But not ready enough, Saul thought with some fear. Would they be able to defend the settlement against a sizeable raid by an enemy that, according to his estimates, outnumbered them five to one?

'What do we do, Mr Rosenblum?' a young man questioned, coming to a skidding halt before Saul, his rifle and bandoleer of spare ammunition in his hands. 'I have heard that we are about to be attacked.'

'You get everyone with a weapon to meet me here at the stables in five minutes,' Saul said calmly. 'I will brief you then on your duties.'

The young defender took heart from the experienced former soldier's calm tone and hurried away, leaving Saul to unsaddle his hard worked horse.

Within a few short minutes a party of nine men and seven women gathered outside the stables. Saul stepped out and gazed around at the ragged militia. They stood silent and grimfaced but Saul was pleased at the way they bore their fear – it did not show.

'To all intents and purposes,' Saul said, addressing his army, one woman translating his words to Yiddish, 'it seems we may be under attack at any time. But more likely tonight.'

The young men and women still held their fear in check. Indeed, a fierce determination to defend their village crept across their faces.

'I will assign you your tasks and appoint leaders who will report to me.' Saul continued his briefing, nominating each person by name for a specific task. 'We will add to our numbers by taking any able-bodied person who can hold an axe, pitchfork or anything else that can be converted into a weapon. The extras will be dispersed amongst those with the guns to bolster numbers.'

When the briefing was over, each nominated team leader scoured the settlement for the volunteers Saul had identified to supplement his small force. When they reported back to him, Saul took their section to a pre-planned defensive position around the settlement. By day the tactically sited outposts had a clear field of fire and anyone attempting to approach the village could be shot down. But by night this would be more difficult, almost impossible, and that is why Saul knew their enemy would attack during the hours of darkness. He walked the perimeter of the village, stopping to identify in depth points that could be defended. His overall plan had his rifles as far forward as possible and a second line of defenders providing positions to fall back, shrinking the perimeter. The defence called for every ounce of tactical knowledge Saul had. The Palestinians were no fools if they were able to ambush Ivan, he realised as he stood gazing out across a recently ploughed field to the distant hills shimmering under the late afternoon sun.

As Saul stood making his observations he had a brief chance to think about his old friend. Ivan was dead and there was nothing he could do about that. When it was safe they would go back and retrieve his body. Grief was something Saul knew he would have to put into the future – the time beyond that when his cold-blooded instincts were required for the sake of their very survival. He did not care if they thought he was heartless for the decisions that he must make. He was their military leader and knew that the orders he would give may bring death to some in the name of the community's survival – that was the way of war. He dreaded the coming of the night and the decisions that would bring. He did not share the apparent optimism of his militia. Had he believed in the God of his ancestors, he might have prayed for a miracle. Instead, he would rely on the hitting power of the Lee Enfield .303 rifles in the hands of his young defenders. It might have been good to have the ancient biblical Joshua with him right now, he thought with a rueful smile. At least he knew how to fight.

In the hall Jakob sat at the battered wooden table and told the gathered community leaders what Saul had reported.

'What if he is wrong?' Aaron Herzog said to the gathering. 'What proof does he have of an attack on us?'

'Because he told me,' Jakob replied with a sigh. 'And I trust the young man's opinion. According to my son, he was a good soldier in South Africa and I heard through friends in the army that he was recommended for their country's highest award for bravery. If Saul Rosenblum thinks that we are going to be attacked, then I believe him. We have been fortunate to receive early warning to prepare our defence.'

'I see no proof,' Herzog persisted, but his argument was gathering little support as it was well known that he and Saul despised each other. 'I say that we should go out immediately and bring back Ivan's body for a fit and proper burial. He was, after all, a devout man.'

This brought a chuckle from a few in the meeting.

'Ivan was devout to the vodka,' someone muttered, causing the chuckle to escalate to a ripple of laughter. 'But we will miss his presence amongst us.'

'I would suggest that we gather the women and children to a place of safety in the settlement,' Jakob said, quietly drawing back the attention of the meeting.

The men nodded, some tugging at long beards. Only Aaron appeared to disagree. If he had his way, the Australian would be ejected from the settlement. From what he had learned, Saul Rosenblum was a man who had no real belief in the spirituality of his ancestors. Nor was his mother even Jewish. The likes of the Australian had no place in the new Zion.

On the perimeter Saul waited patiently. He knew with

certainty that the time of blooding for his small force was only hours away. How would they cope? The next few hours would answer his unspoken question.

It was approaching midday in Ireland.

Patrick finished his packing, leaving only his pistol on top of the bed. It was time to say goodbye to his friend Father Eamon O'Brien and then make his way to the Fitzgerald manor.

From the tiny window of his hotel room Patrick surveyed the countryside. The weather was boiling up for another heavy cloudburst, which would bring cold driving rain to the village and fields. He walked back to his bed and sat on the edge, staring at the revolver. He had failed either to convince his cousin Martin to desist in his seditious activities against the British Crown or to adequately explain his feelings to his wife. Since his visit he had no word from her.

'Damn!' he swore savagely and screwed up his face in anger. Why could Catherine not see his love for her? Or was it that he had been too long under the influence of war to truly be able to express his deepest emotions?

The peat digger closed the door of his tenement house behind him and with hands in pockets hunched against the biting wind. The upraised collar of his coat helped both to protect his face and neck and disguise his features. He hugged the wall of the narrow cobbled street as he strolled casually towards the edge of the village.

If the intelligence was correct, Norris was due this

evening and Sean wanted to be pre-positioned to make his meeting with the British landlord. But it was a meeting that Sean knew only he would walk away from. Then he would go in search of the traitorous Major Duffy and make his score two for the night.

FORTY-NINE

A moonless night came to the settlement.

Saul had issued his orders and the village lay in darkness, his tiny force deployed to strategic points around the village to cover as much of the perimeter as possible. Saul knew that it was not enough, but he had at least trained his militia in night firing and demonstrated to them how easy it was to fire too high in the dark. They had soon learned in range practice to keep the rifle barrels down and fire low.

Those not armed – the older men, women and children – had been confined to a storage building made of heavy stone and easily barricaded. Aaron Herzog was amongst the frightened settlers huddled between bales of straw and crates of farming supplies. He had refused to learn how to use a rifle as he did not believe in violence, and Saul had not pressed the point.

Saul checked the rope he had laid on the ground

between the outposts established just after last light. In the dark, each of the outposts could be found by following the waist-level rope he had hung to wooden markers. It was time to inspect the positions and Saul commenced with an outpost manned only by one person. It was a site less likely to be exposed to an attack but critical in the defence of the interlocking fire zones Saul had designated each position. He was duly challenged for the password and, on giving the correct reply, moved forward cautiously and bumped into one of the defenders.

'It is you, Mr Rosenblum?'

He recognised the frightened voice of the pretty young girl who had been in tears at the range only days earlier. 'How are you holding up?' he asked.

'I see nothing in the dark,' the girl said. 'I am very frightened. Do you think I will be killed?' she asked in a rush of tight words.

'How old are you?' Saul asked gently.

'I am seventeen,' she replied.

'Then you will live to be seventy and have many children born on this land,' Saul said with a smile she could not see. 'That is a promise.'

The young girl's voice seemed to relax just a little. 'Will they really attack us if they think we know they are out there?' she asked.

Saul considered her question. 'I wish that they would instead show some sense and return to their village, but I feel they are stupid enough to attempt an attack on us, so be vigilant.'

'Mr Rosenblum?'

'What, Elsa?' Saul responded.

'Can you stay with me, if they come?' she blurted. 'I would feel safer knowing that you were beside me.'

Saul felt a lump in his throat. How could he tell her that he expected many of them to die before the sun rose on the next day and that she might be one of them? It had taken a lot for Saul to adjust to the idea that women would also be fighting alongside the men to defend the settlement. Jakob had quietly insisted, telling Saul biblical stories about the Hebrew women of old and how they had stood beside their men.

'I will try,' he said, and reached out instinctively as a father would to touch the face of the young girl with the palm of his hand. He felt the wetness of the tears that flowed down her cheeks as Elsa gripped his wrist tightly.

'I would like to tell you something,' Elsa said. 'But I do not know how to say it.'

'Tell me tomorrow, when this is all over,' Saul replied as he self-consciously drew away his hand. 'I must go now and check the others but I promise I will be back tonight.'

Elsa nodded and watched the Australian disappear silently. She settled in to watch her area of responsibility to the front, feeling the reassuring cold wood of the rifle tucked loosely into her shoulder. But the shallow trench that had been hastily dug after last light felt like a grave. Would she have the courage to tell Saul of her feelings, she wondered.

When Saul had completed his rounds to each outpost, reassuring his defenders, he returned to report to Jakob.

'You know that we don't have enough people with rifles to defend the village,' Saul said bitterly as he slumped against a wall, rifle between his knees. It was dark in the hall except for the flickering light of a candle, and with the windows and doors barricaded no light could be seen from

444

outside. Jakob sat at the big table with a book open before him. 'We could have done with bayonets and a machine gun or two,' Saul added with a sigh.

'That is all we could afford,' Jakob answered with a shrug. 'We must trust in God's protection. He will not desert us.'

'You sound like that sanctimonious bastard Herzog,' Saul said. 'I got to see a lot of dead Dutchmen who figured the God of their Old Testament was on their side.'

'Ah, but God has sent you to us,' Jakob countered gently with a twinkle of a smile. 'That is the way He works. He will not desert His chosen people in their dire hour of need.'

Saul glanced at the old man. There was something gentle and wise about the former jewel trader that endeared him to all those he met. 'Rather have Ivan with me right now,' Saul answered. 'But he is probably introducing the archangels to the joys of vodka.'

'That you believe that much, my young friend, is a sign that you have not completely deserted the ways of your father.'

Saul frowned. 'Don't misinterpret my bad jokes as faith, Jakob,' he said. 'But I do believe in the people you have gathered here. Don't ask me why – I just do.'

Jakob nodded. No matter what Saul believed in, it was more important right now to believe in the young former soldier's skills. Such a responsibility was God given.

Elsa tried to fight off the sleep that came to her, despite the fear she felt for the unknown. On his last round of inspection Saul had told her it was midway between midnight and dawn. But involuntarily her eyes closed and for a time she was in a world of serene happiness, dreaming of the snow-fields of her village. Saul was beside her and smiling. He held out his hand . . .

She came awake instantly as the world around her exploded with screams and rifle shots. Blinking desperately to clear her eyes, she could see the myriad burning torches waving in the dark. It seemed that they were all in front of her and suddenly a figure loomed out of the dark only feet away.

Elsa surprised herself by swinging her rifle around and firing. The shadowy figure disappeared momentarily only to rise again from the earth. In shock, Elsa had forgotten to work the bolt to eject the spent cartridge and chamber another round and there was no time to do so before the figure was before her.

'Jesus! You almost shot me,' Saul exclaimed. 'The enemy are out there to your front,' he said as he took up a position beside the young woman.

Saul quickly surveyed the scene. There must be hundreds of them, he thought with a sinking feeling. But the attackers had lit firebrands and unwittingly disclosed their positions as they came in a human wave of blood-curdling, ululating cries, firing wildly. The attackers were shooting high. Saul could hear the thwack of their bullets hitting the stone walls of the village behind him. Already his militia were firing steadily into the ranks crossing the ploughed paddock. For a second he hoped that they just might cripple the attack. It all depended on how well he had trained his small army in using their rifles at night. Each shot of their limited supply of ammunition had to count. But the attackers were also returning fire as they kept coming in what appeared to be an unstoppable wave.

The firebrands began to fall in showers of sparks as the defenders' rifle fire bit into the closely packed formation of attackers. Saul recklessly stood up to observe the flow of battle. It seemed as if the Arabs had concentrated their assault in one formation in order to overwhelm the villagers. If so, then he could draw in the reserve of rifles he had positioned at the other ends of the village. But if he were wrong, and the attackers had placed a force to the other side of the village, then gathering his reserve to the main front would leave them extremely vulnerable. It was a gamble, but Saul also knew that if he did not stem the flow of Palestinians to his front, they were lost anyway.

Saul made his decision and moved quickly to bring up his reserve who scrambled to take up positions next to their comrades in the now less thinly spread front line. The attackers were only a hundred yards or so out when they were met with heavier gunfire than they had experienced from the outset. Saul commanded the deployment from beside Elsa's position where she kept up a steady and disciplined rate of fire, calmly reloading the magazine as it emptied and then continuing to shoot into the flickering wave of torches. Saul could hear the war cry of the Palestinians, goading them to a victory. But the attack was wavering as many turned to flee the murderous fire. It was obvious that they had underestimated the new settlers' capacity to defend themselves. But those who did get close enough hurled their firebrands towards the front line of the defending militia. They landed in a shower of sparks, giving some weak light for the attackers to see their enemy.

A sudden drop-off in rifle fire and new screams and curses to Saul's left flank alerted him that some of his young militia were now engaged in a desperate and vicious hand-to-hand battle. Without hesitating he ran to bolster their attempt to stem any collapse of the defence.

As Saul stumbled into position, a huge Arab in a distinctive white robe swung an ancient scimitar sword. The man's bearded face flashed. A mask of hate and blood lust, he was mere feet from Saul who desperately brought up his rifle to parry the blade. Sword and rifle met in a bone shaking crash, dislodging the rifle from Saul's grip. It clattered to the earth and the swordsman skilfully changed foot, this time readying to deliver a killing blow from the side.

In the blink of an eye Saul realised that there was nothing he could do to prevent the sword slicing through him. The triumphant expression on the Arab's face confirmed that he was a dead man.

As if in slow motion, Saul saw the barrel of a rifle thrust into the Arab's side, and the triumph on the man's face suddenly turned to anguished pain. Saul did not even hear the sharp discharge of the rifle as its projectile ripped through the man's heart and lungs, flinging him sideways. When Saul swung to glimpse his saviour he saw the pinched face of Elsa, her eyes as big as saucers in the semi-dark. He was almost ready to curse her for leaving her position but the terror written across her pretty face was enough to quell his anger.

Without a word he scooped up his weapon and was not disappointed when an attacker stumbled forward to be cut down with a bullet from Saul's rifle only a pace away. Around him, Saul could hear man-to-man fighting. Grunting, cursing and screaming, men kicked, punched, bit and stabbed each other to death to the sound of metal crashing down on metal. The occasional shot indicated to Saul that one or two of his militia had been able to disengage themselves for enough time to reload and fire. Screaming defiance, Saul waded into the melee swinging his rifle like a club.

It seemed an eternity until there were no shots or curses left.

'They have gone,' an awed voice said in the dark as the sound of someone sobbing followed.

Panting, Saul staggered back to a group of men and women as they emerged from their positions, seeking each other to celebrate their survival.

'Get back to your positions,' Saul rasped. 'They might be reforming for another attack.'

Reluctantly, the young defenders returned to their allocated defences while Saul tried to establish how many had been killed and wounded. He moved from position to position as they waited in exhaustion. When he had ensured each man and woman had ammunition and water to drink, he again sought Elsa out.

'Just thought I should thank you for what you did earlier,' he said quietly. 'If you hadn't been nearby I was definitely a dead man.'

Elsa blushed at his words, grateful for the darkness. 'I was doing what you taught me to do,' she replied modestly.

'And didn't I tell you to remain at your post – regardless of anything,' Saul growled gently. 'You disobeyed my orders.'

Elsa hung her head. Did he not know that his life was precious to more than just himself? If he had been killed the others might have broken and run. He was the rock on which the safety of the *moshava* now depended. 'You are a stupid man, Mr Rosenblum,' she snapped. 'It was my duty to make sure that you were not killed.'

Saul was taken aback by her anger. The girl had spirit, he thought, and he now felt just a little remorse for being so hard on her in the past. If the truth be known, he had been frightened that she might suffer the same fate as Karen and Anna – and that he could not endure again.

Without replying, he walked away. Elsa felt tears welling in her eyes. The events of the night were closing in and flashes of what had happened, only a short time earlier, began to erode her nerves. She trembled uncontrollably and her teethed chattered. Dropping her rifle Elsa hugged herself, tears finally flowing. Soon the morning would come and the result of the night before would be evident.

When the sun rose over the battlefield Saul was unsurprised to see that no bodies of the slain enemy were left in the ploughed paddock. The Arabs had taken their dead and wounded under cover of darkness.

But fourteen bodies remained at the edge of the village where the close quarter fighting had occurred. Five of the bodies were of the defenders, four men and one woman, who lay scattered in death with the many, terrible wounds a testimony to how hard they had fought.

Saul supervised the removal of all bodies with the help of grieving settlers who had come out of the sanctuary of the storage shed whilst the remaining militia stood half their number to guard against a daylight attack. Saul sent out a patrol of three to sweep the area beyond the village for any sign of the Palestinian attackers. Then he sent his exhausted defenders into the village to sleep. He reissued their arms to others to put up a pretence of defence should they still be under observation from the attackers. But for himself there was no luxury of rest. The village was still under threat and there was much to do to ensure the safety of these people whose lives Jakob had entrusted to his skills and experience of war.

Saul's mind and body were numb with weariness and he hardly registered Jakob's presence when he came to him sometime before noon.

'Go and sleep,' Jakob had gently commanded. 'We will wake you if anything happens.'

Saul nodded gratefully and stumbled away to a sheltered,

shady spot behind a stone building. He slumped to the earth and curled up with thoughts still racing through his mind. Had he checked to see if his patrols were still out beyond the village sweeping the area as an early warning to a future attack? Had he repositioned and strengthened his defensive positions? Had he . . . Saul fell into a deep sleep.

Later that day Elsa found Saul behind the stone building. She stood and watched him, wondering how he could appear so peaceful. Her hands still trembled, although not as badly as hours before. Healing sleep had come to her eventually and it was now late afternoon, that gentle time of the day when the searing heat gave way to a wonderful coolness before the chill of night took hold.

With a start, Saul awoke. It was dark and he experienced a pang of guilt for sleeping so long when he should have been out supervising the defence. But even more alarming was the realisation that a warm body was curled into his.

'Elsa,' he said in an awed whisper, as his eyes adjusted to the darkness and he recognised the head that lay against his chest.

She stirred at the sound of her name but remained asleep. Saul eased them into a sitting position, propped against the now icy cold wall. The scent of her hair was strong and Saul felt a confusion of emotions. But for the sleeping young woman there was no confusion. Elsa expected to be with this man until they grew old – or died – together.

FIFTY

Sean O'Donohue crouched behind a hedgerow within sight of the old Fitzgerald manor. The cold drizzle could have made the waiting miserable but he was hardly aware of the discomfort, so focused was he on the task ahead.

An hour passed and the light was waning as the feeble sun set behind the low scudding clouds. Sean stretched and stamped his feet, burying himself in his heavy coat to ward off the chill. The waiting had been longer than he anticipated and now the cold and wet was beginning to permeate his thinking, dulling his responses.

Then the carriage came into view, rumbling down the rough road to the house and onto the gravel driveway. Sean found himself holding his breath as the man he had been waiting for stepped down. 'Norris,' he hissed.

Their information had been right and the great irony

was that the coachman who had delivered Norris to the manor was part of the conspiracy. Sean slipped the revolver from his pocket, anxious to move. But the carriage was still in the driveway and he would have to remain where he was until the driver took it to the stables where he would wait to take Sean back to the village. At least he would not have to walk back in the dark, Sean consoled himself.

Once the carriage had disappeared behind the house, Sean rose to make his way to the front door. But he froze when he caught the movement from the corner of his eye. From down the lane in the last light of the day a figure was trudging towards the house. From the cover of the hedge Sean peered intently and recognised Major Duffy. So he would kill both of them, Sean thought with bitter satisfaction. The devil had ordained this day to him.

Patrick hesitated at the door. This was the moment of truth that he feared. Would Catherine return with him to England and then home to Sydney? He took a breath to steady the trembling in his hands and knocked.

When the door was opened Patrick felt a long contained rage well up. Brett Norris stood blocking the way.

At first Norris did not seem to recognise the man who stood in the drizzling rain. Then a sneer curled on his lips. 'Duffy!'

Patrick had to control a sudden urge to smash the face of the man who had taken Catherine from him. 'Norris, what are you doing here?'

'I thought you would know. I own the house, old chap,' Norris replied calmly as he let his first reaction of shock subside. He knew better than to allow a rival to unsettle him. 'I should ask you the same question.'

'You know why I am here,' Patrick growled. 'So let me pass to see my wife.'

'I would, except that Catherine does not appear to be in residence.'

'I don't believe you,' Patrick snarled and stepped forward, brushing Norris aside. 'Where is she?'

Norris closed the door behind him. 'You can search as much as you like. In fact, my housekeeper does not seem to be around either. Rather odd.'

'Catherine,' Patrick called. But his voice echoed in the empty rooms. 'Catherine,' he called again as he made his way through the house.

Norris stood back, bemused. But he too was mystified as to where Catherine might be.

Patrick eventually made his way back to Norris who leant by the front door, puffing on a cigar.

'Satisfied?' Norris asked.

Patrick was at a loss for words. His initial rage to strike out had dissipated with his growing concern for Catherine.

'I would ask you to leave my house, if you please,' Norris stated. 'If you do happen to bump into your wife, please tell her I have returned.'

Patrick swung on Norris and with one hand gripped him by the throat, causing Norris to step back in fear at the killing rage that had exploded in the emerald green eyes. 'Believe me,' Patrick snarled, 'if you ever go near my wife again, I will kill you.' Patrick released his grip and turned to walk away.

Norris massaged his throat as Patrick opened the front door then pulled it behind him. The Englishman cursed himself for his stupid provocation. He should have remembered that Patrick Duffy was a man who lived his life killing others in the name of the Crown.

Sean O'Donohue had planned to simply knock on the door and when it was opened commence firing at both men inside. He would rely on the element of surprise, which had in the past worked well for him. But before he could act, the door opened and Patrick stepped out. At the appearance of the armed peat digger, Patrick instinctively reached for the revolver in the pocket of his coat.

Even as Sean brought up his own pistol to fire, Patrick had his gun out and pointed at the Irishman. Both men stood a mere ten paces apart, their pistols aimed and levelled. An instinct to survive made both pause before pulling the trigger.

'I didn't come to kill you,' Sean lied through dry lips. 'So you can step aside and let me finish a job that I doubt you really wish to stop me doing.'

'Kill Norris?' Patrick asked calmly.

Sean nodded. He was sweating despite the cold and drizzle, but Duffy appeared so deadly calm – almost amused by the situation – while it was completely unnerving to the young Irish assassin, who now realised just how dangerous this man was. 'I know that Norris stole your wife,' Sean said with just a little difficulty as he imagined Patrick's finger squeezing the trigger.

'But to let you pass,' Patrick said quietly, 'would be aiding in a murder.'

'You aren't the police,' Sean snapped. 'So why should you care what happens to this bastard who deals arms to anyone with the money?'

'You're right, I don't care about Norris,' Patrick said. 'But you have put me in a very difficult position. There will be an inquiry into his death and, as I have been here, I will be suspected. On those grounds alone I cannot let you pass although I admit I would be the first to shout you a round of drinks at O'Riley's pub for killing the man. But right now is a bit inconvenient for me. So I suggest that we put down our weapons and go on our separate ways.'

Sean attempted to lick his lips, strangely dry in the drizzling rain. He could feel the pressure mounting in the confrontation and fully knew that in an exchange of gunfire at such close range he might be killed or wounded. Sean had a strong sense of survival and knew only too well that the Australian facing him had the edge with his years of handling weapons.

Very carefully, Sean began to lower his pistol and as he did he realised with horror that Patrick had fired. The lead bullet took Sean in the chest and he crumpled to the wet gravel drive.

Patrick did not lower his gun as he walked towards the fallen man. 'You can go to your Maker in the knowledge that what you set out to do will be finished,' he said gently, squatting beside Sean. 'And they will raise their glasses to you down at O'Riley's when the news is announced of your success.'

Sean closed his eyes and with a last breath went to his death, mumbling a prayer for his soul. Then Patrick picked up Sean's pistol and broke it open to ensure that the chambers were primed.

Inside, Norris heard the shot and fear gripped him. He had been warned before he left England that his life might be in danger from Irish rebels targeting English landlords and now he bitterly regretted not heeding the advice of the police. Remembering the loaded shotgun in the library, he shook off his fear and rushed to the room where he found the lethal, double-barrelled weapon. Quickly, he snapped it open to ensure both barrels were charged. Then he heard the front door open. Norris slipped behind the desk to wait in the dark. No matter who came through the door he would open up with both barrels and the concentrated blast at close range would pepper any man with a hail of deadly lead shot.

Cautiously, Patrick searched each room. He was once again the man who had hunted his Bedouin enemies in the deserts of the Sudan. But this time his enemy was the man who had taken the most precious woman in his life and Patrick no longer recognised the rule of law. He had not believed Sean O'Donohue when he said that Patrick was safe from him. Patrick was a soldier and knew well that the Irishman would have hunted him down after he killed Norris. Killing the peat digger had been a pre-emptive act of self-defence.

The library was where he suspected that he would find Norris, because he knew from past visits with old Fitzgerald himself that it had a gun cabinet. In the dark Patrick made his way to the room and stood beside the open door, waiting with the patience of the hunter for his prey.

Norris knew that his adversary was just outside the door. He had heard the slow but careful footsteps in the hallway. Then they had stopped. The waiting game lasted for several minutes as the tension mounted.

It was Brett Norris who broke. 'Whoever you are, I must warn you that I am armed and that you should leave immediately,' he called in a voice on the verge of cracking.

But there was no answer – just a terrible silence. Norris could no longer stand it. He fired blindly at the open door as if the shot might frighten off whoever was just outside.

Patrick felt the impact of the shot slamming into the wall on the opposite side of the hallway. A shotgun, he thought. And only one barrel discharged. Norris still had another shot left.

Patrick made his move and hurled himself inside the room, flattening on the floor. He felt the second load of shot fill the air above his head. Norris had missed and the discharge lit the room like a strike of lightning. Patrick came to his feet, noting from where the muzzle blast had originated. The Irish rebel's pistol emptied into the space behind the desk and he heard Norris cry out.

Then silence.

Patrick lit a match. It flared, and he saw Norris sprawled on his back. Two of the bullets had found their mark, one taking the man in the head. The match flickered and Patrick turned his back on the room. He had murdered a man in cold blood but felt no remorse for his action. In the past he had killed many of the Queen's faceless enemies and the grateful government had rewarded him with medals and promotion. But killing Norris was personal. Nothing and no-one was a greater threat to the happiness of his family than Norris. For a fleeting moment Patrick thought about his grandmother's reputation for ruthlessness when it came to keeping her family together. He had no doubt that if Lady Enid had been in the same situation – and given the same opportunity – she too would have killed Brett Norris. Maybe he was more like his mother's side than his father's, he thought as he stepped from the manor into the drizzle of the night.

Patrick dropped the pistol he had used to kill Norris beside the dead Irish rebel. Now it was time to return to the village and report that he had stumbled across the killing of a prominent English industrialist but had been fortunate enough to kill the assassin. In the interests of a clean investigation he would surrender his pistol and an autopsy would confirm from which pistols the bullets had come. Sean's pistol was a different calibre to Patrick's and this alone would tell the story. Patrick doubted that he would be questioned at length on the matter even if it was known that he had a motive to kill Norris. Some would have considered it a matter of honour anyway.

'Patrick.'

Slowly, Patrick turned to face the voice that came out of the dark. A sick feeling welled up in his stomach. Had there been a witness to all that had occurred?

'Marty, what are you doing here?' Patrick asked as he focused on the shadowy shape of the former priest.

'I delivered Norris to his death,' Martin answered. 'But I never imagined that it would be at your hands. I think your system of British justice would call it murder.'

Martin came forward and even in the dark Patrick could make out his coachman's garb.

'Why is it that you did not stop me from killing your comrade?' Patrick asked as Martin gazed down at the body of Sean between them.

'I gave him last rites after you went inside the house,' Martin said sadly, ignoring his cousin's question. 'I still believe that we have a soul despite my excommunication and I was taught that it lingers for a short time after death. If that is so, then I might have done some good for the poor, misguided lad.'

'Did you witness me killing him?' Patrick asked.

Martin nodded. 'It was either you or him, Patrick. But I never expected to see you here in this place at this time.'

'What are you going to do?' Patrick asked.

'Nothing. Just disappear from the county until the investigation into the killings runs its course. Maybe go to Dublin.'

'Nothing else?'

Martin looked up at Patrick and the Australian could make out an expression of inconsolable sadness.

'May God forgive us both,' Martin said. 'For we have damned ourselves forever in what we have both done.'

'I thought killing Norris was what you had planned to do anyway,' Patrick said in a puzzled voice. 'So why do you say that I am condemned?'

'Because my motives were at least in the right cause,' Martin answered. 'Yours were motivated by human weakness. For that you are damned.'

'You still talk like a priest – or a Druid maybe,' Patrick said with a slight edge of anger in his voice. 'Strange for one who betrayed the oath of his office.'

'This is not the time or place to debate philosophical matters,' Martin cautioned. 'I think that you should be reporting the matter to the constabulary before any suspicion falls on you.'

'And if I need a witness to corroborate what I tell them?' Patrick asked defiantly. 'Would you step forward?'

'I might give my life for you,' Martin answered. 'But I won't condone your mortal sin.'

'Then that is it,' Patrick sighed. 'It might be that we will meet again.'

Martin held out his hand and Patrick took it. 'In the next life,' Martin said in parting. 'After we have done our penance for our sins.'

Martin waited until Patrick was swallowed by the night. He did not take the coach back to the village as he and Sean had originally planned. Instead, he set out to seek a safe house a few miles away until he could make his way to Dublin.

Patrick trudged along the lane to the village where he woke the local constable and reported the matter. As he predicted, no suspicion fell on him. In fact, he was lauded as a hero by the local military commander for his action in killing the Fenian rebel.

Before the news of how he had killed one of their favourite sons could reach the patrons of O'Riley's, Patrick was gone. He left the village with some reluctance, knowing whatever Catherine's reasons for disappearing, he could only wait for her to contact him. It was time to return to England and make arrangements to sail to Sydney and his family.

FIFTY-ONE

The whirling, dust-filled draught of air twisted across the dry plains to taper out into the azure sky. Wallarie paused in his hunt to see which way the dust devil would go. It posed no threat. He continued to scan the sparse brigalow scrub for his prey: a great red kangaroo. But when he turned his attention back to the big marsupial, it was gone.

Wallarie cursed his eyesight. Time had blurred the world around him and he knew that alone he could not survive as his ancestors had done for countless generations. Muttering swear words in the English he had learned from his white brother, Tom Duffy, so long ago, he tramped back to his campsite with little else than a slow moving lizard he had clubbed in his hunt for food. But at least he knew they were coming, he thought. The woman he had waited so long to meet would be here soon with the others.

~

Helen was pleased to once again meet Patrick's legendary and, some would say, colourful aunt.

'It is good to see you again, Mrs Tracy,' Helen said as they stood on the verandah of the sprawling main house of the Balaclava station, set like an oasis on the dry plains. 'It has been a while since we last spoke.'

Beside Kate stood a young and handsome man she introduced as her son, Matthew. Helen was impressed by both his manner and his bearing. She had also heard much about his exploits in South Africa and was finally meeting the boy who had broken Fenella's heart. But being impressed by his physical appearance did not take away her sense of loyalty to her niece.

After organising the stabling of their horse and buggy Karl soon joined them. He removed his floppy hat and dusted it against the side of his trousers.

With formalities over Kate ushered her visitors inside to meet the station manager and his wife, a couple in their late middle age who looked as if they had been born to the arid lands. The manager's wife escorted Helen and Karl to their quarters, a simple room with two single beds and a weather-beaten wardrobe in the corner. The beds sagged and a posy of withering wildflowers sat forlornly in an empty jar beside the beds on a crude bedside table. But the room was clean.

At six all gathered in the dining room to share a roasted haunch of Balaclava beef served with station-grown vegetables. Wine was also served from a precious supply kept for special occasions. With the station manager at the head of the table, his wife to one side and Kate on the other, the ramifications on trade following the newly formed Commonwealth of Australia were discussed, along with news from the war in South Africa and the price of cattle.

Anything and everything was spoken of except why they had gathered at Balaclava, as if any mention of the subject of Wallarie might cause the curse to manifest itself in the room.

Neither Kate nor Karl and Helen had any idea of what they were supposed to do except wait. After a pleasant evening at the dinner table the men huddled together on the verandah with their pipes whilst the women shared a conversation on family and the hardships of living so far from the comforts of civilisation. Eventually all retired to their respective rooms.

Kate lay in her uncomfortable bed, staring at the ceiling. The subject of Patrick and his absence had arisen in her conversation with Helen, who mentioned that she had heard very little from her half brother since he had been wounded and sent to England to recuperate. Kate now wondered what was happening to her nephew, the illegitimate son of her much loved brother, Michael Duffy. So many terrible tragedies over the years had come to both her family, and the Macintoshes.

She started to doze, the gentle, familiar night sounds of the country lulling her into a soothing sleep. As a young woman she had spent her early years forging her financial empire by trekking with her bullock teams to the Palmer River goldfields and even now Kate required little excuse to leave the comforts of town to return to the country. She had grown to love it with a passion.

Suddenly Kate was awakened fully by a noise alien to the calls of the night birds.

'Mrs Tracy,' she heard from outside her window. 'You 'wake, Mrs Tracy?'

Kate slipped from the bed and pulled a shawl around her shoulders to pad to the window.

'What is it, Nerambura?' she asked. 'I thought you were over at Glen View.'

Nerambura stood in the dark outside the window with his hat in his hands in the European manner. 'I come to get you,' he whispered. 'Wallarie wants to see you.'

Kate felt her heart skip a beat. 'Wait for me by the tank stand,' she replied. 'I will be with you in a short while.'

The man she had heard so much about – and yet had never met – was commanding her presence. But why her? She buttoned a long-sleeved shirt and tucked it into her trousers. And why under such mysterious circumstances was she being summoned?

As she dressed, Kate felt no fear. Just a wondrous anticipation of finally getting to meet the legendary warrior who had once ridden with her oldest brother, Tom, as a bushranger in Burkesland over a quarter of a century before.

When Kate appeared, Nerambura was waiting with two saddled horses. He passed the reins of a gelding to her. 'We ride over to the waterholes 'bout an hour away,' he said as he swung onto his mount with the ease of an expert horseman.

A couple of hundred yards out from the shallow banks of the dry creek bed Kate saw the glow of a campfire.

'That's him,' Nerambura said quietly. 'He wants to see you alone.'

Kate tried to ascertain the expression on Nerambura's face but it was too dark. Had it been fear or awe, she wondered. In her own heart she felt a tremendous awe for the events unfolding.

Kate slipped from her horse and Nerambura took the reins. To avoid stumbling in the dark she walked carefully towards the glowing beacon of the fire.

Wallarie sat cross-legged on the other side of the gently crackling flames. Kate felt strangely deferential, as if waiting for a headmaster to bid her to enter his room. She could see Wallarie's long grey beard touching his chest and when she looked into his eyes noticed that they had an opaqueness about them.

'You Tom Duffy's sister,' Wallarie said. 'You sit down.'

Obediently Kate sank to the earth on the opposite side of the fire. She no longer felt any apprehension but instead a new peace. It was as if this time and place had always been ordained by unseen and unexplained forces that few men of reason believed in.

'You got any baccy?' Wallarie asked unexpectedly, and sighed when Kate apologised for not having any.

'Maybe you bring baccy next time,' he said. 'Good stuff that baccy.'

Just as Kate was beginning to wonder if the old man would ask her anything more meaningful, a strange sound caught her attention.

At first she did not know where it came from, but then Kate noticed the slight rise and fall of Wallarie's scrawny chest. He was chanting, and the rhythm of his song became hypnotic as Wallarie sang to the ancestor spirits.

Transfixed by his eerie song, and a little exhausted from the difficult ride, Kate did not realise that the sound was drawing her soul to another place and time. She was no longer sure whether it was her imagination or even that she might be asleep and dreaming, but suddenly the old Aboriginal was gone. In his place stood a young and tall Aboriginal warrior, with long spears in one hand and fighting sticks tucked into the human hair belt about his waist. Kate recognised Wallarie as that young warrior and beside him materialised an old Aboriginal man daubed in ochre and feathers.

Kate also recognised Wallarie's companion, although so many years had passed since he had first come to her when she was a young woman trekking with Luke Tracy to Glen View in search of her father's grave. Then he had come to her in the early hours of the morning and shown her the tragic slaughter of the Nerambura clan: the many scattered bodies of the men, women and children who had once been part of Wallarie's extended family. Now only Wallarie remained alive, the last of the tribe.

Kate was vaguely aware that she was travelling through time and space and always the eerie chant came to her. And she saw her brothers, Tom and Michael side by side, as she remembered them as young men. Death had brought them together in the world she had entered with Wallarie. She wanted to reach out and touch them but they smiled and faded from her sight. Kate felt the tears streaming down her face for what had been taken from her life so violently. How could the night be so bright, she heard her own dis-embodied voice ask, as she was swept along on a journey that knew no time or space.

'Wake up, Mrs Tracy.' Kate heard the voice calling to her as if down a long tunnel.

She stirred and blinked against the blazing light that seared her eyes, groaning as she attempted to sit up from where she lay in the red earth beside the dry creek. A total confusion overwhelmed her.

'Where? What?' was all she could utter as the morning sun continued to blind her. 'Where is Wallarie?' she finally asked Nerambura Duffy, who crouched beside her.

'Gone,' the young man replied with a shrug. 'Maybe flew away.'

Kate sat up and brushed down her trousers. Her head felt fuzzy but all that had occurred in the night was still fresh in her memory. Nerambura gave her his hand to assist her to her feet and she stood uncertainly, gazing around at the scrubby plain. It was a normal day in a normal world where the sun travelled the cloudless, blue sky, radiating an infernal heat and baking the plains below.

Nerambura handed Kate a water bag and she gulped down the cool liquid with gratification.

'He told me everything,' Kate said quietly as they walked together towards their saddled mounts grazing a short distance away. 'Wallarie will be back.'

Nerambura did not question Kate as to what his kinsman had told her. It was not his place to ask the words of one as magical as Wallarie. In time, Mrs Tracy would tell him what he was supposed to know. That was the way of Wallarie.

'We were worried,' Helen said, hurrying towards the dusty figure dismounting in front of the homestead. 'You were not in your room when we rose this morning and nobody seemed to know where you were.'

Kate passed the reins to Nerambura who led the horse away. 'I went for a ride last night,' she replied without concern for the worried expression on Helen's face. 'I met Wallarie.'

'Wallarie!' Helen gasped. 'You have spoken to him?'

'He has told me what we must do,' Kate said wearily. 'Then the spirits of his ancestors will be at peace.'

As Karl walked up he overheard Kate's last statement. 'What does he want?' he asked.

'Not much,' Kate answered. 'Just that no woman ever enter the cave on Glen View, and that all men remain out of it, with the exception of Nerambura who is initiated. He has said that for a woman to enter the sacred place is taboo and would result in that woman going mad and dying a violent death.' Kate could see the disbelief on Karl's face. 'As far as I know, no woman has ever entered the cave – not even Matilda, who is Nerambura's mother. It is something that I do not confess to understand but that does not mean I cannot accept it. I think that you will be able to keep people away from the cave when you establish your mission station on that tract of Glen View. Wallarie says he wants to come home to die amongst the spirits of his people.'

'I think that he should be instructed in the grace of Our Saviour for the sake of his eternal soul,' Karl muttered and Kate flashed him an angry look.

'I think that Wallarie should be left alone to live out his life according to the beliefs that he holds sacred,' she snapped.

'Mrs Tracy is right,' Helen intervened. 'There will be other heathen souls to save. From what I have seen of some of the stockmen here I would include their souls as well. Is there anything else?' Helen asked, turning to Kate.

'Nothing to be dealt with by you,' Kate replied. 'Just something that I must do to make things right.'

By her tone, Helen realised that whatever Kate referred to was a matter for her alone and she let the subject drop. Together they walked to the homestead where they were met by a cheery station manager who declared a late breakfast had been spread out for them.

A few days later Kate returned to her home in Townsville while Matthew remained at Balaclava to assist with the branding of stock. Kate would be glad to have him back with her in the weeks ahead. Although his terrible experiences of war had changed him forever, she still saw him as the little boy whose shoes she had once laced and whose face she would wipe with her handkerchief, much to his dismay.

Kate sat in the library, which doubled as an office from which to manage her widely dispersed enterprises. A cooling breeze wafted the scent of frangipani flowers into the spacious, shady room that opened onto the broad verandah. Wallarie's request was the reason she had penned the letter to her nephew, Patrick Duffy. She addressed it to his home in Sydney although she knew he was most probably still in England. Eventually he would return and read her words which set out why Nerambura Duffy should be granted rights to share Glen View with Patrick's family.

Kate used the pad of blotting paper to dry the ink on the delicate envelope and placed it aside. Listening to the crackling of palm fronds as the breeze fluttered through the majestic trees, Kate sighed for the battle she knew that she would be facing with her nephew over the issue. Despite being Duffy in name, Patrick was in most ways a Macintosh.

The thought rekindled an almost forgotten conversation with Matilda from a long time ago. Nerambura's mother had been sent over to Balaclava on a task at a time when Kate had been visiting her property. Matilda had taken her aside and announced Catherine's pregnancy. The baby would become Catherine's firstborn, George. As happy as Kate had been for Patrick and Catherine with the news, she had hardly taken much notice of Matilda's ominous warning; she thought the child had been conceived in the sacred cave.

'Baal,' Matilda had scowled. 'No good for Mr Duffy. Evil spirits live near the sacred place. Child be born a devil spirit.'

Normally such an event could be dismissed as the superstitious ramblings of a woman steeped in ignorance, but now, remembering Matilda's fearfully delivered words almost fifteen years later, Kate was not so sure. If George had been conceived in the cave, as Matilda had suspected, then under the beliefs held by Wallarie, Catherine was doomed to go mad and die a horrible death.

Kate could feel the hair on the back of her neck bristle. She was suddenly very afraid for Patrick and Catherine but fought to reassure herself that her fears were just as bad as the superstitious beliefs of her Celtic ancestors with their banshees and leprechauns.

Shaking her head she rose from the desk, determining to rid herself of such thoughts. Instead she would go shopping in town for a new dress. From what she had heard of George, he was no biblical devil. He might be a strange boy – but not a devil!

Kate picked up the envelope to be posted to Sydney. For now, she would worry about the old warrior's final request, to be fought out between her and Patrick when he returned.

A world away, a weather-beaten Irish fisherman puffed on his pipe as he rowed steadily towards the rocky shore below the cliff, overlooking the Atlantic Ocean. It was a good place for mackerel and his son prepared the tackle for the schools that swam in the light swell. The fisherman sighed in contentment at the peace God had brought to this day. A rare vista of blue sky and fluffy white clouds hung over a still sea.

'Da!' his son shouted, pointing towards the rocks around fifty yards from their boat. 'I think I see a lady.'

The fisherman followed his son's finger to something being washed gently against a rocky sea ledge. He first noticed the fiery red hair, drifting like seaweed in the water as the body rolled on each small breaking wave.

The fisherman groaned. Recovering the body meant spoiling what was promising to be a good day of fishing. But he had a duty to the law – and some poor colleen, who did not belong to the sea, needed a proper place of burial in a churchyard.

In England, Patrick received a letter from Father Eamon O'Brien informing him that Catherine's body had been found in the sea just a couple of miles from the Fitzgerald manor. He further wrote that it appeared she must have fallen and would be granted a Church burial in the parish graveyard.

Patrick knew that had there been any hint of suicide she would have been denied such a burial. As it was, no-one would ever really know what brought about his wife's death. After all, there was no such thing as the power of a curse.

EPILOGUE

I sit in the red earth on the land of my ancestor sprits. I cannot see the plains anymore although I feel them, hear them and smell them. The ancestor spirits are all around me and I talk to them in the night when they come to me in my dreams.

'But you don't believe in blackfella curse and want to go into the cave. Ha! You should not disturb the old ones. They got power over the living. And you got questions about Matthew, Patrick and all the others. That take a long time. Mebbe, I think 'bout telling you. Mebbe not.'

AUTHOR'S NOTE

From the hills and plains of India, the prairies of Canada, the fern forests of New Zealand and the Outback frontier of Australia, the tough colonials volunteered to fight in far-off South Africa in the last year of the nineteenth century. They went to fight for the British Empire against men not unlike themselves – independent-minded farmers of Dutch stock known as Boers – and it would become the first war of the twentieth century as the campaign extended into 1902. Like the Korean conflict of the early 1950s, it would become a 'forgotten war'. Yet, in the South African campaign of 1899–1902, the world saw the trend for conflicts for the next one hundred years: war waged against a civilian population to meet strategic needs, and the technology of weapons of mass destruction employed on the battlefield, such as machine guns and quick-firing artillery.

It was a war where Britain initially saw serious military set-backs and any victories were given wide media coverage to allay the fears of the tax-paying public at home. Sadly, the outstanding tenacity of the colonial defenders of the Elands River siege gained little attention or recognition from the British commanders. But the brilliant Boer commander General Smuts would later comment:'Never in the course of this war did a besieged force endure worse sufferings ... [They had shown] magnificent courage, albeit fortified by dugouts and drink, and had taught local Boers a proper appreciation of the Australians.' Flattery may come from friends and allies but praise is best expressed by your enemies.

I found Craig Wilcox's book *Australia's Boer War: The War in South Africa, 1899–1902* (Oxford University Press, 2002) a great source of information on the Australian involvement in that campaign. I would recommend it as a starting point to any student interested in the subject.

The Palestinian aspect of this novel is grounded in the history of the Zionist state of Israel. There is a misconception by many that the terrible Holocaust of World War Two began the mass migration of displaced Jewish people to Palestine. In fact a half-century earlier, Jewish men and women were fleeing bloody pogroms in Russia and settling in the Ottoman-controlled territory of Palestine. But it was a young Jewish journalist from Vienna named Theodor Herzl, covering the infamous Captain Alfred Dreyfus case in France, who recognised that something had to be done to free the Jews of Europe from their two thousand year history of bloody persecution. He put forward his ideas for a Jewish state at the first Zionist Congress in Basel in 1897. At first Argentina was mooted as a place to found a Jewish state but later in 1906 Palestine was formally nominated as the home of people of Jewish beliefs. And so the first settlers after the Russian pogroms of the 1880s drifted to Palestine to seek a new life free of persecution. The rest is the tragic history that extends into our lives in the twenty-first century.

Not to be forgotten in history is the unsung role of Australia's economic gift to the world – the humble gum tree. Because of its ability to live in arid and supposedly infertile land, it has been planted from Africa to Israel to the United States of America to reclaim land for agriculture.

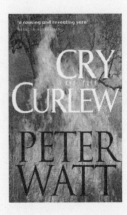

Peter Watt
Shadow of the Osprey

Soldier of fortune Michael Duffy returns to colonial Sydney on a
covert mission and with old scores to settle, still enraged by a bitter
feud between his family and the ruthless Macintoshes.

The Palmer River gold rush lures American prospector Luke Tracy
back to Australia's rugged north country in his elusive search for
riches and the great passion of his life, Kate O'Keefe.

From the boardrooms and backstreets of Sydney to the hazardous
waters of the Coral Sea, the sequel to *Cry of the Curlew* confirms
the exceptional talent of master storyteller Peter Watt.

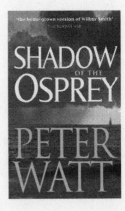

Peter Watt
Flight of the Eagle

Captain Patrick Duffy's passions are inflamed by the mysterious Irishwoman Catherine Fitzgerald, further pitting him against his father, Michael Duffy, and his adoring but scheming grandmother, Lady Enid Macintosh.

On the rugged Queensland frontier, Native Mounted Police trooper Peter Duffy is torn between his loyal bond with Gordon James, the love of his sister, Sarah, and the blood of his mother's people, the Nerambura tribe.

Two men, the women who love them and a dreadful curse that still inextricably links the lives of the Macintoshes and Duffys culminate in a stunning addition to the series featuring *Cry of the Curlew* and *Shadow of the Osprey*.

Peter Watt
Papua

'*Papua* is a rousing historical adventure' GOLD COAST BULLETIN

Two men, bitter enemies, come face to face on the battlefields of France. Jack Kelly, a captain in the Australian army, shows unexpected compassion towards his prisoner Paul Mann, a high-ranking German officer. Neither expect to ever see each other again.

With the Great War finally over, both soldiers return home. But war has changed everything. In Australia, Jack is alone with a son he does not know and in Germany, Paul is alarmed by the growing influence of an ambitious young man named Adolf Hitler...

A new beginning beckons them both in a beautiful but dangerous land – Papua.

A powerful novel with 'plenty of plot twists and sweaty jungle intrigue' SUN HERALD, from the author of *Cry of the Curlew, Shadow of the Osprey* and *Flight of the Eagle*.

PHOTO: DEAN MARTIN